ELSIE'S
CHILDREN

The Original
ELSIE DINSMORE
COLLECTION

ELSIE'S
CHILDREN

Book Six

Martha Finley

HENDRICKSON
PUBLISHERS

Elsie's Children

Hendrickson Publishers Marketing, LLC
P. O. Box 3473
Peabody, Massachusetts 01961-3473

ISBN 978-1-59856-405-1

Printed in the United States of America

Original publication date—1877

First Hendrickson Edition Printing—September 2009

Preface

*The bearing and training of a child
is woman's wisdom.*

—TENNYSON

ith this volume, bringing the story of Elsie and her children down to the present time, the series closes.

It was not by request of the author's personal friends, that either this or any one of the previous volumes was written, but in acquiescence to the demands of the public—the friends and admirers of Elsie herself. We know that as child, as young girl, as wife and mother, she has had many friends who have been loath to part with her. May they find neither Elsie nor her children less lovable in this, than in the earlier volumes, and may their society prove sweet, comforting and helpful to many readers and friends both old.

—M.F.

Chapter First

Of all the joys that brighten suffering earth,
What joy is welcom'd like a newborn child.

—MRS. NORTON

There was a merry scene in the nursery at Viamede, where the little Travillas were waiting for their morning half hour with "dear mamma." Mammy came in smiling and mysterious, her white apron thrown over something held carefully in her arms and bade the children guess what it was.

"A new dolly for me?" said Vi. "I'm going to have a birthday tomorrow."

"A kite," ventured Harold. "No, a balloon."

"A tite! A tite!" cried little Herbert, clapping his little hands.

"Pshaw! It's nothing but a bundle of clothes mammy's been doing up for one of you girls," said Eddie. "I see a bit of lace or work, or something, hanging down below her apron."

"Is it a new dress for Vi, mammy?" asked Elsie, putting her arm about her sister and giving her a loving kiss.

"Yah, yah; you ain't no whar nigh it yet, chillens," laughed mammy, dropping into a chair, and warding off an attempt on the part of little Herbert to seize her prize and examine it for himself.

"Oh, it's alive," cried Harold, half breathlessly, "I saw it move!" Then as a slight sound followed the movement, "A baby! A baby!" they all exclaimed. "Oh, mammy, whose is it? Where did you get it? Oh, sit down and show it to us!"

"Why, chillen, I reckon it 'longs to us," returned mammy, complying with the request, while they gathered closely about her with eager and delighted faces.

"Ours, mammy? I'm so glad it is to be our very own," said Harold, eyeing it with both curiosity and interest.

"So am I, too," remarked Violet, "but it's got such a red face and hardly any hair on the top of its tiny head."

"Well, don't you remember that's the way Herbie looked when he first came?" said Eddie.

"And he grew very white in a few weeks," remarked Elsie. "But is it our own mamma's baby, dear mammy?"

"Yes, honey, dat it am; sho's yer born 'nother dear for ole mammy, de bressed little darlin'," she answered, pressing the little creature to her heart.

The information was received with a chorus of exclamations of delight and admiration.

"Tate a bite of cacker, boy," said Herbert, offering a piece of a cracker which he was eating with most evident enjoyment.

Mammy explained, amid the good-natured laughter of the older children, that the newcomer had no teeth and couldn't eat anything but milk.

"Oh, poor 'ittle fing!" he said, softly touching its velvet cheek. "Won't 'oo tum and pay wis Herbie?"

"No, she can't play," said Violet. "She can't walk and she can't talk."

"Where's our mamma, mammy?" asked Eddie, glancing at the clock. "It's past her time. I wonder, too, she didn't come to show us the new baby herself."

"She's sick, chile," returned mammy, a grave and anxious look coming into her old eyes.

"Mamma sick?" exclaimed little Elsie, "Oh, may I go to her?"

Mammy shook her head. "Not jes now, honey darlin', byme by, when she's bettah."

"Mamma sick?" echoed Violet, "Oh, I'm so sorry!"

"Don't fret, chillen, de Lord make her well again soon," said mammy, with cheerful hopefulness. She could not bear to see how sad each little face had grown, how the young lips quivered, and the bright eyes filled with tears; for dearly, dearly, they all loved their sweet, gentle mother.

"Herbie wants mamma," sobbed the baby boy, clinging to his eldest sister.

"Don't cry, dear," Elsie said touchingly, hugging him close and kissing away his tears. "We'll all ask God to make her well, and I'm sure He will."

"Why! Why! What's the matter here?" cried a cheery voice, as the door opened and Mr. Travilla stepped into their midst. "What's the matter with papa's darlings?" he repeated, gathering them all into his arms, and caressing each in turn.

"Is mamma, dear mamma, very sick?" they asked. Vi immediately added in joyous tones, "No, no, she isn't, or papa wouldn't look so happy."

"I am very happy," he said with emotion, glancing toward the bundle in mammy's lap. "We are both very happy over the new treasure God has given us; and I trust she will soon be well."

"Can we go and speak to her?" they asked.

"After a while," he said. "She is trying to sleep now. What do you think of your little sister?"

"Sister," cried Elsie. "Oh, that is nice! I thought it was a boy. What's her name, papa?"

"She has none yet."

"I sorry for her," remarked Herbert, gazing with curious interest at the tiny creature. "I sorry for her 'cause can't walk, can't talk, can't eat good fings, dot no teef to eat wis. Do, boy, try to eat cacker, cacker dood, Herbie likes," and breaking off a fragment, he would have forced it into the wee mouth if papa and mammy had not interfered for its protection.

"No, no, my son, you would choke her," said Mr. Travilla, gently drawing him away.

"It isn't a boy; it's a girl, Herbie," corrected Harold.

"Oh!" cried Vi, who was gently feeling the top of the tiny head. She looked aghast at her father, "Oh, papa, its head's rotten!"

"No, daughter, don't be alarmed," he said smiling slightly. "There's nothing wrong there; all young babies' heads are soft like that on the top."

"Oh, are they?" she said with a sigh of relief. "I was afraid it would spoil soon and we couldn't keep her."

"No, she seems to be all right," he said with a grave and tender smile. "God has been very good to us."

"Yes, papa. Oh such a pretty darling as she is!" said Elsie.

"Yes, indeed," chimed in the others. Vi added, "And I'm so glad she's a girl 'cause now we have two sisters, Elsie, same as the boys."

"Oh, but we have three now!" said Eddie, laughing good-naturedly at Vi's confused look.

"Oh, yes," she acknowledged, then brightening, "but we have three brothers, and you have two; so it's even all around after all, isn't it, papa?"

The children were full of delight over their new treasure, and eager to show it to grandpa, grandma, Aunt Rosie, Aunt Wealthy, and Aunt May; regretting much that the rest of their friends had left Viamede before the advent of the little stranger.

She proved a frail, gentle creature, with violet eyes and pale golden hair, so fair and delicate that Lily was the name that most readily suggested itself and the one finally settled upon as really hers.

Lily became a great favorite with them all, but Violet claimed a special property in her because as she would say, "the darling came to us almost on my birthday and she's just the sweetest, prettiest birthday present mamma ever gave me."

The weather was growing warm at Viamede and Aunt Wealthy and the little Duncans found the heat oppressive; so when Lily was three weeks old and dear mamma was able to be up again, looking bright and well, that party bade goodbye and set out on their return to Lansdale.

The Dinsmores and Travillas lingered until the middle of May, when they too set their faces northward, not parting company till very near to Ion and the Oaks.

Chapter Second

Envy is but the smoke of low estate,
Ascending still against the fortunate.

—BROOKE

*I*t was dark and raining a little when the carriage turned into the avenue at Ion; but the front of the house was ablaze with lights. The hall door stood wide open, and a double line of servants in holiday attire, each dark face dressed in smiles, stood waiting to welcome the weary travelers home.

There were many hearty shakings and kissings of hands; many frequent exclamations: "God bless you, Massa and Missus!" "Tank de Lord you's got home again, honey. We's been pinin for you darlins and for de sight of de new baby," and with the last words the voices were lowered at a sign from Aunt Chloe, in whose arms the little Lily lay quietly—sleeping sweetly.

There was some fretting among the weary little ones, but mamma and nurses were kind and gentle, and a good supper and bed soon cured all their troubles for that night.

Wee Elsie was roused from her slumbers by a gentle shake, and sitting up in bed, found the sun shining and Vi standing by her side with eager, excited face. "Come, come to the window!" she cried.

"It does seem as if I must be dreaming; it wasn't there before, I'm sure."

"What?" asked Elsie, springing out upon the floor and hurrying after Vi to the window from which she had witnessed the burning of the schoolhouse.

"There!" exclaimed Elsie, clasping her hands in a sort of ecstasy of delight, "Oh, aren't papa and mamma good? How did they ever come to think of it? And how could they get it done while they were away?"

"Grandpa, Uncle Horace, and Cal," suggested Vi. "Oh, aren't you glad? Aren't you glad Elsie?"

"I should think so! And the boat is ever so pretty. Let's hurry and get dressed and go down and see it up close."

Rowing and sailing upon the bayou and lake had been the children's greatest pleasure at Viamede, their greatest regret in leaving it. Knowing this, their ever-indulgent parents had prepared a pleasant surprise for them, causing a small tract of barren land on the Ion estate to be turned into an artificial lake. It was this, shining in the golden beams of the morning sun, and a beautiful boat moored to the hither shore that had called forth from the lips of the little girls those exclamations of almost incredulous wonder and delight.

"Yes, I'll ring for Dinah," cried Vi, skipping across the room and putting out her hand to lay hold of the bell pull.

"Wait, Vi, our prayers first, you know," said the young Elsie.

"Oh, yes! I do want to thank God for being so good to us—the pretty lake and boat and all."

"Dear kind parents, safe journey home, too, and oh, more things than we can count," added Elsie, as they knelt down side by side.

This duty performed with no irreverent haste, the maid was summoned and a careful dressing made in time to take a walk before mamma would be ready to see them.

They found their father on the lower veranda talking with the overseer, while Solon stood waiting with Beppo's bridle in his hand, the horse pawing the ground with impatience.

Eddie was there, too, caressing Bruno who seemed as glad to be at home again as any of the rest. Uttering a joyous bark, he left his young master and bounded to meet the little girls.

Mr. Travilla turned at the sound and with a kind fatherly smile, held out his hands.

"Oh, papa," they cried, running to him, "how good of you to have made it for us!"

"Good morning, my darlings," he said, giving and receiving caresses, "but what ever are you talking about?"

"Why the lake, papa, the lake and the boat."

"Lake?" exclaimed Eddie, "why, where?"

"Oh, you couldn't see it from your windows," said Elsie. "Papa, papa, may we go now and look at it, please, papa?"

"Yes," he said, taking a hand of each. "Larkin, I'll see you again after breakfast. Come, Eddie, my son, you, too, and Bruno."

A brisk five minutes' walk brought them to the shore of the lake, a tiny one, scarce a quarter of a mile in circumference, not very deep and the water so clear that the pebbly bottom could be distinctly seen. And there were gold and silvery fish, too, gliding hither and thither, while a pretty, brightly painted rowboat lying at the water's edge rocked gently in the morning breeze.

Eddie hailed the scene with a shout of delight; the little girls danced about gleefully, Vi clapping her hands and asking eagerly if they might get into the boat now.

Papa looked at his watch, "Yes, there will be time for a row, one trip around the lake. Step in, all of you, and I will take the oars."

Vi was quite ready and Eddie gallantly handed her in, then turned and offered his hand to Elsie. She demurred. "But, mamma! Shouldn't we have mamma with us the first time?" she looked up inquiringly into her father's face.

"Yes, yes, of course!" cried the others, making haste to step ashore again. "We want dear mamma with us the very first time."

Papa smiled approval. "Then we will go back," he said, "and after breakfast, if mamma is willing, we will all come and take a row together. The boat is large enough to carry us all at once."

Mamma's consent was readily obtained, for to please her children was her great delight. So, shortly after breakfast they all repaired to the lake and rowed around and across it several times, a merry, happy party.

At Roselands the family was gathered about the breakfast table and the principal topic of conversation was the return of the party from Viamede. Calhoun had been to the Oaks the previous evening and learned of their safe arrival.

"We must all go this morning and call upon them," said Mr. Dinsmore.

"We'll divide our forces," said Cal, laughing. "Suppose grandpa, mother, and Aunt Enna go first to the Oaks, and we younger ones to Ion?"

"Very well," replied the old gentleman, "I shall spend an hour with my son, then ride over to see Elsie and her little flock. How many of you young folks want to go to Ion in the first division?"

"I" "And I!" "And I!" cried one and then another.

"But you can't go all at once," returned their grandfather, looking around on them with an amused smile. "The carriage is roomy, but, really, you are too many for it. Besides, wouldn't there be some danger of overwhelming your cousins?"

"Well, I'm going, let who will stay at home," observed Molly Percival with cool decision. "The boys can ride—I mean Cal and Art, and Dick and Wal; they all have ponies and the two carriages will hold the rest of us if we crowd a little."

"I'm not going to be bothered with Bob or Betty," said her mother. "They may go with you or wait till another time."

"Then they'll wait," remarked Isadore Conly, "for I shall wear my best silk suit, and I have no notion of being tumbled."

"Last year's suit is quite good enough for the occasion," said her mother. "They're only cousins."

"But rich ones, that can afford to dress, and I'll not go a step if I have to look shabby."

"Nor I," chimed in her sister. "So, mamma, you may as well resign yourself to the situation. It's no good finding fault or objecting," she added with a little laugh.

"Have your own way, then," returned her mother indifferently, "but remember there will be no more dresses this season."

"Dear me, why aren't we rich as the Travillas?" pouted Isadore. "I do think things are very unequally divided in this world."

"Never mind. The wheel of fortune often takes a turn," said her mother. "You may have money left you some day (some of your father's relations arc still rich); and you may make a grand match."

"How long will it take you girls to don your finery?" asked Cal, pulling out his watch. "We'd better start as soon as we can; the sun will be getting hot."

"I'm done," said Molly, jumping up, "and I'll be ready by the time the carriage can be brought to the door. Come Isa and Virgy, you've eaten enough. Cousin Elsie will be sure to treat us to something good." And she ran merrily from the room.

Molly, just turned thirteen, and already as tall as her mother, was a bright, lively girl, full of fun and frolic. She was not a beauty, but had clear complexion and fine, dark eyes; and good humor and intelligence lent a charm to her face that made it more that ordinarily attractive.

Dick had always been fond of her and was beginning to take a brotherly pride in her good looks and intellectual gifts.

Enna's feelings toward her were divided between motherly pride and affection on the one hand, and on the other the dread of being made to appear old by the side of so tall a daughter—dread that made her jealous of Dick, also.

The Conly girls, too, were growing fast, giving promise of fair, graceful womanhood. Isadore was particularly of great beauty, which her mother fondly hoped would be the means of securing her a wealthy husband, for Mrs. Conly's affections were wholly set upon the things of this life. By her and her sister Enna, wealth and beauty were esteemed the highest good, and their children were trained in accordance with that view. The moral atmosphere of this house was very different from that of Ion. At Ion the lives and conversation of the parents were such as to leave no doubt in the minds of their children that to them the things of time and sense were as nothing in comparison with those of eternity.

Enna followed her daughter into the dressing room they used in common.

"Wear the very best you have, Molly," she said. "I don't want you looked down upon as a poor relation, or to have it said that the Conlys dress better than my children."

"I'm sure they don't," said Molly, ringing for the maid, "though they'd like to if they could, and are always jealous when grandpa makes me a present."

"Of course they are, and they manage to get more than their fair share, too," acquiesced the mother in a tone of irritation. "But you see to it that they don't get ahead of you at Ion. Remember, Elsie is as rich as a Jew, and likes the credit of being generous; so, keep on the right side of her if you want all the handsome presents."

"I'm sure she is generous and doesn't give only for the credit of it," said Molly.

"Don't give me any impudence," returned her mother sharply. "Rachel," to the maid, who just then came in answer to the bell, "dress Miss Molly first, and be quick about it."

Enna superintended the business in person, and in a way that sorely tried the temper and nerves of both Molly and the maid. The child's sash must be tied and retied, her hat bent this way and that, her collar and brooch changed again and again, till she was ready to cry with impatience. When, at last, she started for the door, she was called back, and Rachel ordered to change her tiny slippers with walking boots.

"I don't want to wear them!" cried Molly, fairly stamping with impatience. "The heels are so high and narrow, I can't bear them."

"They're just the style and make your foot look beautiful," said her mother. "Sit down and let Rachel put them on you."

"Grandpa says they're dangerous, and so does Dr. Barton, too," grumbled Molly.

"Put them on her, Rachel," commanded Enna. "Molly, behave yourself, or you'll stay at home."

The child submitted rather sullenly, muttering that she would be late.

Rachel was fastening the second boot, when Isadore and Virginia were heard running down the stairs, calling out that the carriage was at the door.

"There! I knew you'd make me late!" cried Molly. "Oh, Rachel, do hurry!"

"Yes, Miss Molly, best I kin; dat's de las' button."

Up sprang Molly, and away in hot haste. She gained the landing, caught her heel in the carpet on the first step of the next flight, and a wild shriek rang through the house, accompanied by the sound of a heavy body tumbling and rolling down the stairs.

Echoing the scream, Enna rushed out into the upper hall.

Calhoun, at the foot of the stairs, was picking Molly up.

"Is she hurt? Is she killed?" asked the mother. "Molly, how did you come to be so awkward?"

"I wasn't! It was those heels. I knew they'd throw me down some day!" cried the child in tones of mingled anger, fright, and pain.

"H'm! You're not killed, haven't even had the temper knocked out of you," remarked Enna, going back to her dressing.

"Poor child, you must be hurt," said Calhoun, laying her gently on a sofa, "but no bones broken, I surely hope?"

"I—I don't know," sobbed Molly. "It's my back. Oh, dear! Oh, dear!"

"Oh, Molly, are you much hurt? Shall I go for the doctor?" asked Dick, coming to her side pale with fright. "Mac's right here at the door, ready saddled and bridled, and—"

"Go for the doctor?" interrupted Molly. "No, indeed! It's very good of you, Dick, but I don't want him; I am going to Ion with the rest of you. I'm ready now."

"You don't look much like it; you're pale as a ghost," he said.

Calhoun added, "You'd better lie still for a while, Molly. Dick or I will take you over this evening, if you find yourself able to go then."

"Thank you, but I'm going to go to Ion now," she answered with decision, getting up and taking Dick's arm.

He helped her to the carriage, where Isadore, Virginia, and some of the younger ones sat waiting, and placed her in it.

She wiped away her tears and tried to smile, while answering the questions and condolences of the others, and the party moved on.

By the time the carriage reached Ion, most of them had nearly forgotten Molly's accident, till Elsie remarked that she was looking pale, and asked if she were quite well.

That brought out the story of her fall.

Elsie heard it with grave concern but asked few questions, as Molly seemed annoyed that the subject had been introduced. It was a habit of her mother's to scold her for awkwardness, and the child was sensitive on that point.

When the young people had left and the older members of the Roselands family called, Elsie seized a favorable opportunity to speak of Molly's pale looks. She urged the importance of calling in a physician so that if there were any reason to apprehend serious results from the fall, measures might be promptly taken to avert the danger.

"She can't have been seriously hurt," returned Enna coldly, "or she wouldn't have been ready to get into carriage the next minute and ride over here."

"By the way," remarked her father, "I haven't heard what caused her fall."

"She's an awkward child, always tumbling about," returned Enna, reddening.

"Especially since she wears those fashionable boots with the high narrow heels," he remarked.

"Had she them on when she fell?"

Enna reluctantly admitted that such was the fact.

"I'll send them into town today, with orders that full half the heel shall be taken off," he said with angry decision.

Chapter Third

'Tis a goodly scene—
Yon river, like a silvery snake, lays out
His coil i' the sunshine lovingly.

—HUNT

The family at Ion presently fell into the old routine of study, work, and play, Elsie resuming the duties of governess; but as the heated term drew on, she and the little ones, especially the babe, began to droop.

"You must go north for the summer," said Dr. Barton. "Start as soon as possible and don't return till October."

"Would you recommend the seashore?" asked Mr. Travilla.

"H'm! That might answer very well, but cool mountain air would, I think, be better."

"Oh, then, mamma!" cried Vi, who was present and had been an eager but hitherto silent listener. "Won't you accept Aunt Lucy's invitation?"

"Perhaps, daughter," Elsie said smiling quite indulgently into the bright little face, "but we will take time to consider what will be best."

"Where is that?" asked the doctor. "Lucy Ross, I suppose, but I've forgotten where they live."

"On the banks of the Hudson, a few miles south of Newburgh; the Crags they call their place, and a beautiful one it is. 'Twas only yesterday I received a letter from Lucy, urging us to come and spend the summer with her."

"I should say go by all means," said the doctor, taking leave.

There were reasons for hesitation on the part of the careful parents of which the physician knew nothing. The young Rosses, all unused to control, were a willful set not likely to exert a beneficial influence over the children—that was the hesitation of the two parents.

However, the final decision was in favor of the visit; and a few days later they set out upon their journey, Mr. Horace Dinsmore taking charge of them, as business made it inconvenient for Mr. Travilla to leave just at that time.

From New York they passed up the Hudson in a steamboat. The carriage from the Crags was found in waiting at the landing, and a short drive brought them to the house, which stood high up above the river, in the midst of magnificent mountain scenery.

The Ion children, taught from early infancy to notice the beauties of nature, were in ecstasies of delight. They were exclaiming anew at every turn in the road, calling each other's, mamma's, or grandpa's attention to the sparkling river, the changing shadows of the mountainsides, here a jutting crag, there a waterfall or secluded glen. Having rested the previous night, sleeping soundly at a hotel, they were not wearied with travel but seemed fresher now than when they left their home.

Lucy and her little flock, gathered on the front porch to receive their guests, gave them a warm welcome. The two ladies had lost none of the affection for each other, which had been one of the happinesses of their childhood and early youth. Each loved the children of the other for the mother's sake if not their own. They numbered the same, but Sophie, Lucy's youngest, was now in her fifth year, and baby Lily was greeted with many expressions and demonstrations of delight.

Lucy excused her husband's absence—he was away on business, she said, but would be at home before night.

"Where's Phil?" asked Eddie, turning to Gertrude.

"Oh, he's at boarding school, don't you know?" she answered. "He'll be home for vacation; but that doesn't begin for two weeks yet."

Mr. Dinsmore tarried for a few days, then returned to the neighborhood of Philadelphia, where he had left his wife and Rosie, who were visiting their northern relatives.

Miss Fisk was still governess at the Crags, and when the children had had a week of play together, it was thought best by the mammas that two hours each morning should be devoted to lessons.

Knowing Miss Fisk to be not only well educated and refined, but also a conscientious and good woman, Elsie was willing to entrust her children to her care; the more so, because Lily in her feeble state, required much of her own time and attention.

In the midst of a beautiful grove of oaks and maples, on the side of a hill, scarce more than a stone's throw from the mansion, and within full view of its windows, stood a small brick building owned by Mr. Ross. It was used as a summer schoolroom for the children.

It was a cool shady spot, enlivened by the songs of the wild birds who built their nests in the trees and the musical tinkle of a little waterfall that came tumbling down from the heights above not half a dozen yards from the door.

Mr. Ross had furnished the room with comfortable and convenient chairs and desks, and Lucy had made it pretty and tasteful with white muslin curtains and neatly papered walls of a neutral tint, enlivened by a few brightly colored pictures. Woodwork and floor were stained a rich dark brown, bright soft rugs were scattered here and there. Altogether, the place was as inviting as a lady's parlor.

The Ion children were well content to spend here two or three hours of that part of the day when the sun was too hot for them to be exposed to its rays with safety and comfort. The others found lessons made much more agreeable by the companionship of their new guests. And Miss Fisk was glad to take them under her charge, because by their intelligence they added greatly to the interest of her work, while their respectful, obedient behavior exerted an excellent influence upon her own pupils.

Before leaving home, Elsie, after careful and prayerful consideration, thought it best to have a plain talk with her older children about the temptations that were likely to assail them during their visit to the Crags.

They had had some past experience with the ways of Lucy's children, and she knew they had not forgotten it. Reminding them of the Bible declaration that "evil communications corrupt good manners," she bade them, while refraining as far as possible from judging their little friends, at the same time to carefully avoid following their example in anything they knew to be wrong.

"Mamma," said Vi, "perhaps sometimes we mightn't know if it was wrong!"

"I think you will, daughter, if you take a moment to think; and if you are doubtful, you may be pretty sure it is wrong."

"Mamma, we mustn't tell tales to you?"

"No, dear, but perhaps you can consult me without that; and do not forget that you can always lift up your heart to God for help to know and do right."

"Yes, dear mamma," returned the little girl thoughtfully, "and I do believe Elsie will 'most always be there and know what's right."

"I'm not sure," said her sister, with a grave shake of her head. "I wish we could always have mamma by to tell us."

"But mamma cannot be with you always, my darlings," Elsie said, regarding them with yearning tenderness. "And so, as your papa and I have often told you, you must learn to think and decide for yourselves—about some things now, and about other things as you grow older and wiser. Some things the Bible tells us plainly, and in regard to those we have nothing to do but obey."

Chapter Fourth

*A child left to himself bringeth his
mother to shame.*

—PROVERBS 29:15

*L*ucy, too, had a talk with her children, in which she begged them quite pathetically, not to disgrace her before the expected guests, Mr. Dinsmore especially, who was so very strict in his ideas of how children ought to be brought up, and how they should behave.

They promised readily enough to "behave splendidly" and for a few days did so astonishingly well that, as she laughingly said, "she began to grow frightened lest they were becoming too good to live."

But she need not have been alarmed; the reaction was not long in coming and was sufficient to relieve all apprehension that they were in immediate danger from a surplus of goodness.

It began on the morning after Mr. Dinsmore's departure. Gertrude was late to breakfast, and when reproved by her mother, answered in a manner so disrespectful as to quite astonish the young Travillas. They expected to see her banished at once from the table and the room; but her mother only looked grave and said in a tone of displeasure, "Gertrude, I cannot have you speak to me in that way. Don't do it again."

"I don't care. You needn't scold so about every little trifle then," muttered the delinquent in an undertone, pulling the dish of meat toward her, helping herself and spilling the gravy on the clean, bright tablecloth.

Mrs. Ross did not seem to hear. She was spreading a piece of bread with the sweetest and freshest butter for Sophie.

"I don't want it; I want waffles!" screamed the child, snatching up the bread the instant it was laid on her plate, and dashing it on the carpet.

"You are not well this morning, dear, and mamma thinks waffles might make her darling worse," said Lucy in a soothing tone. "Come now, be a good baby and eat the bread. Shall mamma spread another piece?"

"No, no, naughty mamma! I'll jus' frow it on the floor if you do," cried the child, bursting into angry sobs and tears.

"Shall mamma have some toast made for her?" she said coaxingly.

"No, no! Waffles! And butter on waffles, and 'lasses on butter, and sugar on 'lasses!"

The mother laughed. It seemed to irritate the child still further; and she screamed louder than ever, slid down from her chair and stamped her foot with rage.

Mrs. Ross was deeply mortified at the exhibition. "Pick her up and carry her to the nursery," she said to a servant.

Sophie kicked and struggled, but the girl—a strong and determined one—carried her away by main force.

"I'm dreadfully ashamed of her, Elsie," Lucy said, turning to her friend, "but she's a nervous little creature and we must try to excuse her."

"A few hearty slaps would reverse the nervous currents and do her an immense amount of good, Mrs. Ross," remarked the governess in her slow, precise way.

"Slaps of any kind, Miss Fisk," returned Lucy reddening, "I don't approve of corporal punishment, as I have told you more than once. I was never whipped, and I don't intend that any of my children shall be."

"Most assuredly not, but I was recommending it, not as a punishment for disobedience or ill temper, but simply as a remedial agent. I have never experienced anything of the kind myself, Mrs. Ross, but have heard it remarked that nervousness occasions greater suffering than is generally understood by the term pain; therefore, I suggest it as I should the amputation of a diseased member when necessary in order to preserve life."

"Permit me to remark," returned Lucy, "that unasked advice is seldom acceptable, and now a truce to discussion, if you please. My dear Elsie," turning to Mrs. Travilla, "I beg you to excuse our ill-manners. It strikes me that none of us is behaving quite as we ought this morning. Hal and Archie, what's wrong between you now?" The two boys, seated side by side, were scowling at each other and muttering angrily half under their breath.

"Why, ma, he went and took the very piece of meat I just said I was going to have," whimpered Archie, digging his fists into his eyes.

"Well, I don't care," retorted Harry, "I'd as good a right as you, and I was ready first."

"Give him a part of it, can't you?" said his mother.

"'Tain't more'n I want myself."

"I won't have it after it's been on his plate," exclaimed the boys one after the other.

"Boys, I'm ashamed of you!" said Lucy, "I wish your father were here to keep you straight. You don't dare behave so before him. I'm sure your little friends would never act so. Don't you see how your naughtiness astonishes them? Vi, would you talk to your mamma as my children do to me?"

The large, bright blue eyes opened wide upon the questioner in half-incredulous, reproachful surprise, then turned upon the beautiful gentle face of Mrs. Travilla with an expression of ardent affection mingled with admiration and respect. "Oh, Aunt Lucy! Could you believe I'd do that to my mamma?"

The very thought of so wounding that tender mother heart was evidently so full of pain to the little one that Elsie could not refrain from responding to the appeal. "Mamma knows you would not, darling."

"Oh, no, mamma, 'cause I love you!" cried the child, her young face growing bright with smiles.

"Atmospheric influences have often a great deal to do with these things; do you not find it so?" Elsie said, turning to her friend.

"Yes, I have noticed that!" Lucy said, catching gladly at the suggestion. "And the air is certainly unusually oppressive this morning. I feel nervous myself. I think we'll have a gust before night."

The last words were spoken in an undertone, but the quick ear of Gertrude caught them. "Then I shan't go to school," she announced decidedly.

"Nonsense," said her mother, "'twon't be here till afternoon, probably not till night, if at all."

"Now, ma, you're just saying that. Aunt Elsie, do you really think it won't come soon?"

Glancing through the open window at the mountains and the sky, Elsie answered that she saw no present indications of a storm. There was nothing to suggest it but the heat and closeness of the air.

"Are you afraid of thunder, Aunt Elsie?" asked little Harry.

"Lightning, you silly boy," corrected Gertrude. "Nobody's afraid of thunder."

"Yes, you are," he retorted. "You just ought to see, Ed, how scared she gets," and Harry laughed rather scornfully.

Gertrude was ready with an indignant retort, but her mother stopped her. "If you are really brave, Gertrude, you can have an excellent opportunity to show it when the storm comes." Then to Harry, "Let your sister alone, or I'll send you to your room."

The gust, a very severe one, came in the afternoon. Before it was fairly upon them, Lucy, herself pale with terror, had collected her children in a darkened room and seated them all on a feather bed. They remained there during the storm, half stifled by the heat, the little ones clinging to their mother, hiding their heads in her lap and crying with fear.

Elsie and her children formed a different group. The mother was the central figure here also, her darlings gathered closely about her, in her dressing room—at a safe distance from the open windows. They watched with awed delight the bursting of the storm clouds over the mountaintops, the play of the lightning, the sweep of the rain down from the heights into the valleys and river below. They listened to the crash and roar of the thunder as it reverberated among the hills, one echo taking it up after another, and repeating it to the next, till it sounded like the explosions of many batteries of heavy artillery, now near at hand, now farther and farther away.

"Mamma, isn't it grand?" exclaimed Eddie in one of the brief pauses in the wild uproar of the violent summer elements.

"Yes," she said, "the thunder of His power, who can understand?"

"Is it God, mamma? Does God make it?" asked little Herbert.

"Yes, dear. 'When He uttereth his voice, there is a multitude of waters in the heavens, and He causeth the vapors to ascend from the ends of the earth; He maketh lightning with rain, and bringeth forth the wind out of His treasures.'"

"We needn't be 'fraid mamma?"

"No, darling, no, for God is our Father; He loves us and will take care of us."

The storm was very violent while it lasted, but soon passed away. The sun shone out, and a beautiful rainbow spanned the eastern sky above the tops of the mountains.

Elsie's children clapped their hands in ecstasy, and ran to call their little friends to enjoy the sight with them. Mrs. Ross followed, looking so pale and exhausted, that Elsie inquired with concern if she were ill.

"Oh, it was the storm!" she said. "Wasn't it fearful? I was sure the house would be struck and some of us killed. Weren't you frightened?"

"No," Elsie said, with a kindly reassuring smile, "I presume my nerves are stronger than yours; and I am not timid in regard to thunder and lightning. Besides, I know so well that He who guides and controls it is my Father and my Friend. Come, look at His bow of promise."

The children were in a group about the window, gazing and admiring.

"Let's ask mamma for the story of it," Vi said.

"The story of it?" repeated Archie Ross.

"Don't you know about Noah and the flood?"

"I never heard it."

"Oh, Archie, it's in the Bible; grandma told it to us once," exclaimed his sister Gertrude.

"I didn't hear it, anyhow," persisted the boy. "Do, Vi, coax Aunt Elsie to tell it."

The petition was readily granted. Mrs. Travilla was an inimitable storyteller, and Lucy, whose knowledge of Scripture history was but superficial, listened to the narrative with almost as much interest and pleasure as did the children.

"I would give anything for your natural talent for storytelling, Elsie," she said at its conclusion.

"Oh, another! Another! Please tell us another!" cried a chorus of young voices.

Mrs. Travilla drew out her watch, and holding it up with a smile said, "Not just now, my dears; see it is almost teatime, and," she added playfully, "some of us have need to change our dresses and smooth our tangled tresses."

"That is true," said Lucy, rising hastily, "and I expect my husband home. I must send the carriage off at once to the depot, for the train is nearly due."

Thereupon a cry was raised among the Rosses as they flew after their mother. "I want to go for papa!" "And I!" "It's my turn, I say, and I will go!" "No, you shan't, for it's mine."

Chapter Fifth

She led me first to God;
Her words and prayers were my
young spirit's dew.

—PIERPONT

"Hello! This looks like a welcome; every one of you has been crying!" Mr. Ross said, catching up Sophie in his arms, and glancing upon his group of children, after an affectionate greeting to his wife and a cordially kind one to their guest.

"What's the trouble? So sorry papa was coming home, eh?"

"No, no, that wasn't it, papa," they cried, crowding around him, each eager to claim the first caress. "It wasn't that, but we wanted to go for you, and mamma wouldn't let us."

"Yes," said Lucy, "they all wanted to go, and as that couldn't be, and no one would give up to the others, I kept them all at home."

"Quite right," he said gravely. "I'm afraid you hardly deserve the pretty gifts I have brought."

"Oh, yes, yes, papa, we'll be good next time! Indeed we will! Mamma, coax him!"

"Yes, do let them have them, Phil," urged his wife. "What would be the use of keeping the things back after spending your money for them?"

"To teach them a good lesson. I'm afraid both you and I are foolishly indulgent, Lucy."

"Oh, they'll be good next time."

"This once, then, but only this once; unless they keep their word," he said, producing his gifts—a book or toy for each of his own children, and a package of sweetmeats which he divided among all present.

He had brought a new dog home with him, but no one but Eddie had noticed it yet. He was stroking and patting it, saying, "Poor fellow, what kind of dog are you?"

"A French poodle," said Mr. Ross, coming up to them. "He's a good watch dog, and excellent for scaring up the wild ducks for the sportsmen. Do you and your papa keep up the shooting lessons, master Eddie?"

"Yes, sir, papa has always said he meant to make me as good a shot as himself, and mamma says it was never his way to give up till a thing's thoroughly done," returned the boy, proudly.

"And you don't equal him as a shot yet, eh?"

"No, sir! No, indeed! Why even cousin Cal Conly—a big man— can't shoot as well as papa."

"What an ugly dog!" exclaimed the other children, gathering round.

"What did you buy it for, papa?" asked Gertrude.

"Not for beauty, certainly," laughed Mr. Ross, stroking and patting the shaggy head of the dog, who was covered with curly hair of a dirty white, mottled with dull brown, "but for worth which is far better. Isn't it, Ranger?"

A wag of his bushy tail was Ranger's only reply.

"Will he bite?" asked little Herbert, shrinking back as the newcomer turned toward him.

"Tramps and burglars, but not good children," replied Mr. Ross. "You needn't be afraid of him, my little man."

Through the evening there was a great deal of romping between the children and the new dog, but little Elsie seemed unusually quiet, scarcely stirring from her mother's side. She was suffering with a toothache, but kept her trouble to herself; principally, because she had a great dread of the dentist's instruments.

But in the night, the pain grew so severe that she could not keep from crying and groaning. She did not want to wake anyone, so buried her face in the pillow to smother the sound of her sobs; but presently a gentle hand touched her caressingly, and mamma's sweet voice asked, "What ails my little daughter?"

"Oh, mamma, I did not mean to wake you!" cried the little girl, sitting up with her hand pressed to her cheek, "but the pain was so bad I couldn't help making a noise."

"My poor dear little girl! Did you think your mother would want to sleep when her child was in pain?" Elsie said, clasping her in her arms. "No, indeed! So do not try to bear any pain alone another time."

Mamma's loving sympathy was very sweet; the pain was soon relieved, too, by some medicine she put into the tooth; and presently all was forgotten in sound refreshing sleep.

Elsie came into her mamma's dressing room the next morning, along with the others, looking bright and well as was her wont, yet with the boding fear that something would be said to her about having the troublesome tooth extracted.

However, to her relief the subject was not broached at all; they had their usual reading and prayer, recitation of verses and talk with mamma about the lessons contained in them, and then the breakfast bell summoned them to their usual morning meal.

The tooth was quiet for a few days, then ached again for several hours harder than ever.

"Couldn't my little girl pluck up courage enough to have it out?" asked the mother tenderly.

"Oh, mamma, don't say I must! Please, don't! I'm so frightened at the very thought!'

"Ah, if I could only bear it for you, my darling! But you know I cannot."

"No, dear mamma, and I couldn't be so selfish as to let you, if I could. But must I have it out?"

"I have not said so; I should far rather my dear daughter would say must to herself."

"Ought I, mamma?"

"Ought you not? The tooth has become only a source of pain and trouble to you. If left, it will cause the others to decay, and decayed teeth injure the health. Health is one of God's best gifts and it is our duty to use every means in our power to preserve it."

"Yes, mamma, but oh, I'm so afraid!" cried the child, trembling and weeping.

"My darling, resolve to do your duty with God's help, and He will fulfill His promise to you. 'As thy days so shall thy strength be.'"

Little Elsie had long ago given her heart to Jesus. Love to Him was the ruling motive of her life, and to please and honor Him she was ready to do or endure anything. "I will try, mamma," she said, "and you, too, will ask God to help me?"

Mamma gave the promise, sealing it with a tender, motherly kiss.

Mr. Ross was going down to New York the next morning, and it was arranged that his wife, Mrs. Travilla, and little Elsie should accompany him.

Mrs. Ross had some shopping to do, but would first take the two Elsies to her dentist, so that the little girl's trial might be over as soon as possible and would be able to enjoy some sight seeing afterward. Baby Lily was better and could be safely entrusted for the day to Aunt Chloe's faithful care.

The plan was concealed from the Ross children because, as their mother said, "It was the only way to have any peace." So they were allowed to sleep until the travelers had taken an early breakfast and gone.

The little Travillas however were up and saw the departure, bidding a cheerful goodbye to "mamma and sister Elsie," sending wistful, longing looks after the carriage as it rolled away, but making no complaint that they were left behind.

"Poor dear Elsie!" Vi said with tears in her eyes. "It's just dreadful that she must have that bad, old tooth extricated."

"Extracted," corrected Eddie. "Vi, you seem to forget what mamma says—that you should never use a big word unless you are sure you have it right, or when a little one would do as well."

"What little one?"

"Pulled."

"Couldn't it be pulled and not come out?"

"Well then, you might say pulled out."

"I like the other word best," persisted Vi. "But you needn't be particular about words when Elsie's going to be so dreadfully hurt."

Herbert burst out crying at that.

"Why, Herbie, what ails you?" asked Vi, putting her arms round his neck and giving him a kiss.

"I don't want the man to hurt my Elsie," sobbed the little fellow. "Maybe dey'll kill her."

"Oh, no, they won't! Mamma will never let them do that. They'll only take away the naughty tooth that hurts her so."

"Come, let's go and walk round the pretty garden," said Eddie, taking Herbert's hand. "Mamma said we may do so."

The breakfast bell called them in to find the Rosses making a perfect bedlam in their anger and disappointment at being left behind by their parents. Sophie was screaming and stamping with rage, the boys and Kate were whimpering and scolding, and Gertrude walking about with flashing eyes was saying, "I'll never forgive mamma for this! No, I never will, for she'd promised to take me along next time she went to the city."

Violet, Eddie, and Harold, hearing these words, looked at each other in horrified silence. "How could she speak so of her own mother?"

Miss Fisk came in, in her quiet, deliberate way and stood looking for a moment from one to another of her pupils in a sort of amazed, reproving silence that presently had the effect of quieting them down a little. Then she spoke.

"Young ladies and young gentlemen, I am astonished— especially at your expressions and behavior, Miss Gertrude Ross! How you can permit yourself to indulge in such invectives against parents so extremely indulgent as Mr. and Mrs. Ross, I cannot possibly conceive."

Sophie, whose screams had sunk to sobs, now permitted the servant to lift her to her high chair; Kate and the boys slunk shamefacedly into their seats at the table; and Gertrude, muttering something about "people not keeping their promises," followed their example.

"Come, sit down my dears," Miss Fisk said, turning to Violet and her brothers. "The tempest seems to have nearly subsided and I hope will not resume its violence."

Herbie was clinging to Vi in a frightened way, sobbing, "I want mamma!" and Harold's eyes were full of tears. It took coaxing and soothing to restore equanimity. Then the breakfast proceeded, everybody seeming to grow brighter and more good humored with the satisfying of the appetite for food.

Vi was a merry little creature, a veritable bit of sunshine wherever she went. And under the influence of her bright looks and ways, sweet rippling laughter and amusing speeches, the whole party at length grew quite merry—especially after Miss Fisk announced that there would be no lessons that day but instead a picnic in the woods.

Chapter Sixth

By sports like these are all their cares beguil'd,
The sports of children satisfy the child.

—Goldsmith

"Good! Good!" cried all the children. "Oh, delightful! But where are we going?"

"To the grove adjacent to the schoolhouse," replied the governess. "We could not find a lovelier spot, and its proximity to the mansion renders it most eligible."

"'Proximity, eligible, adjacent,' what do you mean by those words, Miss Fisk?" asked Gertrude, a little contemptuously.

"I desire that you consult one of our standard lexicographers. You will then be far more likely to retain the definitions in your memory," returned the governess, ignoring the tone of her pupil.

Gertrude shrugged her shoulders, with great impatience, muttering audibly, "I wish you'd talk like other people, and not like a dictionary."

"You quarrel with my phraseology, because you do not understand it," observed Miss Fisk nonchalantly, "which is very irrational; since, were I never to employ, in conversing with you, words beyond your comprehension, you would lose the advantage of being induced to increase your stock of information by a search for their meaning."

"If that's why you do it, you may as well give it up at once," returned Gertrude, "for I don't care enough about your meaning to take half that trouble."

"Miss Gertrude, permit me to remark that you are lacking in respect to your instructor," returned Miss Fisk, reddening.

"Do you mean that it is convenient, because of being so near this house, Miss Fisk?" asked Eddie quite respectfully.

"Yes, convenient and safe, on which account both Mrs. Travilla and Mrs. Ross stipulated that our picnic for today should be held there."

"Well, let's go right away," said Gertrude, jumping up and pushing back her chair.

"Immediately, Miss Ross," corrected the governess. "Right away is exceedingly inelegant."

"How tiresome!" muttered Gertrude. Then, aloud to Violet, as the governess left the room, "I say, Vi, does your mamma reprove you for saying 'right away'?"

"I don't remember that I ever said it. Mamma—"

"Said it?" interrupted Gertrude, with a twinkle of fun in her eyes. "Why don't you say 'used the expression,' my dear?" mimicking Miss Fisk's tones. "You should never condescend to make use of a nickel word, when a fifty cent one would express your sentiments fully as correctly, or per chance even more so."

Vi could not help joining in the laugh with which Gertrude concluded, though feeling rather ashamed of herself, as she seemed to see the grave look of disapproval mamma would have given her if present.

"Oh, Gertrude," she said, "we oughtn't to—"

"Yes, we ought," returned Gertrude as they ran out of the room together. "Mamma always laughs when I take off on old finicky

Fisk. She wouldn't want me to talk like her for the world. Would your mamma wish you to?"

"No, but she never says—"

"'Right away?' No, of course she would not. She says 'immediately' or 'at once' or something that sounds nice. Well, so will I when I'm grown up."

Miss Fisk was on the porch taking an observation of the weather, the children crowding about her, clamoring to be allowed to set out immediately for the grove. The day was fine and there seemed every indication that it would continue so.

"Yes," said the governess, "you may request your maids to see that you are suitably arrayed for the occasion, and as promptly as possible. We will repair to the appointed place—taking our departure in precisely thirty minutes."

The children were ready and impatiently waiting when Miss Fisk came down from her room, "suitably arrayed for the occasion."

They set out at once, the whole party in high good humor. The boys carried their balls, marbles, and fishing rods; the girls had their dolls and a set of toy dishes to play tea-party with.

Miss Fisk had a bit of fancy work and a book, and two servants brought up the rear with camp chairs, an afghan, and rugs to make a couch for the little ones when they should grow sleepy. A grand luncheon was in the course of preparation by the cook, and was to be sent down to the grove by the time the young picnickers were likely to feel an appetite for it.

The boys took the lead, bounding on some distance ahead, with Ranger in their midst. They were in no mood just then to be sitting still; so, depositing their fishing tackle in the schoolhouse, they went roving about in search of more active amusement than that of catching trout.

"That'll be good fun when we want to sit down and rest," said Eddie.

"Oh, I see a bird's nest, and I'm going to have it!" exclaimed Archie, beginning to climb a tree.

"Oh, don't," cried Harold. "Mamma says it's very cruel and wicked to rob the poor little birds."

"Pooh! You're a baby!" answered Archie, half breathlessly, pulling himself up higher and yet higher. "There, I'll have it in a minute," reaching out his hand to lay hold of the branch that held the nest.

Ranger was barking loudly at the foot of the tree, Harry and Eddie were calling Archie to "Take care!" and he hardly knew how it was himself, but he missed the branch, lost his hold of the tree, and fell, lighting upon Ranger's back.

The boy gave a scream, the dog a yelp, and the rest of the party came running to ask what ever was the matter.

Archie picked himself up, looking quite crestfallen, and the fright of the others was turned to laughter as they discovered that he had received no damage beyond a slight scratch on his hand and a small tear in his jacket.

Miss Fisk, making him promise not to repeat the experiment, went back to her seat under the trees and the book she had brought from the house for her own enjoyment.

The morning passed without any further incident worth recording, the children amusing themselves with various quiet plays—the girls keeping house, each under her own particular tree, and exchanging visits; the boys catching trout, which they sent to the house to be cooked for dinner. They wanted to make a fire and cook them themselves, but Miss Fisk wisely forbade it.

She would have had the meal served in the schoolhouse, but yielded to the clamor for an outdoor repast. Several desks were brought out into the shade of the trees, a dainty tablecloth spread over them, and the party presently sat down to a delightful collation, to which all the children brought keen appetites.

Ranger had disappeared. They missed him as they were leaving the table.

"Where can he have gone?" Harry was saying, when Vi cried out, "Oh, yonder he is! And he has a dear little bird in his mouth! Oh, you wicked, cruel dog!" And running to him, she tried to take it from him.

He dropped it and snapped at her, Eddie jerking her back just in time to save her from his teeth, while Archie, who was very fond of Vi, struck the dog a blow with a stick, crying furiously, "You just do that again, sir, and I'll kill you."

Ranger then flew at him, but the boy avoided the attack by jumping nimbly behind a tree.

The other children were screaming with fright, and a catastrophe appeared imminent, but one of the maids came running with some tempting morsels for Ranger, which appeased his wrath, and the danger was averted.

Ranger's attention currently being absorbed with the satisfying of his appetite, the children now looked about for the bird. It was not quite dead, but soon breathed its last in Vi's lap with her tears dropping fast upon it.

"Oh, don't Vi!" said Archie. "I can't bear to see you feel so sorry. And the bird isn't being hurt now, you know; 'twon't ever be hurt any more, will it, Ed?"

"No," said Harry, "we might as well let the dog have it."

"No, no!" said Eddie. "It would just encourage him to catch another."

"So it would," said Gertrude. "Let's make a grand funeral and bury it at the foot of a tree. If we only knew now which one it used to live in."

The motion was about to be carried by acclamation, but Vi entered a decided protest. "No, no, I want to keep it."

"But you can't, Vi," remonstrated Eddie, "dead things have to be buried, you know."

"Not the skin and feathers, Eddie; they do stuff them sometimes and I'll ask mamma to let me have this one done."

"Oh, what's the use?" expostulated Gertrude. "It's only a common robin."

"But I love it—the poor dear little thing—and mamma will let me, I know she will," returned Vi, wiping away her tears as though comforted by the very thought.

The other children wandered off to their play leaving her sitting where she was, on a fallen tree, fondling the bird. But Archie soon came back and seated himself by her side.

"Such a pity, isn't it?" he said. "I hate that Ranger, don't you, Vi?"

"No, I hope not, Archie," she answered doubtfully. "Folks kill birds to eat them and maybe 'tain't any worse for dogs," she added, with a fresh burst of tears. "Poor little birdie! Maybe there are some young ones in the nest that have no mamma now to feed or care for them."

"That old Ranger! And he snapped at you, too. Here he comes again. I'll kill him!" cried the boy with vehemence. "Oh, no, I know what I'll do! Here, Ranger! Here, Ranger!" and starting up, he rushed away in a direction to take him farther from the schoolhouse and the rest of his party.

He had spied in the distance a farmer's boy, a lad of fourteen, with whom he had some slight acquaintance. "Hello, Jared Bates!" he shouted.

"Well, what's wantin'?" and Jared stood still, drawing the lash of his carter's whip slowly between his fingers. "Hurry up now, for I've got to go back to my team. Whose dog's that?" as Ranger came running up and saluted him with a sharp, "bow, wow, wow!"

"Ours," said Archie, "and I'm mad at him 'cause he killed a bird and tried to bite Vi Travilla, when she went to take it from him."

"Like enough," returned Jared, grinning, "but what about it?"

"I thought maybe you'd like to have him."

"So I would; what'll you sell him for?"

"Ten cents."

"I hain't got but two."

"Haven't you, Jared? Truly, now?"

"No, nary red, 'cept them," and diving into his pantaloons' pocket, Jared produced a handful of odds and ends—a broken knife, a plug of tobacco, some rusty nails, a bit of twine—from which he picked out two cent pieces. There, them's um, and they's all I got in the world," he said gravely, passing them over to Archie.

"Well, it's very cheap," observed the latter, pocketing the cash, "but you can have him. Goodbye!" And away he ran back to the spot where he had left Vi and her bird.

"You're a green 'un!" laughed Jared, looking after him; then, whistling to the dog to follow, he went on his way.

Chapter Seventh

*But this I say, he which soweth sparingly
shall reap also sparingly; and he which soweth
bountifully shall reap also bountifully.*

—2 Corinthians 9:6

*A*ll the children, Gertrude excepted, were gathered on the front porch, Vi with the dead bird in her hands, when the carriage drove up with the returning travelers.

There was a chorus of welcome, and most of the young faces were bright and happy. Elsie's little troop had nothing but smiles, caresses, and loving words for her, and tender, anxious inquiries about "sister Elsie."

"Is the tooth out? Did the dentist hurt much?"

"It was hard to bear," she said, "but the doctor was very kind, and tried not to hurt her. And, oh, mamma had made her such a lovely present for being brave and willing to have her tooth out." She took out a beautiful little gold watch and chain from her bosom, and held them up to their admiring gaze.

"Oh, I'm so glad, so glad! Dear mamma, how good of you!" cried Vi, without a touch of envy, embracing first her sister, and then her mother.

Eddie and the two younger ones seemed equally pleased, and "sister Elsie" allowed each in turn to closely inspect her treasure.

In the meantime, Mr. and Mrs. Ross had been busy bestowing caresses and small gifts upon their children, who received them with noisy glee mingled with some reproaches because they had been left at home.

"Come, come, no complaints," said their father. "I think you have fared well—a holiday, a picnic, and these pretty presents. Where's Gertrude?"

"Sure enough, where is she?" asked Lucy, looking round from one to another.

"She's mad because you did not take her along," remarked Harry. "She says you didn't keep your promise, mamma."

"Dear me, I'd forgotten all about it!" exclaimed Mrs. Ross. "I should have taken her, though, but there wasn't time to get her up and dressed."

"Gertrude! Gertrude!" called Mr. Ross, in tones of authority. "Gertrude, come here at once and show yourself, young lady."

At that the child came out slowly from the hall—whence she had been watching the scene through the crack behind the door—looking red and angry.

"What's the matter with you?" asked her father, with some displeasure in his tone.

"Nothing, I'm not crying."

"Nor pouting, either, I suppose? What's all this nonsense about?"

"Mamma promised to take me along the next time she went to the city."

"Perhaps she will the next time."

"But this was the next time, because she promised it when she went before and took Kate."

"Well, such promises are always conditional. She took no one this time but me, and there was a good reason why."

Gertrude smiled slightly, then laughed outright, as she glanced up into his face, saying, "I thought it was you, papa, who took mamma."

"Oh, now you begin to look something like the little girl I'm used to hearing called Gertrude Ross, the one I like to buy presents for. The other one that was here just a moment ago gets nothing bought with my money."

"See here," said her mother, and with a cry of delight Gertrude sprang forward and caught from her hand a watch and chain very nearly the counterparts of those little Elsie was displaying to her sister and brother.

"Oh, joy, joy!" she cried, dancing up and down. "Thank you, papa! I'd rather have this than a dozen visits to New York. See, Kate, isn't it a beauty?"

"Yes," returned her sister sullenly, "but I don't see why you should have a watch and I only this ring. You're hardly more than a year older than I am and not a bit better girl."

"Come, come, don't pout, Kitty," said her father, stroking her hair. "Your time will come. Harry's and Archie's, too; even little Sophie's," he added, catching the household darling up in his arms to give her a hug and a kiss.

It was not until tea that Mr. Ross missed his dog. "Where's Ranger?" he asked of one of the servants.

"That, sir, I don't know," she answered. "Sure he went to the picnic wid the rest of the childer, an' it's mesilf as hasn't seen him since."

"Harry," stepping out on the porch where the children, except the very little ones—who had already been sent up to bed—were sitting listlessly about, too weary with the day's sports to care for any more active amusement, "where's Ranger?"

"Ranger?" cried Harry with a start, "Why, sure enough, I haven't seen him since we came home! And I don't think he came with us, either."

"No, he didn't," answered several young voices.

"I wonder where he can be," pursued Harry. "Shall I go and look for him, papa?"

Mr. Ross was about to say yes when his eye fell upon the face of his youngest son, who, he noticed, looked very red and somewhat troubled.

"What do you know about it, Archie?" he asked. "Can you tell us what has become of Ranger?"

"He behaved very bad indeed, papa," stammered the boy. "He killed a dear little bird and tried to bite Vi, and me too—so I sold him."

The truth was finally out and Archie heaved a sigh of relief.

"Sold him?" repeated his father in a sharp tone of mingled surprise and displeasure.

"Yes, sir, to Jared Bates for two cents. Here they are. I suppose they belong to you," said the little fellow, tugging at his pocket.

"For two cents!" exclaimed Mr. Ross laughing in spite of himself. "You'll never grow rich, my boy, making such bargains as that. But see here," he added, growing grave again, "whose dog was it?"

"I—I thought it was ours, papa."

"Ours? Yours to play with, but only mine to sell or give away. You'll have to go to Jared tomorrow, return his two cents, and tell him the dog is mine, and you sold what did not belong to you."

"Oh, where's my bird?" cried Violet, reminded of it by this little episode. "I laid it down to look at Elsie's watch and it's gone! Mamma, mamma, I'm so sorry!"

"I am too, dear, for your sake," the mother said, putting an arm about her and kissing the wet cheek, for the tears had begun to flow again. "Was it the bird Ranger killed?"

"Yes, mamma, I was going to ask you to get it stuffed for me."

"Some cat has got it, no doubt," said Mr. Ross. "But don't cry. It couldn't hurt it, you know, after it was dead."

"If it only had a heaven to go to," sobbed Vi.

"Perhaps it has," said the gentleman kindly. "I really don't think," turning to Mrs. Travilla, "that the Bible says anything to the contrary. It seems to me to simply leave the matter in doubt."

"I know," she answered thoughtfully, "that is the generally accepted belief that there is no hereafter for the lower animals; yet it has occurred to me, too, that the Bible does not positively assert it. And some of the poor creatures have such a suffering life in this world that it makes my heart ache to think there is no other for them."

"Papa," asked Archie, "don't you think Ranger deserved to be sold for killing that bird and trying to bite Vi?"

"That's a question you should have propounded before selling him; that, and another—perhaps 'may I sell him'?"

"I wish you'd let Phelium go and buy him back," remarked the boy, looking uncomfortable at the thought of having to do the errand himself.

"No, sir," returned the father decidedly. "The mischief you have done, you must undo yourself. Ah, Harry, go and ask if any letters came today."

"I asked," said Gertrude. "There was just one, from Phil," and she drew it from her pocket and handed it to her father.

"What does he say?" Mrs. Ross inquired when he had glanced over it.

"Not much, except that he's to be here tomorrow and wants the carriage sent to the depot for him," he answered, handing it to her.

"Good!" said Gertrude, with much satisfaction. "We always have more fun when Phil's at home."

"Except when he picks a quarrel with you or some of us," remarked Harry.

"For shame, Harry!" said his mother. "The quarrels, if there are any, are as likely to be begun by you, as anyone else."

Lucy was proud and fond of her first-born, and always ready to shield him from blame. He was in his mother's eyes as the king, who could do no wrong; but to the others he was a spoiled child—a willful, headstrong, domineering boy.

Yet, he was not without his good qualities—brave, frank, affectionate, and generous to a fault. Many hearts besides those of his doting parents were drawn to him in sincere affection, Elsie's among the rest. Yet she dreaded exposing her little sons to Phil's influence. She was especially concerned for Edward, as nearer Phil's age; and because, though much improved by good training, his natural disposition was very similar. But she had not seen Philip for two years, and hoped he might have changed for the better.

It seemed so at first. He was a bright, handsome youth, and came home in fine spirits, and with a manner full of affection for parents, brothers, and sisters. She did not wonder at Lucy's fond pride in her eldest son. "Phil," said his mother, following him into his room that night, "you have made a good impression, and I'm very anxious you shouldn't spoil it; so do try to keep on your good behavior while the Travillas stay."

"I intend to, Mrs. Ross," he returned, with a laugh. "Elsie, little Elsie's been my little lady love since the first time my eyes lighted on her, and I know that if I want to secure the prize, I've got to keep on the right side of her father and mother."

Lucy laughed. "You are beginning early, Phil," she said. "I advise you to not say a word of your hopes in their hearing for ten years to come."

"Trust me for managing the thing, ma," he returned, nodding his head wisely. "But do you s'pose now, they'd be so outrageously unreasonable as to expect a fellow to be quite perfect?" he queried, striking a match and lighting a cigar.

"Phil! Phil! Throw that away!" she said, trying to snatch it from him.

He sprang nimbly aside. "No, you don't, ma! Why shouldn't I smoke like my father? Ministers smoke, too, and lots of good people."

"But you're too young to begin yet, and I know your Aunt Elsie would be horrified. She'd think you a very fast boy and hurry away with her children, lest they should be contaminated by your bad example."

"Well," he answered, puffing away, "I'll not let her or them know I ever indulge. I'll only smoke up here and at night, and the smell will be off my breath by morning."

"I wish you'd give it up entirely. Where did you ever learn it?"

"Comes natural! I guess I inherited the taste. But nearly all the fellows at school do it—on the sly."

"Ah, Phil, I'm afraid you're a sad fellow!" Lucy said, shaking her head reprovingly; but he could see the smile shining in her fond, admiring eyes, and lurking about the corners of her mouth.

"Oh, come now, ma, I'm not so bad—not the worst fellow in the world. I wouldn't do a mean thing to anyone."

"No, of course not," she replied, kissing him good night, and leaving him with a parting "Don't forget to say your prayers, Phil."

Mr. and Mrs. Ross were not Christian parents. Careful and solicitous about the temporal welfare of their children, they gave little thought to their spiritual needs. Lucy taught them, in their infancy, to say their prayers before lying down to rest at night. As they grew older she sent them to Sunday school, took them to church on pleasant Sabbath mornings, when it was convenient, and she felt inclined to go herself, and provided each one with a copy of the Bible.

This was about the extent of the religious training they received, and it was strongly counteracted by the worldly atmosphere of their home, the worldly example set them by their parents, and the worldly maxims and precepts constantly instilled into their young minds.

From these they learned to look upon the riches, honors, and pleasures of earth as the things to be most earnestly coveted, most worthy of untiring efforts to secure.

Life at the Crags was a strange puzzle to the Ion children—no blessing asked at the table, no gathering of the family morning or evening for prayer or praise or the reading of God's Word.

"Mamma, what does it mean?" they asked. "Why doesn't Uncle Philip do as papa does?"

Elsie scarce knew how to answer them. "Don't let us talk about it, dears," she said, "but whatever others may do, let us serve God ourselves and seek His favor above everything else; for 'in His favor is life' and 'His loving kindness is better than life.'"

Chapter Eighth

To each his sufferings: all are men
Condemn'd alike to groan;
The tender for another's pain,
The unfeeling for his own.

—GRAY

*T*he weather was delightful. Because of Phil's return, the children were excused altogether from lessons and nearly every day was taken up with picnics, riding, driving, and boating excursions up and down the river.

They were never allowed to go alone on the water or behind any horse but "old Nan," an old slow-moving creature that Phil said "could not be persuaded or forced out of a quiet even trot that was little better than a walk, for more than five consecutive minutes."

The mothers were generally of the party—Lily continuing so much better that Elsie could leave her, without anxiety, in the faithful care of her old mammy—and always one or two trusty servants were taken along.

One day Philip got permission to take old Nan and the phaeton and drive out with the two older girls, Gertrude and Elsie.

They were gone several hours and on their return, while still some miles from home were overtaken by a heavy shower, from which they took refuge in a small log house standing a few yards back from the road.

It was a rude structure built in a wild spot among the rocks and trees, and evidently the abode of pinching poverty; but everything was clean and neat. The occupants were an elderly woman reclining in a high backer wooden rocking chair with her feet propped up on a rude bench, and a young girl who sat sewing by a window overlooking the road. She wore an air of refinement and spoke English more correctly and with a purer accent than sometimes is heard in the abodes of wealth and fashion.

Gertrude ran lightly in with a laugh and jest, Elsie following close at her heels.

The girl rose, and setting out two unpainted wooden chairs, invited them to be seated, remarking as she resumed her work, that the shower had come up very suddenly, but she hoped they were not wet.

"Not enough to hurt us," said Gertrude.

"Hardly at all, thank you," said Elsie. "I hope our mammas will not be alarmed about us, Gerty."

"I don't think they need to be so long as there's no thunder and lightning," answered Gertrude. "Ah, see how it is pouring over yonder on the mountain, Elsie?"

The pale face of the woman in the rocking chair, evidently an invalid, had grown still paler and her features worked with emotion.

"Child! Child!" she cried, fixing her wild eyes on Elsie, "who— are you?"

"They're the young ladies from the Crags, mother," said the girl soothingly.

"I know that, Sally," she answered peevishly, "but one's a visitor, and the other one called her Elsie. She's just the age and very image of—child, what is your family name?"

"Travilla, madam," the little girl replied, with a look of surprise.

"Oh, you're her daughter. Yes, of course. I might have known it. And so she married him, her father's friend and so many years older."

The words were spoken as if to herself and she finished with a deep drawn sigh.

This woman had loved Travilla—all unsuspected by him, for he was not a conceited man—and there had been a time when she would have almost given her hopes for heaven for a return of her affection.

"Is it my mother you mean? Did you know her when she was a little girl?" asked Elsie, rising and drawing near the woman's chair.

"Yes, if she was Elsie Dinsmore and lived at Roselands—how many years ago? Let me see. It was a good many—long before I was married to John Gibson."

"That was mamma's name and that was where she lived, with her grandpa, while her papa was away in Europe so many years," returned the little Elsie. Then she asked with eager interest, "But how did you happen to know her? Did you live near Roselands?"

"I lived there; but I was only a person of no consequence—only a poor governess," returned the woman in a bitter tone, an expression of angry discontent settling down upon her features.

"Are you Miss Day?" asked Elsie, retreating a step or two with a look as if she had seen a serpent.

Her mother had seldom mentioned Miss Day to her, but from her Aunts Adelaide and Lora she had heard of her many acts of cruelty and injustice to the little motherless girl committed to her care.

"I was Miss Day. I am Mrs. Gibson now. I will admit I was a little hard on your mother sometimes, as I see you've been told; but I'd a great deal to bear, for they were a very proud, haughty family—those Dinsmores. I was not treated as one of them, but as a sort of upper servant, though a lady by birth, breeding, and education," the woman remarked, her tone growing more and more bitter as she proceeded.

"But was it right? Was it just and generous to vent your anger upon a poor little innocent girl who had no mother and father there to defend her?" asked the child, her soft eyes filling with tears.

"Well, maybe not, miss; but it is the way people generally do. Your mother was a good little thing, provokingly good sometimes; pretty, too, and heiress, they said, to an immense fortune. Is she rich still? Or did she lose it all in the war?"

"She did not lose it all, I know," said Elsie, "but how rich she is I do not know. Mamma and papa seldom talk of any but the true riches."

"Just like her, for all the world!" muttered the woman. Then aloud and sneeringly, "Pray what do you mean by true riches?"

"Those treasures which can never be taken from us, treasures laid up in heaven where neither moth nor rust doth corrupt and thieves break not through to steal."

The sweet child voice ceased and silence reigned in the room for a moment, while the splashing of the rain upon the roof could be distinctly heard.

Mrs. Gibson was the first to speak again. "Well, I'd like to have that kind, but I'd like wonderfully well to try the other for a while first."

Elsie looked at the thin and sallow face with its hollow cheeks and sunken eyes, and wished mamma were here to talk of Jesus to this poor woman, who surely had but only little time to prepare herself for another world.

"Is your mother at the Crags?" asked Mrs. Gibson, turning to her again.

Elsie answered in the affirmative, adding that they had been there for some time and would probably remain a week or two longer.

"Do you think she would be willing to come here to see me?" was the next question posed, almost eagerly put.

"Mamma is very kind and I am sure she will come if you wish to see her," answered the child.

"Then, tell her I do. Tell her I, her old governess, am sick and poor and in great trouble."

Tears rolled down her cheeks and for a moment her eyes rested upon her daughter's face with an expression of keen anguish. "She's going blind," she whispered in Elsie's ear, drawing the child toward her, and nodding in the direction of Sally, stitching away at the window.

"Blind! Oh, how dreadful!" exclaimed the little girl in low moved tones, the tears springing to her eyes. "I wish she could go to Dr. Thomsom."

"Dr. Thomson! Who is he?"

"An oculist. He lives in Philadelphia. A friend of mamma's had something growing over her eyes so that she was nearly blind, and he cut it off and she can see now as well as anybody."

"I don't think that is the trouble with Sally's; though, of course, I can't tell. But she's always had poor sight, and now that she has to support the family with her needle, her eyes are very nearly worn out."

Sally had been for several minutes making vain attempts to thread a needle.

Elsie sprang to her side with a kindly, eager "Let me do it, won't you?"

It was done in a moment, and the girl thanked her with lips and eyes.

"It often takes me a full five or ten minutes," she said, "and sometimes I have to get mother to do it for me."

"What a pity! It must be a great hindrance to your sewing work."

"Yes, indeed, and my eyes ache so that I can seldom sew or read more than an hour or two at a time. Ah, I'm afraid I'm going to lose the sight in them altogether.

The tone was inexpressibly mournful, and Elsie's eyes filled again.

"Don't fret about it," she said, "I think—I hope you can be cured."

The rain had nearly ceased, and Philip, saying the worst was over, and they were in danger of being late at dinner, hurried the girls into the phaeton.

"What was that woman whispering to you?" asked Gertrude, as soon as they were a good distance away.

Elsie looked uncomfortable. "It was something I was to tell mamma," she replied.

"But what is it?"

"I'm afraid she wanted to keep it a secret from you, Gerty, or she would have spoken out loud."

"I think you're being mean and unaccommodating," retorted Gertrude, beginning to pout.

"No, she isn't," said Philip pompously. "She's honorable, and one of the few females who can keep a secret. But I overheard it, Elsie, and feel pretty sure that the reason she whispered it was to keep the poor girl from hearing. It's very natural she shouldn't want her to know she's afraid her sight's leaving her."

"Oh, yes, I suppose that was it!" returned Elsie. "But you were very wise to think of it, Phil."

"Don't flatter him," said Gertrude. "He thinks a great deal too much of himself already."

Dinner was just ready when they reached home, and both of their mammas were on the porch looking for them.

"So there you are at last! What detained you so long?" said Mrs. Ross.

"Went farther than we intended, and then the rain, you know," said Philip.

"And, oh, we had an adventure!" cried the girls, and hastened to tell it.

Mrs. Travilla had not forgotten her old governess, and though no pleasant recollection of her lingered in her memory, neither was there any dislike or revengeful feeling there. She heard of her sorrows with commiseration and rejoiced in the ability to alleviate them.

"That Mrs. Gibson!" exclaimed Lucy, "I've seen her many a time at the door or window, in driving past, and have often thought there was something familiar in her face, but never dreamed who she was. That hateful Miss Day, as I used to call her. Elsie, I wouldn't do a thing for her, if I were you. Why she treated you with absolute cruelty."

"She was sometimes unjust and unkind." said Mrs. Travilla, smiling at her friend's vehemence, "but probably my sensitiveness, timidity, and stupidity were often very trying."

"No such thing! You'll excuse me for contradicting you, but everybody that knew you then would testify that you were the sweetest, dearest, most patient, industrious little thing that ever was made."

Elsie laughed and shook her head. "Ah, Lucy, you always flattered me; never were jealous even when I was held up to you as a pattern, an evidence that yours was a remarkably sweet disposition. Now, please tell me, what you know about these Gibsons."

"Not much. They came to that hut years ago, evidently very poor, and quite as evidently—so reports say—having seen better days. The husband and father drank deeply, and the wife earned a scanty support for the family by sewing and knitting. That is about all I know of them, except that several of their children died of scarlet fever within a few days of each other, soon after they came to the neighborhood. And that a year ago last winter, the man, coming home drunk, fell into a snow drift, and the next day was found frozen to death. I was told at that time they had two children—a son who was following in his father's footsteps, and this daughter."

"Poor woman!" sighed Elsie. "She is sorely tried and afflicted. I must go to her at once."

"Do, mamma, and get a doctor for her," said little Elsie. "She looked so sick and miserable."

Mrs. Ross offered her carriage, and the shower having cooled the air, Elsie went, shortly after the conclusion of the meal.

Chapter Ninth

I'll not chide thee;
Let shame cover when it will,
I do not call it.

—Shakespeare

"*I* never saw such a likeness in my life!" said Mrs. Gibson, looking after the phaeton as it drove away. "She's the very image of her mother. I could just have believed it was the very little Elsie Dinsmore I used to teach more than twenty years ago."

"She's quite lovely!" exclaimed Sally with great enthusiasm. "Mother, did you see what a pretty watch she had?"

"Yes," gloomily, "some folks seem to have nothing but prosperity, and others nothing but poverty and losses and crosses. They're as rich as Midas and we have hardly enough to keep us from starving."

"Better times may come," said Sally, trying to speak hopefully. "Tom may reform and go to work. I do think, mother, if you'd try to—"

"Hush! I'm a great deal better to him than he deserves at all."

It was some moments before Sally spoke again, then it was only to ask, "Will you have your dinner now, mother?"

"No, there's nothing in the house but bread and potatoes, and I couldn't swallow either. Dear me, what a table they used to set at Roselands! There was enough to tempt the appetite of an epicure."

"I must rest my eyes a little. I can't see any longer," said the girl, laying down her work and going to the door.

"It's just dreadful," sighed the mother, "but don't get discouraged. These people will help us and it is possible some skillful oculist may understand your case and be able to help you."

The girl's eyes were fixed upon the distant mountaintops where, through a rift in the clouds, the sun shone suddenly out for a moment. "'I lift up mine eyes unto the hills whence cometh my help,'" she murmured softly to herself. Then from a full heart went up a strong cry, "Oh, God, my Father, save me, I beseech thee, from this bitter trial that I so dread! Nevertheless, not as I will, but as Thou wilt. Oh, help me to be content with whatsoever Thou shalt send!"

"Sally, you're standing there for a long time." It was the mother's querulous voice again.

The girl turned toward her, answering in a patient tone. "Yes, mother, it rests my eyes to look at the sky and the mountains or any distant object."

"You'd better get yourself something to eat. It must be six or eight hours at least since breakfast."

An hour later Sally, again busied with her sewing by the window, lifted her head at the sound of wheels and exclaimed in a low tone, "There is the same carriage again! It has stopped and a lady is getting out of it."

But turning her head, she perceived that her mother, who was now lying on the bed, had fallen asleep. Dropping her work, she stepped quickly to the door in time to prevent a rap.

She recognized the lady at once from her likeness to her namesake daughter, and holding out her hand with a joyful and admiring smile said, "Mrs. Travilla, is it not? Thank you for coming; I am so glad, and mother will be so delighted to see you; but she is sleeping just now."

She had spoken softly, and Elsie answered in the same subdued tone, as she took the offered hand, then stepped in and sat down in a chair the girl hastened to set for her. "That is just as well; we must not wake her."

A long talk followed in which Elsie by her ready tact and sweet sympathy, free from the slightest approach to patronage, drew from the girl the story of their sorrows, privations, and fears for the future.

Her mother had been gradually failing for some time, though she really did not know what was the nature of the disease. For a while they had contrived by their united efforts to make the two ends meet; but now that all depended upon her, with her poor sight, it was no longer possible.

"How are your eyes affected?" asked Elsie.

"The sight is dim. I can scarcely see to set my stitches. I have great difficulty in threading a needle; I always had. I could never read fine print, never read through a long sentence without shutting my eyes for an instant or looking off the book. It has always been an effort to see, and now I am forced to use my eyes so constantly that they grow worse and pain me very much. At times a mist comes over them so that I cannot see at all until I rest them a little. Indeed, I often seem to be going blind and I'm afraid I shall," she added, with a tremble in her tones, a tear rolling down her cheek. But she hastily wiped it away.

"My poor child, I hope not," Elsie said, laying a hand softly on hers. "There have been wonderful cures of diseased eyes. You must go to an oculist."

"The expense would be far beyond our means."

"You must let me assume that. No, don't shake your head. I have abundant means. The Lord has given me far more of this world's goods than I ought to use for myself or my family and I know it is because He would have me be His steward."

The girl wept for joy and thankfulness.

"Oh, how kind you are!" she cried. "I believe the Lord sent you and that my sight will be spared, for I have prayed so that it might—that He would send me help somehow. But mother, how can she do without me?"

"I will see that she has medical advice, nursing, everything she needs."

Sally tried to speak her thanks but tears and sobs came instead.

The sound woke Mrs. Gibson. "Elsie Dinsmore!" she cried in feeble but excited tones, with difficulty raising herself to a sitting posture. "I should have known you anywhere."

"I cannot say the same; you are much changed," Elsie said, going to the bedside and taking the thin feverish hand in hers.

"Yes, I've grown an old woman, while you are fresh and young; and no wonder, for your life has been all prosperity—mine, nothing but trouble and trial from beginning to end."

"Oh, mother, dear, we have had a great many mercies," said Sally, "and your life is not ended. I hope your good times are yet to come."

"Well, maybe so, if Mrs. Travilla can help us to the medical aid we need, and put us in the way of earning a good living afterward."

"I shall do my best for you in both respects," Elsie said kindly, accepting a chair Sally set for her near the bed.

Chapter Tenth

When we see the flower seeds wafted,
From the nurturing mother tree,
Tell we can, wherever planted,
What the harvesting will be;
Never from the blasting thistle,
Was there gathered golden grain,
Thus the seal the child receiveth,
From its mother will remain.

—Mrs. Hale

For once Mrs. Gibson had the grace to feel a passing emotion of gratitude to this kind benefactor, and shame that she herself had been so ready with fault finding instead of thanks.

As for Sally, she was so completely overcome by the events of the previous day, dropped into a chair, hid her face, and cried heartily.

"Come, don't be a fool," her mother said at last. "There's too much to be done to waste time in crying."

Sally rose hastily, removed the traces of her tears, and began setting the table for their morning meal.

"How soon are you going over to the Crags?" her mother asked at its conclusion.

"Just as soon as I can get the things cleared away and the dishes washed, if you think you can spare me."

"Of course I can. I feel well enough this morning to help myself to anything I'm likely to want."

There was still half an hour to spare before breakfast when, after a round of five or six miles on their ponies, Philip and Elsie reached the Crags.

"What shall you do with yours?" asked Philip, remarking upon that fact.

"Read," she answered, looking back at him with a smile as she tripped lightly up the stairs.

Dinah was in waiting to smooth her hair and help her change the pretty riding hat and habit for a dress better suited to the house; then Elsie, left alone, seated herself by a window with her Bible in her hand.

For a moment her eyes rested upon the blue distant mountains, softly outlined against the deeper blue sky, watching the cloud shadows floating over the nearer hills and valleys—here richly wooded, there covered with fields of waving grain. All the while her ears were drinking in with delight many a sweet rural sound—the songs of the birds, the distant lowing of cattle, and bleating of sheep—her heart swelling with ardent love and thankfulness to Him who had given her so much to enjoy.

Dinah had left the door open, that the fresh air might course freely through the room, and Gertrude coming some minutes later in search of her friend, stood watching Elsie for a little while quite unperceived.

"Dear me!" she exclaimed at length, "How many times a day do you pore over that book?"

Elsie looked up with a smile as sweet as the morning. "I am allowed to read it as often as I please."

"Allowed? Not compelled? Not ordered?"

"No, only I must have a verse ready for mamma every morning."

"Getting one ready for tomorrow?"

"No, just reading. I had time for only a verse or two before my ride."

"Well, that would be plenty for me. I can read it, too, as often as I like, but a chapter or two on Sunday generally does me for all the week. There's the bell; come, let's go down."

Vi met them at the door of the breakfast room. "Oh, Elsie, did you have a pleasant ride? Is Sally Gibson coming soon?"

"I don't know. Mamma said I need not wait for an answer."

There was time for no more, and Vi must put a restraint upon herself, repressing excitement and curiosity for the present, as mamma expected her children to be very quiet and unobtrusive at the table when away from home.

Vi was delighted when just as they were leaving the table, a servant announced that a young person, who called herself Miss Gibson, was asking for Miss Travilla. Vi never liked waiting, and was always eager to carry out immediately any plan that had been set on foot.

Mrs. Gibson was not troubled with any delicacy of feeling about asking for what she wanted, and had made out a list of things to be provided for herself and Sally, which the girl was shamed to show, so extravagant seemed its demands.

When urged by her benefactor, she mentioned a few of the most necessary articles, modestly adding that the generous gift Mrs. Travilla had already bestowed ought to be sufficient to supply all else that might be required.

Elsie, seating herself at her writing desk and taking out pen, ink, and paper, looked smilingly into the faces of her two little girls.

"What do you think about it, dears?"

"Oh, they must have more things—a good many more; and we want to help pay for them with our own money."

"You see, Miss Sally, they both will be sadly disappointed if you refuse to accept their gifts," said Elsie. "Now I'm going to make out a list and you must help me, lest something should be forgotten. Mrs. Ross has kindly offered us the use of her carriage, and we will drive to the nearest town and see what we can find there. The rest we will order from New York."

The list was made out amid much innocent jesting and merry laughter of both mother and children—Sally a deeply interested and delighted spectator of their pleasing exchange. The mother was so sweet, gentle, and affectionate, the children so respectful and loving to her, so kind and considerate of each other.

In fact, the girl was so occupied in watching them that she was not aware till Mrs. Travilla read it over aloud that this new list was longer and more extravagant than the one she had suppressed.

"Oh, it is too much, Mrs. Travilla!" she cried, the tears starting to her eyes.

"My dear child," returned Elsie, playfully, "I'm a willful woman and will have my own way. Come, the carriage is in waiting and we must go."

The shopping expedition was quite a frolic for the children and a great treat to poor, overworked Sally. "She looks so shabby. I'd be ashamed to go with her to the stores or anywhere, or to have her ride in the carriage with me," Gertrude had said to Vi as the little girls were having their hats put on.

Vi answered indignantly, "She's clean and tidy; and she isn't vulgar or rude, and I do believe she's good. And mamma says dress and riches don't make the person."

And that seemed to be the feeling of all. Elsie, too, had purposely dressed herself and her children as plainly as possible so that Sally, though painfully conscious of the deficiencies in her attire, soon forgot all about them and gave herself up to the thorough enjoyment of the pleasures provided for her.

She felt that it would be very ungrateful did she not share the hearty rejoicing of the children over "her pretty things" as they eagerly selected and paid for them with their own pocket money. The children seemed fully to realize the truth of the Master's declaration, "It is more blessed to give than to receive."

Vi would have had the making of the new dresses begun at once, wanting Sally to return with them to the Crags, and let Dinah fit her immediately, but was overruled by her mamma.

"No, dear, Sally must go home to her sick mother now; and Dinah shall go to them after dinner."

"But, mamma, I want to begin my part. You know you said I could hem nicely, and might do some on the ruffles or something."

"Yes, daughter, and so you shall; but you must rest awhile first."

Violet had often to be held back in starting upon some new enterprise, and afterward encouraged or compelled to persevere. Elsie was more deliberate at first, more steadfast in carrying out what she had once undertaken. Each had what the other lacked. Both were winsome and lovable, and they were extremely fond of one another—scarcely less so of their brothers and the darling baby sister.

"When may I begin, mamma?" asked Violet somewhat impatiently.

"After breakfast tomorrow morning you may spend an hour with your needle."

"Only an hour, mamma? It would take all summer at that rate."

"Ah, what a doleful countenance, daughter mine!" Elsie said laughingly, as she bent down and kissed the rosy cheek. "You must remember that my two little girls are not to carry the heavy end of this, and the sewing will be done in good season without overworking them. I could not permit that. I must see to it that they have plenty of time for rest and for healthful play. I appoint you one hour a day, and shall allow you to spend one more, if you wish, but that must be all."

Violet had been trained to cheerful acquiescence in the decisions of her parents, and now put it into practice; yet, she wished very much that mamma would let her work all day for Sally, till the outfit was ready. She was sure she would not tire of it; but she soon learned anew the lessons she had learned a hundred times before—that mamma knew best.

The first day she would have been willing to sew a little longer after the second hour's task was done; the next, two hours were fully sufficient to satisfy her appetite for work. On the third, it was weariness before the end of the first hour; on the fourth, she would have been glad to beg off entirely. Her mother said firmly, "No, dear, one hour's work is not too much for you, and you know I allowed you to undertake it only on the condition that you would persevere to the end."

"Yes, mamma, but I am very tired, and I think I'll never undertake anything again," and with a sigh the little girl seated herself and began her task.

Mamma smiled sympathetically, softly smoothed the golden curls, and said in her gentle voice, "'Let's not be weary in well-doing'! Do you remember the rest?"

"Yes, mamma, 'For in due season we shall reap, if we faint not.' And you told us to faint was to get tired and stop. But mamma, what shall I reap by keeping on with this?"

"A much needed lesson in perseverance, for one thing, I hope; and for another, the promise given in the forty-first Psalm, 'Blessed is he that considereth the poor; the Lord will deliver him in time of trouble. The Lord will preserve him, and keep him alive; and he shall be blessed upon the earth; and thou wilt not deliver him unto the will of his enemies. The Lord will strengthen him upon the bed of languishing: thou wilt make all his bed in his sickness.'

"How would you like to hear a story while you sit sewing by my side?"

"Oh, ever so much, mamma! A story! A story!" And all the little flock clustered about mamma's chair, for they dearly loved her stories.

This was an old favorite, but the narrator added some new characters and new scenes, spinning it out, yet keeping up the interest, till it and the hour came to an end very nearly together.

Then the children, finding that was to be all for the present, scattered to their play.

Mrs. Ross had come in a few minutes before, and signing to her friend to proceed, had joined the group of listeners.

"Dear me, Elsie, how can you take so much trouble with your children?" she said. "You seem to be always training and teaching them in the sweetest, gentlest ways; and, of course, they're good and obedient. I'm sure I love mine dearly, but I could never have the patience to do all you do."

"My dear friend, how can I do less, when so much of their future welfare, for time and for eternity, depends upon my faithfulness?"

"Yes," said Lucy softly, "but the mystery to me is, how you can keep that in mind all the time, and how you can contrive always to do the right thing?"

"I wish I did, but it is not so; I make my mistakes."

"I don't see it. You do wonderfully well anyhow, and I want to know how you manage it."

"I devote most of my time and thoughts to it. I try to study the character of each child. And above all, I pray a great deal for wisdom and for God's blessing on my efforts—not always on my knees—for it is a blessed truth, that we may lift our hearts to Him at any time and in any place. Oh, Lucy," she exclaimed with tearful earnestness, "if I can but train my children for God and heaven, what a happy woman I shall be! The longing desire of my heart for them is that expressed in the stanza of Watts' 'Cradle Hymn':

Mayst thou live to know and fear Him,
Trust and love Him all thy days,
Then go dwell forever near Him,
See His face and sing His praise!"

Chapter Eleventh

Beware the bowl! Though rich and bright,
Its rubies flash upon the sight,
An adder coils its depths beneath,
Whose lure is woe, whose sting is death.

—Street

Mrs. Ross had found a nurse for Mrs. Gibson and a seamstress to help with the sewing. A good many of the garments were ordered from New York ready made, and in a few days the invalid was comfortably established in the seaside cottage recommended by Dr. Morton.

In another week, Sally found herself in possession of a wardrobe that more than satisfied her modest desires. She called at the Crags in her new traveling dress to say goodbye, looking very neat and ladylike—happy, too, in spite of anxiety in regard to her sight.

Not used to the world, timid and retiring, she had felt a good deal of nervous apprehension about making the journey alone. But business called Mr. Ross to Philadelphia and he offered to take charge of her and see her safe in the quiet boarding place already secured by Mrs. Edward Allison, to whom Elsie had written on her behalf.

Adelaide had never felt either love or respect for the ill-tempered governess of her younger brothers and sisters, but readily undertook to do a kindness for her child.

"Have you the doctor's address?" Mr. Ross asked, when taking leave of the girl in her new temporary quarters.

"Yes, sir; Mrs. Travilla gave it to me on a card, and I have it safe. I have a letter of introduction, too, from Dr. Morton. He says he is not personally acquainted with Dr. Thomson, but knows him well by reputation; and if anybody can help me, he can."

"That is encouraging, and I hope you will have no difficulty in finding the place. It is on the next street and only a few blocks from here."

Sally thought she could find it readily. Mrs. Travilla had given her very careful directions about the streets and numbers in Philadelphia; besides, she could inquire if she were at a loss.

When Mr. Ross returned home, he brought someone with him at the sight of whom the Ion children uttered a joyous cry; and who, stepping from the carriage, caught their mamma in his arms and held her to his heart, as if he meant never to let her go.

"Papa! Papa!" cried the children. "We did not know you were coming; mamma did not tell us. Mamma, did you know?"

Yes, mamma had known; they saw it in her smiling eyes. And now they knew why it was that she had watched and listened so eagerly for the coming of the carriage—even more so than Aunt Lucy, who was expecting Uncle Philip, and who was very fond of him, too. But then, he had left her only the other day, and mamma and papa had been parted for weeks.

Mr. Travilla had rented a furnished cottage at Cape May and had come to take them all there. The doctors thought that would be best for Lily now.

The young folks were greatly pleased, and ready to start at once. They had enjoyed their visit to the Crags, but had missed papa sadly; and now they would have him with them all the time—

grandpa and the whole family from the Oaks, too, for they were occupying an adjoining cottage. And the delicious salt sea breeze, oh, how pleasant it would be!

Mrs. Ross was sorry to part with her guests. She had hoped to keep her friend with her all summer; but she was a good deal comforted in her disappointment by the knowledge that her mother and Sophy and her children would soon take their places.

As for young Philip he was greatly vexed and upset. "It is really too bad!" he said, seeking little Elsie out, and taking a seat by her side.

She was on the porch at some little distance from the others, and busied in turning over the pages of a new book her papa had brought her.

"What is too bad, Phil?" she asked, closing it, and giving her full attention to him.

"That you must be hurried away so soon. I've hardly been home two weeks, and we hadn't seen each other for two years."

"Well, a fortnight is a good while. And you will soon have your cousins here—Herbert and Meta."

"Herbert!" he interrupted impatiently. "Who cares for him? And Meta—prying, meddling, telltale Meta is worse than nobody. But there! Don't look so shocked, as if I had said an awfully wicked thing. I really don't hate her at all, though she got me in trouble more than once with grandma and Aunt Sophy that winter we spent at Ashlands. Ah, a bright thought strikes me!"

"Indeed! May I have the benefit of it?" asked the little girl, smiling archly.

"That you may. It is that you might as well stay on another week, or as long as you will."

"Thank you, but you must remember the doctor says we should go at once, on baby's account."

"I know that, but I was speaking only of you personally. Baby doesn't need you, and papa could take you to your father and mother after a little while."

"Let them all go and leave me behind? Oh, Phil, I couldn't think of such a thing!"

The Travillas had been occupying their seaside cottage for two weeks when a letter came from Sally Gibson. This was the first she had written them, though she had been notified at once of their change of address. She'd been told that they would be glad to hear how she was and what Dr. Thomson thought of her case, and a cordial invitation to come to them to rest and recuperate as soon as she was ready to leave her physician.

Elsie's face grew very bright as she read.

"What does she say?" asked her husband.

"There is first an apology for not answering sooner (her eyes were so full of belladonna that she could not see to put pen to paper, and she had no one to write for her). Then, a burst of joy and gratitude—to God, to the doctor, and to me—'success beyond anything she had dared to hope,' but she will be with us tomorrow and tell us all about it."

"And she won't be blind, mamma?" queried Violet, joyously.

"No, dear; I think that she must mean that her eyes are cured, or her sight made better anyway in some way."

"Oh, then, I'll just love that good doctor!" cried the child, clasping her hands in delight.

The next day brought Sally, but they scarcely recognized her, she had grown so plump and rosy; and there was a light in the eyes that looked curiously at them through glasses clear as crystal.

Mrs. Travilla took her by both hands and kissed her sweetly.

"Welcome, Sally, I am glad to see you, but should scarcely have known you had we met in a crowd. You are looking so well and happy."

"And so I am, my dear, kind friend," the girl answered with emotion. "I can see! I can see to read fine print that is all a blur to me without these glasses. And all the pain is gone—the fear, the distress of body and mind. Oh, the Lord has been good to me! And the doctor is so kind and interested! I shall be grateful to him and to you as long as I live!"

"Oh, did he make you those glasses? What did he do to you?" asked the eager, curious children. "Tell us all about it, please."

But mamma said, "No, she is too tired now. She must go to her room and lie down and rest until she can join us at teatime."

Little Elsie showed her the way, saw that nothing was wanting that could contribute to her comfort, then left her to her repose.

It was needed after all the excitement and the hot, dusty ride in the cars; but she came down from it quite fresh, and as ready to pour out the whole story of the experiences of the last two weeks as the children could desire.

When tea was over, they clustered round her on the cool, breezy veranda overlooking the restless, murmuring sea, and by her invitation, questioned her to their heart's content.

"Is he a nice, kind, old man, like our doctor at Ion?" began little Harold.

"Quite as nice and kind I should think, but not very old."

"Did he hurt you very much?" asked Elsie, who had great sympathy for suffering, whether mental or physical.

"Oh, no, not at all! He said directly that the eyes were not diseased; the trouble was malformation and could be remedied by suitable glasses. And oh, how glad I was to hear it!"

"I thought mamma read from your letter that he put medicine in your eyes."

"Yes, belladonna, but that was only to make them sick so that he could examine them thoroughly and measure them for glasses."

Turning to Mrs. Travilla, she said, "He is very kind and pleasant to everyone so far as I could see. He makes no difference between rich and poor, but is deeply interested in each case in turn—always giving his undivided attention to the one he has in hand at the moment, putting his whole heart and mind into the work."

"Which is doubtless one great reason why he is so successful," remarked Elsie, adding, "Remember that, my children. Half-hearted work accomplishes little for this world or the next."

"Weren't you afraid the first time you went?" asked timid little Elsie.

"My heart beat pretty fast," said Sally smiling. "I am rather bashful you see, and worse than that, I was afraid the doctor would say like others, that it was the nerve and I would go blind, or that some dreadful operation would be necessary. But, after I had seen him and found out how kind and pleasant he was, and that I'd nothing painful or dangerous to go through, and might hope for good sight at last, I didn't mind going at all."

"It was a little tedious sitting there in the outer office among strangers with no one to speak to, and with nothing to do for hours at a time, but that was nothing compared to what I was to gain by it."

Then the children wanted to know what the doctor measured eyes with, and how he did it. Sally amused them very much by telling how she had to say her letters every day and look at the gaslight and tell what shape it was, and on and on.

"The doctor told me," she said, addressing Mrs. Travilla, "that I would not like the glasses at first, hardly anyone does; but I do, though not so well, I dare say, as I shall after a while when I get used to them."

Mrs. Gibson's health was improving so that she was in a fair way to recover and as she was well taken care of and did not need her daughter, Sally felt at liberty to stay with these kind friends and enjoy herself.

She resolved to put away care and anxiety for the future, and take full benefit of her present advantages. Yet there was one trouble that would intrude itself and rob her of half her enjoyment. Tom, her only and dearly beloved brother, was traveling the downward road, seeming wholly given up to the dominion of the love of strong drink and kindred vices.

It was long since she had seen or heard from him and she knew not where he was. He had been in the habit of leaving their poor home on the Hudson without deigning to give her or his mother any information as to whither he was bound or when he would return. Sometimes he came back in a few hours, and then again, sometimes he stayed away for days, weeks, or months.

One day Elsie saw Sally turn suddenly pale while glancing over the morning paper. There was keen distress in the eyes she lifted to hers as the paper fell from her nerveless hand.

"Poor child! What is it?" Elsie asked with a motherly compassion, going to her and taking the cold hand in hers. "Is there anything that I can relieve or help you to bear?"

"Tom!" and Sally burst into hysterical weeping.

He had been arrested in the city of Philadelphia for drunkenness and disorderly conduct, fined, and sent to prison till the amount should be paid.

Elsie did her best to comfort the poor sister who was in an agony of shame and grief. "Oh," she sobbed, "he is such a dear fellow if only he could let drink alone! But it's been his ruin, his ruin!

"He must be so disgraced that all his self-respect is gone and he'll never hold up his head again or have the heart to try to do better."

"Don't despair, poor child!" said Elsie, "he has not fallen too far for the grace of God to reclaim him. 'Behold the Lord's hand is not shortened, that it cannot save; neither His ear heavy, that it cannot hear.'"

"And oh, I cry day and night to Him for my poor Tom, so weak, so beset with temptations!" exclaimed the girl. "And will He not hear me at last?"

"He will if you ask in faith, pleading the merits of His Son," returned her friend in moved tones.

"He must be saved!" Mr. Travilla said with energy, when Elsie repeated to him this conversation with Sally. "I shall take the next train for Philadelphia and try to find him."

Tom was found, his fine paid, his release procured, his rags exchanged for neat gentlemanly attire, and hope of better things for this world and the next set before him. With self-respect and manhood partially restored by all this and the kindly, considerate, brotherly manner of his benefactor, he was persuaded to go with the latter to share with Sally for a few weeks, the hospitality of that pleasant seaside home.

He seemed scarcely able to lift his eyes from the ground as Mr. Travilla led him onto the veranda where the whole family was gathered eagerly awaiting his coming. But in a moment Sally's arms were around his neck, her kisses and tears warm on his cheek, as she sobbed out in excess joy, "Oh, Tom, dear Tom, I'm so glad to see you!"

Then Mrs. Travilla's soft white hand grasped his in cordial greeting, and her low, sweet voice bade him welcome. The children echoed her words, apparently with no other thought of him than that he was Sally's brother and it was perfectly natural he should be there with her.

So he was soon at ease among them; but felt very humble, kept close by Sally and used his eyes and ears far more than his tongue.

His kind entertainers exerted themselves to keep him out of the way of temptation and help him to conquer the thirst for intoxicating drink, Mrs. Travilla giving Sally carte blanche to go into the kitchen and prepare him a cup of strong coffee whenever she would.

"Sally," he said to his sister one evening when they sat alone together on the veranda, "what a place this is to be in! It's like a little heaven below. There is so much peace and love; the moral atmosphere is so sweet and pure. I feel as though I had no business here, such a fallen wretch as I am!" he concluded with a groan, hiding his face in his hands.

"Don't, Tom, dear Tom!" she whispered, putting her arm about his neck and laying her head on his shoulder. "You've given up that dreadful habit. You're never going back to it?"

"I don't want to! God knows I don't!" he cried as in an agony of fear. "But that awful thirst—you don't know what it is! And I'm weak as water. Oh, if there was none of the accursed thing on the face of the earth, I might hope for salvation! Sally, I'm afraid of myself, of the demon that is in me!"

"Oh, Tom, fly to Jesus!" she said, clinging to him. "He says, 'In Me is thine help.' 'Fear not; I will help thee,' and He never yet turned a deaf ear to any poor sinner that cried to Him for help. Cast thyself wholly on Him and He will give you strength. For 'everyone that asketh, receiveth; and he that seeketh, findeth; and to him that knocketh, it shall be opened.'"

There was a moment of silence, in which Sally's heart was going up in earnest prayer for him. Then, Mr. Travilla joined them and addressing Tom said, "My wife and I have been talking about your future; indeed, Sally's also. We suppose you would like to keep together."

"That we should," they said.

"Well, how would you like to emigrate to Kansas and begin life anew, away from all the old associates? I need not add that if you decide to go, the means shall not be wanting."

"Thank you, sir. You have been the best friends to us both, and to our mother, you and Mrs. Travilla," said Tom, with emotion. "This is just what Sally and I have been wishing we could do. I understand something of farming and should like to take up a claim out there in some good location where land is given to those who will settle on it. And if you, sir, can conveniently advance the few hundred dollars we shall need to carry us there and give us a fair start, I shall gladly and thankfully accept it as a loan, hoping to be able to return it in a year or two."

This was the arrangement made and preparations to carry it out were immediately set on foot. In a few days the brother and sister bade goodbye to their kind entertainers. Their mother, now nearly recovered, joined them in Philadelphia, and the three together turned their faces westward.

In biding adieu to Elsie, Sally whispered with tears of joy the good news that Tom was trusting in a strength mightier than his own. And so, as years rolled on, these friends were not surprised to hear of his steadfast adherence to the practice of total abstinence from all intoxicating drinks, and his growing prosperity.

Chapter Twelfth

You may as well
Forbid the sea to obey the moon,
As, or by oath, remove, or counsel, shake
The fabric of her folly.

—SHAKESPEARE

carcely had the Gibsons departed when their places were more than filled by the unexpected arrival of a large party from Roselands comprising of Mr. Dinsmore and his daughter, Mrs. Conley and her entire family, with the exception of Calhoun, who would follow shortly.

They were welcomed by their relatives with true Southern hospitality and assured that the two cottages could readily be made to accommodate them all comfortably.

"What news of Molly?" was the first question after the greetings had been exchanged.

Mrs. Conly shook her head and sighed, "She hasn't been able to set her foot on the floor for weeks, and I don't believe she ever will. That's Dr. Pancoast's opinion, and he's good authority. 'Twas her condition that brought us north. We've left her and her mother at the Continental in Philadelphia."

"There's to be a consultation tomorrow of all the best surgeons in the city. Enna wanted me to stay with her till that was over, but I couldn't think of it with all these children fretting and worrying to get down here out of the heat. So I told her I'd leave Cal to take care of her and Molly."

"Dick's with them, too. He's old enough to be useful now, and Molly clings to him far more than to her mother."

"Isn't it dreadful," said Virginia, "to think that that fall down the stairs has made her a cripple for life, though nobody thought she was much hurt at first?"

"Poor child! How does she bear it up?" asked her uncle.

"She doesn't know how to bear it at all," said Mrs. Conly. "She nearly cries her eyes out."

"No wonder," remarked the grandfather. "It's a terrible prospect she has before her, to say nothing of the present suffering. And her mother has no patience with her, pities herself instead of the poor child."

"No," said Mrs. Conly, "Enna was never known to have patience with anybody or anything."

"But Dick's good to her," remarked Isadore.

"Yes," said Arthur, "it's really beautiful to see his devotion to her and how she clings to him. And it's doing the lad good—making a man of him."

"Surely Enna must feel for her child!" Elsie said, thinking of her own darlings and how her heart would be torn with anguish at the sight of one of them in so distressing a condition.

"Yes, of course, she cried bitterly over her when first the truth dawned upon her that Molly was so dreadfully injured. But, of course, that couldn't last and she soon took to bewailing her own hard fate in having such a burden on her hands—a daughter who must always live single and could never be anything but a helpless invalid."

Elsie understood how it was, for had she not known Enna from a child? Her heart ached for Molly, and as she told her own little ones of their poor cousin's hopeless, helpless state, she mingled her tears with theirs.

"Mamma, won't you 'vite her to come here?" pleaded Harold.

"Yes, dear mamma, do," urged the others, "and let us all try to amuse and comfort her."

"If I do, my dears, you may be called upon at times to give up your pleasures for her. Do you think you will be willing to do so?"

At that the young faces grew very grave, and for a moment no one spoke. Quick, impulsive Violet was the first to answer.

"Yes, mamma, I'm willing. I do feel so sorry for her I'd do anything to help her bear her pain."

"Mamma," said Elsie, softly, "I'll ask Jesus to help me, and I'm sure He will."

"So am I; and I think Vi means to ask His help, too?"

"Oh, yes, mamma, I do!"

"And I," "And I," "And I," responded the others.

So the invitation was sent for Molly and her mother and brother to come and pay as long a visit as they would.

A letter came in a few days, accepting it and giving the sorrowful news that all the surgeons agreed in opinion that the poor girl's spine had been so injured that she would never again have any use of her lower limbs.

It was Mrs. Conly who brought the letter to her niece, it having come in one addressed to her. She expressed strong sympathy for Molly, but was much taken up with the contents of another letter received by the same mail.

"I've just had a most generous offer from Mr. Conly's sister, Mrs. Delaford," she said to her niece. "She has no children of her own, is a widow and very wealthy. She's very fond of my Isadore, who is her godchild and namesake. She offers now to clothe and educate her, with the view of making the child her heir, and also to pay for Virgy's tuition, if I will send them both to the convent where she herself was educated."

"Aunt Louise, you will not think of it, surely?" cried Elsie, looking much disturbed.

"And why not, pray?" asked Mrs. Conly, drawing herself up, and speaking in a tone of mingled hauteur, pique, and annoyance.

"You would not wish them to become Roman Catholics, would you?"

"No, of course not; but that need not follow."

"It is very apt to follow."

"Nonsense! I should exact a promise that their faith would not be interfered with."

"But would that avail, since 'no faith with heretics,' has been for centuries the motto of the 'infallible, unchangeable,' Church of Rome?"

"I think you are inclined to see danger where there is none," returned the aunt. "I would not for the world be as anxious and fussy about my children as you are about yours. Besides, I think it quite right to let their father's relatives do for them when they are both able and willing."

"But Aunt Louise—"

"There! Don't let us talk any more about the matter today, if you please," interrupted Mrs. Conly, rising. "I must go now and prepare for my bath. I'll be in again this evening to see Enna and the others. They'll be down by the afternoon train. Good morning."

And she sailed away, leaving Elsie sad and anxious for the future of her young cousins.

"What is it, daughter?" Mr. Dinsmore asked, coming in a moment later. "I have seldom seen you look so disturbed."

Her face brightened, as was its wont under her father's greeting, but this time only momentarily.

"I am troubled, papa," she said, making room for him on the sofa by her side. "Here is the note from Enna. The doctors give Molly no hope that she will ever walk again. One cannot help feeling very sad for her, poor child! And besides, something Aunt Louise has been telling me makes me anxious for Isadore and Virginia."

He was scarcely less concerned than she, when he heard what that was. "I shall talk to Louise," he said. "It would be the height of folly to expose her girls to such influences. It is true I once had some thoughts of sending you to a convent school, under the impression that the accomplishments were more thoroughly taught there than in the Protestant seminaries. But with the light I have since gained upon the subject, I know that it would have been a fearful mistake."

"Dear papa," she said, putting her hand into his and looking at him with loving eyes, "I am so thankful to you that you did not— so thankful that you taught me yourself. The remembrance of the hours we spent together as teacher and pupil has always been very sweet to me."

"To me, also," he answered with a smile.

The expected quests arrived at the appointed time—Enna looking worn, faded, and fretful; Dick, sad and anxious; and poor Molly, weary, exhausted, and despairing—as if life had lost all brightness to her.

Her proud spirit rebelled against her helplessness, against the curious, even against the pitying looks it attracted to her from strangers in the streets and public conveyances.

The transit from one vehicle to another was made in the strong arms of a stalwart Negro whom they had brought with them from Roselands. Dick followed closely to guard his sister from accident and shield her as much as possible from observation, while Enna and Cal brought up the rear.

A room on the ground floor had been appropriated to Molly's use, and thither she was carried at once and gently laid upon a couch. Instantly her cousin Elsie's arms were about her, her head pillowed upon the gentle breast, while tears of loving sympathy fell fast upon her poor, pale face, mingled with tender caresses and whispered words of endearment.

It did the child good. The tears and sobs that came in response relieved her aching heart of half its load. But it vexed Enna.

"What folly, Elsie!" she said. "Don't you see how you're making the child cry? And I've been doing my best to get her to stop it; for, of course, it does no good, and only injures her eyes."

"Forgive me, dear child, if I have hurt you," Elsie said low and tenderly, as she laid Molly's head gently back against the pillows."

"You haven't! You've done me good!" cried the girl, flashing an indignant glance at Enna. "Oh, mother, if you treated me so, it wouldn't be half so hard to bear!"

"I've learned not to expect anything but ingratitude from my children," said Enna, coldly returning Elsie's kind greeting.

But Dick grasped his cousin's hand warmly, giving her a look of grateful affection, and accepted with delight her offered kiss.

"Now, I will leave you to rest," she said to Molly, "and when you feel like seeing your cousins, they will be glad to come in and speak to you. They are anxious to do all they can for your entertainment while you are here."

"Yes, but I want to see grandpa and Uncle Horace now, please; they just kissed me in the car, and that was all."

They came in at once, full of tender sympathy for the crippled, suffering girl.

"They're so kind," sobbed Molly, as they quietly left the room.

"Yes, you can appreciate everybody's kindness but your mother's," remarked Enna in a piqued tone. "And everybody can be sorry for you, but my feelings are lost sight of entirely."

"Oh, mother, don't!" sighed Molly. "I'm sure I've enough to bear without your reproaches. I'd appreciate you fast enough if you were such a mother as Cousin Elsie."

"Or as Aunt Louise, why don't you say?" said Mrs. Conly, coming in, going up to the couch, and kissing her. "How d'ye do, Enna?"

"Yes, even you are sorrier for me than mother is, I do believe!" returned Molly, bursting into tears. "And if it was Isa or Virgy you'd be ever so good to her, and not scold her as mother does me."

"Why, I'm just worn out and worried half to death about that girl," said Enna in answer to her sister's query. "She'll never walk a step again—all the doctors say that." At these words Molly was almost convulsed with sobs, but Enna went on relentlessly. "And when they asked her how it happened, she up and told them her high-heeled shoe threw her down, and that she didn't want to wear them, but I made her do it."

"And so you did, and I only told it because one of the doctors asked if I didn't know they were dangerous. When I said yes, he wanted to know how I came to be so foolish as to wear them."

"And then he lectured me," Enna went on, "as if it was my fault, when of course it was her own carelessness. For if it wasn't, why haven't some of the rest of us fallen down? Accidents happen when nobody's to blame."

"I came near falling the other day, myself," said Mrs. Conly, "and I'll never wear a high, narrow heel again, nor let one of my girls do so. Now I'm going out. You two ought to take a nap—Molly especially, poor child! I'm very sorry for you, but don't cry any more now. It will only hurt your eyes."

Mrs. Conly was to stay to tea and spend the evening. Stepping into the parlor, she found all the adult members of the family there.

"I want to have a talk with you, Louise," her brother said, seating her comfortably on a sofa and drawing up a chair beside her.

"And I think I know what about," she returned with heightened color, glancing toward Elsie, "but let me tell you beforehand, Horace, that you may as well spare yourself the trouble. I have already accepted Mrs. Delaford's offer."

"Louise! How could you be so hasty in so important a matter?"

"Permit me to answer that question with another," she retorted, drawing herself up haughtily. "What right have you to call me to account for so doing?"

"Only the right of an older brother to take a fraternal interest in your welfare and that of an uncle for his nieces."

"What is it, mother?" asked Calhoun.

She told him in a few words, and he turned to his uncle with the query why he so seriously objected to her acceptance of what seemed so favorable an offer for the girls.

"Because I think it would be putting in great jeopardy the welfare of your sisters, both temporal and spiritual."

"What nonsense, Horace!" exclaimed Mrs. Conly angrily. "Of course I shall expressly stipulate that their faith is not to be interfered with."

"And just as much, of course, that very promise will be given and systematically broken without the slightest compunction; because, in the creed of Rome, the end justifies the means and no end is esteemed higher than that of adding members to her own communion."

"Well," said Louise, "I must say you judge them hardly. I'm sure there are at least some pious ones among them and, of course, they wouldn't lie."

"You forget that the more pious they are, the more obedient they will be to the teachings of their church. And when she tells them it is a pious act to be false to their word or oath, for her advancement, or to burn, kill, and destroy, or break any other commandment of the decalogue, they will obey—believing that thus they do God service.

"Really, the folly of Protestant parents who commit their children to the care of those who teach and put in practice, too, these two maxims, so utterly destructive of all truth and honesty, all confidence between man and man—'the end sanctifies the means,' and 'no faith with heretics'—is to me perfectly astounding."

"So you consider me a fool," said Mrs. Conly, bridling. "Thanks for the compliment."

"It is you who make the application, Louise," he answered. "I had no thought of doing so, and still hope you will prove your wisdom by reconsidering and letting Mrs. Delaford know that you revoke your decision."

"Indeed, I shall not; I consider that I have no right to throw away Isadore's fortune."

"Have you then a greater right to imperil her soul's salvation?" he asked with solemn earnestness.

"Pshaw! What a serious thing you make of it," she exclaimed loudly, yet with an uneasy and a troubled look.

"Uncle!" cried Calhoun in surprise. "Do you not think there have been and are some real Christians in the Roman Catholic church?"

"No doubt of it, Cal; some who, in spite of her idolatrous teachings, worship God alone and put their trust solely in the atoning blood and imputed righteousness of Christ. Yet who can fail to see in the picture of Babylon the Great so graphically drawn in Revelation, a faithful picture of Rome? And the command is, 'Come out of her, my people, that ye be not partakers of her sins, and that ye receive not of her plagues.'"

Mr. Dinsmore paused, but no one seeming to have anything to say in reply, went on to give his sister a number of instances which had come to his knowledge, of the perversion of Protestant girls while being educated in convents.

"Well," she said at last, "I'm not going to draw back now, but I shall be on the watch and if they do begin to tamper with my girls' faith, I'll remove them at once. There now, I hope you are satisfied!"

"Not quite, Louise," he said. "Remember that they are accomplished proselytizers and may have the foundations completely and incurably undermined ere you suspect that they have begun."

Chapter Thirteenth

Affliction is the wholesome soil of virtue;
When patience, honor, sweet humility,
Calm fortitude, take root, and strongly flourish.

—MALLET AND THOMSON'S ALFRED

A bath, a nap, and a dainty supper had refreshed Molly somewhat before the children were admitted to her room; but they found her looking pale and thin, and oh, so sorrowful, so different from the bright, merry, happy "Cousin Molly" of six months ago.

Their little hearts swelled with sympathetic grief, and tears filled their eyes as one after another they took her hand and kissed her lovingly.

"Poor child, I so solly for oo!" said Herbert, and Molly laughed hysterically, then put her hands over her face and sobbed as though her heart would break. First, it was the oddity of being called "child" by such a mere baby; then, it was the thought that she had become an object of pity to such a one.

"Don' ky," he said, pulling away her hand to kiss her cheek. "Herbie didn't mean to make oo ky."

"Come, Herbie dear, let us go now; we mustn't tease poor, sick cousin," whispered his sister Elsie, drawing him gently away.

"No, no! Let him stay. Let him love me," sobbed Molly. "He is a dear little fellow," she added, returning his caresses, and wiping away her tears.

"Herbie will love oo, poor old sing," he said, stroking her face, "and mamma and papa, and all de folks will be ever so dood to oo."

Molly's laugh was more natural this time, and under its enlivening influence, the little ones grew quite merry, really amusing her with their prattle, until their mammy came to take them to bed.

Little Elsie was beginning to say good night, too, thinking there was danger of wearying the invalid, but Molly said, "I don't wonder you want to leave me—mother says nobody could like to stay with such a—" she broke off suddenly. Again she hid her face in her hands and wept bitterly.

"Oh, no, no! I was only afraid of tiring you," Elsie said, leaning over her and stroking her hair with a soft, gentle touch. "I should like to stay and talk if you wish, to tell you all about our visit to the Crags, and mamma's old governess, and—"

"Oh, yes, do! Anything to help me forget, even for a few minutes. Oh, I wish I was dead! I wish I was dead! I can't bear to live and be a cripple!"

"Dear Molly, don't cry. Don't feel so dreadfully about it!" Elsie said, weeping with her. "Jesus will help you bear it. He loves you and is sorrier for you than anybody else is. He won't let you be sick or in pain in heaven."

"No, He doesn't love me! I'm not good enough. And if He did, He wouldn't have let me get such a dreadful fall."

Little Elsie was perplexed for the moment, and knew not what to answer.

"Couldn't He have kept me from falling?" demanded Molly, almost fiercely.

"Yes, He can do everything."

"Then, I hate Him for letting me fall!"

Elsie was inexpressibly shocked. "Oh, Molly!" in an awed, frightened tone, was all that she could say.

"I'm awfully wicked, I know I am; but I can't help it. Why did He let me fall? I couldn't bear to let a dog be so dreadfully hurt, if I could help it!"

"Molly, the Bible says 'God is love.' And in another place, 'God so loved the world, that He gave His only begotten Son, that whosoever believeth in Him should not perish, but have everlasting life.' 'God commendeth His love toward us, in that while we were yet sinners, Christ died for us.' He must have loved you, Molly, when He died that dreadful death to save you."

"Not me."

"Yes, if you will believe. 'Whosoever believeth.'"

"It was just for everybody in a lump," said Molly, sighing wearily. "Not for you or me, or anybody in particular—at least not for anybody that's living now. Because we weren't made then, so how could He?"

"But mamma says He knew He was going to make us, just the same as He does now. And that He thought of each one and loved and died for each one just as much as if there was only one."

"Well, it's queer if He loved me so well as that, and yet would let me fall and be so awfully injured. What's this? You didn't have it before you came north," taking hold of the gold chain about Elsie's neck.

Out came the little watch and Elsie told about the tooth and the trip to New York to have it extracted.

"Seems to me," was Molly's comment, "you have all the good things—such as a nice mother and everything else. Such a good father, too; and mine was killed when I was a little bit of a thing, and mother's so cross.

"But Dick's good to me, dear old Dick," she added, looking up at him with glistening eyes as he came in and going up to her couch, asked how she was doing.

"You'd better go to sleep now," he said. "You've been talking quite a while, haven't you?"

At that Elsie slipped quietly away and went in search of her mother.

She found her alone on the veranda looking out meditatively upon the restless moonlit waters of the sea.

"Mamma," said the child softly, "I should like a stroll on the beach with you. Can we go alone? I want to talk with you about something."

"Come, then, daughter," and hand in hand they sought the beach, only a few yards distant.

It was a clear, still night, the moon nearly full, and the cool salt breeze from the silver-tipped waves was exceedingly refreshing after the heat of the day, which had been one of the hottest of the season.

For a while they paced to and fro in silence; then, little Elsie gave her mother the substance of her conversation with Molly in which the latter expressed her disbelief in God's love for her because He had not prevented her fall. "Mamma," she said in conclusion, "how I wished you were there to help make her understand."

"Poor child!" said the mother, in low, moved tones. "Only He who permitted this sore trial can convince her that it was sent in love."

"But you will talk to her, mamma?"

"Yes, when a suitable opportunity offers; but prayer can do more for her than any words of ours addressed to her."

The presence of Molly and her mother proved a serious drawback to the enjoyment of the party during the remainder of their sojourn at the seashore. The burden fell heaviest upon Elsie and her children, as the principal entertainers. And the mother had often to counsel patience and forbearance, and to remind her darlings of their promise to be ready to do all they could for the comfort and happiness of the sufferer.

All made praiseworthy efforts to fulfill their engagement. And Elsie and Vi, particularly the former, as nearest to Molly in age, and therefore most desired by her as a companion, gave up many a pleasure excursion for her sake, staying at home to talk with and amuse her when all the rest were out driving or boating.

Chapter Fourteenth

Ah! Who can say, however fair his view,
Through what sad scenes his path may lie?

*M*rs. Conly adhered to her resolve in regard to the education of
her daughters. And about the middle of September left with them
and her younger children for a visit to Mrs. Delaford, at whose
house the wardrobes of the two girls were to be made ready for
their first school year at the convent chosen by their aunt.

Arthur went with them as their escort. A week later the rest of
the Roselands party returned home and early in October the Oaks
and Ion rejoiced in the return of their families.

Lily had been so benefited by the trip that Elsie felt warranted
in resuming her loving employment as acting governess to her
older children.

They fell into the old round of duties and pleasures, as loving and
happy a family as one might wish to see. This was a striking and
most pleasant contrast to the one at Roselands—that of Enna and her
offspring, where the mother fretted and scolded, and the children,
following her example, were continually at war with one another.

Only between Dick and Molly there was peace and love. The poor
girl led a weary life pinned to her couch or chair, wholly dependent

upon others for the means of locomotion and for anything that was not within reach of her hand.

She had not yet learned submission under her trial, and her mother was far from being any assistance in bearing it. Molly was greatly depressed in spirits, and her mother's scolding and fretting were often almost beyond endurance.

Her younger brother and sister thought it a trouble to wait on her and usually kept out of her way. But Dick, when present, was her faithful slave, always ready to lift and carry her, or to bring her anything she wanted. But much of Dick's time was necessarily occupied with his studies and in going to and from his school, which was two or three miles distant.

He was very thoughtful for her comfort and it was through his suggestion that their grandfather directed that one of the pleasantest rooms in the house, overlooking the avenue so that all the coming and going could be seen from its windows, should be appropriated to Molly's use.

There Dick would seat her each morning, before starting for school, in an invalid's easy chair presented to her by her Cousin Elsie, and there he would be pretty sure to find her on his return. Unless, as occasionally happened, their grandfather, Uncle Horace, Mr. Travilla, or some one of the relatives had taken her out for a drive.

One afternoon about the last of November, Molly, weary of sewing and reading, weary, inexpressibly weary, of her confinement and enforced quietude, was gazing longingly down the avenue. She was wishing that someone would come to take her out for an airing, when the door opened and her mother came in dressed for the open air, in hat, cloak, and furs.

"I want you to button my glove, Molly," she said, holding out her wrist. "Rachel's so busy on my new silk, and you have nothing to do. What a fortunate child you are to be able to take your ease all the time."

"My ease!" cried Molly bitterly, "I'd be gladder than words can tell to change places with you for a while."

"Humph! You don't know what you're wishing! The way I have to worry over my sewing for four beside myself is enough to try the patience of a saint. By the way, it's high time you began to make yourself useful in that line. With practice, you might soon learn to accomplish a great deal, having nothing to do but stick at it from morning to night."

Molly was in the act of buttoning the second glove. Tears sprang to her eyes at this evidence of her mother's heartlessness, and one bright drop fell on Enna's wrist.

"There, you have stained my glove!" she exclaimed angrily. "What a baby you are! Will you have done with this continued crying?"

"It seems very easy for you to bear my troubles, mother," returned poor Molly, raising her head proudly, and dashing away the tears. "I will try to learn to bear them, too, and never again appeal to my mother for sympathy."

"You get enough of that from Dick. He cares ten times as much for you as he does for me—his very own mother."

At that moment Betty came running in. "Mother, the carriage is at the door, and grandpa's ready. Molly, grandpa says he'll take you, too, if you want to go."

Molly's face brightened, but before she could speak, Enna answered for her. "No, she can't. There isn't time to get her ready."

Mrs. Johnson hurried from the room, Betty following close at her heels, and Molly was left alone in her grief and weariness.

She watched the carriage as it rolled down the avenue, then turning from the window, indulged in a hearty cry.

At length, exhausted by her emotion, she laid her head back and fell asleep in her chair.

How long she had slept she did not know. Some unusual noise downstairs woke her, and the next moment Betty rushed in screaming, "Oh, Molly, Molly, mother and grandfather's killed—both of 'em! Oh dear! Oh dear!"

For an instant Molly seemed stunned; she scarcely comprehended Betty's words. Then, as the child repeated, "They're killed! They're both killed. The horses ran away and threw 'em out," she too uttered a cry of anguish, and grasping the arms of her chair, made desperate efforts to rise. But all was in vain, and with a groan she sank back, and covering her face with her hands, shed the bitterest tears her impotence had ever yet cost her.

Betty ran away again, and she was all alone. Oh, how hard it was for her to be chained there in such an agony of doubt and distress! She forcibly restrained her groans and sobs, and listened intently.

The Conlys, except Cal, were still up north. The house seemed strangely quiet, only now and then a stealthy step or a murmur of voices and occasionally a half-smothered cry from Bob or Betty.

A horseman came dashing furiously up the avenue. It was her uncle, Mr. Horace Dinsmore. He threw himself from the saddle and hurried into the house, and the next minute two more followed at the same headlong pace.

These were Cal and Dr. Barton, and they dismounted in hot haste and disappeared from her sight beneath the veranda. Certainly something very dreadful had happened. Oh, would nobody come to tell her?

The minutes dragged their slow length along, seeming like hours. She lay back in her chair in an agony of suspense, the perspiration standing in cold drops on her brow.

But the sound of wheels roused her and looking out she saw the Oaks and Ion carriages drive up, young Horace and Rosie alight from one, Mr. Travilla and Elsie from the other.

"Oh!" thought Molly, "Cousin Elsie will be sure to think of me directly and I shall not be left much longer in this horrible suspense."

Her confidence was not misplaced. Not many minutes had elapsed when her door was softly opened, a light step crossed the floor and a sweet fair face, full of tender compassion, bent over the grief-stricken girl.

Molly tried to speak; her tongue refused its office. But Elsie quickly answered the mute questioning of the wild, frightened, anguished eyes.

"There is life," she said, taking the cold hands in hers, "life in both, and 'while there is life there is hope.' Our dear old grandfather has a broken leg and arm and a few slight cuts and bruises, but is restored to consciousness now, and able to speak. Your poor mother has fared still worse, we fear, as the principal injury is to the head, but we will hope for the best in her case also."

Molly dropped her head on her cousin's shoulder while a burst of weeping brought partial relief to the overburdened heart.

Elsie clasped her arms about her and strove to soothe and comfort her with familial caresses and endearing words.

"If I could only nurse mother now," sobbed the girl, "how glad I'd be to do it. Oh, cousin, it almost breaks my heart now to think how I've vexed and worried her since—since this dreadful trouble came to me. I'd give anything never to have said a cross or disrespectful word to her. And now I can do nothing for her! Nothing! Nothing!" and she wrung her hands in grief and despair.

"Yes, dear child, there is one thing you can do," Elsie answered, weeping with her.

"What is that?" asked Molly, half incredulously, half hopefully, "What can I do to help her as I am chained here?"

"Pray for her, Molly. Plead for her with Him unto whom belong the issues from death; to Him who has power in heaven and in earth and who is able to save to the uttermost."

"No, no, even that I can't do," sobbed Molly. "I've never learned to pray, and He isn't my Friend as He is yours and your children's!"

"Then first of all make Him your Friend. Oh, He is so kind and merciful and loving! He says 'Come unto Me, all ye that labor and are heavy laden, and I will give you rest.' 'Him that cometh to Me, I will in no wise cast out.'"

"Oh, if I only knew how!" sighed Molly. "Nobody needs such a Friend more than I. I'd give all the world to have Him for mine."

"But you cannot buy His friendship—His salvation. It is 'without money and without price.' What is it to come to Him? Just to take Him at His word, give yourself to Him and believe His promise that He will not cast you out."

There was a tap at the door and young Rosie came in, put her arms round Molly, kissed her, and wept for her.

Then young Horace followed and after that his father. Both seemed to feel very much for Molly and to be anxious to do everything in their power to help and comfort her.

Mr. Dinsmore was evidently in deep grief and soon withdrew, Elsie going with him. They stood together for a few minutes in the hall.

"My dear father, how I feel for you!" Elsie said, laying her hand on his arm and looking up at him through gathering tears.

"Thank you, my child; your sympathy is always sweet to me," he said. "And you have mine; for I know this trial touches you also though somewhat less nearly than myself."

"Is grandpa suffering much?" she asked.

"Very much; and at his old age— But I will not anticipate sorrow; we know that the event is in the hands of Him who doeth all things well. Ah, if he were only a Christian! And Enna! Poor Enna!"

Sobs and cries coming from the nursery broke upon the momentary silence that followed the exclamation from Horace.

"Poor little Bob and Betty. I must go to them," Elsie said, gliding away in the direction of the sounds, while Mr. Dinsmore returned to the room where his father lay groaning with the pain of his wounds. Mr. Travilla, Calhoun, and the doctor were with him, but he was asking for his son.

"Horace," he said, "can't you stay with me?"

"Yes, father, night and day while you want me."

"That's right! It's a good thing to have a good son. Dr. Barton, where are you going?"

"To your daughter, sir, Mrs. Johnson."

"Enna! Is she much hurt?" asked the old man, starting up, but falling back instantly with almost a scream of pain.

"You must lie still, sir, indeed you must," said the doctor, coming back to the bed. "Your life depends upon your keeping quiet and exciting yourself as little as possible."

"Yes, yes, but Enna?"

"Has no bones broken."

"Thank God for that! Then she'll do. Go, doctor, but don't leave the house without seeing me again."

They were glad he was so quickly satisfied, but knew he would not be if his mind were quite clear.

Dick had come home in strong excitement, rumors of the accident having met him on the way. The horses had taken fright at the sudden shriek of a locomotive, and the breaking of a defective bit had deprived the old gentleman of the power to control them. They ran madly down a steep embankment, wrecking the carriage and throwing both passengers out upon a bed of stones.

Pale and trembling the lad went straight to his mother's room where he found her lying moaning on the bed, recognizing no one, unconscious of anything that was going on about her.

He discovered that he loved her far more than he would have believed. He thought she was dying, and his heart smote him as memory recalled many a passionate, undutiful word he had spoken to her. Often, it is true, under great provocation; but, oh, what would he not now have given to recall them.

He had much ado to control his emotion enough to ask the doctor what he thought of her case. He was somewhat comforted by the reply.

"The injury to the head is very serious, yet by no means despair of her life."

"What can I do for her?" was the boy's next question in an imploring tone as though he would esteem it a boon to be permitted to do something for her relief.

"Nothing. We have plenty of help here, and you are too inexperienced for a nurse," Dr. Barton said, not unkindly. "But see to your sister, Molly," he added. "Poor child! She will feel this sorely."

The admonition was quite superfluous. Dick was already hastening to her.

Another moment and she was weeping out her sorrow and anxiety on his shoulder.

"Oh, Dick," she sobbed, "I'm afraid I can never speak to her again, and—and my last words to her, just before she went, were a reproach. I said I'd never ask her for her sympathy again; and now I never can. Oh, isn't it dreadful, dreadful!" and she wept as if her very heart would break.

"Oh, don't, Molly!" he said hoarsely, pressing her closer to him and mingling his tears with hers. "Who could blame you, you poor suffering thing! And I'm sure you must have been provoked to it. She hadn't been saying anything kind to you?"

Molly shook her head with a fresh burst of grief. "No, oh, no! Oh, if we'd parted like Cousin Elsie and her children always do—with kind and loving words and caresses!"

"But we're not that sort, you know," returned Dick with an awkward attempt at consolation. "And I'm a great deal worse than you, a great deal, for I've talked up to mother many a time and didn't have the same excuse."

There was sickness at Pinegrove. Mrs. Howard was slowly recovering from an attack of typhoid fever. This was why she had not hastened to Roselands to the assistance of both her injured father and sister.

And Mrs. Rose Dinsmore was at Ashlands, helping Sophy nurse her children through the scarlet fever. And so, Mrs. Conly being still absent up north, the burden of these new responsibilities must fall upon Mr. Horace Dinsmore and his three children.

Mr. Dinsmore undertook the care of his father, Mr. Travilla and young Horace engaging to relieve him now and then. Elsie undertook that of Enna. Elsie's children, except the baby who must come to Roselands with mammy, could do without her for a time. It would be hard for both her and them, she knew, but the lesson in self-denial for the sake of others might prove more than compensation. And Enna must not, in her critical state, be left to the care of anyone but family.

Rosie volunteered to see that Molly was not neglected, and to exert herself for the poor girl's entertainment; and Bob and Betty were sent to the Oaks to be looked after by Mrs. Murray and their cousin Horace.

It would be no easy or agreeable task for the old lady, but she was sure not to object in view of the fact that quiet was essential to the recovery of the sufferers at Roselands.

Chapter Fifteenth

Great minds, like heaven,
are pleased in doing good,
Though the ungrateful subjects
of their favors
Are barren in return.

—ROWE

The short winter day was closing in. At Ion, five eager, expectant little faces were looking out upon the avenue where slowly and softly, tiny snowflakes were falling, the only moving thing within range of their vision.

"Oh, dear, what does keep papa and mamma so long!" cried Vi, impatiently. "It seems most like a year since they started."

"Oh, no, Vi, not half a day yet!"

"I don't mean it is, Eddie, but it does seem like it to me. Elsie, do you think anything's happened?"

"One of the horses may have lost a shoe," Elsie said, trying to be very cheerful. She put her arm round Violet as she spoke. "I remember that happened once a good while ago. But if mamma were here, don't you know what she would say, my dear little sister?"

"Yes, 'don't fret; don't meet trouble half way, but trust in God, our Father, who loves us so dearly that He will never let any real harm come to us.'"

"I think our mamma is very wise," remarked Eddie, "so very much wiser than Aunt Lucy, who gets frightened at every little thing."

"Oh, Eddie, dear, would mamma or papa like that?" said Elsie softly.

"Well, it's true," he said, reddening.

"But they've both told us that unkind remarks should not be made even if true, unless it is quite necessary for the situation."

"Oh, why don't papa and mamma come?" "Oh, I wis dey would! I so tired watchin' for 'em!" burst out Harold and Herbert, nearly ready to cry.

"Look, look!" cried the others in chorus, "they are coming! The carriage is just turning in at the gate!"

But it was growing so dark now, and the tiny flakes were coming down so thick and fast, that none of them were quite sure the carriage was their own until it drew up before the door and two dear familiar forms alighted and came quickly up the veranda steps.

They were greeted with as joyous a welcome as if they had been absent for weeks or months, and returned the sweet caresses as lovingly as they were bestowed, smiling tenderly upon each darling of their hearts.

Almost instantly, however, little Elsie perceived something unusual in the sweet, fair face she loved so dearly, and was wont to study with such fond, tender scrutiny.

"Mamma, dear mamma, what ever is wrong?" she asked.

"A sad accident, daughter," Elsie answered, her voice faltering with emotion. "Poor grandpa and Aunt Enna have been badly hurt."

"Our dear grandpa, mamma?" they all asked, lips and voices tremulous with grief.

"No, darlings, not my own dear father," the mother answered, with a heart full of gratitude that it was not he, "but our poor old grandfather who lives at Roselands."

"My dear little wife, you are too much overcome to talk any more just now," Mr. Travilla said, wheeling an easy chair to the fire, seating her in it, and removing her hat and cloak, with all the tender gallantry of the days when he wooed and won his bride. "Let me tell it." He took a seat near her side, lifted "wee bit Herbie" to his knee, and with the others gathered close about him, briefly told how the accident had happened, and that he and their mother had met a messenger coming to acquaint them with the disaster, and summon them to Roselands. Then he gave the children some idea of the present situation of their injured relations.

When he had finished, and his young hearers had expressed their sorrow and sympathy for the sufferers, a moment of silence ensued, broken by Elsie.

"Mamma, who will take care of them?"

"God," said Herbert. "Won't He, papa?"

"But I mean who will nurse them while they are sick," said Elsie.

"My father will take care of grandpa," Mrs. Travilla answered, "Uncle Horace and papa helping when needed."

"And Aunt Enna, mamma?"

"Well, daughter, who do you think should nurse her? Aunt Louise is away, Aunt Lora sick herself, and grandma at Ashlands with Aunt Sophy and her sick children."

"Oh, mamma, it won't have to be you, will it?" the child asked almost imploringly.

"Oh, mamma, no! How could we do without you?" chimed in the others. Herbert added tearfully, "Mamma stay wis us; we tan't do wisout you."

They left their father to cluster about and cling to her, with caresses and entreaties.

"My little darlings," she said, returning their endearments, "can you not feel willing to spare your mother for a little while to poor, suffering Aunt Enna?"

"Mamma, they have plenty of servants."

"Yes, Vi, but she is so very ill that we cannot hope she will get well without more careful, tender nursing than any servant would give her."

"Mamma, it will be very hard to do without you."

"And very hard for me to stay away from my dear children; but what does the Bible say? Seek your own pleasures and profit, and let others take care of themselves?"

"Oh, mamma, no! 'Thou shalt love thy neighbor as thyself.'"

"'Do good to them that hate you,'" quoted Eddie in an undertone.

"But we were not speaking of enemies, my son," his mother said in surprise.

"I think Aunt Enna is your enemy, mamma; I think she hates you," he said, with flashing eyes. "For I've many a time heard her say very hateful things to you. Mamma, don't look so sorry at me. How can I help being angry at people who say unkind things to you?"

"'Forgive and you shall be forgiven,'" she said gently. "'Do good and lend.' Can't you lend your mother for a few weeks, dears?"

"Weeks, mamma! Oh, so long!" they cried. "How can we? Who will take care of us, and hear our lessons and teach us to be good?"

"Dinah will wash and dress you, Elsie will help you little ones to learn your lessons, and I think papa," looking at him, "will hear you recite."

"Yes," he said, smiling on them, "we will do our best, so that dear mamma may not be anxious and troubled about us in addition to all the care and anxiety for the suffering ones at Roselands."

"Yes, papa," they answered, returning his smile half tearfully; then, they questioned their mother as to when she must go, and whether they should see her at all while Aunt Enna was sick.

"I can wait only long enough to take supper with you, and have our talk together afterward," she said, "because I am needed at Roselands. Perhaps papa will bring you sometime to see me for a little while if you will be very quiet. And it may be only for a few days that I shall be wanted there. We cannot tell about that yet."

She spoke cheerfully, but it cost her an effort because of the grieved, troubled looks on her dear little faces.

"But baby, mamma!" cried Vi. "Baby can't do without you!"

"No, she and mammy will have to go with me."

They were not the usual merry party at the tea table, and a good many tears were shed during the talk with mamma afterward.

They all consented to her going, but the parting with her and the thought of doing without her for "so long" was the greatest trial they had ever known.

She saw all the younger ones in bed, kissed each one good night, and, reminding them that their heavenly Father was always with them, and that she would not be too far away to come at once to them if needed, she left them to their sleep.

Elsie followed her mother to her dressing room and watched for every opportunity to assist in her preparations for her absence. They were not many, and with some parting injunctions to this little daughter and the servants, she announced herself ready to go.

Elsie clung to her with tears at the last, as they stood together in the lower hall waiting for the others.

"Mamma, what shall I do without you? I've never been away from you for a whole day in all my life."

"No, dearest, but be my brave, helpful little girl. You must try to fill mother's place to the little ones. I shall not be far away, you know, and your dear father will be here nearly all the time. And don't forget, darling, that your best Friend is always with you."

"No, mamma," said the child, smiling through her tears. "It is so sweet to know that; and please don't trouble about us at home. I'll do my best for papa and the children."

"That is right, daughter. You are a very great comfort to me now and always," the mother said, with a last caress, as her husband joined her and gave her his arm to lead her to the carriage.

"Don't come out in the cold, daughter," he said, seeing the child was about to follow.

Mammy had just come down with the sleeping babe in her arms, warmly wrapped up to shield her from the cold.

Wee Elsie sprang to her side, lifted the veil that covered the little face, and softly touched her lips to the delicate cheek. "Goodbye, baby darling. Oh, mammy, we'll miss her sadly and you, too."

"Don't fret, honey, 'spect we all be comin' back soon," Aunt Chloe whispered, readjusting the veil, and hurrying after her mistress.

Elsie flew to the window, and watched the carriage roll away down the avenue, till lost to sight in the darkness, tears tumbling in her eyes, but a thrill of joy mingling with her grief. "It was so special to be a comfort and help to dear mamma."

She set herself to considering how she might be the same to her father and brothers and sister, what she could do now.

She remembered that her father was very fond of music and that mother often played and sang for him in the evenings. He had said he would probably return in an hour. Going to the piano, she spent the intervening time in the diligent practice of a new piece of music he had brought her a day or two before.

At the sound of the carriage wheels, she ran to meet him, her face bright with welcoming smiles.

"My little sunbeam," he said, taking her in his arms. "You have been nothing but a comfort and blessing to your mother and me, since the day you were born."

"Papa, how kind of you to tell me that!" she said, her cheek flushing and her eyes glistening.

He kept her with him till after her usual hour for retiring, listening to, and praising her music and talking with her quite as if she were fit to be a companion for him.

Both the injured ones were very ill for some weeks, but by means of competent medical advice and careful nursing, their lives were saved. Yet, neither of them recovered entirely from the effects of the accident.

Mr. Dinsmore was feeble and ailing, and walked with a limp for the rest of his days. Enna, though her bodily health was quite restored, rose from her bed with an impaired intellect, her memory gone, her reasoning powers scarcely equal to those of an ordinary child of five or six.

She did not recognize her children, or indeed anyone. She had everything to relearn and went back to childish amusements—dolls, dollhouses, and other toys.

The sight was inexpressibly painful to Dick and Molly, far worse than following her to her grave.

She remained at her father's, a capable and kind woman being provided to take constant care of her. Bob and Betty stayed on at the Oaks, their uncle and aunt bringing them up with all the care and kindness bestowed upon their own children. Dick and Molly made their home at Ion.

Molly was removed thither as soon as the present danger to her mother's life was past, the change being considered only temporary at the time. Afterward it was decided to make it permanent, in accordance with the kind and generous invitation of Mr. and Mrs. Travilla to her and her brother, and their offer to become responsible for the education and present support of both.

Little Elsie was bravely and earnestly striving to fill her mother's place in the household. She was making herself companionable to her father. She was helping Eddie, Vi, and Harold with their lessons; comforting Herbie when his baby heart ached so sorely with its longing for mamma, and in all his little griefs and troubles; and settling the slight differences that would sometimes arise between the children. She found Molly an additional burden, for she too must be cheered and consoled and was often fretful, unreasonable, and exacting.

Still the little girl struggled on, now feebly and almost ready to despair, now with renewed hope and courage gathered from an interview with her earthly or her heavenly Father.

Mr. Travilla was very proud of the womanly way in which she acquitted herself at this time. He regarded her complete diligence, utter unselfishness, patience, and thoughtfulness for others and did not withhold the reward of well-earned praise. This, with his advice and sympathy, did much to enable her to persevere to the end.

But, oh, what relief and joy when at last the dear mother was restored to them and the unaccustomed burden lifted from the young shoulders!

It would have been impossible to say who rejoiced most heartily in the reunion—father, mother, or children. But every heart leaped lightly, every face was bright with smiles.

Mrs. Travilla knew she was adding greatly to her cares and to the annoyances and petty trials of everyday life in taking Dick and especially Molly into her family, but she realized it more and more as the months and years rolled on. Both had been so spoiled by Enna's unwise and capricious treatment, that it was a difficult thing to control them. And poor Molly's sad affliction caused her frequent fits of depression that rendered her a burden to herself and to others. Also, she inherited to some extent, her mother's infirmities of temper so that her envy, jealousy, and unreasonableness made her presence in the family a trial to her young cousins.

The mother had to teach patience, meekness, and forbearance by precept and example, ever holding up as the grand motive, love to Jesus, and a desire to please and honor Him. Such constant sowing of the good seed, such patient, careful weeding out of the tares, such watchfulness and prayerfulness as Elsie bestowed upon the children God had given her, could not fail of their reward from Him who has said, "Whatsoever a man soweth, that shall he also reap." And as the years rolled on, she had the unspeakable joy of seeing her darlings, one after another gathered into the fold of the

Good Shepherd. One by one consecrating themselves in the dew of their youth to the service of Him who had loved them and washed them from their sins in His own blood.

She was scarcely less earnest and persistent in her efforts to promote the welfare, temporal and spiritual, of Molly and Dick. She far more than supplied the place of the mother, now almost worse than lost to them.

They had always liked and respected her; they soon learned to love her deeply, and grew happier and more lovable under the refining, elevating influence of her conduct and conversation.

She and her husband gave to both Dick and Molly the best advantages of education that money could procure, aroused in them the desire, and stimulated them to earnest efforts to become useful members of society.

Elsie soon discovered that one grand element of Molly's depression was the thought that she was cut off from all the activities of life and doomed, by her sad affliction, to be a useless burden upon others.

"My poor dear child!" she said clasping the weeping girl in her arms. "That would be a sad fate indeed, but it is not yours. There are many walks of usefulness still open to you—literature, several of the arts and sciences, music, painting, authorship, to say nothing of needle work both plain and fancy. The first thing will be a good education in the ordinary sense of the term. And that you can take as easily as one who has the use of all her limbs. Books and masters shall be at your command, and when you have decided to what employment you will especially devote yourself, every facility shall be given you for perfecting yourself in it."

"Oh, Cousin Elsie," cried the girl, her eyes shining, "do you think I could ever write books or paint pictures? I mean, such as would be really worth the doing, such as would make Dick proud of me and perhaps give me money to help him with, because you know the poor fellow must make his own way in the world."

"I scarcely know how to answer that question," Elsie said, smiling at her sudden enthusiasm, "but I do know that patience and perseverance will do wonders, and if you practice them faithfully, it will not surprise me to see you someday turn out a great author or artist."

"But don't fret because Dick has not a fortune to begin with. Our very noblest and most successful men have been those who had to win their way by dint of hard and determined struggling with early disadvantages. 'Young trees root the faster with shaking!'" she added with a smile.

"Oh, then Dick will succeed, I know, dear, noble fellow!" cried Molly flushing with sisterly pride.

From that time she took heart and though there were occasional returns of despondency and gloom, she strove to banish them and was upon the whole brave, cheerful, and energetic in carrying out the plans her cousin had suggested.

Chapter Sixteenth

It is as if the night should shade noonday,
Or that the sun was here, but forced away;
And we were left, under that hemisphere,
Where we must feel it dark for half a year.

—BEN JOHNSON

*S*ince the events recorded in the last chapter, six years rolled their swift, though noiseless round. Six years brought such changes as they must—growth and development to the very young, a richer maturity, a riper experience to those who had already attained an adult life, and to the aged, increasing infirmities, reminding them that their race was nearly run. It may be so with others; it must be so with them.

There had been gains and losses, sickness and other afflictions, but death had not yet entered any of their homes.

At Ion, the emerald, velvety lawn, the grand old trees, the sparkling lakelet, the flower gardens and conservatories bright with rich autumn hues, were looking their loveliest in the light of a fair September morning.

The sun was scarcely an hour high and, except in the region of the kitchen and stables, quiet reigned within and without the mansion. Doors and windows stood wide open and servants were busied here and there cleaning and setting in order for the day, but without noise and bustle. In the avenue before the front entrance stood Solon with the pretty grey ponies, Prince and Princess, ready saddled and bridled. While on the veranda sat a tall, dark-eyed, handsome youth, a riding whip in one hand, the other gently stroking and patting the head of Bruno, as it rested on his knee—the dog receiving the caress with demonstrations of delight.

A light, springing step passed down the broad stairway, crossed the hall, and a slender fairy-like form appeared in the doorway. It was Violet, now thirteen, and already a woman in height, though the innocent childlike trust in the sweet, fair face and azure eyes told another tale.

"Good morning, Eddie," she said. "I am sorry to have kept you waiting."

"Oh, good morning," he cried, jumping up and turning toward her. "No need for apology, Vi, I've not been here five minutes."

He handed her gallantly to the saddle, then mounted himself.

"Try to cheer up, little sister; one should not be sad on such a lovely morning as this," he said as they trotted down the avenue side by side.

"Oh, Eddie," she answered, with tears in her voice, "I do try, but I can't yet. It isn't like home without them."

"No, no indeed, Vi; how could it be? Mr. and Mrs. Daly are very kind, yet not in the least like our father and mother. But it would be impossible for anyone to take their places in our hearts or home."

"The only way to feel at all reconciled is to keep looking forward to the delight of seeing them return with our darling Lily well and strong," Vi said, struggling bravely with her tears.

Eddie answered, "I cannot help hoping that that may be in spite of all the discouraging things the doctors have said."

Lily, always frail and delicate, had drooped more and more during the past year. And only yesterday the parents had left with her for the North, intending to try the effect of different watering places, in the faint hope that the child might yet be restored to health, or her life at least prolonged for a few years.

They had taken with them their eldest daughter, an infant son, and several servants.

Aunt Chloe and Uncle Joe were not of the party, increasing infirmities compelling them to stay behind at home.

The separation from her idolized mistress caused the former many tears, but she was much comforted by Elsie's assurance that to have her at home to watch over the children there would be a great comfort and relief from anxiety on their account.

It had seemed to Mr. and Mrs. Travilla a very kind providence that had sent them an excellent tutor and housekeeper in the persons of Mr. and Mrs. Daly, their former guests at Viamede.

Since the winter spent together there, an occasional correspondence had been kept up between the two families. Learning from it that Mr. Daly was again in need of a change of climate just as they were casting about for some suitable persons to take charge of their house and children during their contemplated absence from home, Elsie suggested to her husband that the situations should be offered to him and his wife.

Mr. Travilla approved, the offer was made at once, and promptly and thankfully accepted.

Frank Daly, now a fine lad of eleven, was invited to come with his parents, and to share his in his father's instructions.

They had now been in the house for more than a week, and seemed eminently suited to the duties they had undertaken. Yet, home was sadly changed to the children, deprived for the first time in their lives of the parents who they so dearly loved, and who so thoroughly understood and sympathized with them.

Eddie was growing very manly, and he was well advanced in his studies, easy and polished in manner. Vi and the younger ones looked up to him with pride and respect, as the big brother who knew a great deal, and in papa's absence would be their leader and protector.

He, on his part, was fond and proud of them all, but more especially of Elsie and Vi, who grew daily in beauty and grace.

"You can't think how sorely I have missed Elsie this morning," Vi said, breaking a slight pause in the talk, "and yet I am glad she went, too. She will be such a comfort to mamma and Lily, and she promised me to write every day—which, of course, mamma could not find time to do."

"Yes, and her absence will give you an opportunity for practice in that line and in being motherly to Rosie," Eddie said with a smile.

"To Herbie, too," she answered. "We are to meet in mamma's dressing room every morning just as usual, only it will be a strange half hour without mamma. But we will say our verses to each other, talk them over and read together."

"Yes, I promised mamma that I would be with you. Which way now?" he asked as they came to the crossroads.

"To the Oaks. I want to see grandpa. A caress, or even a word or smile from him would do me good this morning."

"He may not be up."

"But I think he will. You know he likes to keep early hours."

Mr. Dinsmore was up and pacing the veranda thoughtfully to and fro, as the young riders came into his line of sight.

He welcomed them with a smile, and lifting Vi from her pony, held her close to his heart as something very dear and precious.

"My darling," he said, "your face is sad this morning, and no wonder. Yet, cheer up, we will hope to see our dear travelers at home again in a few weeks, our poor fading flower restored to bloom and health."

He made them sit down and regale themselves with some fine fresh oranges, which he summoned a servant to bring. Their grandma, aunt, and uncle joined them presently and they were urged to stay to breakfast, but declined. "The little ones must not be left alone this first morning without papa and mamma."

On their return, Rosie—a merry, healthy, romping child of five, with a rich, creamy complexion, dark hair and eyes, forming a strong contrast to Vi's blonde beauty—came bounding to meet them.

"Oh, Vi, I've been wanting you! You'll have to be mamma to us now, you know, till our real own mamma comes back. And, Eddie, you'll have to be the papa. Won't he, Vi? Come let's all go to mamma's dressing room; my verse is ready."

"What is your verse, Rosie?" Violet asked when they reached the room, sitting down and drawing the child to her side.

"Take me in your lap like mamma does and I'll say it."

"Now then," Vi said, complying with the request.

"'When my father and my mother forsake me then the Lord will take me up.'"

"Who taught you that, dear?" asked Vi, with a slight tremble in her low sweet tones.

"Cousin Molly. I was crying for mamma and papa and she called me in there and told me I mustn't cry, 'cause Jesus loves me and will never, never go away from me."

"That's like my verse," said Herbert. "Mamma gave it to me for today. 'I will never leave thee, nor forsake thee.'"

"And mine," said Harold, "'Lo, I am with you always, even unto the end of the world.'"

"'This God is our God forever and ever; He will be our guide even unto death,'" repeated Vi quite feelingly.

"That's a nice one," said Rosie.

"Yes," said Eddie, "and this is a nice one for us to remember just now in connection with the dear ones on their journey, and for ourselves when we go away. Yes, now, and at all times. 'Behold I am with thee, and will keep thee in all places whither thou goest, and will bring thee again into this land.'"

"Isn't the Bible the sweetest book!" exclaimed Vi. "The Book of books—it has been a comforting word for everybody and in every time of need."

The breakfast bell rang.

"Oh, dear!" cried Rosie, clinging to Violet, her chest heaving with sobs. "How can we go to the table and eat without papa and mamma?"

"Don't cry, little dear, don't cry. You know they want us to be cheerful and make it pleasant for Mr. and Mrs. Daly," the others said, and with a great effort the child swallowed her sobs. Then, wiping away her tears, she allowed Vi to lead her down to the breakfast room.

Mrs. Daly met them with a smiling face and kind motherly greeting. Mr. Daly had a pleasant word for each and talked so entertainingly all through the meal that not a one had scarcely time for sad or lonely thoughts.

Family worship followed immediately after breakfast, as was the custom of the house. Mr. Daly's prayers were short, comforting them all, and simple enough for even little Rosie to understand.

There was still time for a walk before school, but first Vi went to Molly to ask how she was and to carry her a letter from Dick which had come by the morning mail.

Dick was in Philadelphia studying medicine. He and Molly corresponded regularly and she knew no greater treat than a letter from him. Vi was glad she could carry it to her this morning. It was so great a pleasure to be the bearer of anything so welcome.

There were no more pleasant or better-furnished rooms in the house than those appropriated to the use of the poor, dependent, crippled cousin. Molly—herself tastefully and becomingly dressed, blooming, bright, and cheerful—sat in an invalid chair by the open window. She was reading, and so absorbed in her book that she did not hear the light step of her young relative.

Vi paused in the doorway a moment, thinking what a pretty picture Molly made—with her intellectual countenance, clear complexion, rosy cheeks, bright eyes and glossy braids—framed by the vine-wreathed window.

Molly looked up and laying aside her book, "Ah, Vi, this is kind!" she said. "Come in, do; I'm ever so glad to see you."

"And what of this?" asked Vi, holding up the letter.

"Oh, delightful! Dear old fellow to write so soon. I was not expecting it till tomorrow."

"I knew you'd be glad," Vi said, putting it into her hand, "and now I'll just kiss you good morning and run away, that you may enjoy it fully before lesson time."

Rosie's voice was summoning Vi. The children were on the veranda ready for their morning walk, waiting only for "Sister Vi."

"Let's walk to the Oaks," said Rosie, slipping her hand into Vi's. "It's a nice shady walk, and I like to throw pebbles into the water. But I'll feed the fishes first. See what a bag full of crumbs mammy has given me."

Violet was very patient and indulgent toward the little sister, yet obliged to cut short her sport with the pebbles and the fishes, because the hour for lessons drew near.

Chapter Seventeenth

The lilies faintly to the roses yield,
As on the lovely cheek they struggling vie,
And thoughts are in thy speaking eyes revealed,
Pure as the fount the prophet's rod unseal'd.

—HOFFMAN

"*D*r. Arthur lef 'dis for you, Miss Wi'let," said one of the maids, meeting her young mistress on the veranda and handing her a note.

"Cousin Arthur? Was he here?"

"Yes, miss. He axed for you, but hadn't no time to stop, not even to see po' Miss Molly. 'Spect somebody's mighty sick."

Arthur Conley had entered the medical profession, and for the last two years had been practicing in partnership with Dr. Barton.

Vi glanced quickly over the note and hastened to Eddie, who she found in the schoolroom—its sole occupant at the moment.

"Here's a note from Isa, asking us to bring Rosie and come to Roselands for the rest of the day, after lessons are done. She thinks I must feel lonely. It is very kind, but what shall I do about it? Rosie would enjoy going, but would it be kind to you or the boys or Molly?"

"I might take the boys over to the Oaks, but I don't know— oh, I think Molly would probably prefer solitude, as I happen to know that she has some writing to do. Well, what now?" seeing a hesitating, perplexed look on Vi's face.

"I cannot ask permission of papa or mamma."

"No, of course not. We must go to Mr. Daly for that now."

"I don't like it," she answered, coloring. "It does seem as if nobody has the right to control us except our father and mother and our grandparents."

"Only that they have given him the right for the present time, Vi."

Mr. Daly came in at that instant and Vi, placing the note in his hand, said, "Will you please look at this, sir, and tell me if I may accept the invitation?"

"I see no objection," he said, returning it with a kindly smile, "provided your lessons are well recited."

Mr. Daly was an excellent teacher, thoroughly prepared for his work by education, native talent for imparting the knowledge he possessed, love for the employment, and for the young ones entrusted to his care.

The liking was mutual, and study hours were soon voted only less enjoyable than when mamma was their loved instructor.

Molly occupied her place in the schoolroom as regularly as the others. It adjoined her apartments and her wheeled chair required a very slight exertion of strength on the part of friend or servant to propel it from room to room.

Molly had already made herself a very thorough French and German scholar, and was hoping to turn her ability to translate to good account in the way of earning her own support. There was no pauper instinct in the girl's noble nature, and able and willing as her cousin was to support her, she greatly preferred to earn her own living, though at the cost of much wearisome labor of hand and brain.

She was not of those who seem to forget that the command "six days shalt thou labor and do all thy work," is equally binding with that other, "in it (the seventh day) thou shalt not do any work." This lesson—that industry is commanded, idleness forbidden—was one which Elsie had ever been careful to instill into the minds of her children from their earliest infancy. Nor was it enough, she taught them, that they should be doing something. They must be usefully employed, remembering that they were but stewards who must one day give an account to their Lord of all they had done with the talents entrusted to them.

"Is Dick well? Was it a nice letter?" Violet asked, leaning over Molly's chair when lessons were done.

"Oh, very nice! He's well and doing famously. I must answer it this afternoon."

"Then you will not care for company?"

"Not particularly. Why?"

Vi told of her invitation.

"Go, by all means," said Molly. "You know Virgy has a friend with her, a Miss Reed. I want you to see her and tell me what she's like."

"I fear you'll have to see her yourself to find that out. I'm no portrait painter," Violet said with a smile as she ran lightly away to order the carriage and see to her own grooming and Rosie's.

They were simple enough—white dresses with blue sashes and ribbons for Vi, the same but pink for Rosie.

Miss Reed, dressed in a stiff silk and loaded with showy jewelry, sat in the drawing room at Roselands in a bay window overlooking the avenue. She was gazing eagerly toward its entrance, as though expecting someone.

"Yes, I've heard of the Travillas," she said in answer to a remark from Virginia Conly who stood by her side almost as showily attired as Miss Reed. "I've been told she was a great heiress."

"She was; and he was rich, too; though I believe he lost a good deal during the war."

"They live splendidly, I suppose?"

"They've everything money can buy, but are nearly breaking their hearts just now over one of their little girls who seems to have some incurable disease, poor thing."

"Is that so? Well, they ought to have some trouble as well as other folks. I'm sorry though, for I'd set my heart on being invited there and seeing how they live."

"Oh, they're all gone away except Vi and Rosie and the boys. But maybe Vi will ask us there to dinner or tea. Ah, here they come!"

"What splendidly matched horses! And what an elegant carriage!" exclaimed Miss Reed, as a beautiful barouche drawn by a pair of fine bays came bowling up the avenue.

"Yes, they've come. It's the Ion carriage."

"But that's a young lady Pomp's handing out of it!" exclaimed Miss Reed the next moment. "And I thought you said it was only two children you expected, Virginia."

"Yes, Vi's only thirteen," answered Virginia running to the door to meet her. "Vi, my dear, how good of you to come. How sweet you look!" kissing her. "Rosie, too," bestowing a caress upon her also. "Pink's so becoming to you, little dear, and blue equally so to Vi. This is my friend Miss Reed, Vi. I've been telling her about you."

Violet gave her hand, then drew back blushing and slightly disconcerted by the almost rude stare of the black eyes that seemed to be taking an inventory of her personal appearance and attire.

"Where is Isa?" she asked.

"Here, and very glad to see you, Vi," answered a silvery voice. A tall, queenly looking girl of twenty in rustling black silk and with roses in her hair and at her throat took Violet's hand in hers and kissed her on both cheeks; then, letting her go, saluted the little one in like manner.

"Why don't you do that to me? Guess I like kisses as well as other folks. Ha! Ha!" cried a shrill voice. A little withered up, faded woman with a large wax doll in her arms came skipping into the room.

Her hair, plentifully sprinkled with grey, hung loosely about her neck, and she had bedecked herself with ribbons and faded artificial flowers of every hue.

"Well, Griselda," she continued, addressing the doll, which she bounced in her arms, regarding it with a look of fond admiration, "we don't care, do we, dear? We love and embrace one another and that's enough."

"Oh, go back to your own room," said Virginia in a tone of annoyance. "We don't want you here."

"I'll go when I get ready, and not a minute sooner," was the rejoinder in a peevish tone. "Oh, here's visitors! What a pretty little girl! What's your name, little girl? Won't you come and play with me?

"I'll lend you Grimalkin, my other wax doll. She's a beauty—almost as pretty as Griselda. Now, don't get mad at that, Grissy, dear," kissing the doll again and again.

Rose was frightened and clung to her sister, trying to hide behind her.

"It's Aunt Enna. She won't hurt you," whispered Vi. "She never hurts anyone unless she is teased or worried into a passion."

"Won't she make me go with her? Oh, don't let her, Vi."

"No, dear, you shall stay with me. And here is the nurse come to take her away," Violet answered, as the poor lunatic was led from the room by her constant attendant.

"Dear me!" exclaimed Miss Reed, who had not seen or heard Enna before. Turning to Virginia, she asked. "Does she belong in the house? Aren't you afraid of her?"

"Not at all; she's perfectly harmless. She is my mother's sister and lost her reason some years ago by an accidental injury to the head."

"I wonder you don't send her to an asylum."

"Perhaps it might be well," returned Virginia indifferently, "but it's not my affair."

"Grandpa would never hear of such a thing!" said Isadore indignantly.

"Mamma would not either, I am certain of that," said Violet. "Poor Aunt Enna! Should she be sent away from all who love her just because she was unfortunate to have an accident?"

"Everyone to their taste," remarked the visitor, shrugging her shoulders.

Vi inquired for her Aunt Louise and the younger members of the family, and was told that they and the grandfather were passing the day at Pinegrove.

"I was glad they decided to go today," said Isadore, seating Vi and herself comfortably on a sofa; then, taking Rose on her lap and caressing her, "because I wanted you here, and to have you to myself. You see these two young ladies," glancing smilingly at her sister and guest, "are so fully taken up with each other, that for the most of the time I am quite alone, and must look for entertainment elsewhere than in their company."

"Yes," said Virginia, with more candor than politeness, "Josie and I are all sufficient for each other, are we not, *mon amie*?"

"Very true, *ma chere*, yet I enjoy Isa's company, and am extremely delighted to have made the acquaintance of your charming cousin," remarked Miss Reed, with an insinuating bow directed to Violet.

"You do not know me yet," said Vi, modestly. "Though so tall, I am only a little girl and do not know enough to make an interesting companion for a young lady."

"Quite a mistake, Vi," said Isadore rising. "But there is the dinner bell. Come let us try the soothing and exhilarating effect of food and drink upon our flagging spirits. We will not wait for Art. There's no knowing when he can leave his patients, and Cal's away on business."

On leaving the table, Isadore carried off her young cousins to her apartments. Rose was persuaded to lie down and take a nap, while the older girls conversed together in an adjoining room.

"Isn't it delightful to be at home again, after all those years in the convent?" queried Vi.

"I enjoy home, certainly," replied Isa, "yet I deeply regretted leaving the sisters; for you cannot think how good and kind they were to me. Shall I tell you about it? About my life there?"

"Oh, do! I should so like to hear it."

Isadore smiled at Violet's eager tone, the bright, interested look, and at once began a long and minute description of the events of her school days at the nunnery, ending with a eulogy upon convent life in general and the nuns who had been her educators in particular. "They lived such holy, devoted lives, were so kind, so good, so self-denying."

Violet listened attentively, making no remark, but Isadore read disapproval more than once in her speaking countenance.

"I wish your mamma would send you and Elsie there to finish," remarked Isa, breaking the pause that followed the conclusion of her narrative. "Should you not like to go?"

"No, oh, no, no!"

"Why not?"

"Isa, I could never, never do some of those things you say they require—bow to images or pictures, or kneel before them, or join in prayers or hymns to the Virgin."

"I don't know how you could be so very wicked as to refuse. She is the queen of heaven, and mother of God."

"Isa!" and Violet looked inexpressibly shocked.

"You can't deny it. Wasn't Jesus God?"

"Yes, He is God. 'In the beginning was the Word, and the Word was with God, and the Word was God.' 'And the Word was with God, and the Word was God.' 'And the Word was made flesh, and dwelt among us.'"

"Ah! And was not the Virgin Mary His mother?"

Vi looked perplexed for a moment, then brightening, "Ah, I know now," she said. "Jesus was God and man both."

"Well?"

"And—mamma told me—Mary was the mother of his human nature only, and it is blasphemous to call her the mother of God. And to do her homage is idolatry."

"So I thought before I went to the convent," said Isadore, "but the sisters convinced me of my error. Vi, I should like to show you something. Can you keep a secret?"

"I have never had a secret from mamma. I do not wish to have any."

"But you can't tell her everything now while she's away, and this concerns no one but myself. I know I can trust your honor," and taking Vi's hand, she opened a door and drew her into a large closet, lighted by a small circular window quite high up on the wall. The place was fitted up as an oratory, with a picture of the Virgin and child, and a crucifix, standing on a little table with a prayer book and rosary beside it.

Vi had never seen such things, but she had heard of them and knew what they signified. Glancing from the picture to the crucifix, she started back in horror, and without a word hastily retreated to the dressing room, where she dropped into a chair, pale, trembling, and distressed.

"Isadore, Isadore!" she cried, clasping her hands, and lifting her troubled eyes to her cousin's face, "have you—have you become a Roman Catholic?"

"I am a member of the one true church," returned her cousin coldly. "How bigoted you are, Violet. I could not have believed it of so sweet and gentle a young thing as you. I trust you will not consider it your duty to betray me to mamma?"

"Betray you? Can you think I would? So Aunt Louise does not know? Oh, Isa, can you think it right to hide it from her—your own mother?"

"Yes, because I was directed to do so by my father confessor; and because my motive is a good one; and 'the end sanctifies the means.'"

"Isa, mamma has taught me, and the Bible says it too, that it is never right to do evil that good may come out of it."

"Perhaps you and your mamma do not always understand the real meaning of what the Bible says. It must be that many people misunderstand it, else why are there so many denominations of Protestants, teaching opposite doctrines, and all professing to get them from the Bible?"

Violet in her extreme youth and want of information and ability to argue was not prepared with a ready answer.

"Does Virgy know?" she asked.

"About my change of views and my oratory? Yes, she knows."

"And does she—"

"Virgy is altogether worldly, and cares nothing for religion of any kind."

Vi's face was full of distress. "Isa," she said, "may I ask you a question?"

"What is it?"

"When you pray, do you kneel before that—that—that—"

"Crucifix? Sometimes, at others before the Virgin and child."

Vi shuddered. "Oh, Isa, have you forgotten the second commandment? 'Thou shalt not make unto thee any graven image or likeness of anything that is in heaven above, or that is in the earth; thou shalt not bow down thyself to them nor serve them.'"

"I have not forgotten, but am content to do as the church directs," returned Isadore, coldly.

"Isa, didn't they promise Aunt Louise that they would not interfere with your religion?"

"Yes."

"And they broke their promise. How can you think they are good?"

"They did it to save my soul. Was not that a good and praiseworthy motive?"

"Yes; but if they thought it their duty to try to make you believe as they do, they should not have promised not to do so."

"But in that case I should never have been placed in the convent, and they would have had no opportunity to labor for my conversion."

Earnestly, constantly had Elsie endeavored to obey the command, "Therefore shall ye lay up these my words in your heart and in your soul, and bind them for a sign upon your hand, that they may be as guards between your eyes. And ye shall teach them to your children, speaking of them when thou sittest in thy house, and when thou walkest by the way, when thou liest down, and when thou risest up."

Thus Violet's memory was stored with verses, and those words from Isaiah suggested themselves as a fit comment upon Isadore's last remark. "Woe unto them that call evil good and good evil; that put darkness for light and light for darkness; that put bitter for sweet and sweet for bitter."

Chapter Eighteenth

But all's not true that supposition saith,
Nor have the mightiest arguments most faith.

—DRAYTON

Examples I could cite you more;
But be contented with these four;
For when one's proofs are aptly chosen,
Four are as valid as four dozen.

—PRIOR

*I*sa's conversion, Isa's secret, weighed quite heavily upon the heart and conscience of poor Violet, as the child had never been burdened with a secret before.

She thought Aunt Louise ought to know, yet was not at all clear that it was her duty to tell her. She wished it might be discovered in some way without her telling, for it was a dreadful thing for Isa to be left to go on believing and doing as she did. Oh, if only she could be talked to by someone old enough and wise enough to convince her of her errors!

Isadore with the zeal of a young convert, had set herself the task of bringing Vi over to her new faith. The opportunity afforded by the absence of the vigilant parents was too good to be lost, and should be improved to the utmost.

She made daily errands to Ion, some trifling gift to Molly often being the excuse. She was sweet and gracious to all, but devoted herself especially to Violet, insisting on sharing her room when she stayed overnight, coaxing her out for long walks and drives, rowing with her on the lake, learning to handle the oars herself in order that they might go alone.

And all the time she was on the watch for every favorable opening to say something to undermine the child's faith, or bias her mind in favor of the tenets of the church of Rome.

Violet grew more and more troubled and perplexed, and now not on Isa's account alone. She could not give up the faith of her fathers, the faith of the Bible. (To that inspired Word she clung as to the Rock which must save her from being engulfed in the wild waters of doubt and difficulty that was surging around her.) But neither could she answer all of Isadore's questions and arguments. And there was no one to whom she might turn in her bewilderment, lest she should betray her cousin's secret.

She prayed for guidance and help, searching the Scriptures and "comparing spiritual things with spiritual," and thus was kept from the snares laid for her inexperienced feet. She stumbled and walked with uncertain step for a time, but did not fall.

Those about her, particularly Eddie and her old mammy, noticed the unwonted care and anxiety in her innocent face, but attributed it wholly to the unfavorable news in regard to Lily's condition, which reached them from time to time.

The dear invalid was reported as making little or no progress toward recovery, and the hearts of brothers and sisters were deeply saddened by the unhappy tidings.

Miss Reed was still at Roselands and had been brought several times by Virginia for a call at Ion. At length, Violet having written for and obtained permission of her parents, and consulted Mrs. Daly's convenience in reference to the matter, invited the three girls for a visit of several days, stipulating, however, that it was not to interfere with lessons.

To this the girls readily assented. "They would make themselves quite at home and find their own amusement. It was what they should like above all things."

The plan worked well, except that under this constant association with Isadore, Vi grew daily more careworn and depressed. Even Mr. Daly noticed it, and spoke to her of Lily's weakened state as hopefully as truth would permit.

"Do not be too troubled, my dear child," he said, taking her hand in a kind fatherly manner. "She is in the hands of One who loves her even better than her parents, brothers, and sisters do, and will let no real evil come nigh her. He may restore her to health, but if not—if He takes her from us, it will be to make her infinitely happier with Himself; for we know that she has given her young heart to Him."

Violet bowed a silent assent, then hurried from the room—her heart too full for speech. She was troubled, sorely troubled for her darling, suffering little sister, and with this added anxiety, her burden was hard indeed to bear.

Mr. Daly was reading in the library that afternoon, when Violet came running in as if in haste, a flush of excitement on her fair face.

"Ah, excuse me, sir! I fear I have disturbed you," she said, as he looked up from his book. "But, oh, I'm glad to find you here for I think you can help me! I came to look for a Bible and concordance."

"They are both here on this table," he said. "I am glad you are wanting them, for we cannot study them too much. But in what can I help you, Vi? Is it some theological discussion between your cousins and yourself?"

"Yes, sir. We were talking about a book—a recent storybook that Miss Reed admires—and I said mamma would not allow us to read it because it teaches that Jesus Christ was only a good man. Miss Reed said that was her belief, and yet she professes to believe the

Bible. I wish to show her that it teaches that He was very God as well as man."

"That will not be difficult," he said, "for no words could state it more directly and clearly than these, 'Christ, who is over all, God blessed forever.'" And opening the Bible at the ninth chapter of Romans, he pointed to the latter clause of the fifth verse.

"Oh, let me show her that!" cried Vi.

"Suppose you invite them in here," he suggested, and she hastened to do so.

Miss Reed read the verse as it was pointed out to her. "I don't remember noticing that before," was all she said.

Silently Mr. Daly turned over the leaves and pointed out the twentieth verse of the first epistle of John, where it is said of Jesus Christ, "This is the true God and eternal life," and then to Isaiah 9:6. "For unto us a Child is born, unto us a Son is given; and the government shall be upon His shoulder; and His name shall be called Wonderful, Counselor, the Mighty God, the Everlasting Father, the Prince of Peace," and several other passages equally strong and explicit in their declaration of the divinity of Christ. "Well," said Miss Reed, "if He was God, why didn't He say so?"

"He did, again and again," was the reply. "Here in John 8:58 we read, "Jesus said unto them, 'Verily, verily, I say unto you, before Abraham was, I am.'"

"I don't see it!" she said sneeringly.

"You do not? Just compare it with this other passage in Exodus 3:14–15. 'And God said unto Moses, I AM THAT I AM: and He said, thus shalt thou say unto the children of Israel, the Lord God of your fathers, the God of Abraham, the God of Isaac, and the God of Jacob, hath sent me unto you; this is My name forever, and this is My memorial unto all generations.' The Jews who were present understood those words of Jesus as an assertion of His divinity and took up stones to cast at Him."

Isadore seemed interested in the discussion, but Virginia showed evident impatience. "What's the use of bothering ourselves about it?" she exclaimed at length. "What difference does it make whether we believe in His divinity or deny it?"

"A vast difference, my dear young lady," said Mr. Daly. "If Christ be not divine, it is idolatry to worship Him. If He is divine, and we fail to acknowledge it and to trust in Him for salvation, we must be eternally lost for 'neither is there salvation in any other; for there is none other name under heaven given among men, whereby we must be saved.' 'But whosoever believeth in Him shall receive remission of sins.'"

Virginia fidgeted uneasily and Miss Reed inquired with affected politeness if that were all.

"No," he said, "far from it. Yet, if the Bible be—as I think we all acknowledge—the inspired Word of God, one plain declaration of a truth should be as authoritative as a dozen."

"Suppose I don't believe it is all inspired?" queried Miss Reed.

"Still, since Jesus asserts His own divinity, we must either accept Him as God or believe Him to have been an imposter and therefore not even a good man. He must be to us everything or nothing. There is no neutral ground. He says, 'He that is not with Me is against Me.'"

"And there is only one true church," remarked Isadore, forgetting herself, "the holy Roman church, and none without her limits can be saved."

Mr. Daly looked at her in astonishment. Violet was at first greatly startled, then inexpressibly relieved. Since Isa's secret being one no longer, a heavy weight was removed from her heart and her young conscience.

Virginia was the first to speak. "There!" she said, "you've let it out yourself. I always knew you would sooner or later."

"Well," returned Isadore, drawing herself up haughtily, determined to put a brave face upon the matter, now that there was no retreat. "I'm not ashamed of my faith, nor afraid to attempt its defense against any who may see fit to attack it," she added with a defiant look at Mr. Daly.

He smiled a little sadly. "I am very sorry for you, Miss Conly," he said, "and do not feel at all belligerent toward you; but let me entreat you to rest your hopes of salvation only upon the atoning blood and imputed righteousness of Jesus Christ."

"I must do works also," she said.

"Yes, as an evidence, but not as the ground of your faith. We must do good works not that we may be saved but because we are saved. 'If a man love Me, he will keep My words.' Well, my little Vi, what is it?" for she was looking at him with eager, questioning eyes.

"Oh, Mr. Daly, I want you to answer some things Isa has said to me. Isa, I have never mentioned it to anyone before. I have kept your secret faithfully till now that you have told it yourself."

"I don't blame you, Vi," she answered, coloring. "I presume I shall be blamed for my efforts to bring you over to the true faith, but my conscience acquits me of any bad motive. I wanted to save your soul. Mr. Daly, I do not imagine you can answer all that I have to bring against the claims of Protestantism. Pray, tell me where was that church before the Reformation came?"

"Wherever the Bible was made the rule of faith and practice," he said, "there was Protestantism though existing under another name. All through the dark ages, when Popery was dominant almost all over the civilized world, the light of the pure gospel—the very same that the Reformation spread abroad over other parts of Europe—burned brightly among the secluded valleys of Piedmont. And twelve hundred years of bloody persecution on the part of the apostate Rome could not quench it."

"I know that Popery lays great stress on her claims to antiquity. But Paganism is older still, and evangelical religion—which, as I have already said, is Protestantism under another name—is as old as the Christian Era, as old as the human nature of its founder, the Lord Jesus Christ."

"You are making assertions," said Isadore bridling, "but where are your proofs?"

"They are not wanting," he said. "Suppose we undertake the study of ecclesiastical history together and see how Popery was the growth of centuries, as one error after another crept into the Roman church."

"I don't believe she was ever the persecutor you would make her out to have been," said Isadore.

"Popish historians bear witness to it as well as Protestant," he answered.

"Well, it's persecution to bring up those old stories against her now."

"Is it? When she will not disavow them, but maintains that she has always done right? And more than that, tells us she will do the same again if she ever has the power."

"I'm sure all Roman Catholics are not so cruel as to wish to torture or kill their Protestant neighbors," cried Isadore indignantly.

"And I quite agree with you there," he said. "I have not the least doubt that many of them are very kind-hearted; but I was speaking, not of individuals, but of the Roman church as such. She is essentially a persecuting power."

"Well, being the only true church, she has the right to compel conformity to her creed."

"Ah, you have already imbibed something of her spirit. But we contend that she is not the true church. 'To the law and to the testimony; if they speak not according to this word, it is because there is no light in them.' Brought to the touchstone of God's revealed word, she is proved to be reprobate silver—her creed spurious Christianity. In Second Thessalonians, second chapter, we have a very clear description of her as that 'Wicked whom the Lord shall consume with the spirit of His mouth, and shall destroy with the brightness of His coming.' Also, in the seventeenth chapter of Revelation, where she is spoken of as 'Babylon the great, the mother of the harlots and abominations of the earth.'"

"How do you know she is meant there?" asked Isadore, growing red and angry.

"Because she, and she alone, answers to the description. It is computed that fifty million Protestants have been slain in her persecutions. May it not then be truly said of her that she is drunken with the blood of the saints?"

"I think what you have been saying shows that the priests are right in teaching that the Bible is a dangerous book in the hands of the ignorant, and should therefore be withheld from the laity," retorted Isadore hotly.

"But," returned Mr. Daly, "Jesus said, 'search the Scriptures; for in them ye think ye have eternal life; and they are they which testify of Me.'"

Chapter Nineteenth

Let us go back again, mother,
Oh, take me home to die.

"And so, Isa, my uncle's predictions that your popish teachers would violate their promise not to meddle with your faith have proved only too true," said Calhoun Conly, stepping forward as Mr. Daly finished his last quotation from the Scriptures.

In the heat of their discussion, neither the minister nor Isadore had noticed his entrance, but he had been standing there, an interested listener, long enough to learn the facts of his sister's conversion.

"They richly deserve the blame, and you cannot prevent it from being given them," he answered firmly and with flashing eyes. "I have come by my mother's request to take you and Virginia home, inviting Miss Reed to accompany us."

"I am ready," said Isadore, rising, the others doing likewise.

"But you will stay to tea?" Violet said. "Cal, you are not in too great haste for that?"

"I'm afraid I am, little cousin," he answered with a smile of acknowledgment of her hospitality. "I must meet a gentleman on business, half an hour from now."

Vi expressed her regrets, and ran after the girls, who had already left the room to prepare for their drive home.

They seemed in haste to get away.

"We've had enough of Mr. Daly's prosing about religion," said Virginia.

"I'm sick of it," chimed in Miss Reed. "What difference does it make what you believe, if you're only sincere and live right?"

"'With the heart man believeth unto righteousness,'" said Violet, "and 'the just shall live by faith.'"

"You're an apt pupil," sneered Virginia.

"It's mamma's doing that my memory is stored with verses," returned the child, reddening.

Isadore was silent and gloomy and took leave of her young cousin so coldly as to quite sadden her sensitive spirit.

Violet had enjoyed being made much of by Isa, who was a beautiful and brilliant young lady, and this sudden change in her manner was far from pleasant. Still the pain it gave her was greatly overbalanced by the relief of having her perplexities removed, her doubts set free.

Standing on the veranda, she watched the carriage as it rolled away down the avenue. Then she hailed with delight a horseman who came galloping up, alighted and, giving the bridle to Solon, turned to her with open arms and a smile that proclaimed him the bearer of good tidings before he uttered a word.

"Grandpa," she cried, springing to his embrace, "oh, is Lily better?"

"Yes," he said, caressing her; then, turning to greet Rosie and the boys who came running at the sound of his voice, he declared, "I have had a letter from your mother in which she says the dear invalid seems decidedly better."

"Oh, joy! joy!" cried the children, Rosie hugging and kissing her grandfather, the boys capering about in a transport of gladness.

"And will they come home soon, grandpa?" asked Eddie.

"Nothing is said about that but I presume they will linger up north till the weather begins to grow too cool for Lily," Mr.

Dinsmore answered, shaking hands with Mr. Daly, who, hearing his voice on the veranda, stepped out to inquire for news of the absent ones.

While they talked together Vi ran away in search of Aunt Chloe.

She found her on the back veranda enjoying a chat with Aunt Dicey and Uncle Joe.

"Oh, mammy, good news, good news!" Vi cried, half breathless with her haste and happiness. "Grandpa had a letter from mamma and our darling Lily is better, much better."

"Bress de Lord!" exclaimed her listeners in chorus.

"Bress His holy name! I hope de chile am gwine to discover her health agin," added Uncle Joe. "I'se been a prayin' pow'ful strong for her."

"'Spect der is been more'n you at dat business, Uncle Joe," remarked Aunt Dicey. "'Spect I knows one ole un dat didn't fail to disremember de little darlin' at de throne ob grace."

"De bressed lamb!" murmured Aunt Chloe, dropping a tear on Violet's golden curls as she clasped her to her heart. "She's de Lord's own, and He'll take de bes' care of her in dis world and in de nex'; be sho' ob dat honey. Ise mighty glad for her and my dear missus and for you, too, Miss Wi'let. You's been frettin' yo' heart out 'bout Miss Lily."

"I've been very anxious about her, mammy, and something else has been troubling me, too, but it's all right now, too," Violet answered with a glad look. Then, releasing herself, she ran back to her grandfather.

She had seen less than usual of him for several weeks past, and wanted an opportunity to pour out all her heart to him.

He had gone up to Molly's sitting room and she followed him there.

With Rosie on his knee, Harold and Herbert standing on either side, and Eddie sitting near, he was chatting merrily with his crippled niece, who was as bright and cheery as any of the group, all of whom were full of joy over the glad tidings he had brought with him.

"Grandpa," said Vi, joining them, "it seems a good while since you were here for more than a short call. Won't you stay now for the rest of the day?"

"Yes, and I propose that we drive down to the lake—Molly and all—and have a row. I think it would do you all good. The weather is delightful."

The motion was carried by acclamation. Molly's maid was summoned. Eddie went down to order the carriage and the rest scattered to prepare for the day's expedition.

It was a lovely October day, the air balmy, the woods gorgeous in their richly colored autumn robes—gold, scarlet, crimson, russet, and green mingled in bright profusion. The slanting beams of the descending sun fell across the lakelet like a broad band of shimmering gold, and here and there lent an added glory to the trees. The boat glided swiftly over the rippling waters, now in sunshine, now in shadow, and the children hushed their merry chatter, silenced by the beauty and stillness of the scene.

Tea was waiting when they returned and on leaving the table the younger ones bade good night and went away with Vi to be put to bed.

She had a story or some pleasant talk for them every night, doing her best to fill mamma's place.

Vi was glad to find her grandpa alone in the library when she came down again.

"Come, sit on my knee as your dear mamma used to do at your age," he said, "and tell me what you have been doing these past weeks while I have seen so little of you."

"It is so nice," she said as she took the offered seat, and he passed his arm about her, "so nice to have a grandpa to love me, especially when I've no father or mother at home to do it."

"So we are mutually satisfied," he said. "Now what have you to tell me? Any questions to ask? Any doubts or perplexities to be cleared away?"

"Grandpa, has anybody been telling you anything?" she asked.

"No, nothing about you, my little cricket."

"Then I'll just tell you all." And she gave him a history of Isadore's efforts to convert her and their effect upon her. She also told of the conversation of that afternoon in which Mr. Daly had answered the questions of Isadore that had most perplexed and troubled her.

Mr. Dinsmore was grieved and distressed by Isa's defection from the evangelical faith and indignant at her attempt to lead Vi astray also.

"Are you fully satisfied now on all the points?" he asked.

"There are one or two things I should like to ask you about, grandpa," she said. "Isa thinks a convent life so beautiful and holy, so shut out from the world with all its cares and wickedness, she says. It's so quiet and peaceful, so full of devotion and the self-denial the Lord Jesus taught when He said, 'If any man will come after me, let him deny himself and take up his cross and follow Me.' Do you think leaving one's dear home and father and mother, and brothers and sisters to be shut up for life with strangers in a convent was the cross He meant, grandpa?"

"No, I am perfectly sure it was not. The Bible teaches us to do our duty in the place where God puts us. It recognizes the family relationships, teaches the reciprocal duties of kinsmen—parents and children, husbands and wives—but has not a word to say to monks and nuns.

"It bids us take up the cross God lays upon us, and not one of our own invention; nor did any one of the holy men and women it tells of live the life of a recluse. Nor can peace and freedom from temptation and sin be found in a convent any more than elsewhere, because we carry our evil natures with us wherever we go.

"No, peace and happiness are to be found only in being 'followers of God as dear children,' doing our duty in that station in life where He has placed us. Our motive should be to love Him, leading us to desire above all things to live to His honor and glory."

Violet sat with downcast eyes, her face full of earnest thought. She was silent for a moment after Mr. Dinsmore had ceased speaking; then, lifting her head and turning to him with a relieved look, "Thank you, grandpa," she said. "I am fully satisfied on that point. Now, there is just one more. Isa says that divisions among Protestants show that the Bible is not a book for common people to read for themselves. They cannot understand it right. If they did, they would all believe alike."

Mr. Dinsmore smiled. "Who is to explain it, then?"

"Oh, Isa says that is for the priests to do; and they and the people must simply accept the decisions of the church."

"Well, my child, it would take too much time to tell you just how impossible it is to find out what are the authoritative decisions of the Roman church on more than one important point. One council would contradict another; one pope would affirm what his predecessors had denied, and vice versa. Why, even councils contradict popes and popes, councils.

"As to the duty of studying the Bible for ourselves—we have the Master's own command: 'Search the Scriptures'—which settles the question at once for all His obedient disciples. And no one who sets himself to the work humbly and teachably, looking to the Holy Spirit for enlightenment will fail to find the path to heaven. 'The way-faring men, though fools shall not err therein.' Jesus said 'the Comforter which is the Holy Ghost, whom the Father will send in My name, He shall teach you all things.'

"And, my child, none of us is responsible for the interpretation that his neighbor puts upon God's Word as His letter is addressed to us all. Each of us must give account of himself to God."

Violet's doubts and perplexities had vanished like morning mist before the rising sun. Her natural happiness of spirits returned, and she became again, as was her wont, the sunshine of the house, full of life and hope, with a cheery word and sunny smile for everyone—from Mr. Daly down to Rosie, and from Aunt Chloe to the youngest child in the quarter.

She had not been so happy since the departure of her parents.

Eddie, Molly, and the younger ones reflected in some measure her bright hopefulness and the renewed ardor with which she pursued her studies. For some days all went on prosperously at Ion.

Then came a change.

One evening Vi, having seen Rosie to bed and bade Harold and Herbert good night also, returned to the schoolroom where Eddie and their cousin were busied with their preparations for the morrow's recitations.

She had settled herself before her desk and was taking out her books when the sound of horses' hooves coming swiftly up the avenue caused her to spring up and run to the window.

"It is grandpa," she said. "He seldom comes so late. Oh, Eddie!" and she dropped into a chair, her heart beating wildly.

"Don't be alarmed, Vi," Eddie said, rising and coming toward her, his own voice trembling with apprehension. "It may be good news again."

"Oh, do you think so? Can it be?" she asked.

"Surely, Vi, uncle would not come as fast as possible if he had bad news to bring," said Molly. "Perhaps it is that they are coming home. It is getting so late in the fall now that I'm expecting every day to hear that."

"Let's go down to grandpa," cried Vi, rising, while a faint color stole into her cheek which had grown very pale at the thought that the little darling sister might be dead or dying. "No, no," as a step was heard on the stairs, "he is coming to us."

The door opened and Mr. Dinsmore entered. One look into his grief-stricken face and Violet threw herself into his arms and wept upon his chest.

He soothed her with silent caresses, his heart almost too full for speech. But, at length, "It is not the worst," he said in low, moved tones. "She is alive but has had a relapse. They are bringing her, our little Lily, home."

"Home to die!" echoed Violet's heart, and she clung about her grandfather's neck, weeping almost convulsively.

Tears coursed down Molly's cheeks also; and Eddie, hardly less overcome than his sister, asked tremulously, "How soon may we expect them home, grandpa?"

"In about two days, I think. My dear children, we must school ourselves to meet Lily with calmness and composure lest we injure by exciting and agitating her. We must be prepared to find her more feeble than when she went away and much exhausted by the fatigue of the journey."

Worse than when she went away? And even then the doctors had no hope! It was almost as if they already saw her lying lifeless before them.

They wept themselves to sleep that night and in the morning it was as though death had already entered the house. A solemn stillness reigned in all its rooms, and the quiet tread, the sad, subdued tones, the oft falling tear, attested to the warmth of affection in which the dear, dying child was held.

A parlor car was speeding southward. Its sole occupants were a noble-looking man; a lovely matron; a blooming, beautiful girl of seventeen; a rosy babe in his nurse's arms; and a pale, fragile, golden-haired, blue-eyed child of seven. She was lying now on the couch with her head in her mother's lap, now resting in her father's arms for a little.

She seemed the central figure of the group. All eyes turned ever and again upon her in tenderest solicitude. Every ear attentive to her slightest complaint, every hand ready to minister her every want.

She was very quiet, very patient, answering their anxious, questioning words and looks with many a sweet, affectionate smile or whisper of grateful appreciation of their ministry of love.

Sometimes she would beg to be lifted up for a moment that she might see the rising or setting sun, or gaze upon the autumnal glories of the woods. And as they grew near their journey's end she would ask, "Are we almost there, papa? Shall I soon see my own sweet home and dear brothers and sisters?"

At last the answer was "Yes, my darling, in a few moments we shall leave the car for our own easy carriage, and one short stage will take us home to Ion."

Mr. Dinsmore, his son, and Arthur Conley met them at the station and told how longingly their dear ones at home were looking for them.

The sun had set, and shadows began to creep over the landscape as the carriage stopped before the door and Lily was lifted out, borne into the house, and gently laid upon her own little bed.

She was nearly fainting away with fatigue and weakness, and dearly as the others were loved, father and mother had no eyes for any but her. There was no word of greeting as the one bore her past. The others hastily followed with the doctor and grandfather to her room.

But Elsie and Vi quickly locked in each other's arms, mingling their tears together, while Rosie and the boys gathered round, waiting their turn.

"Oh!" sobbed Rosie, "mamma didn't speak to me; she didn't even look at me. She doesn't love me anymore, nor my papa either."

"Yes, they do, little dear," Elsie said, leaving Violet to embrace the little sister. "And sister Elsie loves you dearly; Harold and Herbert, too; as well as our big oldest brother," smiling up at Eddie through her tears, as he stood by her side.

He bent down to kiss her sweet lips.

"Lily?" he said in a choking voice.

With a great effort Elsie controlled her emotion, and answered low and tremulously, "She is almost done with pain. She is very happy—no doubt, no fear, only gladness that soon she will be

> *Safe in the arms of Jesus,*
> *Safe on his gentle breast.*"

Eddie turned away with a broken sob. Vi uttered a low cry of anguish, and Rosie and the boys broke into a wail of sorrow.

Till that moment they had not given up hope that the dear one might even yet be restored.

In the child's sickroom, the golden head lay on a snow-white pillow. The blue eyes were closed and the breath came in pants from the pale, parted lips.

Cousin Arthur had his finger on the slender wrist, counting its pulses while father and grandfather stood looking on in anxious solicitude. The mother bent low over her fading flower asking in tender whispered accents, "Are you in pain, my darling?"

"No, mamma, only so tired, so tired!"

Only the mother's quick ear, placed close to the pale lips, could catch the low-breathed words.

The doctor administered a cordial, then a little nourishment was given, and the child fell asleep.

The mother sat watching her, lost to all else in the world. Arthur came to her side with a whispered word about her own need of rest and refreshment after her fatiguing journey.

"How long?" she asked in the same low tone, glancing first at the white face on the pillow, then quickly back up at him.

"Some days, I hope. She is likely now to sleep for hours. Let me take your place."

Elsie bent over the child, listening for a moment to her breathing; then, accepting his offer, followed her husband and father from the room.

Rosie, waiting and watching in the hall without, sprang to her mother's embrace with a low, joyful cry. "Mamma, mamma! Oh, you've been gone so long! I thought you'd never come back."

"Mamma is very glad to be with you again," Elsie said, holding her close for a moment; then, giving her to her father, she sought the others—all near at hand, and waiting eagerly for a sight of her loved face, a word from her gentle lips.

They were all longing for one of their confidential talks, Violet, perhaps, more than the others. But it could not be now. The mother could scarcely allow herself time for a little rest ere she must return to her station by the side of the sickbed.

But Molly was not forgotten or neglected. Elsie went to her with kind inquiries, loving cheering words, and a message from Dick, whom she had seen a few days before.

"How kind and thoughtful for others she is! How sweet and gentle, how patient and resigned. I will try to be more like her. How truly she obeys the command 'be compassionate, be courteous.' But why should one so lovely, so devoted a Christian, be visited with so sore a trial? I can see why my trials were sent. I was so proud and worldly. They were necessary to show me my need of Jesus, but she has loved and leaned upon Him since she was a little child—oh why?" Molly quietly asked herself as Elsie left her alone.

Chapter Twentieth

Let them die,
Let them die now, thy children!
So thy heart
Shall wear their beautiful image all undimm'd
Within it to the last.

—MRS. HEMANS

Lily seemed a little stronger in the morning and the brothers and sisters were allowed to go in by turns and speak to her.

Violet chose to be the last, thinking that would, perhaps, secure a little longer interview.

Lily with mamma by her side lay propped up with pillows—her eyes bright, a lovely color on her almost transparent cheek, her luxurious hair lying about her like heaps of shining gold, her red lips smiling a joyous welcome, as Vi stooped over her.

Could it be that she was dying?

"Oh, darling, you may get well even yet!" cried Vi, in tones tremulous with joy and hope.

Lily smiled and stroked her sister's face lovingly with her little, thin, white hand.

Violet was startled by its scorching heat.

"You are burning up with fever!" she exclaimed, tears gushing from her eyes.

"Yes, but I shall soon be well," said the child clasping her sister close. "I'm going home to the happy land to be with Jesus, Vi. Oh, don't you wish you were going, too? Mamma, I'm tired; please tell Vi my verse."

"'And the inhabitant shall not say, I am sick; the people that dwell therein shall be forgiven their iniquity,'" the mother softly repeated in a low and sweet voice.

"For Jesus' sake," softly added the little dying one. "He has loved me and washed me from my sins in His own blood."

Vi fell on her knees by the bedside, and buried her face in the sheets, vainly trying to stifle her bursting sobs.

"Poor Vi," sighed Lily. "Mamma, comfort her."

Mamma drew the weeper to her heart and spoke tenderly to her of the loving Savior and the home He has gone to prepare for His people.

"Our darling will be so safe and happy there," she said, "and she is glad to go, to rest in His bosom and wait there for us, as, in His own good time, He shall call one after another to Himself.

> 'Tis there we'll meet,
> At Jesus' feet,
> When we meet to part no more."

Tears were coursing down the mother's cheeks as she spoke, but her manner was calm and quiet.

To her, as to her child standing upon the brink of Jordan, heaven seemed very near, very real. While mourning that soon that beloved face and form would be seen no more on earth, she rejoiced with joy unspeakable for the blessedness that should be hers forever and forevermore.

There were no tears in Lily's eyes. "Mamma, I'm so happy," she said smiling. "Dear Vi, you must be glad for me and not cry so. I have no pain today and I'll never have any more when I get home where the dear Savior is. Mamma, please read about the beautiful city."

Elsie took up the Bible that lay beside the pillow. And opening to the Revelation, read its last two chapters—the twenty-first and the twenty-second.

Lily lay intently listening; Violet's hand fast clasped in hers.

"Darling Vi," she whispered, "you love Jesus, don't you?"

Violet nodded assent; she could not speak.

"And you're willing to let Him have me, aren't you, dear?"

"Yes, yes," but the tears fell fast. "Oh, what shall I do without you?" she cried with a choking sob.

"It won't be long," said Lily. "Mamma says it will seem only a very little while when it is past."

Her voice sank with the last words, and she closed her eyes with a weary sigh.

"Go, dear daughter, go away for the present," the mother said to Violet, who instantly obeyed.

Lily lingered for several days, suffering little except for weakness. She was always patient and cheerful, talking so joyfully of "going home to Jesus," that death seemed robbed of all its gloom. For it was not of the grave they thought in connection with her, but of the glories of the upper sanctuary, the bliss of those who dwell forever with the Lord.

Father, brothers and sisters often gathered for a little while about her bed, for she dearly loved them all. But the mother scarcely left her day or night. The mother whose gentle teachings had guided her childish feet into the path that leads to God, whose ministry of love had made the short life bright and happy in spite of weakness and pain.

It was in the early morning that the end came.

She had been sleeping quietly for some hours, sleeping while darkness passed away till day had fully dawned and the eastern sky was flushing with crimson and gold.

Her mother sat by the bedside gazing with tender glistening eyes upon the little wan face, thinking how placid was its expression, what an almost unearthly beauty it wore, when suddenly the large azure eyes opened wide, gazing steadily into hers, while the sweetest smile played about the lips.

"Mamma, dear mamma, how good you've been to me! Jesus is here. He has come for me. I'm going now. Dear, darling mamma, kiss me goodbye."

"My darling! My darling!" Elsie cried, pressing a kiss of passionate love upon the sweet lips.

"Dear mamma," they faintly whispered—and were still.

Kneeling by the bedside, Elsie gathered the little wasted form in her arms, pillowing the beautiful golden head upon her bosom, while again and again she kissed the pale brow, the cheeks, the lips. Then, laying her down gently she stood gazing upon her with unutterable love and mingled joy and anguish.

"It was well with the child," and no rebellious thought arose in her heart; but, oh, what an aching void was there! How empty were her arms, though so many of her darlings were still spared for her.

A quiet step drew near, a strong arm was passed about her waist, and a kind hand drew her head to a resting place on her husband's shoulder.

"Is it so?" he said in moved tones, gazing through a mist of tears upon the quiet face of the young sleeper. "Oh, darling, our precious lamb is safely folded in at last. He has gathered her in His arms and is carrying her in His bosom."

They laid her body in the family burial ground and mamma and the children went very often to scatter flowers upon the graves, reserving the fairest and sweetest for the little mound that looked so fresh and new.

"But she is not here," Rosie would say, "she's gone to the dear home above where Jesus is. And she's so happy. She'll never be sick any more because it says, 'Neither shall there be any more pain.'"

Lily was never spoken of as lost or as dead. She had only gone before to the happy land where they all were journeying and where they should find her again, blooming and beautiful. They spoke of her often and with cheerfulness, though tears would sometimes fall at the thought that the separation must be so long.

Elsie was much worn out with the long nursing that she would not resign to other hands; and, as Mr. and Mrs. Daly were well pleased to have it so arranged, they still retained their current posts in the household.

But the children again enjoyed the pleasant evening talks and the prized morning half hour with mamma. They might go to her at other times also, and it was not long before Vi found an opportunity to unburden her mind by a full account of all the doubts and perplexities that had so troubled her. She also recounted the manner in which they had been removed, to her great comfort and peace.

It was in the afternoon of the second day after the funeral. The two older girls were alone with their mother in her boudoir.

Elsie was startled at the thought of the peril her child had been in.

"I blame myself," she said, "that I have not guarded you more carefully against these fearful errors. We will now take up the subject together, my children and I, and study it thoroughly. And we will invite Isa and Virgy to join with us in our search after truth."

"Molly also, mamma, if she is willing," suggested her namesake daughter.

"Certainly, but I count her among my children. Ah, I have not seen her for several days! I fear she has been feeling neglected. I will go to her now," she added, rising from the couch on which she had been reclining. "And you may both go with me, if you wish."

Isa had been with Molly for the last half hour. "I came on that unpleasant business of making a call of condolence," she announced on her entrance. "But they told me Cousin Elsie was lying down to rest and her girls were with her—Elsie and Vi—so, not wishing to disturb them, I'll visit with you first, if you like."

"I'm glad to see you," Molly said. "Please be seated."

Isadore seemed strangely embarrassed and sat for some moments without speaking.

"What's the matter, Isa?" Molly asked at length.

"I think it was really unkind in mamma to send me on this errand. It was her place to come, but she said Cousin Elsie was so bound up in that child that she would be overwhelmed with grief. And she (mamma) would not know what to say. She always found it the most awkward thing in the world to try to console people under such afflictions."

"It will not be at all necessary," returned Molly dryly. "Cousin Elsie has all the consolation she needs. She came to me for a few minutes the very day Lily died, and though I could see plainly that she had been weeping, her face was perfectly calm and peaceful. And she told me that her heart sang for joy when she thought of her darling's blessedness."

Isa looked very thoughtful.

"I wish I were sure of it," she said unconsciously. "She was such a dear little thing."

"Sure of what?" cried Molly indignantly. "Can you doubt for a moment that that child is in heaven?"

"If she had only been baptized into the true church. But there, don't look so angry! How can I help wishing it when I know it's the only way to truly be saved?"

"But you don't know it! You can't know it, because it isn't so. Oh, Isadore, how could you turn Roman Catholic and then try to turn Violet?"

"So you've heard about it? I supposed you had," said Isadore coloring. "I suppose, too, that Cousin Elsie is very angry with me, and that is why I thought it so unkind in mamma to send me in her place, making an excuse of a headache. It was not a bad enough one to prevent her coming, I'm sure."

"I don't know how Cousin Elsie feels about it, or even whether she has heard it," said Molly. "Though I promise she has, as Vi never conceals anything from her."

"Well, I've only done my duty and can't feel that I'm deserving of blame," said Isadore. "But such a time as I've had of it since my conversion became known in the family!"

"Your perversion, you should say," interrupted Molly. "Was Aunt Louise angry?"

"Very, but principally, I could see, because she knew grandpa and Uncle Horace would reproach her for sending me to the convent."

"And did they?"

"Yes, grandpa was furious, and of course uncle said, 'I told you so.' He has only reasoned with me, though he let me know he was very much displeased about Vi. Cal and Art, too, have undertaken to convince me of my errors, while Virginia sneers and asks why I could not be content to remain a Protestant. Altogether, I've had a sweet time of it for the last two weeks."

"There's a tap at the door. Will you please open it?" asked Molly.

It was Mrs. Travilla, Elsie, and Violet whom Isadore admitted. She recognized them with a deep blush and an embarrassed, deprecating air. For the thought instantly struck her that Vi had probably just been telling her mother what had occurred during her absence.

"Ah, Isa, I did not know you were here," her cousin said taking her hand. "I am very pleased to see you."

The tone was gentle and kind and there was not a trace of displeasure in look or manner.

"Thank you, cousin," Isa said, trying to recover her composure. "I came to—mamma has a headache, and sent me—"

"Yes, never mind. I know all you would say," Elsie answered, tears trembling in her soft hazel eyes, but a look of perfect peace and resignation on her sweet face. "You feel for my sorrow, and I thank you for your sympathy. But, Isa, the consolations of God are not small with me, and I know that my dear little one is safe with Him.

"Molly, my child, how are you today?"

"Very well, thank you," Molly answered, clinging to the hand that was offered her, and looking up with dewy eyes into the calm, beautiful face bending over her. "How kind you are to think of me at such a time as this. Ah, cousin, it puzzles me to understand why afflictions should be sent to one who already seems almost an angel in goodness."

Elsie shook her head. "You cannot see my heart, Molly, and the Master knows just how many strokes of His chisel are needed to fashion the soul in His image. He will not make one too many! Beside should I grudge Him one of the many darlings He has given me, or her the bliss He has taken her to? Ah, no, no! His will be done with me and my own."

She sat down upon a sofa, and making room for Isa, who had been exchanging greetings with her younger cousins, invited her to a seat by her side.

"I want to talk with you," she said gently. "Vi has been telling me everything. Ah, do not think I have any reproaches for you, though nothing could have grieved me more than your success in what you attempted with Vi."

She then went on to give, in her own gentle, kindly way, good and sufficient reasons for her dread and hatred of—not Catholics—but Popery. She concluded by inviting Isa to join with them in a thorough investigation of its claims.

Isa consented, won by her cousin's generous forbearance and affectionate interest in her welfare, and arrangements were made to begin the very next day.

Molly's writing desk stood open on the table by her side, and Violet's bright eyes catching sight of the address on a letter lying there exclaimed, "Oh, cousin, have you heard? And is it good news?"

"Yes, I have," replied Molly, a flush of pride and pleasure mantling her cheek. "I should have told you at once, if—under ordinary circumstance—but—" and her eyes filled as she turned them upon Mrs. Travilla.

"Dear child, I am interested now and always in your plans and pleasures," responded the latter, "and shall heartily rejoice in any good that has come to you."

Then Molly, blushing and happy, explained that she had been using her spare time for months past in making a translation of a French story. She had offered it for publication, and, after weeks of anxious waiting, had that morning received a letter announcing its acceptance, and enclosing a check for a hundred dollars.

"My dear child, I am proud of you—of the energy, patience and perseverance you have shown," her cousin said warmly, and with a look of great gratification. "Success, so gained, must be very sweet, and I offer you my hearty congratulations."

The younger cousins added theirs, Elsie and Vi rejoicing as at a great good to themselves, and Isa expressing extreme surprise at the discovery that Molly had attained to so much knowledge, and possessed sufficient talent for such an undertaking.

Chapter Twenty-First

*T*he winter and spring passed very quietly at Ion. At Roselands there was more merriment, the girls going out frequently and receiving a good deal of company at home.

Virginia was seldom at Ion, but Isadore spent an hour there almost every day pursuing the biblical investigation proposed by her cousin Elsie.

She was an honest and earnest inquirer after truth, and at length acknowledged herself entirely convinced of the errors into which she had been led and was entirely restored to the evangelical faith. And more than that, she became a sincere and devout Christian— much to the disgust and chagrin of her worldly minded mother and Aunt Delaford, who would have been far better pleased to see her a mere butterfly of fashion as were her younger sister and most of her younger friends.

But to her brother, Arthur, and at both the Oaks and Ion, the change in Isa was a source of deep joy and thankfulness.

Also, it was a means of leading Calhoun, who had long been halting between two opinions, to come out decidedly upon the Lord's side.

Old Mr. Dinsmore had become quite infirm and Cal now took entire charge of the plantation. Arthur was busy in his profession, and Walter was at West Point preparing to enter the army.

Herbert and Meta Carrington were up north—the one attending college and the other at boarding school. Old Mrs. Carrington was still living, making her home at Ashlands. Through her the Rosses were frequently heard from.

They were still enjoying a large measure of worldly prosperity—Mr. Ross being a very successful merchant. He had taken his son Philip into partnership a year ago and Lucy's letter spoke much of the lad as delighting his father and herself by his business ability and shrewdness.

They had their city residence as well as their country place. Gertrude had made her debut into fashionable society in the fall and spent a very happy winter. The occasional letters she wrote to the younger Elsie were filled with descriptions of the balls, parties, operas, and theatricals she attended, the splendors of her own attire, and the elegant dresses worn by others.

It may have been that at another time Elsie, so unaccustomed to worldly pleasures, would have found these subjects interesting from their very novelty; but now, while the parting from Lily was so recent, when her happy death had brought the glories of heaven so near, how frivolous they seemed.

These events had more attraction for excitable, excitement-loving Violet. Yet, even she, interested for the moment, presently forgot them again as something reminded her of the dear little sister who was not lost but gone before to the better land.

Vi had a warm, loving heart. No one could be fonder of home, parents, and brothers and sisters than she; but, as spring drew on, she began to have a restless longing for change of scene and employment. She had been growing fast and felt both weak and languid.

Both she and Elsie had attained their full height, Vi being a trifle the taller of the two. They grew daily in beauty and grace and were not lovelier in person than in character and mind.

They were as open as the day with their gentle, tender mother and their fond, proud father. He was proud of his lovely wife and his sons and daughters, whose equals he truly believed were not to be found anywhere throughout the whole length and breadth of the land. So Vi was not slow in telling of her desire for change.

It was on a lovely evening in May when all of the family were gathered on the veranda, serenely happy in each other's company. The babe was in his mother's arms, Rosie on her father's knee, the others grouped about them, doing nothing but enjoying the rest and quiet after a busy day with books and work.

Molly in her wheelchair was there in their midst, feeling quite like one of them, looking as contended and even blithesome as any of the rest. She was feeling very glad over her success in a second literary venture, thinking of Dick, too, and how delightful it would be if she could only talk it all over with him.

He had told her in his last letter that she was making him proud of her. What a thrill of delight the words had given her!

"Papa and mamma!" exclaimed Violet, breaking a pause in the conversation. "Home is very dear and sweet, and yet—I'm afraid I ought to be ashamed to say it—I want to go away somewhere for a while, to the seashore, I think; that is, if we can all go and be together."

"I see no objection if all would like it," her father said with an indulgent smile. "What do you say to the plan, little wife?"

"I echo my husband's sentiments as a good wife should," she answered with something of the sportiveness of other days.

"And we echo yours, mother," said Edward, "do we not?" as he appealed to the others.

"Oh, yes, yes!" they cried. "A summer at the seashore, by all means."

"In a cottage home of our own, shall it not be, papa?" added Elsie.

"Your mamma decides all such questions," was his smiling rejoinder.

"I approve the suggestion. It is far preferable to hotel life," she said. "Molly, my child, you are the only one who has not spoken."

Molly's bright face had clouded a little. "I want you all to go and enjoy yourselves," she said, "though I shall miss you sadly."

"Miss us! Do you then intend to decline going along with us?"

Molly colored and hesitated. "I've become such a troublesome piece of furniture to move," she said half in jest, bravely trying to cover up the real pain that came with the thought.

"That is nothing," said Mr. Travilla, so gently and tenderly that happy, grateful tears sprang to her eyes. "You go, of course, with the rest of us—unless there is some more important objection—such as disinclination on your part. And even that should, perhaps, be overruled for the change, I think, would do you good."

"Oh, Molly, you will not think of staying behind, would you?"

"We should miss you sadly," said Elsie and Vi.

"And if you go you'll see Dick," suggested Eddie.

Molly's heart bounded at the thought. "Oh," she said, her eyes sparkling, "how delightful that would be! And since you are all so kind, I'll be glad, very glad to go."

"Here comes grandpa's carriage. I'm so glad!" exclaimed Herbert, the first to spy it as it turned in at the avenue gate. "Now I hope they'll say they'll all go, too."

He had his wish. The carriage contained Mr. and Mrs. Dinsmore, and their son and daughter. It soon appeared that they had come to propose the very thing Herbert desired—that adjacent cottages at the seashore should be engaged for the two families and that all spend the summer pleasantly there together.

It was finally arranged that the Dinsmores should precede the others by two or three weeks, then Mr. Dinsmore would return for his daughter and her family. Then, Mr. Travilla would follow a little later in the season.

Also, it was decided that the second party should make their journey by water. It would be easier for Molly and newer to all than the land route that they had taken much more often in going north.

"Dear me, how I wish we were rich!" exclaimed Virginia Conly when she heard of it the next morning at breakfast from Cal, who had spent the evening at Ion. "I'd like nothing better than to go north for the summer—not to the dull, prosaic life in a cottage though, but to some of the grand hotels where people dress splendidly and have dances and all sorts of merry times. If I had the means I'd go to the seashore for a few weeks and then off to Saratoga for the rest of the season. Mamma, couldn't we manage it somehow? You ought to give Isa and me every advantage possible, if you want us to make good matches."

"I shouldn't need persuasion to gratify you if I had the money, Virginia," she answered dryly, and with a significant glance at her father and sons.

There was no reason from them, for none of them felt able to supply the coveted funds.

"I think it very likely Cousin Elsie will invite you to visit them," remarked Arthur at length, breaking the silence that had followed his mother's remarks.

"I shall certainly accept if she does," said Isa, "for I should dearly like to spend the summer with her and her family there."

"Making garments for the poor, reading good books, and singing psalms and hymns," remarked Virginia with a contemptuous sniff.

"Very good employments, all of them," returned Arthur quietly, "though I feel safe in predicting that a good deal more time will be spent by the Travillas in swimming, riding, driving, boating, and fishing. They are not ascetics, but the most cheerful, happy family I have ever come across."

"Yes, it's quite astonishing how easily they've taken the death of that poor, little child," said Mrs. Conly ill naturedly.

"Mother, how could you even say such a thing!" exclaimed Arthur, indignant at the insinuation.

"Oh, mamma, no one could think for a moment it was from want of affection!" cried Isadore.

"I have not said so. But you can't tell me, I suppose, how Molly assured you her cousin had no need of any consolation?"

"Yes, mother, but it was that her motherly grief was swallowed up in the realizing sense of the bliss of her dear, departed child. Oh, they all talk of her to this day with glad tears in their eyes—sorrowing for themselves but rejoicing for her."

Elsie did give a cordial invitation to her aunt and the two girls to spend the summer with her. It was accepted at first, but declined afterward when a letter came from Mrs. Delaford inviting them to join her in some weeks' sojourn, at her expense, first at Cape May and afterward at Saratoga.

It would be the merry life of dressing, dancing, and flirting at great hotels for which Virginia hungered, and so Virginia and her mother snatched at it with great eagerness.

Isadore would have preferred to be with the Travillas, but Mrs. Conly would not hear of it.

Aunt Delaford would be mortally offended. And the idea of throwing away such a chance! Was Isa crazy? It would be well enough to accept Elsie's offer to pay their traveling expenses and provide each with a handsome outfit, but her cottage would be no place to spend the summer when they could do so much better. There would be few gentlemen there. Elsie and Mr. Travilla were so absurdly particular as to whom they admitted to an acquaintance with their daughters. If there was the slightest suspicion against a man's moral character, he might as well wish for the moon as for entrance to their house—or so much as a bowing acquaintance with Elsie and Vi. It was really too absurd.

"But, mamma," expostulated Isadore, "surely you would not be willing that we should associate with anyone who was not of irreproachable character?"

Mrs. Conly colored and looked annoyed.

"There is no use in being too particular, Isadore," she said. "One can't expect perfection. Young men are very apt to be a little wild, and they often settle down afterward into very good husbands."

"Really, I don't think any the worse of a young fellow for sowing a few wild oats," remarked Virginia, with a toss of her head. "They're a great deal more interesting than your good young men."

"Such as Cal and Art," suggested Isa, smiling slightly. "Mamma, don't you wish then that they'd be a little wild?"

"Nonsense, Isadore! Your brothers are just what I would have them to be! I don't prefer wild young men, but I hope I have sense enough not to expect everybody's sons to be as good as mine and charity enough to overlook the imperfections of those who are not."

"Well, mamma," said Isadore with great and grave seriousness, "I have talked this matter over with Cousin Elsie, and I think she takes the right view of it. The rule should be as strict for men as for women. The sin that makes a woman an outcast from decent society should receive the same condemnation when committed by a man. A woman should require the same absolute moral purity in the man she marries as men do in the women they choose for wives. So long as we are content with anything less, so long as we smile on men whom we know to be immoral, we are in a measure responsible for their vices."

"I endorse that sentiment," said Arthur, coming in from the adjoining room. "It would be a great restraint upon men's vicious inclinations, if they knew that indulgence in vice would shut them out of ladies' society."

"A truce on the subject—I'm tired of it," said Virginia. "Is it decided, mamma, that we take passage in the steamer with the Travillas?"

"Yes, and now let us turn our attention to the much more agreeable topic of dress. There are a good many questions to settle in regard to it—what we must have, what can be got here, and what after we reach Philadelphia."

"And how one dollar can be made to do the work of two," added Virginia, "for there are loads and loads of things I must have in order to make a respectable appearance at the watering places."

"And we have just two weeks in which to make our arrangements," added her mother.

Chapter Twenty-Second

Such sheets of fire, such bursts of horrid thunder
Such groans of roaring wind and rain, I never
Remember to have heard.

—SHAKESPEARE

Early in the morning of a perfect June day, the numerous parties arrived at the wharf where the steamer lay that was to carry them all to Philadelphia.

The embarkation was made without incident. Molly had had a nervous dread of her share in it, but under her uncle's careful supervision was conveyed safely on board.

The weather was very warm for so early in the season, the sea perfectly calm, and as they steamed out of the harbor a pleasant breeze sprang up and the voyage began most prosperously.

There were a hundred lady passengers, and not more than a dozen gentlemen. But to Virginia's delight one of the latter was a dashing young army officer with whom she had a slight acquaintance.

He caught sight of her directly, hastened to greet her, and they were soon promenading the deck together, engaged in an evident flirtation.

Mr. Dinsmore, seated at some little distance with his daughter and her children about him, watched his niece's proceedings with a deepening frown. He was not pleased with either her conduct or her new companion.

At length, rising and approaching his sister, he asked, "Do you know that young man, Louise?"

"Not intimately," she returned, bridling. "He is Captain Brice of the army."

"Do you know his character?"

"I have heard that he belongs to a good family and I can see that he is a gentleman. I hope you are satisfied, brother."

"No, I am not, Louise. He is a wild and a reckless fellow, fond of drink, gambling—"

"And what of it?" she interrupted. "I don't suppose he's going to teach Virginia to do either."

"He is no fit associate for her or for any lady. Will you interpose your authority?"

"No, I won't. I'm not going to insult a gentleman and I'm satisfied that Virginia has sense enough to take care of herself."

"Waiving the question whether a man of his character is a gentleman, let me remark that it is not necessary to insult him in order to put a stop to this. You can call your daughter to your side, keep her with you, take an early opportunity to inform her of the man's reputation and bid her discourage his attentions. If you do not interfere," he added in his determined way, "I shall take the matter into my own hands."

"Isadore," said Mrs. Conly, "go and tell your sister I wish to speak to her."

Virginia was extremely vexed at the summons, but obeyed it promptly.

"What can mamma want? I was having such a splendid time," she said peevishly to her sister when they were out of the captain's hearing.

"It is more Uncle Horace than mamma."

Virginia reddened. She well knew her uncle's opinions and she was not entirely ignorant of the reputation of Captain Brice.

She feigned ignorance, however, listened with apparent surprise to her uncle's account of him, and promised sweetly to treat him with the most distant politeness in the future.

Mr. Dinsmore saw through her, but what more could he do, except keep a strict watch over both?

The captain, forsaken by Virginia, sauntered to the deck and presently approached an elderly lady who sat somewhat apart from the rest, lifted his cap with a smiling, "How do you do, Mrs. Noyes?" Taking an empty chair by her side, he entered into a desultory conversation.

"By the way," he said, "what an attractive family group is that over yonder," with a slight motion of his head in the direction of the Travillas. "The mother is my ideal of a lovely matron, in appearance at least. I have not the happiness of her acquaintance, and the daughters both are models of beauty and grace. Mrs. Noyes, they are all from your neighborhood, I believe?"

"Yes, I have a calling acquaintance with Mrs. Travilla. She was a great heiress. She has peculiar notions—rather puritanical—but is extremely agreeable for all that."

"Could you give me an introduction?"

She shook her head. "I must beg you to excuse me from such a thing."

"But why?"

"Ah, captain, do you not know that you have the reputation of being a naughty man? Not very, but then, as I have told you, the mother is very strict and puritanical in her ideas. The father is the same. I should only offend them without doing you any good. The girls would not dare or even as much as wish to look at or speak to you."

Growing red and angry, the captain stammered out something about being no worse than most of the rest of the world.

"Very true, no doubt," she said, "and please understand that you are not tabooed by me. I'm not so strict. But perhaps," she added laughing, "it may be because I've no daughters to be endangered by young fellows who are as handsome and fascinating as they are naughty." He bowed his acknowledgments; then, as a noble looking young man was seen to approach the group with the manner of one on a familiar footing, inquired, "Who is that fellow that seems so much at home with them?"

"His name is Leland, Lester Leland. He's the nephew of the Leland who bought Fairview from the Fosters some years ago. He's an artist and poor—the nephew—he had to work his own way in the world, has to yet for that matter. I should wonder at the notice the Travillas take of him, only that I've heard he's one of the good sort. Then, besides, you never know, he may make a good reputation some day."

"A pious fortune hunter, I presume," sneered Brice, rising to give his seat to a lady. Then, with a bow, he turned and walked away.

Mr. Dinsmore was taking his grandsons over the vessel, showing them the engine and explaining its complicated machinery.

Edward, who had quite a mechanical turn, seemed to understand it nearly as well as his grandfather. Both Harold and Herbert—bright, intelligent boys of ten and twelve, looked and examined with much interest, asking sensible questions and listening attentively to the replies.

They were active, manly little fellows, not foolhardy or inclined to mischief, nor was their mother the over-anxious kind. She could trust them. And when the tour of inspection with their grandpa was finished, they were allowed to roam about the steamer by themselves.

Captain Brice took advantage of this to make acquaintance with them and win their hearts by thrilling stories of buffalo hunts and encounters with wolves, grizzly bears, and Indians, in which he invariably figured as the conquering hero.

He thought to make them stepping stones to an acquaintance with their sisters. He congratulated himself on his success when, on being summoned to return to their mother, they asked eagerly if he would not tell them more tomorrow.

"Just try me, my fine fellows," he answered, laughing heartily.

"Mamma, what do you want with us?" they asked, running up to her. "A gentleman was telling us such nice stories."

"I think the call to supper will come very soon," she said. "I want you to smooth you hair and wash your hands. Dinah will take you to your stateroom and see that you have what you need."

"I'm afraid we're going to have a gust," remarked Isadore as the lads hurried away to do their mother's bidding. "See how the clouds are gathering yonder in the northwest?"

"A thunder storm at sea, how romantic!" said Virginia. "'Twill be something to talk about all for the rest of our lives."

"Silly child!" said her mother. "To hear you talk, one would think there was no such thing as any real danger in the world."

"Pshaw, mamma! We're hardly out of sight of land—our own shores," she retorted.

"That would but increase our danger if the storm were coming from the opposite direction," said her uncle. "Fortunately, it is from a quarter to drive us out to sea."

"Do you think it will be a gust, grandpa?" asked Violet, a little anxiously.

"I fear so. The heat has become so oppressive, the breeze has entirely died down, and the clouds look threatening. But, my child, do not fear. Our Father, God, rules upon the sea as well as the land, the stormy wind fulfilling His word."

The storm came up rapidly, bursting on them in its fury before they had left the tea table. The lightning's flash and the crash and roll of the thunder followed in quick succession. The stentorian voices of the officers of the vessel, shouting their orders to the crew, the heavy hasty tramp of the men's feet, the whistling of the wind through the rigging, the creaking of the cordage, the booming of the sea mingling with the terrific thunder claps and the down pouring of the rain all combined in an uproar fit to cause the stoutest heart to quake.

Faces grew pale with fear. The women and children huddled together in frightened groups; the men looked anxiously at each other, and between the thunder peals, spoke in low tones of the danger of being driven out to sea. They asked each other of the captain's skill, on what part of the coast they were, and whether the vessel was strong enough to outride the tempest, should it continue very long.

"Oh, this is dreadful! I'm afraid we shall all go to the bottom if it keeps on much longer," Mrs. Conly was saying to her niece, when there came a crash as if the very sky were falling—as if it had come down upon them. There was a shock that threw some of them from their seats, while others caught at the furniture to save themselves. The vessel shivered from stem to stern, seemed to stand still for an instant, then rushed on again.

"It struck! We're lost!" cried a number of voices, while many women and children screamed, and some fainted.

"Courage, my friends!" called Mr. Dinsmore in loud clear tones that could be distinctly heard by all above the storm. "All is not lost that is in danger. And the 'Lord's hand is not shortened that it cannot save; neither His ear heavy that it cannot hear.'"

"Yes, it is time to pray," said an excited, answering voice. "The lightning has struck and shivered the mast. And look how it has run along over our heads and down yon mirror, as you may see by the melting of the glass. It has doubtless continued on to the hold and set fire to the cotton stored there." The speaker—a thin, nervous looking man who was pushing his way through the throng—added this in a whisper close to Mr. Dinsmore's ear.

"Be quiet!" said the latter sternly. "These women and children are sufficiently frightened already."

"Yes, and I don't want to scare 'em unnecessarily, but we'd better be prepared for the worst."

Elsie had overheard the whispers and her cheek paled, a look of keen distress coming over her face as she glanced from one to another of her loved ones. They were dearer by far than was her own life.

But she showed no sign of agitation. Her heart sent up one swift cry to Him to whom "all power is given in heaven and in earth," and faith and love triumphed over her fear. His love to her was infinite and there was no limit to His power. She would trust Him that all would be well whether in life or death.

"'Even the wind and the sea obey Him,'" she whispered to Violet who was asking with pale trembling lips, "Mamma, mamma, what will become of us?"

"But mamma, they say the vessel is loaded with cotton, and that the lightning has probably set it on fire."

"Still, my darling, He is able to take care of us. 'It is nothing with Him to help whether with many or with them that have no power.' He is the Lord our God, my dear one."

Her father came to her side. "Daughter my dear, dear daughter!" he said with emotion, taking her in his arms as was his habit in her early years.

"Oh, grandpa, take care of mamma, whatever becomes of us!" exclaimed Elsie and Vi together.

"No, no!" she said. "Save my children and never mind me."

"Mamma, you must be our first care!" said Eddie rather hoarsely.

"Your sisters, my son, and your brothers. Leave me to the last," she answered firmly.

"We will hope to save you all," Mr. Dinsmore said, trying to speak cheerfully. "But, if you perish, I perish with you."

"Horace, is it true? Is it true that the vessel is on fire?" gasped Mrs. Conly, clutching his arm and staring him in the face with eyes wild with terror.

"Try to calm yourself, Louise," he said kindly. "We do not know certainly yet, though there is reason to fear it may be so."

"Horrible!" she cried, wringing her hands. "I can't die! I've never made any preparations for death. Oh, save me, Horace, if you can! No, no, save my girls, my poor dear girls, and never mind me."

"Louise, my poor sister," he said, deeply moved, "we will not despair yet of all being saved. But try to prepare for the worst. Turn now to Him who has said, 'Look unto Me and be ye saved all ye ends of the earth.'"

Virginia had thrown herself upon a sofa, in strong hysterics, and Isadore stood over her with smelling salts and a fan.

Mrs. Conly hurried back to them with tears rolling down her cheeks.

"Oh, what is to be done?" she sighed, taking the fan from Isadore's hand. "If only Cal and Art were here to look after us! Your uncle has his hands full with his daughter and her children."

"Mamma, let us ask God for help. He and He only can give it," whispered Isadore.

"Yes, yes, ask Him! You know how and He will hear you. Virgy, my child, try to calm yourself."

Isa knelt by her sister's side. There were many on their knees crying for succor in this very hour of terrible danger.

The storm was abating. The rain had nearly ceased to fall and the wind to lash the waves into fury. The flashes of lightning were fewer and fainter and the heavy claps of thunder had given place to distant mutterings. They would not be wrecked by the fury of the tempest. Yet, alas, there still remained the fearful danger of devouring fire.

It was a night of terror. No one thought of retiring, and few but young children closed an eye.

Every precaution was made for taking to the water at a moment's warning. Those that had life preservers—and all of this party were supplied with them—brought them out and secured them to their persons. Boats were made ready to launch, and those who retained sufficient presence of mind and forethought, selected and kept close at hand such valuables as it seemed possible they might be able to carry about them.

The Travillas kept together, Mr. Dinsmore with them. So was young Leland also.

He was to them only an ordinary friend, but one of them he would have died to save. And almost he would have done it for the others for her sake.

Poor Molly had never felt her helplessness more than now—fastened to her chair as with bands of steel, there was less hope of escape for her than for any of the others.

Her thoughts fled to Dick in that first moment of terror, to Dick who loved her better than any other earthly thing. Alas, he was far away. But, there was One near, her Elder Brother, who would never leave her. With that thought, she grew calm and strong to wait and endure.

But her uncle did not forget her. With his own hands, he fastened a life preserver about her.

"My poor helpless child," he said low and tenderly, "do not fear that you will be forgotten should there be any chance for rescue."

"Thank you, kind uncle," she said with tears in her eyes, "but leave me to the last. My life is worth so much less than theirs," glancing toward her cousins. "Only Dick would mourn my loss—"

"No, no, Molly, we all love you!" he interrupted.

She smiled a little sadly, but went on, "And it would be more difficult to save me than two others."

"Still, do not despair," he said. "I will not leave you to perish alone. And I have hope that in the good providence of God, we shall all be saved."

Gradually the screaming, sobbing, and fainting gave place to a dull, despairing waiting—waiting with a trembling, sickening dread for the worst.

Rosie had fallen asleep upon a sofa with her head in her eldest sister's lap, Vi on an ottoman beside them, tightly clasping a hand of each.

Elsie had her babe in her arms. He was sleeping sweetly, and laying her head back, she closed her eyes. Her thoughts flew to Ion, to the husband and father who would perhaps learn tomorrow of the loss of all his treasures.

Her heart bled for him, as she seemed to see him bowed down with heart-breaking sorrow.

Then arose the question, What should the end bring to them—herself and her beloved children?

For herself she could say, "Though I walk through the valley of the shadow of death, I will fear no evil; for Thou art with me." Elsie, Vi, and Eddie she had good reason to hope were true Christians. But Harold and Herbert? A pang shot her heart. Good, obedient children though they were, she knew not that they had ever experienced that new birth without which none can enter heaven.

Jesus said, "Verily, verily, I say unto thee, except a man be born again, he cannot see the kingdom of God."

"Mamma, what is it?" Eddie asked, seeing her glance anxiously from side to side.

"Your little brothers! I do not see them. Where have they gone?"

"They went into their stateroom a moment ago. They were right here. Shall I call them?"

"Yes, yes, I must speak to them."

They came at once in answer to Eddie's summons.

Herbert's eyes were full of tears, not of terror or grief; there seemed a new and happy light in each boyish face.

"Mamma," whispered Harold, putting his arm around her neck, his lips to her ear, "we went away to be alone, Herbie and I. We knew what made you look so sorry at us—because you were afraid we didn't love Jesus. But we do, mamma, and we went away to give ourselves to Him. We mean to be His always, whether we live or die."

Glad tears rolled down her cheeks as she silently embraced first one and then the other.

And so slowly the night wore away. There was a reign of terror for hours while every moment they were watching with despairing hearts for the smell of fire or the bursting out of flames from the hold. Their fears gave way to a faint hope as time passed on and the catastrophe was still delayed. A hope grew gradually stronger and brighter, till at last it was lost in glad certainty.

The electricity, it appeared, had scattered over the iron of the machinery instead of running on down into the hold.

Some said, "What a lucky escape!" Others said, "What a kind providence."

Chapter Twenty-Third

Sacred love is basely bought and sold;
Wives are grown traffic, marriage is a trade.

—RANDOLPH

They came safely into port. A little crowd of eager, expectant friends stood waiting on the wharf. Among them was a tall, dark-eyed young man with a bright, intellectual face whom Molly, seated on the deck in the midst of the family group, recognized with almost a cry of delight.

The instant a plank was thrown out, he sprang on board, and in another moment she was in his arms sobbing, "Oh, Dick, Dick, I thought I'd never see you again!"

"Why?" he said with a joyous laugh. "We've not been so long or so far apart that you need have been in despair of that."

Then, as he turned to exchange greetings with the others, his ear caught the words, "We had an awful night, expecting every moment to see flames bursting out of the hold."

"What?—what does it mean?" he asked, grasping his uncle's hand, while his cheek paled and he glanced hastily from side to side.

"We have had a narrow escape, Dick," replied Mr. Dinsmore.

The main facts were soon given, the details as they drove to the hotel. Dick rejoiced with trembling, as he learned how, almost, he had lost these dear ones.

A few days were spent in Philadelphia, and then Mr. Dinsmore and the Travillas sought their seaside homes. Dick went with them.

Mrs. Dinsmore and her daughter Rose, who had been occupying their cottage for a week or more, hailed their coming with joy.

The Conlys would linger some time longer in the city, laying in a stock of finery for the summer campaign. Then, joined by Mrs. Delaford, they too would seek the seashore.

The cottages were quite out of the town, built facing the ocean and as near it as consistent with safety and comfort.

The children hailed the first whiff of the salt sea breeze with eager delight. They were down upon the beach within a few minutes of their arrival. And until bedtime left it only long enough to take their tea, finishing their day with a long moonlit drive along the shore.

They each were given perfect liberty to enjoy themselves to the full. The only restrictions were that they were not to go into danger, or out of sight of the house, or to the water's edge unless accompanied by some older member of the family or a trusted servant.

The next morning they were all out again for a ramble before breakfast. Immediately after prayers Vi, Rosie, Harold, and Herbert, with a man servant in attendance, returned to the beach.

The girls were collecting shells and seaweed; the boys were skipping stones on the water. Ben, the servant, watched the sport with keen interest and occasionally joined in it.

Absorbed in their amusements, none of them noticed the approach of a handsome young man in undress uniform.

He followed them for some moments in a careless way, as if he were but casually strolling in the same directions. Yet, he was watching with close attention every movement of Vi's graceful figure.

She and Rosie were unconsciously widening the distance between their brothers and themselves, not noticing that the boys had become stationary.

Perceiving this, and that they were now out of earshot, the stranger quickened his pace, and coming up behind the lads, hailed them with "So here you are, my fine fellows! I'm pleased to meet you again!"

"Oh," exclaimed Herbert, looking round, "It's the gentleman that tells such nice stories! Good morning, sir. We're glad to see you, too."

"Yes, indeed," assented Harold, offering his hand, which the stranger grasped and shook heartily. "We're having a splendid time skipping stones. Did you ever do it?"

"I did, many a time when I was a little chap like you. I used to be a famous hand at it." Let's see if I can equal you now."

He was soon apparently as completely engrossed with the sport as any of them. Yet through it all, he was furtively watching Vi and Rosie as they strolled slowly onward—now stooping to pick up a shell, or pausing a moment to gaze out over the wide expanse of water, then sauntering on again in careless, aimless fashion. They were thoroughly enjoying the entire freedom from ordinary tasks and duties.

The boys knew nothing about their new companion except what they had seen of him on board the vessel. Their mother had not understood who was their story-telling friend, and in the excitement of the storm and the hasty visit to the city, he had been quite forgotten by all three. Nor were any of the family aware of his vicinity. Thus it happened that the lads had not been warned against him.

Vi, however, had seen him with Virginia and knew from what passed directly afterward between her grandfather and aunt (though she did not hear the conversation) that the stranger was not one of whom Mr. Dinsmore approved.

Not many minutes had passed before she looked back, and seeing that she had left her brothers some distance behind, hastily began to retrace her steps—Rosie with her.

The instant they turned to do so, the captain, addressing Harold, artfully inquired, "Do you know that young lady?"

"I should think so! She's my own sister," said the boy proudly. "The little one is, too."

"Pretty girls, both of them. Won't you introduce me, young sir?"

"Yes, I suppose so," returned the boy a little doubtfully. Taking a more critical survey of his new acquaintance than he had thought necessary before, "You—you're a gentleman and a good man, aren't you, Mr. —?"

"Don't I look like it?" laughed the captain. "Would you take me for a rogue?"

"I—I don't believe you'd be a burglar or a thief, but—but—"

"Well?"

"Please, don't think I mean to be rude, sir, but you broke the third commandment a minute ago."

"The third? Which is that? I really don't remember."

"I thought you'd forgotten it," said Herbert.

"It's the one that says, 'Thou shalt not take the name of the Lord thy God in vain,'" answered Harold in low reverent tones.

"I own to being completely puzzled," said the captain. "I certainly haven't been swearing."

"No, not exactly; but you said, 'by George,' and 'by heaven,' and mamma says such words are contrary to the spirit of the command. And no one who is a thorough gentleman and Christian will ever use them."

"That's a very strict rule," he said, lifting his cap and bowing low to Violet, who was now close at hand.

She did not seem to notice it, or to see him at all.

"Boys," she said with gentle gravity, "let us go home now."

"What for, Vi? I'm not tired of the beach yet," objected Herbert.

"I have something to tell you, something else to propose. Won't you come with me?"

"Yes," and with a hasty "goodbye" to the captain, they joined their sisters who were already moving slowly toward home.

"What have you to tell us, Vi?" asked Harold.

"That I know grandpa does not approve of that man, and I am quite sure mamma would not wish you to be with him. The sun is getting hot and there are Dick and Molly on the veranda. Let's go and talk with them for a while. It's nearly time now for our drive."

"Miss Wi'let," said Ben, coming up behind, "dat fellah's mighty pow'ful mad. He swored a big oath dat you's proud as Lucifer."

"Oh, then we won't have anything more to do with him!" exclaimed the boys. Herbert added, "But I do wish he was good for he does tell such famous stories."

They kept their word and were so shy of the captain that he soon gave up trying to cultivate their acquaintance, or to make that of their sisters.

Mrs. Noyes and he were boarding at the same hotel, and from her he learned that Mrs. Delaford and the Conlys were expected shortly, having engaged rooms on the same floor with her.

The information was agreeable, as, though he did not care particularly for Virginia, flirting with her would, he thought, be rather an enjoyable way of passing the time—all the more so because it would be in opposition to Mr. Dinsmore's wishes. The captain knew very well why, and at whose suggestion, Virginia had been summoned away from his society on board the vessel. And he had no love for the man who so highly disapproved of him.

The girl, too, resented her uncle's interference, and, on her arrival, with the perversity of human nature, went farther in her encouragement of the young man's attentions than she perhaps would otherwise have done.

Her mother and aunt looked on with indifference, if not absolute approval.

Isadore was the only one who offered even the slightest remonstrance, and she was cut short with a polite request to "mind her own business."

"I think I am, Virgy," she answered pleasantly. "I'm afraid you're getting yourself into trouble, and surely I ought to try to save you from that."

"I won't submit to surveillance," returned her sister. "I wouldn't live in the same house with Uncle Horace for anything. And if mamma and Aunt Delaford don't find fault, you needn't."

Isadore, seriously concerned for her sister's own welfare, was questioning in her own mind whether she ought to mention the matter to her uncle, when her mother set that doubt at rest by forbidding her to do so.

Isa, who was trying to be a consistent Christian, would neither flirt nor dance, and the foolish, worldly minded mother was more vexed at her behavior than at Virginia's.

Isa slipped away to the cottage homes of the Dinsmores and Travillas whenever she could. She enjoyed the quiet pleasures and the refined and intellectual society of her relatives and the privileged friends, both ladies and gentlemen, whom they gathered about them.

Lester Leland, who had taken up his abode temporarily in that vicinity, was a frequent visitor. He sometimes brought a brother artist with him. Dick's friends came, too, and old friends of the family from far and near.

Elsie sent an early invitation to Lucy Ross to bring her daughters and spend some weeks at the cottage.

The reply was a hasty note from Lucy saying that she deeply regretted her inability to accept, but they were extremely busy making preparations to spend the season at Saratoga and had already engaged their rooms and could not draw back. Besides that,

Gertrude and Kate had set their hearts on going. "However," she added, "she would send Phil in her place. He must have a little vacation and he insisted that he would rather visit their old friends the Travillas than go anywhere else in the world. He would put up at a hotel (being a young man, he would of course prefer that) but hoped to spend a good deal of time at the cottage."

He did so and attached himself almost exclusively to the younger Elsie with an air of proprietorship, which she did not at all relish.

She tried to let him see it without being rude. But the blindness of egotism and vast self-appreciation was upon him and he thought her only charmingly coy, probably with the intent to thus conceal her love and admiration.

He was egregiously mistaken. She found him never the most interesting of companions and at times, an intolerable bore. She was constantly contrasting his conversation—which ran upon trade and money making to the exclusion of nearly everything else except fulsome flatteries of herself—with that of Lester Leland, who spoke with enthusiasm of his art. He was a lover of nature and nature's God and his thoughts dwelt among lofty themes, while at the same time he was entirely free from vanity. His manner was as simple and unaffected as that of a little child.

He was a favorite with all the family, his society enjoyed especially by the ladies.

He devoted himself more particularly to sculpture, but also sketched finely from nature, as did both Elsie and Violet. Violet was beginning to show herself a genius in both that and music. Elsie had recently, under Leland's instructions, done some very pretty wood carving and modeling in clay. This similarity of tastes made them very congenial.

Philip's stay was happily not lengthened, business calling him back to New York.

Letters came now and then from Mrs. Ross, Gertrude, and Kate, telling of their merry life and the events at Saratoga.

The girls seemed to have no lack of gentleman admirers, among whom was a Mr. Larrabee from St. Louis who was particularly attentive to Gertrude.

At length, it was announced that they were engaged to be married.

It was now the last of August. The wedding was to take place about the middle of October and as the intervening six weeks would barely afford time for the preparation of the trousseau, the ladies hurried home to New York.

Then Kate came down to spend a week with the Travillas at their cottage.

She looked tired and worn, complained of ennui, was already wearied of the life she had been leading, and had lost all taste for simple pleasures.

Her faded cheek and languid air presented a strange contrast to the fresh, bright beauty and animation of Elsie and Violet—a contrast that pained the kind motherly heart of Mrs. Travilla, who would have been glad to make all the world as happy as she and her children were.

Elsie and Vi felt a lively interest in Gertrude's prospects and had many questions to ask about her betrothed—"Was he young? Was he handsome? Was he a good man? But oh, that was of course."

"No, not of course at all," Kate answered, almost with impatience. She supposed he was not a bad man; but he wasn't good in their sense of the word—not in the least religious—and he was neither young nor handsome.

A moment of disappointed silence followed this communication. Then Elsie said, a little doubtfully, "Well, I suppose Gerty loves him and is happy in the prospect of becoming his wife?"

"Happy?" returned Kate, with a contemptuous sniff. "Well, I suppose she ought to be; she is getting what she wanted—plenty of money and a splendid establishment. But as to loving Mr. Victor

Larrabee—I could about as soon love a—snake, and so could she. He always makes me think of one."

"Oh, Kate! And will she marry him?" both exclaimed in horror.

"She's promised to and doesn't seem inclined to draw back," replied Kate with indifference. Then, bursting into a laugh, "Girls," she said, "I've had an offer, too, and mamma would have had me accept it, but it didn't suit my ideas. The man himself is well enough. I don't really dislike him, but such a name! Hogg! Only think of it! I told mamma that I didn't want to live in a sty, if it was lined with gold."

"No, I don't believe I could feel willing to wear that name," said Violet laughing. "But if his name suited, would you marry him without loving him?"

"I suppose so. I like riches and mamma says wealthy men as Mr. Hogg and Mr. Larrabee are not to be picked up every day."

"But, oh, it wouldn't be right, Kate! You have to promise to love."

"Oh, that's a mere form!" returned Kate with a yawn. "Gerty says she's marrying for love—not of the man but his money," and Kate laughed as if it were an excellent joke.

The other two girls looked grave and distressed. Their mother had taught them that to give the hand without the heart was folly and sin.

Chapter Twenty-Fourth

There's many a slip
'Twixt the cup and the lip.

The Travillas were all invited to Gertrude's wedding; but as it was to be a very grand affair, the invitation was declined because of their recent bereavement.

Mr. Ross had not seen his intended son-in-law, nor did he know how mercenary were Gertrude's motives. He took for granted that she would not, of her own free will, consent to marry a man who was not at least agreeable to her, though he certainly thought it odd that she should fancy one over forty years older than herself.

He made some inquiries relative to the man's character and circumstances, and learning that he was really very wealthy, and bore a respectable reputation as the world goes, gave his consent to the match.

The preparations went on—dresses and jewels were ordered from Paris, invitations issued to several hundred guests, and the reception rooms of their city residence refurnished for the occasion. Money was poured out without stint to provide the wedding feast and flowers, rich and rare, for the adornment of the house and the persons of the girls.

Gertrude did not seem unhappy, but was in a constant state of excitement. She would not allow herself a moment to think.

Ten days before that appointed for the ceremony, the bridegroom arrived in the city and called upon the family.

Mr. Ross did not like his countenance one bit and wondered more than ever at his daughter's choice.

He waited till Mr. Larrabee was gone, then sent for her to come to him in the library.

She came, looking surprised and annoyed. "What is it, papa?" she said impatiently. "Please be as brief as you can, because I simply have a world of things to attend to."

"So many that you have not a moment to spare for the father you are going to leave so soon?" he said a little sadly.

"Oh, don't remind me of that!" she cried, a sudden change coming over her manner. "I can't bear to think of it!" and creeping up to him, she put her arms around his neck, while a tear trembled in her eye.

"Nor I," he said, caressing her, "not even if I knew you were going to be very happy so far away from me. But I fear you are not. Gertrude, do you love that man?"

"Why, what a question coming from my practical father!" she said, forcing a laugh. "I am choosing for myself, marrying of my own free will. Is that not sufficient for you?"

"I tell you candidly, Gertrude," he answered, "I do not like Mr. Larrabee's looks. I cannot think it possible that you can love him, and I beg of you if you do not love him, to draw back even now at this late hour."

"It is too late, papa," she returned, growing cold and hard. "And I do not wish it. Is this all you wanted to say to me?"

"Yes," he said, releasing her with a sigh.

She glided from the room and he spent the next half hour in pacing slowly back and forth with his hands bowed upon his chest.

The doorbell rang and a servant came in with a calling card.

Mr. Ross glanced at it, read the name with a look of pleased surprise, and said, "Show the gentleman in here."

The next moment the two were shaking hands and greeting each other as old and valued friends.

"I'm very glad to see you, Gordon!" exclaimed Mr. Ross. "But what happy chance brought you here? Were you not residing somewhere in the West?"

"Yes, in St. Louis. And it is not a happy chance, but a painful duty that has brought me to your home tonight."

He spoke hurriedly, as if to be done with an unpleasant task. Mr. Ross's pulse throbbed at the sudden recollection that Larrabee also was a resident of St. Louis.

He turned a quick, inquiring look upon his friend. "Out with it, man! I'm in no mood to wait, whether it be good news or ill."

Gordon glanced toward the door.

Mr. Ross stepped to it and turned the key. Then coming back, seated himself close to his friend with the air of one who is ready for anything.

"Phil, my old chum," said Gordon, clapping him affectionately on the shoulder, "I heard the other day in St. Louis that Larrabee was about to marry a daughter of yours. So I took the first eastern bound train and traveled night and day to get here in time to put a stop to the thing. I hope I am not too late."

"What do you know of the man?" asked Mr. Ross steadily, looking Gordon full in the eye, but with a paling cheek.

"Know of him? I know that he made all his money by gambling and that he is a murderer."

The last word was spoken low and close to the listener's ear.

Mr. Ross started back—horrified—deadly pale.

"Gordon, do you know whereof you affirm?" he asked low and huskily.

"I do. I had the account from one who was an eyewitness to the affair. He is dead now, and I do not suppose it would be possible to prove the thing in a court of justice; but, nevertheless, I assure you it is true."

"It was thirty years ago, on a Mississippi steamer, running between St. Louis and New Orleans, that the deed was done."

"Larrabee, then a professional gambler, was aboard plying his trade. My informant, a man whose veracity I could not doubt, was one of a group of bystanders who saw Larrabee fleece a young man out of several thousand dollars—all he had in the world. Then, enraged by some taunting words from his victim, pulled out a pistol and shot him through the heart, just as they sat there on opposite sides of the gambling table. Then, with his revolver still in his hand, he threatened with terrible oaths and curses to shoot down any man who should attempt to stop him. He rushed on deck, jumped into the river, swam ashore, and disappeared into the woods."

"Horrible, horrible!" groaned Mr. Ross, hiding his face in his hands. "And this murderer, this fiend in human form, would have married my daughter!" he cried, starting up in strong excitement. "Why was he allowed to escape? Where is he now, the ruffian?"

"The whole thing passed so quickly, my informant said, that everyone seemed stunned, paralyzed with horror and fright till the scoundrel had made good his escape. Besides, there were several others of the same stamp on board—desperate fellows probably belonging to the same gang—who were evidently ready to make common cause with the ruffian.

"In those days that part of our country was, you know, infested with desperados and outlaws."

"Yes, yes, but what is to be done now? I shall of course send a note to Larrabee at his hotel telling him that all is at an end between him and Gertrude, forbidding him the house and intimating that the sooner he leaves the vicinity the better. But—Gordon, I can never thank you sufficiently for your kindness. Will you add to it by keeping this thing to yourself for the present? I wouldn't for the world have the story get into the papers."

"Certainly, Ross!" returned his friend, grasping his hand in adieu. "I understand how you feel. There is but one person beside ourselves who knows my errand here and I can also answer for his silence."

"Who is it?"

"Mr. Hogg, a friend of your wife and daughters."

The news brought by Mr. Gordon sent both Gertrude and her mother into violent hysterics. Mr. Ross and an old nurse who had been in the family for years had their hands full for the rest of the night. It was a sore wound to the pride of both mother and daughter.

"The scoundrel! The wretch! The villain!" cried Gertrude. "I can never hold up my head again. Everybody will be talking about me. Those envious Miss Petitts and their mother will say, "It's just good enough for her. It serves her right for being so proud of the grand match she was going to make. Oh, dear, oh, dear! Why couldn't that Gordon have stayed away and held his tongue?"

"Gertrude!" exclaimed her father in anger and astonishment. "Is this your gratitude to him for saving you from being the wife of a gambler and murderer? You might well be thankful to him and to a Higher Power for your happy escape."

"Yes, of course," said Lucy. "But what are we to do? The invitations are all out. Oh, dear dear, was there ever such a wretched piece of business? Phil, it's real good in you not to reproach me."

"'Twould be useless now," he sighed, "and I think the reproaches of your own conscience must be sufficient. Not that I would put all the blame on you, though; a full share of it belongs to me."

By morning both ladies had recovered some degree of calmness, but Gertrude obstinately refused to leave her room or to see anyone who might call—even her most intimate friends.

"Tell them I'm sick," she said. "It'll be true enough, for I have an awful headache."

It was to her mother who had been urging her to come down to breakfast that she was speaking.

"Well, I shall send up a cup of tea," said Mrs. Ross. "But what is this?" as the maid entered with a note. "It's directed to you, Gertrude."

"From him, I presume," Gertrude said, as the girl went out and closed the door. "Throw it into the fire, mother, or I'll send it back unopened."

"It is not his hand at all," said Mrs. Ross, closely scrutinizing the address.

"Then give it to me, please," and almost snatching it from her mother's hand, Gertrude tore it open and glanced hastily over its contents.

"Yes, I'll see him! He'll be here directly and I must look my best!" she exclaimed, jumping up and beginning to take down her hair.

"See him? Gertrude are you mad? Your father will not allow it."

"Mr. Hogg, mother."

"Oh!"

They exchanged glances and smiles. Mrs. Ross hurried down to breakfast, not to keep her husband waiting. Gertrude presently followed all dressed up and in apparently quite merry spirits—a trifle pale, but only enough to make her interesting, her mother said.

Mr. Ross and Philip, Jr., had already gone away to their place of business. Sophie and the younger boys were off to school and only Mrs. Ross and Kate were left. Kate had little to say but regarded her sister with a sort of contemptuous pity.

Gertrude had scarcely finished her meal when the doorbell rang and she was summoned to the drawing room to receive her visitor.

The wedding came off at the appointed time. There was a change of bridegrooms; that was all. And few could decide whether the invitations had all been a ruse, so far as he was concerned—or if that was not so, how the change had been brought about.

In a long letter to Violet Travilla, Kate Ross gave the details of the whole affair.

A strange, sad story it seemed to Vi and her sister. They could not in the least understand how Gertrude could feel or act as she had, and fear she would find, as Kate expressed it, "even a gold-lined sty, but a hard bed to lie in, with no love to soften it."

"Still," they said to each other, "it was better, a thousand times better, than marrying that dreadful Mr. Larrabee."

For Kate had assured them Mr. Hogg was "an honest, honorable man, and not ill-tempered; only an intolerable bore—so stupid and uninteresting."

Chapter Twenty-Fifth

Whatsoever a man soweth, that shall he also reap.

—GALATIANS 6:7

Elsie and her children returned home to Ion healthful and happy with scarce any but pleasing recollections of the months that had just passed.

This was not so with Mrs. Conly and Virginia. They seemed soured and disappointed. Nothing had gone right for them. Their finery was all spoiled and they were worn out—with the journey they said, but in reality far more by late hours and dissipation of one sort and another.

The flirtation with Captain Brice had not ended in anything serious—except the establishment of a character for coquetry for Virginia—nor had several others that followed in quick succession.

The girl had much ado to conceal her chagrin. She had started out with bright hopes of securing a brilliant match, and now, though not yet twenty, began to be haunted with the terrible, boding fear of old maidenhood.

She confided her trouble to her sister, Isadore, one day when a fit of depression had made her unusually communicative.

Isa could scarce forbear smiling, but checked the inclination to do so.

"It is much too soon to despair, Virgy," she said. "But, indeed, I do not think the prospect of living single need make one wretched."

"Perhaps not you who are an heiress, but it's another thing for poor, penniless me."

Isadore acknowledged that that probably did make a difference.

"But," she added, "I hope neither of us will ever be so silly as to marry for money. I think it must be dreadful to live in such close connection with a man you do not love, even if he is rolling in wealth. Suppose he loses his money directly? There you are tied to him for life without even riches to compensate you for your loss of liberty."

"Dear me, Isa, how tiresome! Where's the use supposing he's going to lose his money?"

"Because it's something not at all unlikely to happen. Riches do take wings and fly away. I do not feel certain that Aunt Delaford's money will ever come to me, or that if it does I may not lose it. So I intend to prepare to support myself if it should ever become necessary."

"How?"

"I intend to take up the study of English again, and also higher mathematics, and make myself thorough in them. I am far from being thorough now because they do not teach them thoroughly at the convent. I want be able to command a good position as a teacher. And let me advise you to do the same."

"Indeed, I've no fancy for such hard work," sneered Virginia. "I'd rather trust to luck. I'll be pretty sure to be taken care of somehow."

"I should think if anyone might feel justified in doing that it would be Cousin Elsie," said Isadore. "But Uncle Horace educated her in such a way to make her quite capable of earning her own living, and she is doing the same by every one of her own children."

"Such nonsense!" muttered Virginia.

"Such prudence and forethought, I should say," laughed her sister.

A few days after this, Isadore was calling at Ion and in the course of conversation Mrs. Travilla remarked with concern, "Virginia looks really unhappy of late. Is her trouble anything it would be in my power to relieve?"

"No, unless she would listen to good counsel from you. It is really nothing serious, and yet, I suppose it seems so to her. I'm almost ashamed to tell you, cousin, but as far as I can learn it is nothing in the world but the fear of old maidenhood," Isa answered, half laughing.

Elsie smiled and said, "Tell her from me that there is plenty of time yet. She is two or three years younger than I was when I married, and," she added with a bright, happy look, "I never thought I lost anything by waiting."

"I'm sure you didn't, mamma," said Violet who was present. "But how very odd of Virgy to trouble about that! I'm glad people don't have to marry, because I shall never, never be willing to leave my dear home and my father and mother—especially not to live with some stranger."

"I hope it may be some years before you change your mind in regard to that," her mother responded with a loving look.

Elsie was not bringing up her daughters to consider marriage the chief end of woman. She had, indeed, said scarcely anything on the subject till her eldest was of an age to begin to mix a little in general society. Then, she talked quietly and seriously to them of the duties and responsibilities of the married state and the vast importance of making a wise choice in selecting a partner for life.

In their childhood she had never allowed them to be teased about beaux. She could not prevent their hearing, occasionally, something of the kind. But she did her best to counteract the evil influence. She had succeeded so well in that, and in making home a delight, that her children one and all shunned the thought of leaving it, and her girls were as easy and free from self-consciousness in the society of gentlemen as in that of ladies—never bold or forward. There was nothing in their manner that could give the slightest encouragement to undue familiarity.

And then, both she and their father had so entwined themselves about the hearts of their offspring that all shared the feeling expressed by Violet. They truly believed that nothing less than death could ever separate any of them from these beloved parents.

There was a good deal to bring the subject of marriage prominently before their minds at present. The event of the winter was the bringing home of a wife by their Uncle Horace and Aunt Rosie was to be married in the ensuing spring.

The approaching Centennial was another topic of absorbing interest.

That they might reap the full benefit of the great Exhibition, they went north earlier than usual. The middle of May found them in quiet occupancy of a large, handsome, elegantly furnished mansion in the vicinity of Central Park.

Here they kept open house, entertaining a large circle of relatives and friends drawn thither by a desire to see the great World's Fair.

The Dalys were with them, husband and wife in the same capacities as at Ion, which left Mr. and Mrs. Travilla free to come and go as they wished—with or without the children.

They kept their own carriages and horses and when at home drove almost daily to the Exhibition.

Going there with parents and tutor and being able to devote so much time to it, the young people gathered a great store of general information.

Poor Molly's inability to walk shut her out of several of the buildings, but she gave the more time and careful study to those whose contents were brought within her reach by the rolling chairs.

Her cousins gave her glowing descriptions of the treasures of the Art Building, Horticultural Hall, and Women's Department and sincerely sympathized with her deprivation of the pleasure of examining them for herself.

But Molly was learning submission and contentment with her lot and would smilingly reply that she considered herself highly favored in being able to see so much, since there were millions of people even in this land who could not visit the Exhibition at all.

One morning, early in the season, when as yet the crowd was not very great, the whole family had gone in a body to Machinery Hall to see the Corliss engine in action.

They were standing near it, silently gazing, when a voice was heard in the rear.

"Ah, ha! Ah, ha! Um h'm, ah, ha! What think ye o' that now, my lads? Is it worth looking at?"

"That it is, sir!" responded a younger voice in manly tones, full of admiration, while at the same instant Elsie turned quickly round with the pleasant exclamation, "Cousin Ronald!"

"Cousin Elsie!" he responded as hand grasped hand in cordial greeting.

"I'm so glad to see you!" she said. "But why did you not let us know you were coming? Did you not receive my invitation?"

"No, I did not, cousin, and thought to give you a surprise. Ah, Travilla, the sight of your pleasant face does one good like a medicine. And these bonny lads and lasses, can they be the bairns of eight years ago? How they have grown and increased in number, too?" he said glancing around the little circle.

He shook hands with each, then introduced his sons—two tall, well built, comely young men aged twenty and twenty-two respectively—whom he had brought with him over the sea.

Malcom was the name of the elder; the other he called Hugh.

They had arrived in Philadelphia only the day before and were putting up at the Continental.

"That will not do at all, Cousin Ronald," Elsie said when told this. "You must all come immediately to us and make our house your home as long as you stay."

Mr. Travilla seconded her invitation and, after some urging, it was accepted.

It proved an agreeable arrangement for all concerned. Cousin Ronald was the same genial companion that he had been eight years before. The two lads were worthy of their sire—intelligent and well-informed, frank, simple-hearted, and true.

The young people made acquaintance very rapidly. The Exposition was a theme of great and common interest, discussed at every meal and on the days when they stayed at home for rest. They all found it necessary to do so occasionally; some of the ladies and little ones could scarcely endure the fatigue of attending two days in succession.

Then through the months of July and August they made excursions to various points of interest, usually spending several days at each—sometimes a week or two.

In this way they visited Niagara Falls, Lakes Ontario, George, and Champlain, the White Mountains, and different seaside resorts.

At one of these last, they met Lester Leland again. The Travillas had not seen him for nearly a year but had heard of his welfare through the Lelands of Fairview.

All seemed pleased to renew the old familiar communication. This was an easy matter as they were staying at the same hotel.

Lester was introduced to the Scotch cousins as an old friend of the family.

Mr. Lilburn and he exchanged a hearty greeting and chatted together very amicably, but Malcom and Hugh were only distantly polite to the newcomer and eyed him askance, jealous of the favor shown him by their young lady cousins whose sweet society they would have been glad to monopolize.

But this they soon found was impossible even could they have banished Leland for Herbert Carrington, Philip Ross, Dick Percival and his friends, and several others soon appeared upon the scene.

Elsie was now an acknowledged young lady; Violet, in her own estimation and that of her parents, was still a mere child. But her height, her graceful carriage, and unaffected ease of manner—which was the combined result of native refinement and constant association with the highly polished and educated, united to childlike simplicity of character and utter absence of self-consciousness—led strangers into the mistake of supposing her several years older than she really was.

Her beauty, too, and her genius for music and painting added to her attractiveness; so that altogether the gentlemen were quite as ready to pay court to her as to her sister. Had she been disposed to receive their attentions or to push herself forward in the least, her parents would have found it difficult to prevent her entering society earlier than was good for her.

But like her mother before her, Violet was in no haste to assume the duties and responsibilities of womanhood. Only fifteen she was

> *Standing with reluctant feet*
> *Where the brook and river meet,*
> *Womanhood and childhood fleet.*

Hugh Lilburn and Herbert Carrington both regarded her with covetous eyes and both asked permission of her father to pay their addresses, but received the same answer—that she was too young yet to be approached on that subject.

"Well, Mr. Travilla, if you say that to everyone, as no doubt you do, I'm willing to wait," said Herbert going off tolerably contented.

But Hugh reddened with the sudden recollection that Violet was an heiress and his portion a very moderate one. Then he stammered out something about hoping he was not mistaken for a fortune hunter and that he would make no effort to win her until he was in circumstances to do so with propriety.

"My dear fellow," said Mr. Travilla, "do not for a moment imagine that has anything to do with my refusal. I do not care to find rich husbands for my daughters. If Violet were of proper age, I should have no objection to you as a suitor even though you would be likely to carry her far away from us."

"No, no, sir, I wouldn't," exclaimed the lad warmly. "I like America and I think I shall settle here. And sir, I thank you most heartily for your kind words. But, as I've said, I won't ask again till I can do so with propriety."

Leland, too, admired Violet extremely, but loved her with brotherly affection. It was Elsie who had won his heart.

But he had never whispered a word of this to her, or to any human creature, for he was both poor and proud. He had firmly resolved not to seek her hand until his art should bring him fame and fortune to lay at her feet.

Similar considerations alone held the young Malcom Lilburn back. Each was tortured with the fear that the other would prove a successful rival.

Philip Ross, too, was waiting to grow rich, but he feared no rival in the meantime because he was so satisfied that no one could be so attractive to Elsie as himself.

"She's waiting for me," he said to his mother, "and she will wait. She's just friendly and kind to those other fellows, but it's plain she doesn't care a pin for any of them."

"I'm not so sure of that, Phil," returned Mrs. Ross. "Someone may cut you out. Have you spoken to her yet? Is there a regular engagement between the two of you?"

"Oh, no! But we understand each other—always have since we were mere babies."

Mrs. Ross and her daughters had accompanied Philip to the shore and it pleased Lucy greatly that they had been able to obtain rooms in the same house with their old friends, the Travillas.

Mr. Hogg was of the party also, and Elsie and Violet had now an opportunity to judge of the happiness of Gertrude's married life.

They were not greatly impressed with it. Husband and wife seemed to have few interests in common and to be bored with each other's company.

Mr. Hogg had a fine equipage and drove out a great deal— sometimes with his wife, sometimes without. Both dressed handsomely and spent money lavishly, but he did not look happy and Gertrude, when off her guard, wore a discontented, care-worn expression.

Mrs. Ross was full of care and anxieties and one day she unburdened her heart to her childhood friend.

They were sitting alone together on the veranda upon which Mrs. Travilla's room opened, waiting for the call to the tea table.

"I have no peace with my life, Elsie," Lucy said fretfully. "One can't help sympathizing with one's children and my girls don't seem happy like yours. Kate's lively and pleasant enough in company, but at home she's dull and spiritless. And though Gertrude has made what is considered an excellent match, she doesn't seem to enjoy life. She's easily fretted and wants change and excitement all the time."

"Perhaps matters may improve for her," Elsie said, longing to comfort Lucy. "Some couples have to learn to accommodate themselves to each other."

"Well, I hope it may be so," Lucy responded, sighing as though the hope were faint indeed.

"And Kate may grow happier, too, dear. Lucy, if you could only lead her to Christ, I am sure she would," Elsie went on low and tenderly.

Mrs. Ross shook her head, tears trembling in her eyes. "How can I? I have not found Him myself yet. Ah, Elsie, I wish I'd begun as you did. You have some comfort in your children. I've none in mine. That is," she added hastily, correcting herself, "not as much as I ought to have, except in Phil. He's doing well. Yet, even he's not half as thoughtful and affectionate toward his father and mother as your boys are. But then, of course, he's of a different disposition."

"Your younger boys seem fine lads," Elsie said, "and Sophie has a winning way."

Lucy looked pleased, then sighed, "They are nice children, but so willful; and the boys are so venturesome. I've no peace when they are out of my sight, lest they should be in some danger."

Chapter Twenty-Sixth

Oh, Lord! Methought what pain it was to drown!
—SHAKESPEARE

*A*s naturally as sunflowers to the sun, did the faces of Elsie's little ones turn to her when in her loved presence. At the table, at their sports, their lessons, everywhere and however employed, it was always the same, the young eyes turning ever and anon to catch the tender, sympathetic glance of mamma's.

Cousin Ronald was a great favorite with his young relatives. Harold and Herbert had long since voted him quite equal, if not superior, to Captain Brice as a storyteller. His narratives were fully interesting and, besides, always contained a moral or some useful information.

There were tales of the sea, wild tales of the Highlands and of the Scottish border, stories of William Wallace of the Bruce and the Black Douglass, in all of which the children greatly delighted. Mr. Lilburn's ventriloquial powers were used for their amusement, also. Altogether, they found him a very entertaining companion.

Rosie, holding a shell to her ear one day, was sent into ecstasies of delight by hearing low, sweet strains of music, apparently coming from the inside of it.

At another time, as she stooped to pick up a dead crab while wandering along the beach, she started back in dismay at hearing it scream out in a shrill, tiny voice, "Don't touch me! I'll pinch you if you do."

The merry laugh of the boys told her that it was "only Cousin Ronald," but she let the crab alone, keeping at a respectful distance from its claws. All of this was on the same evening while mamma and Aunt Lucy were chatting together on the veranda waiting for the call to tea.

It sounded presently and Cousin Ronald and the children started on a run for the house, trying to see who would get there first. Harold showed himself the fleetest of foot, Herbert and Frank Daly were close at his heels, while Mr. Lilburn with Rosie in one hand and little Walter in the other came puffing and blowing not far behind.

"Won't you take us for another walk, cousin?" asked Rosie when they came out again after their meal together.

"Yes," he said, "this is a very pleasant time to be down on the beach. Come lads," to Harold and Herbert, "will you go along?"

They were only too glad to accept the invitation and the four sauntered leisurely down to the water's edge where they strolled along watching the incoming tide.

"I love the sea," Rosie said. "I wish we could take it home with us."

"We have a lake and must be content with that," said Herbert, picking up a stone and sending it far out to fall with a splash in among the restless waves. "We can't have everything in one place."

"Have you ever seen a mermaid, Rosie?" asked Mr. Lilburn.

"No, sir, what is it?"

"They're said to live in the sea and to be half fish and half woman."

"Ugh! That's dreadful! I wouldn't like to be half fish. But I wish I could see one. Are there any in our sea here, Cousin Ronald?"

"They're said to have very long hair," he went on, not noticing her query, "and to come out of the water and sit on the rocks sometimes while they comb it out with their fingers and sing."

"Sing! Oh, I'd like to hear 'em! I wish one would come and sit on that big rock way out there."

"Look sharp now and see if there is one there. Hark! Don't you hear her sing?"

Rosie and the boys stood still listening intently, and in another moment strains of music seemed to come to them from over the water from the direction of the rock.

"Oh, I do! I do!" screamed Rosie in delight. "Oh, boys, can you hear her, too? Can you see her?"

"I hear singing," said Harold smiling, "but I think the rock is bare."

"I hear the music, too," remarked Herbert, "but I suppose Cousin Ronald makes it. A mermaid's only a fabled creature."

"Fabled? What's that?"

"Only pretend."

"Ah, now, what a pity!"

At that instant a piercing scream seemed to come from the sea, out beyond the surf, some yards higher up the coast. "Help! Help! I'll drown! I'll drown!"

Instantly Harold was off like a shot, in the direction of the sound, tearing off his coat as he went; while Herbert, screaming "Somebody's drowning! The life boat! The life boat!" rushed off toward the hotel. "Lads! Lads!" cried Mr. Lilburn, putting himself to his utmost speed to overtake Harold in time to prevent him from plunging into the sea. "Are ye mad? Are ye daft? There's nobody there, lads. 'Twas only Cousin Ronald at his old tricks again."

As he caught up to Harold, the boy's coat and vest lay on the ground and he was down beside them, tugging at his boots and shouting, "Hold on! I'm coming," while a great wave came rolling in and dashed over him, wetting him from head to foot.

"No, ye're not!" cried Mr. Lilburn, laying a tight grasp upon his arm. "There's nobody there; and if there was, what could a bit, frail laddie like you do to rescue him? You'd only be dragged under yourself, my young fellow."

"Nobody there? Oh, I'm so glad," cried Harold with a hearty laugh as he jumped up, snatched his clothes from the ground and sprang hastily back just in time to escape the next wave. "But you gave us a real scare this time, Cousin Ronald."

"You gave me one," said Mr. Lilburn, joining in the laugh. "I thought you'd be in the sea and maybe out of reach of help before I could catch up to you. You took no time to deliberate."

"Deliberate when somebody was drowning? There wouldn't have been a second to lose."

"You'd just have thrown your own life away, lad, if there had been anybody there. Don't you know it's an extremely hazardous thing for a man to attempt to rescue a drowning person? They're so apt to catch and grip you in a way to deprive you of the power to help yourself and to drag you under with them.

"I honor you for your courage, but I wish, my boy, you'd promise me never to do the like again; at least, not till you've grown up and have some strength, my boy."

"And have a fellow creature to perish!" cried the boy almost indignantly. "Oh, cousin, could you ask me to be so selfish?"

"Not selfish, lad, only prudent. If you want to rescue a drowning man, throw him a rope or reach him the end of a pole or do anything else you can without putting yourself within reach of his hands."

Rosie, left behind by all her companions, looked this way and that in fright and perplexity, then ran after Herbert. That was the direction to take her to her father and mother.

Mr. Travilla and Eddie had started toward the beach to join the others. They were the first to hear Herbert's cry.

"Oh, it was Cousin Ronald," said Eddie. "Nobody goes bathing at this hour."

"Probably," said his father, "yet—ah, there's the lifeboat out now and moving toward the spot."

With that, they ran in the same direction and came up to Mr. Lilburn and Harold just as the boy had put on his coat and the gentleman had concluded his exhortation.

They all saw at once that Eddie had been correct in his conjecture.

"Hello! Where's the drowning man?" he called. "Or was it a woman?"

"Ask Cousin Ronald," said Harold laughing. "He's better acquainted with the person."

"A hoax, was it?" asked Mr. Travilla. "Well, I'm glad things are no worse. Run home, my son, and change your clothes. You're quite wet."

"I fear I owe you an apology, sir," said Mr. Lilburn, "but the fact is I'd a great desire to try the mettle of the lads. I believe they're brave fellows, both, and not lacking in the very useful and commendable quality called presence of mind."

"Thank you, sir," Mr. Travilla said, turning upon his boys a glance of fatherly pride that sent a thrill of joy to their young hearts.

Chapter Twenty-Seventh

Nursed by the virtues she hath been
From childhood's hour.

—HALLECK

Count all th' advantage prosperous vice attains,
'Tis but what virtue flies from and disdains;
And grant the bad what happiness they would,
One they must want—which is to pass for good.

—ALEXANDER POPE

Mrs. Travilla was sitting on the veranda of the hotel, reading a letter her husband had handed her at the tea table, when Violet came rushing toward her in wild affright.

"Mamma! Mamma! Something's wrong at the water! Something's happened! Herbie just came running up from the beach calling for the lifeboats. Papa and Eddie have gone back with him, running as fast as they can. Oh, I'm afraid Harold or Rosie has fallen into the water!" she added, bursting into hysterical weeping.

Her mother rose hastily, thrusting the letter into her pocket, pale but calm.

"Daughter, dear, we will not meet trouble half way. I do not think it could be they for they are not disobedient or venturesome. But come." And so together they hurried toward the beach.

In a moment they perceived that their fears were groundless, for they could see their dear ones coming to meet them.

Violet's tears were changed to laughter as Harold gave a humorous account of "Cousin Ronald's sell," as he called it. And the latter's praise of the boy's bravery and readiness to respond to the cry for help brought proud, happy smiles to the lips and eyes of both mother and sisters.

Elsie had joined them as had Mrs. Ross and a handsome, richly dressed, middle-aged lady, whom she introduced as her friend, Mrs. Faude, from Kentucky.

They, as Lucy afterward told Elsie, had made acquaintance the year before at Saratoga, and were glad to meet again.

Mrs. Faude was much taken with Elsie and her daughters, pleased, indeed, with the whole family; and from that time forward sought their company very frequently.

Elsie found her to be an entertaining companion, polished in manners, refined, intelligent, highly educated and witty, but very worldly, caring for the pleasures and rewards of this life only.

She was a wealthy widow with but one child, a grown son of whom she talked a great deal. "Clarence Augustus" was evidently, in his mother's eyes, the perfection of manly beauty and grace—a great genius, and indeed everything that could be desired in a man.

"He is still single," she one day said significantly to the younger Elsie, "though I know plenty of girls, desirable matches in every way, who would have been delighted with the offer of his hand. Yes, my dear, I am quite sure of it," she added, seeing a slight smile of incredulity on the young girl's face. "Only wait till you have seen him. He will be here on the morrow."

Elsie was quite willing to wait, and no dreams of Mrs. Faude's idol disturbed either her sleeping or waking hours.

Clarence Augustus made his appearance duly the next day at the dinner table. He was a really handsome man, if regular features and fine coloring be all that is necessary to constitute good looks. But his face wore an expression of self-satisfaction and contempt for others, which was not attractive to the Ion clan.

It soon became evident that to most of the other ladies in the house, he was an object of admiration.

His mother seized upon an early opportunity to introduce him to the Misses Travilla, coming upon them as they stood talking together on the veranda.

But they merely bowed and withdrew, having, fortunately, an engagement to drive at that hour with their parents and cousins along the beach.

"What do you think of him?" asked Violet when they had reached their room.

"He has good features and a polished manner."

"Yes, but do you like his looks?"

"No, I do not desire his acquaintance."

"Nor I. He's not the sort that papa and grandpa would wish us to know."

"No, so let us keep out of his way."

"But without seeming to do so?"

"Oh, yes, as far as we can. We don't wish to hurt his feelings or his mother's."

They carried out their subtle plan of avoidance so skillfully that neither mother nor son was quite sure it was intended. In fact, it was difficult for them to believe that any girl could wish to shun the attentions of a young man so attractive in every way as was Clarence Augustus Faude.

"I should like you to marry one of those girls," the mother said to her son, chatting alone with him in her own room. "You could not do better. They are beautiful, highly educated and accomplished, and will have large fortunes."

"Which?" he added sententiously, with a smile that seemed to say he was conscious that he had only to take his choice.

"I don't care. There's hardly a pin to choose between them."

"Just my opinion. Well, I think I shall go for the dark eyes. You tell me the other is not out yet, and I hear the father refuses, on that plea, to allow anyone to court her—though, between you and me, Mrs. F., I fancy he might make an exception in my favor."

"It would not surprise me, Clarence Augustus," she responded, regarding him with a proud, fond smile. "I fancy he must be aware that there's no better match in the Union. But you have no time to lose. They may leave here any day."

"True, but what's to hinder us from following? However, I will take your advice and lose no time. Let me borrow your writing desk for a moment. I'll ask her to drive with me this morning, and while we're out secure her company for the boating party that's to come off tomorrow."

A few moments later the younger Elsie came into her mother's room with a note written in a manly hand, on delicately perfumed French paper.

"What shall I do about it, mamma?" she asked. "Will you answer it for me? Of course, you know I do not wish to accept."

"I will, daughter," Mrs. Travilla said, "though if he were such a man as I could receive into my family on friendly terms, I should prefer to have you answer it yourself."

Mr. Faude's very handsome carriage and horses were at the door, a liveried servant holding the reins. The gentleman himself waited in the parlor for the coming of the young lady, who, he doubted not, would be well pleased to accept his invitation. He was not kept waiting long. He had, indeed, scarcely seated himself and taken up the morning paper, when Mr. Travilla's Ben appeared with a note, presented it in a grave silence, and with a respectful bow, withdrew.

"Hold on! It may require an answer," Mr. Faude called after him.

"No, sah, Mrs. Travilla say dere's no answer," returned Ben, looking back for an instant from the doorway, then vanishing through it.

"All right!" muttered Clarence Augustus, opening the missive and glancing over the contents, an angry flush suffusing his face as he read.

"What is it? She hasn't declined, surely?" Mrs. Faude asked in an undertone, close at his side.

"Just that. It's from the mother. She thanks me for the invitation, but respectfully declines, not even condescending to a shadow of an excuse. What can it mean?"

"I don't know, I'm sure. But if they knew you had serious intentions—it might make a difference."

"Possibly. I'll soon bring it to the proof."

He rose and went out in search of Mr. Travilla. He found him alone and at once asked his permission to pay court to Elsie.

The request was courteously but decidedly and firmly refused.

"May I ask why?" queried the young man in anger and astonishment.

"Because, sir, it would not be agreeable to either my daughter herself, to her mother, or to me."

"Then I must say, sir, that you are all three hard to please. But pray, sir, what is the objection?"

"Do you insist upon knowing?"

"I do, sir."

"Then let me answer your query with another. Would you pay court to a young woman—however wealthy, beautiful, or high born—whose moral character was not better, whose life had been no purer than your own?"

"Of course not!" exclaimed Faude, coloring violently, "but who expects—"

"I do, sir. I expect the husbands of my daughters to be as pure and stainless as my sons' wives."

"I'm as good as the rest, sir. You'll not find one young fellow in five hundred who has sowed fewer wild oats than I."

"I fear that may be true enough, but it does not alter my decision," returned Mr. Travilla, intimating by a bow and a slight wave of the hand that he considered the interview at an end.

Faude withdrew in anger, but with an intensified desire to secure the coveted prize. The more difficult the acquisition, the more desirable it then seemed to him.

He persuaded his mother to become his advocate with Mrs. Travilla.

She at first fully refused, but at length yielded to his entreaties, and undertook the difficult, and to her haughty spirit, humiliating mission.

Requesting a private interview with Elsie, she told her of the wishes of Clarence Augustus, and pleaded his cause with all the eloquence of which she was mistress.

"My boy would make your daughter a good husband," she said. "Indeed, I think any woman might feel highly honored by the offer of his hand. I do not understand how it is, Mrs. Travilla, that a lady of your sense fails to see that."

"I appreciate your feelings, my dear Mrs. Faude," said Elsie gently. "I am a mother, too, you know. And I have sons of my own."

"Yes, and what possible objection can you have to mine? Excuse my saying it, but the one your husband advanced seems to me simply absurd."

"Nevertheless, it is the only one—except that our child's heart is not enlisted. But either alone would be insuperable."

"She hardly knows him yet, and could not fail to learn to love him if she did. Be persuaded my dear Mrs. Travilla, to give him a chance to try. It is never well to be hasty, especially in declining a good offer. And this, let me tell you, is such an one as you will not meet with every day—lovely and attractive in every way as your daughters are.

"Ours is an old, aristocratic family. There is none better to be found in our state or in the Union. We have wealth, too, and I flatter myself that Clarence Augustus is as handsome a man as you would find anywhere. He is amiable in disposition, also, and would, as I said before, make an excellent husband. Will you not undertake his cause?"

"Believe me, it is painful to me to refuse, but I could not, in good conscience."

"But why not?"

"Simply for the reason my husband gave. We both consider moral purity more essential than anything else in those we admit to even friendly acquaintance with our children, especially our young daughters."

"My son is not a bad man, Mrs. Travilla. Very far from it!" Mrs. Faude exclaimed in the tone of one who considers herself grossly insulted.

"Not, I am sure, as the world looks upon those things," said Elsie. "But the Bible is our standard, and guided by its teachings we desire above all things else, purity of heart and life in those who seek friendship of our children. We especially desire it in those who are to become their partners for life and the future fathers or mothers of their offspring, should it please God to give them any."

"That is certainly looking ahead," returned Mrs. Faude, with a polite sneer.

"Not farther than is our duty, since after marriage it is too late to consider, to any profit, what kind of parent our already irrevocably chosen partner for life will probably make."

"Well, well, everyone to her taste!" said Mrs. Faude, rising to go. "But, had I a daughter, I should infinitely prefer for her husband such a young man as my Clarence Augustus to such as that poor artist who is so attentive to Miss Travilla.

"Good morning. I am sure I may trust you not to blazon this matter abroad?"

"You certainly may, Mrs. Faude," Elsie returned with sweet and gentle courtesy, "and, believe me, it has been very painful to me to speak words that have given pain to you."

"What is it, little wife?" Mr. Travilla asked, coming in a moment after Mrs. Faude's departure and finding Elsie alone and seemingly sunk in a painful reverie.

She repeated what had just passed, adding, "I am very glad now that we decided to return to Philadelphia tomorrow. I could see Mrs. Faude was deeply offended, and it would be unpleasant to both of us to remain longer in the same house. As she and her son go with the boating party today and we leave early in the morning, I trust we are not likely to encounter each other again."

"Yes, it is all for the best," he said, "but I wish I could have shielded you from this trial."

Chapter Twenty-Eighth

The brave man is not he who feels no fear,
For that were stupid and irrational;
But he whose soul its fear subdues,
And bravely dares the
danger nature shrinks from.

—BAILLIE

The Travillas returned home to Ion in the month of November and took up with new zest the old and loved routine of study, work, and play.

Elsie was no longer a schoolgirl, but still devoted some hours of each day to the cultivation of her mind and the keeping up of her accomplishments. She also pursued her art studies with renewed ardor under the tutelage of Lester Leland. Leland's health required a warmer climate than that of his northern home so he had come at the urgent request of his relatives to spend the winter season with them at Fairview.

Elsie had a number of gentlemen friends, some of whom she highly esteemed, but Lester's company was preferred to that of any other.

Malcom Lilburn had grown very jealous of Lester and found it difficult indeed to refrain from telling his love, but he had gone away without breathing a word of it to anyone.

He'd not gone to Scotland, however; he and his father were traveling through the West, visiting the principal points of interest.

They had partly promised to take Ion in their way as they returned, which would probably not be before spring.

Mr. and Mrs. Travilla were not exempt from the cares and trials incident to our fallen state, but no happier parents could be found. They were already reaping as they had sowed. Indeed, it seemed to them that they had been reaping all the way along, so sweet was the return of affection from the clinging, helpless ones—the care of whom had been no less a pleasure than a sacred, God-given duty. With each passing year, the harvest grew richer and more abundant. The eldest three had become companionable and the exchanges between the two Elsies were more like that of sisters than of mother and daughter. The young girls loved their mother's company above that of any other of her sex. "Mamma" was still, as she had ever been, their most intimate friend and confidante.

And was it not wise? Who could be a more tender, faithful, and prudent guide and counselor than the mother to whom she was dearer than life?

It was the same with the others also—both sons and daughters. And they were scarcely less open with their wisely indulgent father.

Life was not all sunshine. The children had their faults that would occasionally show themselves; but the parents, conscious of their own imperfections, were patient and forbearing. They were sometimes tried with sickness, too, but it was borne with cheerful resignation. No one could say what the future held in store for any of them; but God reigned—the God whom they had chosen as their portion and their inheritance forever. And they left all with Him, striving to obey the command to be without carefulness.

The winter passed quickly, almost without incident—save one.

Eddie had been spending the afternoon with his cousins at Pinegrove—some of them were lads near his own age—fine, intelligent, good boys. He had stayed to tea and was riding home alone, except that he had an attendant in the person of a young Negro boy, who rode some yards in the rear.

It was already dark when they started, but the stars shone down from a clear sky and a keen, cold wind blew from the north.

Part of the way lay through woods, in the midst of which stood a hut occupied by a family by the name of Smith, belonging to the class known as "poor whites." They were shiftless, lazy, and consequently, very poor indeed. Many efforts had been put forth on their behalf by the families of the Oaks and Ion and by others also; but thus far with small results, for it is no easy matter to effectually help those who will not try to help themselves.

As Eddie entered the woods, he thought he smelled smoke, and presently a sudden turn in the road brought into view the dwelling of the Smiths all wrapped in flames.

Putting spurs to his horse at the sight, Eddie flew along the road shouting at the top of his lungs, "Fire! Fire! Fire!" Jim, his attendant, followed his good example.

But there was no one within hearing save the Smiths themselves.

The head of the family, half stupefied with rum, stood leaning against the fence, his hands in the pockets of his ragged coat, a pipe in his mouth, gazing in a dazed sort of way upon the work of destruction. All the while the wife and children ran hither and thither, screaming and wringing their hands with never a thought of an attempt to extinguish the flames or save any of their few poor possessions.

"Sam Smith," shouted Eddie, reining in his horse close to the individual addressed, "why don't you drop that old pipe, take your hands out of your pockets, and go to work to put out the fire?"

"Eh!" cried Sam, turning slowly round so as to face his interlocutor, "why—I—I—I couldn't do nothin'; it's bound to go— that house is. Don't you see how the wind's a blowin'? Well, 'tain't much 'count nohow, and I wouldn't care, on'y she says she's left the baby in there—so she does."

"The baby?" and almost before the words had left his lips, Eddie had cleared the rough rail fence at a bound and was rushing toward the burning house.

How the flames crackled and roared, seeming like demons greedily devouring all that came in their way.

"That horse blanket, Jim! Bring it here quick, quick!" he shouted back to his servant. Then to the half-crazed woman, "Where is your baby? Where did you leave it?"

"In there, in there on the bed. Oh, oh, it's burnin' all up! I forgot 'im an' I couldn't get back."

Eddie made one step backward and ran his eye rapidly over the burning pile, calmly taking in the situation, considering whether the chances of success were sufficient to warrant the awful risk.

It was the work of an instant to do that. He snatched the blanket from Jim, wrapped it around his person, and plunged in among the flames, smoke, and falling firebrands, regardless of the boy's frightened protest. "Oh, Mr. Eddie, don't; you'll be killed! You'll burn all up!"

He had looked into the cabin but a day or two before and remembered in which corner stood the rude bed of the family, their only one. He groped his way to it, half suffocated by the heat and smoke, and in momentary dread of the falling in of the roof, reached it at last. Feeling about among the scanty covering laid hold of the child which was either insensible or sound asleep.

Taking the babe in his young, strong arms, while holding it underneath the blanket which he drew closer about his person, he rushed back out again, stepping from the door just as the roof fell in with a giant crash.

The woman snatched her babe and its gallant rescuer fell fainting to the ground. A falling beam had grazed his head and struck him a heavy blow upon his shoulder.

With a cry Jim sprang forward, dragged his young master out of reach of the flying sparks, the overpowering heat, and suffocating smoke; and dropping, blubbering down by his side, tried to loosen his cravat.

"Fetch some wattah!" he called. "Quick dar! You gwine let young Marse Eddie die, when he done gone saved yo' baby from burnin' up?"

"Take the gourd and run to the spring Celestia Ann. Quick, quick as you kin go," said the mother hugging her rescued child and wiping a tear from her eye with the corner of a very dirty apron.

"There ain't none," answered the child. "We uns ain't got nothin' left; it's all burnt up."

But a keen, fresh breeze was already reviving the young hero.

"Take me home, Jim." He faintly said, "Stop that wagon," as one was heard rumbling down the road still at some distance away.

"Hello dar! Jes stop an' take a passenger aboard!" shouted Jim, springing to his feet and rushing into the road, waving his cap above his head.

"Hello!" shouted back the other, "dat you Jim Yates? Burnin' down Smith's house. Dat's a powerful crime, dat is, sah!"

"Oh, go 'long, you fool, Pete White!" retorted Jim as the other drew rein close at his side. "You bet you don't catch dis un a burnin' no houses. 'Spect ole Smith set de fire goin' hisself wid dat ole pipe o' his'n!"

"An' it's clar burnt down to de ground," observed Pete, gazing with eager interest at the smoldering ruins. "What you s'pose dey's gwine to do for sheltah for dem po' chillen?"

"Dat ain't no concern ob mine," returned Jim indifferently. "Ise consarned 'bout getting young Marse Ed'ard safe home, an' don't care nuffin' for all de others in de country. Jes hitch yo' hoss an' help me lift him into de wagon."

"What's de mattah?" queried Pete, leisurely dismounting and slowly hitching his horse to a tree.

"Oh, you hurry up, you ole Petey!" returned Jim impatiently. "Mr. Ed'ard's lyin' dar in de cold. He catch his diff if you's gwine to be all night 'bout gittin to him."

"I'se got de rheumatiz, chile. Ole folks can't turn roun' like young uns," returned Pete quickening his movements somewhat as he clambered over the fence and followed Jim to the spot where Eddie lay.

"Hurt, sah?" he asked.

"A little, I fear I can hardly sit my horse—for this faintness," Eddie answered low and feebly. "Can you put me into your wagon and drive me to Ion?"

"Yes, sah, wid de greatest pleasah in life, sah. Mr. Travilla and de Ion ladies ben berry kind to me an' my ole woman an' de chillen."

Mrs. Smith and her dirty ragged little troop had gathered round, still crying over their fright and their losses, curious about the young gentleman who had saved the baby and was lying there on the ground so helpless.

"Are ye much hurt, Mr. Edward?" asked the woman. "Oh yer mother'll never forgive me fur lettin' ye risk yer life that away!"

"I don't think the injury is serious, Mrs. Smith, at least I hope not. And you were not to blame," he answered, "so make yourself easy. Now, Pete and Jim, give me an arm, each of you."

They helped him into the wagon and laid him down, putting the scorched horse blanket under his head for a pillow.

"Now drive carefully, Pete," he said, trying to suppress a groan. "And, please, look out for the ruts. I'd rather not be jolted."

"And you, Jim, ride on ahead and lead Prince. I want you to get in before us. Ask for father and tell him I've had an accident. Tell him that I'm not seriously hurt but want my mother prepared. She must not be alarmed by seeing me brought in unexpectedly in this state."

His orders were obeyed. Jim reached Ion some ten minutes ahead of the wagon and gave due warning of its approach. He met his master in the avenue and told his story in a straightforward manner.

"Where is Mr. Edward now?" asked Mr. Travilla.

"De wagon's jes down de road dar a piece, sah, be here in 'bout five minutes, sah."

"Then off for the doctor, Jim, as fast as you can go. Here, give me Prince's bridle. Now don't let the grass grow under your horse's feet. Either Dr. Barton or Dr. Arthur—it doesn't matter which—only get him here speedily." And vaulting into the saddle, Mr. Travilla rode back to the house, dismounted, throwing the bridle to Solon, and went in.

Opening the door of the drawing room where the family was gathered, "Wife," he said cheerfully, "will you please step here for a moment?"

She came at once and followed him down the hall, asking, "What is it, Edward?" for her heart warned her that something was wrong.

"Not much, I hope, dearest," he said, turning and taking her in his arms. "Our boy, Eddie, has done a brave deed and suffered some injury by it, but nothing serious, I trust. He will be here in but a few moments."

He felt her cling to him with a convulsive grasp. He heard her quick coming breath, the whispered words, "Oh, my son! Dear Lord, help!" Then, as the rumble of the wagon wheels was heard nearing the door, she put her hand in his, calm and quiet, and went forth with him to meet their wounded child.

His father helped him to alight and supported him up the veranda steps.

"Don't be alarmed, mother, I'm not badly hurt," he said, but staggered as he spoke, and would have fallen but for his father's sustaining arm. By the light from the open door she saw his eyes close and a deadly pallor overspread his face.

"He's fainting!" she exclaimed, springing to his other side. "Oh, my boy, this is no trifle!"

Servants were crowding about them and Eddie was quickly borne to his room, laid upon the bed, and restoratives administered.

"Fire!" his mother said with a start and shudder, pointing to his singed locks. "Oh, where has the child been?"

Her husband told her in a few words.

"And he has saved a life!" she cried with tears of mingled joy and grief, proud of her brave son, though her tender mother's heart ached for his suffering. "Thank God for that, if—if he has not sacrificed his own."

The door opened and Arthur Conly came in.

Consciousness was returning to the lad and looking up at his cousin as he bent over him, he murmured, "Tell mother that I'm not much hurt."

"I have to find that out first," said Arthur. "Do you feel any burns, bruises? Whereabouts are you injured, do you think?"

"Something—a falling beam, I suppose—grazed my head and struck me on the shoulder. I think, too, that my hands and face are scorched."

"Yes, your face is and your hands—scorched? Why, they are badly burned! And your collarbone's broken. That's all, I believe enough to satisfy you, I hope?"

"Quite," Eddie returned with a faint smile. "Don't cry, mother dear. You see it's nothing but what can be made right in a few days or weeks."

"Yes," she said, kissing him and smiling through her tears. "Oh, let us thank God that it is no worse!"

Eddie's adventure created quite a stir in the family, and among outside relatives and friends he was dubbed the hero of the hour. Attention was lavished upon him without stint.

He bore his honors meekly. "Mother," he said privately to her, "I don't deserve all this praise and it makes me ashamed. I am not really brave. In fact, I'm afraid I'm an errant coward. Do you know I was afraid to rush in among those flames, but I could not bear the thought of leaving that poor baby to burn up. You taught me that it was right and noble to risk my own life to save another's."

"That was not cowardice, my dear boy," she said, her eyes shining, "but the truest courage. I think you deserve far more credit for bravery than you would if you had rushed in impulsively without a thought of the real danger you were encountering."

"Praise is very sweet from the lips of those I love, especially my mother's," he responded with a glad smile. "And what a nurse you are, mother mine! It pays to be ill when one can be so tended."

"That is when one is not seriously ill, I suppose?" she said playfully, stroking his hair. "By the way, it will take longer to restore these damaged locks than to repair any of the other injuries caused by your little escapade."

"Never mind," he said, "they'll grow again in time. What has become of the Smiths?"

"Your father has found temporary shelter for them at the quarter and is rebuilding their hut."

"I knew he would; it is just like him—always so kind, so generous."

Chapter Twenty-Ninth

Oh, gentle Romeo,
If thou dost love, pronounce it faithfully.
Or if thou think'st I'm too quickly won,
I'll frown and be perverse, and say thee nay,
So thou wilt woo; but else nor for the world.

—SHAKESPEARE

*O*ne lovely morning in the ensuing spring, the younger Elsie wandered out alone into the grounds and sauntering aimlessly along with a book in her hand, at length found herself standing on the shore of the lakelet.

It was a lovely spot, for the limpid waters reflected grassy banks sprinkled here and there with wild violets and shaded by beautiful trees.

A gentle breeze just ruffled the glassy surface of the pond and rustic seat invited rest. It seemed just the place and time for a reverie, and Elsie, with scarce a glance about her, sat down to that enjoyment. It was only of late that she had formed this habit, but it was growing upon her.

She sat for some time buried in thought, her cheek upon her hand, her eyes upon the ground, and smiles and blushes chasing each other over the fair, sweet face.

The dip of an oar followed instantly by a discordant laugh and a shrill voice saying, "What are you sittin' there for so still and quiet?

Wouldn't you like to get in here with me?" caused her to start and spring to her feet with a cry of dismay.

About an hour before, a little, oddly dressed woman, with grey hair hanging over her shoulders, a large doll in one arm and a sun umbrella in the other hand, might have been seen stealing along the road that led from Roselands to Ion. She kept close to the hedge that separated it from the fields and now and then glanced over her shoulder as if fearing or expecting pursuit.

She kept up a constant gabble—now talking to herself, now to the doll, hugging and kissing it with a great show of affection.

"Got away safe this time, didn't we, Grissy? And we're not going back in a hurry, are we, dear? We've had enough of being penned up in that old house ever so long. Now we'll have a day in the woods, a picnic all to ourselves. Hark! What was that? Did I hear wheels?" Pausing a moment to listen, she said, "No, they haven't found us out yet, Grissy, so we'll walk on."

Reaching the gate leading into the avenue at Ion, she stood a moment peering in between the bars.

"Seems to me I've been here before, must have been a good while ago. Guess I won't go up to the house; they might catch me and send me back. But let us go in, Griselda, and look about. Yonder's a garden full of flowers. We'll pick what we want and nobody'll know it."

Putting down her umbrella and pushing the gate open just far enough to enable her to slip through, she stole cautiously in, crossed the avenue and lawn, and entered the garden unobserved.

She wandered here and there, plucking whatever seized her fancy, till she had an immense bouquet of the choicest blossoms.

At length, leaving the garden, she made a circuit through the shrubbery and finally came out upon the shore of the little lake.

"Oh, this is nice!" she said. "Did I ever see this before? It's cool and shady here. We'll sit down and rest ourselves under one of those trees, Grissy." Then catching sight of a pretty rowboat moored to the shore, "No, we'll jump into this boat and take a ride!" And springing nimbly in, she laid the doll down on one of the seats, the bouquet beside it, saying, "I'm tired carrying you, Griselda, so just lie there and rest." Then quickly loosing the little craft from the moorings and taking up the oars, she pushed off into the deep water.

She laid down the oars presently and amused herself with the flowers, picking them to pieces and scattering the petals in the water. She leaned over the side of the boat, talking to the fishes, and bidding them eat what she gave them, "for it was good, much better and daintier than bread crumbs."

The breeze came from the direction to take her farther from the shore and soon wafted her out to the middle of the lakelet. But she went on with her new diversion, taking no note whatever of her whereabouts.

It was just about this time that Elsie reached the spot and sat down to her daydreams.

Enna, for it was she who occupied the boat, did not see her niece at first. After a little while, growing weary of her sport with the flowers, threw them from her, and took up an oar again. Glancing toward the land as she dipped the oar into the water, her eye fell upon the graceful white-robed figure seated there underneath the trees and she instantly called out to her.

Elsie was much alarmed—concerned for the safety of her poor aunt. There was no knowing what madness might seize her at any moment. No one was within call and, that being the only boat there, there was no way of reaching her until she should return to the shore of her own accord. All this was if, indeed, she was capable of managing the boat so as to reach land and if she desired to do so.

Elsie did not lose her presence of mind. She thought very rapidly. The breeze was wafting the boat farther from her, but nearer to the opposite shore. If let alone, it would arrive there in the course of time and Enna, she perceived, did not know how to propel it with the oars.

"Will you come?" she was asking again. "Will you take a ride in this pretty boat with me?"

"I'll run round to the other side," Elsie called in reply. "I wouldn't bother with those heavy oars if I were you. Just let them lie in the bottom of the boat while you sit still and rest. The wind will carry it to the land."

"All right!" Enna answered, laying them down. "Now you hurry up."

"I will," Elsie said, starting upon a run for the spot where she thought that the boat would be most likely to reach the shore.

She reached it first. The boat being several yards away floating upon very deep water, she watched it a moment anxiously.

Enna was sitting still in the bottom, hugging the doll to her bosom and singing a lullaby to it. Suddenly, as Elsie stood waiting and watching in trembling suspense, she sprang up, tossed the doll from her, leaped over the side of the boat, and disappeared beneath the water.

Elsie tore off her sash, tied a pebble to one end, and as Enna rose to the surface, spluttering and struggling, threw it to her crying, "Catch hold and I will try to pull you out."

"Oh, don't! You will but sacrifice your own life!" cried a manly voice in tones of almost agonized entreaty. Lester Leland came dashing down the bank.

It was too late. Enna seized the ribbon with a jerk that pulled Elsie also into the water. They were struggling together, both in imminent danger of drowning.

It was but an instant before Lester was there also. Death with Elsie would be far preferable to life without her and so he would save her or perish with her.

It was near being the latter. It would have been had not Bruno come to his aid. With the help of the faithful dog, he at length succeeded in rescuing both ladies, dragging them up the bank and laying them on the grass, both in a state of insensibility.

"Go to the house, Bruno. Go and bring help," he said panting, for he was well-nigh overcome by his exertions. The dog bounded away in the direction of the house.

"Lord, grant it may come speedily," entreated the young man, kneeling beside the apparently lifeless form of her whom he loved so well. "Oh, my darling, have those sweet eyes closed forever?" he cried in anguish, wiping the water from her face and chafing her cool hands in his. "Elsie, my love, my life, my all! Oh! I would have died to save you!"

Enna had been missed almost immediately and Calhoun, Arthur, and several servants at once set out in different directions in search of her.

Arthur and Pomp got upon the right scent, followed her to Ion, and joined by Mr. Travilla, soon traced her through the garden and shrubbery down to the lake. They came upon the scene of the catastrophe, or rather the rescue, but a moment after Bruno left.

"Why, what is this?" exclaimed Mr. Travilla in alarm. "Is it Elsie? Can she have been in the water? Oh, my child, my darling!"

Instantly he was down upon the grass by her side, assisting Lester's efforts to restore her to a full and complete consciousness.

For a moment she engrossed the attention of all to the utter exclusion from their thoughts of poor Enna, for whom none of them entertained any great amount of affection.

"She lives! Her heart beats! She will soon recover!" Arthur said presently. "See, a faint color is coming into her cheek. Run, Pomp, bring blankets and more help. They must be carried at once to the house."

He turned to his aunt, leaving Mr. Travilla and Lester to attend to Elsie.

Enna seemed gone. He could not be sure that life was not extinct. Perhaps it were better so, but he would not give up till every possible effort had been made to restore her.

Both ladies were speedily conveyed to the house. Elsie, already conscious, was committed to the care of her mother and Aunt Chloe. Arthur, Dr. Barton, and others used every exertion for Enna's resuscitation. They were at length successful in fanning to a flame the feeble spark of life that yet remained; but fever intervened, and for weeks afterward she was very ill.

Elsie kept her bed for a day, then took her place in the family again, looking quite herself except for a slight paleness. And yet, a close observer might have detected another change—a sweet, glad light in the beautiful, hazel eyes that was not there before.

Lester's words of passionate love had reached the ear that seemed closed to all earthly sound. They were heard as in a dream, but afterward recalled with a full apprehension of their reality and of all they meant to her and to him.

Months ago she had read the same sweet story in his eyes, but how much sweeter by far it was to have heard it from his lips.

She had sometimes wondered that he held his peace so long, and again had doubted the language of his looks. Now those doubts were set at rest and their next meeting was anticipated with a strange flutter of the heart, a longing for, yet half-shrinking from, the words he might have to speak.

But the day passed and he did not come—another and another— and no word from him. How strange! He was still her tutor in her art studies. Did he not know that she was well enough to resume them? If not, was it not his place to inquire?

Perhaps he was ill. Oh, had he risked his health, perhaps his life in saving hers? She did not ask. Her lips refused to speak his name. Would nobody tell her?

At last she overheard her father saying to Eddie, "What has become of Lester Leland? It strikes me as a little ungallant that he has not been in to inquire after the health of your aunt and sister."

"He has gone away," Eddie answered. "He left the morning after the accident."

"Gone away," echoed Elsie's sad, sinking heart. "Gone away, and why so suddenly? What could it mean?" She stole away to her room to indulge, for a brief space, in the luxury of tears; then, with a woman's instinctive pride, carefully removed their traces and rejoined the family with a face all wreathed in smiles.

Chapter Thirtieth

Love is not to be reasoned down or lost,
In high ambition, or a thirst for greatness;
'Tis second life, it grows into the soul,
Warms ev'ry vein, and beats in ev'ry pulse;
I feel it here; my resolution melts.

—ADDISON

Enna lay at the point of death for weeks. Mrs. Travilla was her devoted nurse, scarcely leaving her day or night, and only snatching a few hours of rest occasionally on a couch in an adjoining room.

Mr. Travilla at length remonstrated, "My darling, this is too much. You are risking your own life and health, which are far more valuable than hers."

"Oh, Edward," she answered, the tears shining in her eyes, "I must save her if I can. I am praying, praying that reason may come back and her life be spared till she has learned to know Him, whom to know aright is life eternal."

"My unselfish little wife!" he said embracing her. "I believe your petition will be granted, that the Master will give you this soul for your hire, saying to you as to one of old, 'according to your faith be it unto you.' But, dearest," he added, "you must allow others to share your labor. There are others upon whom she certainly has a nearer claim. Where is Mrs. Conly?"

"Aunt Louise says she has no talent for nursing," Elsie answered with a half smile."

"I am partly of her opinion," he replied playfully; then, more seriously, "Will you not, for my sake and for your children's, spare yourself a little?"

"And your father's," added Mr. Dinsmore, whose step as he entered the room they had not heard.

Elsie turned to him with both hands extended, a smile on her lips, a tear in her eye, "My dear father, how are you?"

"Quite well, daughter," he said, taking the hands and kissing the rich, red lips, as beautiful and sweet now, as in her childhood and youth, "but troubled and anxious about you. Are you determined to be quite obstinate in this thing?"

"No," she said, "I hope not; but what is it you and my husband would have me do?"

"Take your rest at night," answered the one, the other adding, "and go out for a little air every day."

Arthur, coming in at that moment from his morning visit to his patient, joined his entreaties to theirs, and upon his assurance that Enna was improving, Elsie consented to do as they desired.

Still, the greater part of her time was spent at Enna's bedside and her family saw but little of her.

This was a trial to them all, but especially to the eldest who was longing for mamma's dear company. She fully appreciated Molly's and Eddie's companionship, dearly loved that of her father, and esteemed Vi's as sweet, but none could fill her mother's place.

Not even to her, would she have unburdened her heart. She could scarce bear to look into it herself. But the dear mother's very presence, though she might only sit in silence by her side, would be as a balm to her troubled spirit.

She forced herself to be cheerful when with the others and to take an interest in what interested them, but when left alone she would drop her book or work and fall into a reverie. Or she would wander out into the grounds, choosing the most quiet and secluded parts—often the shady banks of the lakelet where she and Lester had passed many an hour together in days gone by.

She had gone there one morning, leaving the others at home busied with their lessons. She was seated on a rustic bench, her book lying unheeded at her feet. She was startled by a sound as of something heavy falling and crashing through the branches of a thick clump of trees on the other side of the lake.

She sprang up and stood looking and listening with a palpitating heart. She could see that a large branch had broken from a tall tree and that it lay upon the ground and—yes, something else lay beside or on it, half concealed from her view by the green leaves and twigs, and—did she hear a groan?

Perhaps it was only fancy, but it might be that lying there was someone in pain and needing assistance.

Instantly she flew toward the spot, her heart beating wildly. She drew near, started back and caught at a young sapling for support. Yes, there lay a motionless form among the fallen branches. It was a man, a gentleman as she discerned by what she could see of his clothing; her heart told her the rest.

In a moment, she was kneeling at his side, gazing into the still, white face. "He is dead; the fall has killed him." She had hope of nothing else. There seemed no possibility of life in that rigid form and deathlike face, and she made no effort to give assistance. She was like one turned to stone by the blow. She loved him and she had lost him—that was all she knew.

But, at length, this stony grief gave place to a sharper anguish. A low cry burst from her lips and hot scalding tears fell upon his face.

They brought him back to consciousness and he heard her bitter sighs and moans. He knew she thought him dead and mourned as for one who was dear.

He was in terrible pain, for he had fallen with his leg bent under him and it was badly broken. But a thrill of joy shot through his whole frame. For a moment more he was able to control himself and remained perfectly still, then his eyelids quivered and a groan burst from him.

At the sound Elsie started to her feet, then bending over him she said, "You're hurt, Lester," unconsciously addressing him for the first time by his Christian name. "What can I do for you?"

"Have me carried to Fairview," he said faintly. "My leg is broken and I cannot rise or help myself."

"What can I do?" she cried. "How can I leave you alone in such pain? Ah!" as steps were heard approaching, "here is grandpa coming in search of me."

She ran to meet him and tell him what had happened.

He was concerned. "Solon is here with the carriage," he said. "I was going to ask your company for a drive, but we will have him take Leland to Fairview first. What could have taken him into that tree?"

The broken limb kept Lester on his back six weeks.

His aunt nursed him with the utmost kindness, but could not refrain from teasing him about his accident, asking what took him into the tree, and how he came to fall. At last, in sheer desperation, he told her the whole story of his love. He told of his hopelessness on account of his poverty, his determination not to go back to Ion to be thanked by Elsie and her parents for saving her life, his inability to go or stay far away from her. And finally he owned that he had climbed the tree simply that he might be able to watch her, himself unseen.

"Well, I must say you are a sensible young man!" laughed Mrs. Leland. "But it is very unromantic to be so heavy as to break the limb and fall."

"True enough!" he said, a flush suffusing his face.

"Well, what are you going to do next?"

"Go off to—Italy, I suppose."

"What for?"

"To try to make fame and money to lay at her feet."

"Well, I think the honest, straightforward, and best course, would be to seek an interview with the parents of the lady. Tell them your feelings toward her, your hopes and purposes, and leave it with them to say whether you shall go without speaking to her."

"They will take me for a fortune hunter, I fear," he said, the color mounting to his very hair.

"I think not, but at all events, I should risk it. I do not pretend to know Elsie's feelings, but if she cares for you at all, it would be treating her very badly indeed to go away without letting her know yours.

"There, I've said my say, and will not mention the subject again till you do. But I will leave you to consider my advice at your leisure."

Lester did so during the next week, which was the last week of enforced quietude. And the more he pondered it, the more convinced was he of the soundness of his aunt's advice. At length, he fully resolved to follow it.

Mr. Travilla had called frequently at Fairview since his accident, always inquiring for him. Eddie had been there, too, on similar errands; but there was never a word from her whose lovely image was ever present to his imagination.

Enna was recovering. There was partial restoration of reason, also. Elsie's prayers had been granted, and though still feeble in intellect, Enna had sense enough to comprehend the plan of salvation and seemed to have entered into the kingdom as a little child—very different, indeed, from the Enna of old. Elsie rejoiced over her with joy akin to that of the angels "over one sinner that repenteth."

Elsie's children were full of happiness in having mamma again at leisure to bestow upon them her accustomed care and attention. Her husband was contented, also, in that he was no longer deprived of the large share of her sweet company.

"Let us have a quiet walk together, little wife," he said to her one lovely summer evening as she joined him on the veranda after coming down from seeing her little ones safe in their nests. "Suppose we call on the Lelands. Lester, I hear, is talking of going north soon, and I believe contemplates a trip to Europe."

"I have not seen him yet to thank him for saving our darling daughter's life, and Enna's, too. Yes, let us go."

Lester and his aunt were alone in the drawing room at Fairview when their visitors were announced.

There seemed a slight air of embarrassment about the young man at the moment of their entrance, but it was dispelled by the kindly warmth of their greeting.

The four chatted together for some time, then Mrs. Leland found some excuse for leaving the room and Mrs. Travilla seized the opportunity to pour out her thanks to Elsie's rescuer from a watery grave.

This made a favorable opening for Lester, and modestly disclaiming any right to credit for what he had done, he frankly told the parents all that was in his heart toward their daughter. He told why he had refrained from speaking before, and his purpose not to seek to win her until he could bring fame and fortune to lay at her feet.

He began in almost painful confusion, but something in their faces reassured him. They expressed neither surprise nor displeasure, though tears were trembling in the soft, hazel eyes of the mother.

Lester had concluded, and for a moment there was silence, then Mr. Travilla said with a slight huskiness in his voice, "Young man,

I like your straightforward dealing; but do you know the worth of the prize you covet?"

"I know, sir, that her price is above rubies, and that I am not worthy of her."

"Well, we will let her be the judge of that," the father answered. "Shall we not, wife?" turning to Elsie with a look that held in it all the homage of the lover, as well as the tender devotion of the husband.

"Yes," she sighed, already feeling the pang of parting with her child.

"Do you mean that I may speak now?" Lester asked, half incredulous of his happiness.

"Yes," Mr. Travilla said. "Though not willing to spare our child yet, we would not have you part in doubt of each other's feelings. And," he added with a kind smile, "if you have won her heart, the want of wealth is not against you. 'Worth makes the man.'"

They walked home together—Elsie and Edward—sauntering along arm in arm, like a pair of lovers.

There was something very lover-like in the gaze he bent upon the sweet, fair face at his side. She was almost sad in her quietness.

"What is it, little wife?" he asked.

"How can we spare her—our darling, our first-born?"

"Perhaps we shall not be called upon to do so; he may not have won her heart."

She shook her head with a faint smile.

"She has tried to hide it—dear innocent child! But I know the symptoms. I have not forgotten." And she looked up into his face, blushing and happy as in the days when he had wooed and won his bride.

"Yes, dearest, what a little while ago it seems! Ah, those were gladsome days to us, were they not?"

"Gladsome? Ah, yes! Their memory is sweet to this hour. Yet I do not sigh for their return; I would not bring them back. A deeper, calmer blessedness is mine now. My dear husband,

> *I bless thee for the noble heart,*
> *The tender and the true,*
> *Where mine hath found the happiest rest*
> *That e'er fond woman's knew;*
> *I bless thee, faithful friend and guide,*
> *For my own, my treasur'd share,*
> *In the mournful secrets of thy soul,*
> *In thy sorrow and thy care."*

"Thank you, my darling," he said, lifting her hand to his lips, his eyes shining. "Yes,

> *We have lived and loved together,*
> *Through many changing years,*
> *We have shared each other's sorrows,*
> *And we've wept each other's tear.*
> *Let us hope the future*
> *As the past has been, may be,*
> *I'll share with thee thy sorrows,*
> *And thou my joys with me."*

For more than forty years,
Yearling has been the leading name
in classic and award-winning literature
for young readers.

Yearling books feature children's
favorite authors and characters,
providing dynamic stories of adventure,
humor, history, mystery, and fantasy.

Trust Yearling paperbacks to entertain,
inspire, and promote the love of reading
in all children.

OTHER YEARLING BOOKS YOU WILL ENJOY

PURE DEAD MAGIC, *Debi Gliori*

THE CITY OF EMBER, *Jeanne DuPrau*

THE TIME HACKERS, *Gary Paulsen*

MOLLY MCGINTY HAS A REALLY GOOD DAY, *Gary Paulsen*

VARJAK PAW, *SF Said*

SHREDDERMAN: SECRET IDENTITY, *Wendelin Van Draanen*

EAGER, *Helen Fox*

HOOT, *Carl Hiaasen*

EOIN McNAMEE

THE NAVIGATOR

illustrated by Jon Goodell

A YEARLING BOOK

Published by Yearling, an imprint of Random House Children's Books
a division of Random House, Inc., New York

Visit us on the Web! www.randomhouse.com/kids

Educators and librarians, for a variety of teaching tools, visit us at
www.randomhouse.com/teachers

The Library of Congress has cataloged the hardcover edition of this work as follows:
McNamee, Eoin.
The navigator / Eoin McNamee.
p. cm.
Summary: Owen has always been different, and not only because his father committed
suicide, but he is not prepared for the knowledge that he has a mission to help the Wakeful—the
custodians of time—to stop the Harsh from reversing the flow of time.
ISBN: 978-0-375-83910-8 (trade)—ISBN: 978-0-375-93910-5 (glb)
[1. Time—Fiction. 2. Fantasy.] I. Title.
PZ7.M4787933Nav 2007
[Fic]—dc22
2006026691
ISBN: 978-0-385-73554-4 (pbk.)
Reprinted by arrangement with Wendy Lamb Books
Printed in the United States of America
April 2008
10 9 8 7 6 5 4 3 2 1
First Yearling Edition

For Owen and Kathleen

There was something different about the afternoon. It seemed dark although there wasn't much cloud. It seemed cold although the sun shone. And the alder trees along the river stirred and shivered although the wind did not seem to blow. Owen came over the three fields and crossed the river just below the Workhouse on an old beech tree that had fallen several years before, climbing from branch to branch with his eyes almost closed, trying not to look down, even though he knew the river was narrow and sluggish at that point and that there were many trailing branches to cling to if he fell. Only when he reached the other side did he dare to look down, and even then the black, unreflecting surface seemed to be beckoning to him so that he turned away with a shudder.

He had woken early that morning. It was Saturday and he had tried to get back to sleep, but that hadn't worked, so he had got up and got dressed. Before his mother could wake, Owen had slipped out of the house and down to Mary White's shop. Mary had run the shop for many years. It was small and packed with goods and very cozy, with good cooking smells coming from the kitchen behind. Mary, who was a shrewd but kindly woman, had smiled at Owen when he came in. Before he had even asked, she handed him a packet of bacon, milk, and half a dozen eggs. He had no money, but then he never had. Mary used to write down what he got in a little book, but now she didn't even bother with that. As always, she could see his embarrassment.

"Stop looking so worried," she had said. "You'll pay it back someday. Besides, you have to be fed, for all our sakes."

She often said mysterious things like that, telling him that it was a pleasure and a privilege to look after him. Owen didn't know what she meant, for no one else seemed to think that way. Sometimes, when he walked through the little town at the bottom of the hill, you would think he had a bad smell the way people shied away from him and whispered behind their hands. It was the same in school. Sometimes it seemed the only reason that anybody ever talked to him was in order to start a fight. He knew that he had no father, and that his clothes were older and more worn than those of the other boys and girls at the school, but something seemed to run deeper than that.

"It's not that they don't like you," Mary had said, in her curious way. "They see something in you that both frightens them and attracts them as well. People don't like things that they don't understand."

When Owen got back to the house, he cooked the bacon and eggs and took them up to his mother. She woke and smiled sleepily at him, as if awakened from a pleasant dream, then looked around her and frowned, as if bad old memories had come flooding back. He handed her the tray and she took it without thanking him, a vague, worried look on her face. She was like that most of the time now.

Then there was the photograph. It had been taken shortly after Owen had been born. His father was holding him in the crook of one arm, his other arm around Owen's mother. He was dark-haired and strong and smiling. His mother was smiling as well. Even the baby was smiling. The sun shone on their faces and all was well with the world. After his father's death, Owen's mother had taken to carrying the photograph everywhere, looking at it so often that the edges had become frayed. As a reminder of happier times, he supposed. Then one day he noticed that she hadn't looked at it. "Where is it?" he had asked gently. "Where is the photograph?"

She looked up at him. "I lost it," she'd said, and her

eyes were full of misery. "I put it down somewhere and I don't remember. . . ."

Now he made a bacon sandwich for himself and took it to his room, where he sat on his wooden chest to eat it. The lock on the trunk was missing and it had never been opened. There was a name on it, J M Gobillard et Fils. It sounded strange and exotic and always made him wish that he was somewhere exciting. Owen knew that his father had brought it back from somewhere and had insisted on it being put in his room, but that was all he knew about it.

He looked around. The only things he really owned in the world were in that room. The old chest. A guitar with broken strings. A dartboard. A set of cards and a battered CD player. There was a replica Spitfire hanging on fishing line from the ceiling. There were a few books on a broken bookcase, a pile of old jigsaws, and a Game Boy.

Owen stood up on the chest and scrambled through the window and onto the branch of a sycamore tree. He swung expertly to the ground from a low branch and set off across the fields.

Owen crossed the burying banks below the mass of the old Workhouse and climbed the sloping bank, passing through the long, tree-lined gully that split the slope. It wasn't that he was hiding from anyone. He just liked the idea of being able to move about the riverbank without anyone seeing him. So he found routes like the gully, or tunnels of hazel and rowan, or dips in the ground that rendered you suddenly invisible. The riverbank was ideal for this. There were ridges and trenches and deep depressions in the ground, as though the earth had been worked over again and again.

It took ten minutes to skirt the Workhouse. It was a tall, forbidding building of cut stone perched on an outcrop of rock that towered above the river. It had been derelict for many years and its roof had fallen in, but something about it made Owen shiver. He had asked many people about its history, but they seemed reluctant to talk. He had asked Mary White about it.

"I bet there are ghosts," he said.

She'd leaned forward in the gloom of her small shop and met his gaze with eyes that seemed suddenly stern and blue in a wrinkled face.

"No ghosts," she had said, giving him a strange look. "No ghosts at the Workhouse. But there are other things. That place has been there longer than anyone thinks."

It took another ten minutes to reach the Den. Owen checked the entrance, as he did every time. A whitethorn bush was bent across it, tied with fishing line. Behind that he had built up a barrier of dried ferns and pieces of bush. The barriers were intact. He moved them carefully aside and rearranged them behind him. He found himself in a clearing just big enough to stand in. The space was lit from above by the sunlight passing through a thick roof of ferns and grass, so it was flooded with greenish light. In front of him was an old wooden door he had pulled from the river after the winter floods. He had attached it to the stone doorway of the Den with leather hinges, but it was still stiff and took all his strength to open.

Inside, things were as he had left them. The Den was roughly two meters square, a room dug into the hillside, its roof supported by old roots. The floor was earth and the walls were a mixture of stones and soil. Owen had found it two years ago while looking for hazelnuts. He had cleared it of fallen earth and old branches and had put an old piece of perspex in a gap in the roof. The roof was under an outgrowth of brambles halfway up the steep part of the slope and the perspex window was invisible while still providing the same greenish light as the space in front of the door.

He had furnished the Den with a sleeping bag and an old sofa that had been dumped beside the river. There were candles for winter evenings, and a wooden box where he kept food. The walls were decorated with objects he had found around the river and in Johnston's yard a quarter of a mile away across the fields. Johnston kept scrap cars and lorries and salvage from old trawlers from the harbor at the river mouth. Owen had often gone to Johnston's, climbing the fence and hunting through the scrap. That was until Johnston had caught him. He winced at the memory. Johnston had hit him hard on the side of the head, then laughed at him as he ran away.

Before that, Johnston used to come to the house three

or four times a year, selling secondhand furniture, but he hadn't been back since he'd caught Owen.

But that had been last year. Now Owen had a lorry wing mirror, a brass boat propeller, a car radio-cassette, and an old leather bus seat with the horsehair filling poking through. He had also found an old wooden dressing table painted pink. He looked at himself in the mirror as he passed. A thin face, his hair needing a cut. He had a wary look. His eyes were a little older than they should be. He made a face at himself in the mirror and the eyes came alive then. He let the mask fall again and saw the same watchful face looking back.

He spent as much time as he could at the Den. Sometimes he felt that people were watching him, whispering that he was the boy whose father had killed himself. *Suicide*—that was the word he heard. He could see it in people's eyes when he went into shops. A strange boy. One day he'd heard a woman whisper behind him, "Like father like son." "He'll go the same way," another voice had said. Sometimes it was just easier to stay away from them.

Owen sat down heavily on the bus seat. He knew he was in trouble. He'd skipped school again that week and spent his day around the harbor, where the river met the sea. He couldn't help it. He kept being drawn back. And yet when he got close to the edge of the dock, he could feel the terrible panic welling up in him. The coldness, the heavy salt greenishness of the water filling his mouth

7

and his lungs, and then the terrible blackness below. Each time he would come to as if he'd been asleep, finding himself many meters from the edge of the dock, his limbs trembling and his mouth dry.

It had been like that for as long as Owen could remember. He wanted to ask his mother if he'd always suffered from such fear, but she seemed so weighed down and lost in her own thoughts that she barely noticed him these days, and when he did ask a question she raised dull, lifeless eyes to him, staring at him as if she was struggling to remember who he was.

That was the worst thing of all, so he had stopped asking questions.

Owen emptied his bag. In the kitchen he had found some cheese and some chocolate biscuits. He took a magazine from the small pile that he kept in the Den. The cheese was a little stale and tasted odd with the chocolate biscuits, but he ate everything and washed it down with milk. Outside, the wind sighed through the trees, but the Den was warm and dry. These were the best times, he thought. No one knew where he was, but he was safe and warm in a secret place that no one else knew about but him.

He had found the Den a few years ago, when things were normal, or almost normal. Those were the days when he'd been able to talk to his mother. About most things, anyway. Except, of course, when he had tried to talk about his father. She would open her mouth as if to reply, but her eyes would cloud over and she'd turn away.

But at least then they had been happy, living together in the small house. "Me and you, son," she would say. "That's how it is, me and you." And he had been glad to have her. In school he had always been a loner. Not that anyone actually bothered him much. They just seemed to think that it was better if he went his way and they went theirs. Fine with him.

But then his mother started to change. She said that something in the house was "weighing on her." That there was something in the air itself that left her unable to think straight. She started to forget things. Little things at first, then it seemed as if she forgot almost everything, wandering through the house vaguely.

Owen read on until the light changed, almost as if a rain cloud had arrived overhead, the light dark but silvery, so he could still see the letters on the page. He listened for the sound of the rain falling, but there was nothing, not even the sound of the wind. In fact, a stillness had fallen outside, so complete that you couldn't hear the sound of birds or insects. Owen decided to investigate. He slipped on his jacket and heaved the old door open. He was careful to replace the branches that hid the door, even though he was aware of their loud rustling in the still air. He paused. There was a sense of expectancy. He began to climb toward the old swing, which was the highest point overlooking the river.

It took ten minutes to get up to the level of the swing tree. The air itself was dense and heavy, and Owen was breathing hard. He skirted the ridge until he got to the swing. It was a piece of ship's cable that had been hung from the branch of an ancient oak protruding over a sheer drop of fifty meters to the river. The rope part of the cable had almost rotted away to expose the woven steel core. No one knew who had climbed the branch to put the cable there, but Owen knew what it felt like to swing on it. It was both terrifying and exhilarating. You knew that if you lost your momentum or your grip there was nothing to save you from the long drop to the stones of the river far below. Local children had used it as a test of nerve for years. For Owen, it wasn't the bone-crunching impact of the stones that he feared but the clammy touch of the water.

For some reason he couldn't explain he felt that there was someone watching. Almost without thinking, he crouched down behind a heap of old stones and peered out over the river. As he did so he saw a part of the bank below him start to move. At least he thought it was part of the bank, but as he looked closer he saw that it was in fact a man. He was wearing some kind of uniform, which might have been blue to begin with but was now faded to a grayish color. There were no insignia on the uniform except for heavy epaulettes on the shoulders. The man's hair was close-cropped and steely gray. In one hand was a narrow, metallic tube, almost gun-shaped, and on his belt there were oddly shaped objects—thick glass bulbs with narrow, blunt metal ends.

There was something else strange about him and it took Owen a little while to work it out. Then he realized what it was. Even though the man was obviously fully grown he was barely a meter and a half tall, just a little taller than Owen himself. The man was staring intently across the river. A small knot of hazel trees on the slope meant that Owen couldn't see what he was looking at, but a dip in the ground led toward the man's position, and Owen crept along it.

As he got closer, he could see how tense the man was, how his left hand gripped the metal tube so tightly that his knuckles were white. As Owen drew level with him he could see that the man was looking in the direction of Johnston's farm and scrapyard. Owen knew that Johnston's scrapyard had been getting bigger, but he hadn't looked at it for a long time and now he saw that it seemed to have expanded to cover field after field. At the fringes of the scrapyard he could see small black figures moving busily to and fro. And as he watched, a figure in white emerged from the fields of scrap and stood facing in the direction of the river. Owen heard a sudden intake of breath from the man in front of him.

"The Harsh!" he exclaimed, then went silent as the cloaked figure raised his right hand in the air. Owen heard an inhuman cry both angry and triumphant, and full of youthful arrogance and ancient fury, a cry that seemed to flow like a raging river until Owen covered his ears and pressed his face to the ground.

And then, as suddenly as it had begun, the cry stopped. Owen looked up. The man in front of him had not moved. If the cry had shaken him, he did not show it. He was waiting for something. The wind had stopped and every branch and leaf was still. The birds and insects made no sound. Even the noise of the river faded away into silence. The man waited and Owen waited with him. The silence stretched on and on. Owen's muscles were taut and his hands were clenched into fists though he didn't know why. And then it came, soundlessly and all-enveloping. A kind of dark flash, covering the sky in an instant, sweeping across the land and plunging everything momentarily into total blackness like the blackness before the world began. And then, just as suddenly, it was gone and the trees and grasses seemed to sigh, the very stones of the land seemed to sigh, as if something precious had gone forever.

"It has begun," the little man said softly to himself, his voice weary. And then there was another great cry, but this time filled with terrible triumph. Owen felt a chill run down his spine and he gasped. In a second the man had turned and taken several swift steps toward him, brandishing the metal tube. But when Owen stood up, the man stopped and rubbed his chin thoughtfully.

"So," he said, as if to himself, "it is to be you. I suppose it had to be."

Owen waited, suppressing the impulse to run. The man strode up to him and took him by the arm.

"We must hurry," he said. "We have a lot to do."

Owen didn't resist. He felt completely bewildered. When the man released his arm he followed. They were going in the direction of the old Workhouse, the small man moving with great speed through the tangles of willow and hazel scrub along the river. After a few minutes, Owen realized that they were following faint paths through the undergrowth, paths that he had never noticed before but which were well traveled. Every so often the man would disappear from sight, but he never got too far ahead. Owen would round a bend to find him waiting.

"What's your name?" Owen said breathlessly as he hurried up to him for the third or fourth time.

"My name . . . ," the man said, stroking his chin and leaning back against a tree as though the matter of his name was worth interrupting his headlong progress for, something that merited sitting down and thinking about.

You either know your name or you don't, Owen thought impatiently. "My name's Owen," he blurted out, hoping to hurry the man along.

"I know your name," the man said in a tone that left Owen in no doubt that he was speaking the truth. "They call me the Sub-Commandant."

A sudden cold breeze made the trees around them rustle. Owen shivered. The man straightened up quickly.

"Let's go," he said urgently, and started out again. Owen followed, almost running.

After ten minutes they were close to the Workhouse. To Owen's surprise the narrow paths had started to widen and there was freshly cut foliage to either side of them. The grass had been stripped from the ground and he could see that the surface of the path underneath was cobbled. But that wasn't all. As they approached the Workhouse, he could hear the sounds of people at work, hammers tapping, wood being sawn, the rumble of masonry. When he rounded the corner he stopped and blinked and rubbed his eyes in amazement. The side of the hill leading to the Workhouse was swarming with people, many of them wearing the same uniform as the Sub-Commandant. And instead of there being a smooth stone face, archways were beginning to appear in the rock. Archways and windows, more and more of them. Men were unblocking entrances and passing the stones from them from hand to hand down the cliff. Other men were using the cut stones to construct a wall at the bottom of the hill. In the oak wood on the other side of the Workhouse teams of women were working with saws at the trees.

Owen realized that he had stopped walking and the Sub-Commandant was now far ahead. He started to run after him but stopped again when he saw the Workhouse. There were people in every window, smoke rising from its chimneys, and from the highest window a black banner with nothing on it stirred in the cold wind.

He realized that he could no longer see the Sub-Commandant and that people were casting curious glances at him. He moved forward, calmly at first and then with increasing panic. On a small rise in the shadow of the Workhouse he saw a man who seemed to be directing the work. He was much taller than the others and was wearing a black suit. The suit was shabby and worn through to the lining, but his hair was cropped and steely gray, and his deep-set, penetrating eyes told you that this was no tramp. As Owen stared at him, he saw the Sub-Commandant emerge from the crowd at the base of the rise. Owen started toward them. As he did so the tall man turned and saw the Sub-Commandant. The two men looked into each other's eyes for a long time, then the tall man strode forward and they embraced. Owen pushed through the people at the bottom of the rise. The tall man turned to look across the river, still holding the Sub-Commandant affectionately by the elbow.

"It has been a long Sleep this time," he said.

"It has been a long watch, Chancellor," the Sub-Commandant replied.

"A long weary one, by your face," the tall man said, glancing at him shrewdly.

"I am tired, but there's no time for that. The Harsh have had a long time to prepare."

"I was worried about that," said the tall man. "We must be quick in our own preparations."

The tall man's eyes swept over the crowd until they reached Owen. It was almost a physical sensation, one that left him feeling uncomfortable, as if his most secret thoughts were suddenly visible. But just as suddenly the sensation stopped and the tall man's eyes were sad.

"I suppose it had to be," he said, sighing, "although I would have preferred somebody else."

"These decisions aren't in our hands," the Sub-Commandant said.

"I know, but I hope we do not have to pay a price for it."

Once again Owen felt that searching gaze sweep over him.

Suddenly a cry went up from the direction of the river. There was a flash of blue light and a sudden smell of burning in the air.

"It begins," the Sub-Commandant said quietly.

"A feint, I would say, nothing more. But we have to be ready. I'll talk to you later."

The tall man grasped the Sub-Commandant's shoulder and strode quickly off. Owen realized that he had

16

moved up the hill as the two men spoke until he found himself standing beside the Sub-Commandant. Despite the man's small stature, Owen had the sensation of being sheltered and protected, more so as the man rested his hand on his shoulder.

"I have a lot to do," the Sub-Commandant murmured, then called, "Cati! Cati!"

A small figure detached itself from a group under the Workhouse walls and ran toward them. Despite the steepness of the slope, the figure came at full speed, taking great leaps and sliding dangerously on the scree. As the figure got closer Owen could see that it was a girl, her long black hair plaited at the back. She was wearing a uniform like the others, but it was covered in badges and brooches. Underneath a peaked cap, her hair was tied in brightly colored braids. Her green eyes watched him warily.

"Cati," the Sub-Commandant said, "I want you to look after young Owen here."

"But I was going to go down to the forward posts, Father!" she exclaimed. "It looks like the Harsh are going to try to cross there!"

"There will be no crossing," the Sub-Commandant said sternly. "At least not yet, but you must do what you are told, Cati. This is no time for disobedience, especially from you."

The girl bit her lip. There were tears in her eyes and two bright points of color burned high up on her cheeks.

"Yes, Father," she said quietly. The Sub-Commandant

turned to her and Owen could see his eyes soften. He put his hands on her shoulders and leaned his forehead against hers. Owen could not hear what he said, but the girl smiled and he could feel the current of warmth between them. The small man cupped the girl's face in his hands and kissed her forehead, and then he turned and was gone. The girl turned to Owen.

"Now, young Owen," she said, putting her hands on her hips, "I hope you're a bit tougher than you look. Come on!" Without looking to see if he was following, she turned and ran back toward the Workhouse, swarming up the slope with fierce agility. Not having a choice, Owen followed. Even so, he found it hard to keep up with her.

As he ran, the workers looked up at him curiously, men and women dressed in many different uniforms. Some of them were gray and worn like the Sub-Commandant's. Others were ornate and colorful. The faces that looked up at him were as varied. There were stern-looking people with straw-blond hair and hooked noses. There were smaller, dark men and women with a cheerful look in their eye who wore copper-colored uniforms and looked as if they would be happier putting down their burdens and joining the two children. There were small, squat people, men with dark curly hair and beards, and others—so many that Owen's head hurt.

"Where did everyone come from?" he said, catching up with Cati. "What's happening? I mean . . ." He stopped. He didn't know which questions to ask first. He felt a sudden impulse to return to the Den, pull the bushes over the entrance and hide. It was all too strange that one minute the riverbank should be just as it always was, and an hour later it looked like a huge armed outpost preparing for war.

"The people have awoken from the Sleep. Or some of them have," Cati said as they passed a group of women who were looking around with dazed eyes, while others rubbed their hands and feet, softly calling their names.

"But where did you all come from? I mean, you weren't here an hour ago."

"We were, you know. Two hours ago. Two years ago. Two hundred years ago. Asleep in the Starry."

"What's the Starry?" Owen began. But he couldn't go on. There was too much to ask.

"Are you hungry?" Cati said. "Come on." She turned sharply left and plunged through an ornate doorway made of a brassy metal with strange shapes etched into it—what seemed like a spindly, elongated aircraft with people sitting on top, tiny men with tubes like the one the Sub-Commandant had carried. There were tiny etched fires and people falling. Cati reached through the doorway and grabbed his shoulder. "Come on!"

Owen found himself on a wide stone stairway that spiraled downward. Every few steps they met a man carrying a barrel or a box on his shoulder, or women walking with rolls of cloth and stores of one kind or another. They all smiled at Cati and she spoke to them by name. The stair seemed to go on forever, until eventually it opened out into a broad corridor that appeared to be a main thoroughfare, for people of every kind were moving swiftly and purposefully through it. Owen felt dizzy. The corridor was lit with an eerie blue light, but he couldn't see where it was coming from.

Cati dived through a side door and Owen found they were now in a vast kitchen. It stretched off into the distance, a place full of the hubbub of cooking, with giant ovens lining one wall, roof beams groaning under the weight of sides of beef, and men stirring great pots. People were baking, stewing, carving, spitting, and all the time shouting and cursing, their faces shining with the heat. To one side of the kitchen, Owen saw a giant trapdoor lying open and a team of coopers opening endless barrels that were being passed up from what must have been a huge cellar below. He saw round cheeses with oil dripping from them, herrings pickled in brine, sides of bacon. There were barrels of honey and of biscuits, and casks of wine carried shoulder high across the kitchen. As he watched, Cati darted across the top of the barrels with a piece of bread in each hand. Before the men could react, she had thrust the bread into the honey and skipped away laughing.

"Here," Cati said, thrusting one of the pieces of bread into his hand. The bread was warm and nutty, and the honey was rich and reminded him of hot summer days spent running through heather moorlands.

"Hello, Contessa," he heard Cati say. Owen turned to see a woman standing beside the girl. She was tall and slender, and her ash-blond hair hung to her waist. She was wearing a plain white dress that fell to her ankles. Her eyes were gray and ageless. Despite the heat of the kitchen, her brow was smooth and dry, and despite all the cooking and frying and battering, there wasn't a trace of a stain on her white dress.

"Hello, Wakeful," the woman said. Her voice was deep and low.

"Contessa is in charge of food and cooking and things," Cati said. "We have to live off supplies until we can plant and get hunting parties out."

"Hunting parties?" Owen said, thinking of the neat fields and little town with its harbor and housing estates. "There's nothing to hunt around here. I mean, it's the twenty-first century. You buy stuff in shops."

Cati and Contessa exchanged a look, then Cati reached out and touched Owen's sleeve. Almost casually, she pushed her finger against the cloth and it gave way, ripping silently. Contessa and Cati exchanged a look. Owen stared, wondering why she had torn his sleeve and how she had managed to do it so easily.

"I know it's all very strange," Contessa said gently, "but if you search in your heart, down deep, I think you'll find that in a way, it mightn't be so strange after all."

Before he could answer, Cati leapt to her feet. "Quick!" she shouted, spraying them both with crumbs. "They'll be raising the Nab. I nearly forgot. Come on!" Tugging at Owen's arm, she ran off.

"Go on," Contessa said. "It's worth seeing." Owen thought there was something he should say, but his mind was blank. With a quick smile he ran after Cati. Contessa watched him go, her face kind but grave.

"Like your father before you, you will be tested," she murmured. "Like your father." With these words, sorrow seemed to fill her face. With a sigh, she turned back to the bustle of the kitchen.

When Owen emerged into the corridor he saw that Cati was almost lost in the crowds ahead. He dashed after her but the flaps of leather coming loose on his trainers made it hard to run. Cati dived through another doorway and Owen, following, found himself on yet another twisting staircase rising upward.

"Hurry up!" Cati shouted back to him. He was panting for breath when he emerged into daylight at the top. He stumbled on the top step and shot forward, landing flat on his face to find himself looking down the sheer wall of the Workhouse to the ground hundreds of meters below. A hand on his collar hauled Owen back. Cati was surprisingly strong and she practically lifted him to his feet before he pushed her hand away.

"I'm all right," he said, trying to sound gruff. "Leave me alone. I can look after myself." If she was offended by his tone, she didn't show it. She met his eyes for a few seconds and he felt that he was being judged by an older and wiser mind, but he thought he saw sympathy there as well. "What is so important, anyway?"

She pointed behind him. Owen saw that they were standing on a flat platform in the middle of the Workhouse roof. The slates on the roof were buckled and covered in mildew, and the stonework was weathered and cracked. In the middle of the platform was a large round hole.

"It's a hole," he said. "I can see that."

"Listen," she said.

At first he could hear a faint rumbling deep in the hole. Then there were deep groaning and complaining noises, as if some very old machinery was grumbling into life. There was a boom that sounded a long way away and then the rumbling got louder and Owen started to feel tremors beneath his feet. As the rumbling grew, the whole building seemed to shake and pieces of crumbling stone began to fall from the parapet.

"What is it?" He looked at Cati, but her attention was on the gaping hole in front of them. More loud groanings and creakings and protesting sounded from the hole, followed by a long, ominous shriek.

"Stand back!" Cati shouted above the noise.

Just as he did, a vast cloud of steam burst upward and then, with terrifying speed, what looked like the top of a lighthouse shot from the hole—a lighthouse that seemed to be perched on top of a column of brass, which was battered and scarred and scratched and dulled as though it was ancient. Owen realized that the thing was coming out of the hole section by section, like a telescope, the sections sliding over each other with deafening groans

23

and shudders and bangs, the whole structure swaying from side to side so that he thought it would fall on top of them. Cati gripped his arm.

"Jump!" she yelled, propelling him forward. The stained brass wall reared dizzily in front of him and he saw himself rebounding off it, being flung over the parapet.

"Grab hold!" Cati shouted, just as Owen was about to hit the wall. Terrified, he glanced down and saw a brass rail coming toward him at great speed. He grabbed it with both hands and Cati pushed him over it. He landed on his back on a narrow walkway as the platform shot upward, swaying and groaning sickeningly.

After what seemed like an eternity, the platform heaved and clanged to a halt. Owen raised himself cautiously on one elbow and looked through the railing. It was a long way down. The figures on the ground below them were tiny. He turned and looked up. The little turreted point that resembled the top of a lighthouse was maybe twenty meters above him. Despite the battered look of the rest of the structure, the glass gleamed softly, as if it had just been polished.

"What is it?" he said, his voice sounding a bit more shaky than he would have liked.

"This is the Nab," Cati said.

"What's that up there?"

"That? That's the Skyward," she said, almost dreamily.

"What's it for?"

"For seeing, if it lets you. For seeing across time."

"You could have killed us," he said, "jumping like that."

"Don't be cross," she said. "I knew you wouldn't jump on your own." Owen opened his mouth, then closed it again. There didn't seem to be anything to say. He looked around and saw that the platform they were on joined two sections of a winding staircase that led to the Skyward. He got to his feet, holding on to the rail. A sudden gust of wind caused the whole structure to sway gently. Owen took a firmer hold and looked out across the river.

Where Johnston's yard had been there were trenches and tall figures in white, although the pale mist that came and went made it difficult to get a proper look at them. But there was no mistaking the defenses that had been thrown up on his own side of the river. Earthworks topped with wooden palisades. Deep trenches. And down near the river, hidden by trees, the flicker of that blue flame. Further in the distance he saw the sun touch the horizon, an orange ball, smoldering and ominous. It reminded Owen that he should be home and his eyes turned to the house on the ridge at the other side of the river.

He blinked and looked again, thinking that he was looking in the wrong place, but he knew from the shape of the mountains in the distance that he was not. He was looking for his house. The long, low house with the slate roof and the overgrown garden that his mother had once kept. The house at the end of the narrow road with several other houses on it. No matter how much he blinked he could not see them. The road, the other houses, his own house where his sad mother wandered the rooms at night—they were all gone, and in their place a wood of large pine trees grew along the ridge. As if they had always grown there.

"It's gone," Owen said, his voice trembling. "The house is gone, my mother . . ."

He felt Cati's arm around his shoulder.

"It's not gone," she said, "not the way you mean it. In fact, in a way it was never really there in the first place. Oh dear, that wasn't really the right thing to say. . . ."

That was enough. Tearing himself away from her, Owen started to run, clattering down the metal stairs of the Nab, out onto the roof, and then down the stone stairs inside the Workhouse. He could hear Cati calling behind him but he didn't stop. Whatever was going on in this place, it was nothing to do with him. He was going to cross the river and get his mother. On he ran, through the busy main corridor now, elbowing people aside, shouting at them to get out of his way, so that they turned to stare after him. The corridor cleared a little as he approached the kitchen, and he was running at full tilt, Cati's cries far behind, when the sole of his right trainer came off and caught under his foot. Arms flailing, he tried to stay upright, but it was no good. With a ripping sound, the sole of the left trainer came off and Owen went crashing to the ground, his head striking the stone floor with a crunch.

He lay there for a moment, sick and dizzy. He put his hand to his head, feeling a large bump starting to rise. He opened his eyes and saw a pair of elegant slippers. He looked up to see Contessa peering down at him with concern. Cati skidded to a halt beside them.

"I—I didn't tell him . . . I mean, I said it would be explained," she stammered. Contessa held up a hand and Cati stopped talking. Owen sat up and Contessa knelt beside him.

"Our house," he said hopelessly, "my mother, they're gone . . ."

"I know," Contessa said gently. "I know. Here. Drink some of this." She pulled a small bottle from the folds of her dress and put it to his lips. The liquid tasted warm and nutty.

"I have to go," he said. "She might be frightened. . . ." But as he spoke, everything seemed to become very far away, even his own voice. His eyelids felt heavier and heavier. He had to fight it. He had to go home. But it seemed that his brain refused to send the order to his legs to move. Instead, strong arms enveloped him and lifted him, and as they did so, he fell asleep.

Owen felt himself coming out of sleep as though he was swimming to the surface of a warm sea. He opened his eyes. It was dark, but it was a strangely familiar dark. Then he realized—he was in his Den. It all came flooding back to him—the Workhouse, Cati. Perhaps he had been asleep and dreamed the whole thing! He felt along the back wall for the store of candles he kept there and lit one. He pulled the sleeping bag around him and sat very still. That was it, he decided. It had all been a very real dream. He felt cold and moved to pull his sleeve down over his forearm. As he did so, the seam disintegrated and the sleeve came away in his hand. He looked down on the floor and saw his trainers, both soles half torn away. It hadn't been a dream! He remembered sitting on the chest in his bedroom that morning and longing for something strange and exotic. Well, what had happened was certainly strange, but he wasn't so sure if he wanted it as much.

He tried to arrange what he knew in his head. The Sub-Commandant. Cati and Contessa. The Workhouse and the Nab. But it was no good. He couldn't make any sense of it. Owen jumped to his feet, and as he did so, he felt his clothes falling away. He looked down. His trousers were hanging in rags; his jacket and T-shirt seemed to have disintegrated.

Owen looked round the walls of the Den. The posters he had hung on the wall had faded, the images indistinct and the paper yellowed. The metal objects did not seem to have suffered as badly, although he noticed that the plastic on the cassette player had faded and warped. Only the brass boat propeller he had found in Johnston's yard seemed to be the same as ever. He tugged at the rotting fabric of his T-shirt in disgust. He couldn't go out without clothes. Then he noticed a neat pile of clothes in the doorway. Owen unfolded it. It seemed to be a uniform of the same faded fabric as the Sub-Commandant had been wearing. There was a pair of boots made of some material that seemed like leather but was not, and which fastened to the knee with brass clips. He imagined what would happen if any of the town children saw him in those clothes—how they would laugh—but a sudden draft on his bare skin made him shiver. He realized that he had no choice but to put on the clothes.

Five minutes later, Owen looked at himself in the mirror. He seemed to look much older. The uniform was a good fit, although it was frayed here and there. He thought he looked like a soldier, somebody who had been in a long war far from home. He heard a noise behind him and turned. Cati was standing in the doorway.

"It suits you," she said.

"This is my place. You have no right to come in here without asking," said Owen, suddenly defensive.

"I was only trying to help. You needed clothes."

"I don't need anything of yours!" he said angrily. "I just want to be left alone."

"Next time I will leave you alone," she snapped back. There were red spots high on her cheeks. "Next time I will leave you alone and you can go around in your bare skin."

They glared at each other for a minute. Then Owen saw a muscle twitch in Cati's face. He felt his own face begin to crease. A few seconds later they were helpless with laughter.

Owen laughed until his sides ached. He and Cati collapsed on the old bus seat, wiping their eyes. They sat for a moment in companionable silence, then Cati leapt to her feet without a word and went back outside. When she came back, she was carrying a basket. Delicious smells rose from it, and Owen stared at it hungrily.

"Contessa sent it," Cati said. She opened the basket and set out the contents neatly on the top of the dressing table. There was fresh, warm bread and sealed bowls of hot stew. There were roast potatoes, cheese sauce, and all sorts of pickles that Owen didn't think that he would like and then discovered he did. They ate without talking, finishing up with two bowls of a delicious substance that was something like custard and something like cream. Owen lay back on the bus seat feeling that suddenly life did not look so bleak after all. But Cati leapt to her feet again.

"Come on," she said briskly. "We have to go to the Convoke."

"I'm too full for a Convoke now, whatever it is."

"I think you'd better come," Cati said, suddenly serious. "You need to know about your mother, apart from anything else."

His mother! Owen sprang to his feet and hurried after her. Outside, it was a cold, crisp night and he could see his breath hanging in the air. He hurried after Cati through the shadows of the trees.

"We've got time," she said. "There are two parts to this Convoke . . . and you're not allowed into the first part."

"Why not?"

She hesitated, then spoke softly, as if she was afraid that she might be overheard. "Well . . . it's actually about you."

"About me?"

"Yes. It's about whether you should be allowed to attend or not. And other things."

"Why wouldn't I be allowed to attend?"

"You'll find out."

Owen was puzzled. What was so special about him that they would waste time talking about whether or not he could attend the Convoke?

"Do you really want to hear the first bit?" Cati asked. "Really?"

"I suppose," he said. "If it's about me, maybe I'd better."

"There's a secret way into the chamber," she said. "I found it ages ago. Come on."

Cati turned onto a path that seemed to lead under the hill. Owen had noticed a gully there before, but it had been choked with trees and undergrowth. Now it had been cleared and the path was smooth underfoot. The path sloped downward and high walls reared on either side, their ancient stones covered in moss and ferns and lichen.

"Where are we going?" Owen said, suddenly aware he was whispering.

"You'll see."

Cati moved swiftly on. It became darker and darker but she did not falter, and Owen began to wonder if she could see in the dark.

After what felt like a long time, Cati stopped so suddenly that Owen ran into her. As his eyes became accustomed to the dark, he saw that they were standing in front of a vast door made of brass and wood, so old and gnarled that it looked like stone. Again, it was decorated with spidery shapes that looked like a child's drawings of boats and planes. As Owen examined it, he realized that the drawings glowed faintly with a blue light he had seen everywhere that day.

Cati took a key from her pocket, a tiny key for a door so vast, but as she held it up he could see that it was ornately worked with complicated-looking teeth. She fitted it into a tiny aperture and turned it, once, twice, three times. There was a sound like heavy, oiled bolts being drawn and then the huge door swung silently open. Cati stepped inside and Owen followed. As they did so the door closed soundlessly behind them. They were now standing in a narrow passage lit by faint blue light coming from the opening at one end. There was an odd smell, musty and old, but sweet as well.

Cati slowly stepped through the opening. Owen hesitated, then with a backward glance at the closed door stepped forward also.

He found himself in a vast chamber, stretching off as far as the eye could see. The ceiling, high above them, was speckled with points of blue light, so it seemed that they stood under a clear night sky. But that was not all. The chamber was filled with innumerable flat couches, each with a single sheet and a pillow. Most of the beds were empty, but as Owen's eyes got used to the dim light, he saw that some of them were still occupied. He looked for Cati, but while he had been standing lost in awe she had moved quietly off. He watched as she moved slowly among the occupied beds, which were scattered among the empty ones. The sleepers seemed to be of all ages, young and old, fair and dark. She stopped by one bed as Owen went toward her. He saw that the figure in the bed was a young man, a little older than him. He had curly dark hair and his breathing was deep and even. Cati reached out and touched his hair, smiling sadly.

"What is this place?" Owen asked.

"The Starry, where we sleep until we are called."

"Who are these people, then?"

"Friends, most of them. When we get the call we are supposed to wake, but some do not wake and we do not know why."

Owen saw that the black-haired boy and two other children—girls with brown hair—were lying in a circle round a woman with work-worn hands and a pleasant face that seemed to be smiling even as she slept. Cati put her hand on the woman's shoulder and bent to kiss her. Owen wanted to ask who she was, but Cati seemed to be almost in a dream and he didn't want to disturb her. He noticed that each pillow had a small blue cornflower placed on it.

"It is our sign of remembering," Cati said. "A sign that we do not forget our friends."

The sweet, musty smell in the air seemed to be getting heavier. If sleep had a smell, this is what it would smell like, Owen thought. His eyelids felt as if there were weights attached to them. The empty beds began to look very inviting.

Suddenly he felt Cati shaking his shoulders. "The Convoke," she said urgently. "Come on. If you stay here, you'll sleep."

34

She led him toward a small doorway that opened onto another one of the winding staircases that were a feature of the Workhouse. The staircase was dark and apparently unused; cobwebs brushed their faces as they climbed, but there must have been a window to the outside world, for Owen felt cold fresh air on his face, chasing away the sleep that had stolen over him in the Starry.

"What is the Starry for?" he said. "Why are they all sleeping? They look as if they've been asleep for years."

"They have," said Cati, sounding sad, "but that's another thing that needs to be explained." And she would say no more about it.

At the top of the staircase was another corridor, then another staircase, then they were under the Workhouse roof. Owen ducked his head to avoid the huge timber beams supporting the roof, half choking on the dust, which rose in great clouds under his feet. Just as he was about to ask where they were, Cati turned and put her fingers to her lips. Following her, he got onto his hands and knees and crawled forward. He saw light coming through a gap in the stone wall in front of him. Cati disappeared into the light and he followed, finding himself in a tiny wooden gallery suspended, it seemed, in midair over great buttresses that went down and down until they reached the floor far below. Owen gasped and grabbed Cati's arm. She made a face at him to be quiet and pointed. Far below them, the Convoke had started.

It was a while before Owen's eyes adjusted to the light and he could make out the scene below. The first thing he noticed were the banners that hung from the ceiling, enormous cloth banners in faded colors that seemed hundreds of meters long. Then he saw that the banners framed a great hall of flagged floors and pillars and stone walls. Massive chains hanging from the roof held globes of blue light and in their glow he could see figures on the ground, some standing, others sitting on a raised dais, and many more standing in a circle around them. He could see that one of the standing figures was the Sub-Commandant and even from far above Owen could tell that the small man was pleading with the figures on the dais.

To the right of these figures was a fireplace where great logs burned, and in front of the fireplace a figure sprawled in a chair. It was too far away to see who it was and Owen was distracted just then as the Sub-Commandant began to speak. His voice was low and even, but there was an intensity to it and Owen guessed that there was some dispute going on.

"You are talking about history in this, Chancellor, but we aren't certain about what took place," he said. Owen could just see Chancellor shake his head as if in sorrow.

"I think that you are the only one who doubts what happened, Sub-Commandant," Chancellor said. "We had the Mortmain and with it the security of the world, or at least as much as was in our power to guarantee. But the Mortmain is gone." His voice was mellow but full of authority, a leader gently rebuking a much-loved but erring lieutenant. Even from his perch in the rooftop, Owen could feel that the crowd in the hall was swayed by him.

"We cannot judge the future by the past," the small man said. "There are many things that we don't know."

"I agree that there are many things we do not know," Chancellor said, "but we have to work with what small knowledge we have. I feel that the boy should not be admitted to our counsel."

The crowd began to murmur this time. Glancing sideways, Owen could see that Cati was worried. Chancellor leaned back in his chair. He looked weighed down by the gravity of the situation. Suddenly Owen heard a woman's voice—a ringing voice with a tone of harsh amusement to it.

"The boy should be allowed in," the voice said.

"You have been listening to our arguments, Pieta?" Chancellor asked.

The woman made a scornful sound. "I have no need to listen to your talk, Chancellor," she said. "I know what is right and so does the man who has watched for us these long years. The boy is allowed into the Convoke by right of who he is." Owen realized that the voice was coming from the chair by the fire.

"Would we leave him outside, parentless and confused?" the Sub-Commandant said softly.

"Is that your final position, Pieta?" Chancellor asked. His voice was low and there was a hint of anger in it.

There was no reply from the chair, but Owen heard a bottle clinking against a glass and there seemed to be a kind of finality to the sound.

Chancellor sighed. "You have the right to ask much for your defense of us. . . ."

"Yes. I have the right, Chancellor."

"I appreciate your reservations, Chancellor," Contessa interjected gently, "but I think justice demands that the boy be brought before us."

"You appeal to justice, Contessa, but are you certain that the boy does not appeal to another part of you?" This new speaker stood up. He was a long-haired man dressed in a uniform of somber but rich red. As he spoke, he swept his hair back over his shoulder. A silence fell over the hall. Contessa did not reply, but Owen could feel a chill stealing through the air.

"That settles it," the woman they called Pieta said. "Bring the damn boy and bring him now. If our resident peacock starts scheming about the thing, we'll never hear the end of it." The man in the colored uniform glared at Pieta and made to speak again, but Chancellor held up his hand.

"Sub-Commandant." His tone was stern.

"I sent Cati to get him," the Sub-Commandant said. "In case he was required," he added smoothly. Chancellor turned his gaze to the Sub-Commandant. Owen shivered. He could only imagine the scrutiny of those piercing eyes.

"While we are waiting," Contessa said, "we should

discuss those who will not wake. The numbers have risen. We're desperately weak, Chancellor." Owen realized that she must have interrupted in order to break Chancellor's searching gaze at the Sub-Commandant. He felt Cati's elbow dig him in the side.

"Come on," she hissed. "Quick!"

Owen and Cati crawled back through the gap in the stone wall. They ran as fast as they could down the staircases, Owen's clothes covered in cobwebs and his hands and elbows grazed from the rough stone walls as he tried to keep his balance. Disheveled and filthy, they practically fell out of the stairway into a brightly lit hall. A young man in the same richly colored uniform as the long-haired man grabbed Owen under the arm and lifted him to his feet. His face seemed friendly but serious.

"Hurry," he hissed. "You do not keep the Convoke waiting."

The wooden door in front of them swung open and Owen was propelled into the hall.

Owen stopped dead. Every eye in the hall was fixed on him. He could see Chancellor standing on the dais. The young man gestured to him impatiently. Somehow, Owen managed to put one foot in front of the other, the crowd parting for him as he did so. He felt his heart beat faster and faster, and as he approached the dais, his foot caught the hem of a woman's cloak. He would have fallen had not a hand reached out and grabbed his elbow. Owen turned and found himself looking into the eyes of a tall older man with a beard and a terrible scar that looked like a burn on one side of his face. The man grinned and winked at him, managing to look both villainous and friendly at the same time. The sight gave Owen heart. At least he wasn't without friends in the hall. He pulled himself upright and strode to the dais, where the Sub-Commandant addressed him.

"You are welcome to the Convoke, young Owen. Have you anything to ask us?" But before Owen could open his mouth the man with the long hair broke in.

"He'll have time enough for questions. For the moment I want to ask him a few things about himself and how he got here."

For the next ten minutes Owen answered questions about where he came from, his school, his friends, his age, and how well he knew the area around the Workhouse. Such was the piercing quality of the man's eyes and his air of command that it was impossible not to reply.

Chancellor was particularly interested in Johnston's scrapyard. Contessa asked him about his home and about his mother, and listened sympathetically as he tried to make things with his mother sound better than they actually were, while feeling that he was letting her down with every word.

"Do you have any great fears, things that terrify you for no apparent reason?" Chancellor asked. His voice was casual, but Owen could feel that the whole Convoke was intent upon the answer. In his mind the image of a deep, still pool of black water formed, and he saw himself

40

bending over it and realizing that there was no reflection. He felt a single bead of sweat run down his spine and his voice dropped to a whisper.

"N-no," he stammered. Before he had time to wonder why he had lied, the man in the red uniform stood up.

"I've had enough of this. Where is the Mortmain? Tell us that, boy. Return it to its rightful owners!"

"Enough, Samual!" the Sub-Commandant said. He didn't speak loudly, but his voice cut through the tension in the room like a whiplash. The man in red sat down again, grumbling.

"That subject should not have been mentioned," the Sub-Commandant went on. "Let the boy ask his questions now."

Owen looked around. A thousand questions swirled in his mind. "Where am I?" he said, and then, with his voice getting stronger, "Who are you? And what has happened to . . . to everything?"

"I will try to answer," Chancellor said, getting to his feet. "There are three parts to your question. As to where you are, you are in the Workhouse, the center of the Resisters to the Harsh and the frost of eternal solitude that they wish to loose upon the earth. We are not the only Resisters. There are pockets elsewhere, perhaps even in other lands, but all hinges on us, on our strength and strategy." There was pride in his voice, even vanity, but sorrow as well.

"As to who we are," he went on, "we are the Wakeful. We sleep the centuries through until we are called. You could say we are the custodians of time. Like everything else, time has a fabric or structure. And sometimes that fabric is weakened or attacked and requires repair or defense. But we do not have much time to explain things, and others can tell you more of us. The most important of your questions is the last. What has happened?"

"I will answer that," the Sub-Commandant said, "since the boy and I both witnessed it, although he did not know it at the time."

"The floor is yours," Chancellor said stiffly.

Once more Owen could feel the people in the hall bend their attention to the slender figure, as if he was going to relate a terrible story that they had heard before but felt compelled to hear again.

"You may perhaps have learned that time is not a constant, that it is relative." Owen nodded, hoping that he looked clever. The words that the Sub-Commandant used were familiar from school, but to tell the truth he hadn't been listening when these things were talked about, and he hadn't understood what he had heard.

"What happened today is an extension of that. Do you remember when you saw that dark flash in the sky?" Owen nodded. "The process is complex and subtle, and many events took place both together and apart. But to put it in the simplest possible terms, a terrible thing has happened. A thing that our enemies have sought to achieve for many eras."

The Sub-Commandant paused. The whole hall seemed to hold its breath and Owen understood that although they knew in their hearts what had happened, it had yet to be confirmed to them. The Sub-Commandant's face was stern and gray and age showed in it, great age.

"They have started the Puissance," he said. "The Great Machine in the north turns again and time is flowing backward."

A shuddering sigh flowed through the hall. Owen stared blankly at the Sub-Commandant. How could time flow backward? What sort of machine were they talking about? He didn't know how long he stood there until the Sub-Commandant stepped forward and gripped him by the shoulders.

"It's a lot for you to understand and I won't trouble you with any more tonight. You'll have questions and we'll answer them as best we can. But for now, I think it is best if you rest."

"Wait!" The man they called Samual rose to his feet. "I have a few more questions." He moved up close to Owen and walked round him, studying him, his eyes glittering with dislike. "What is your understanding of your father's death?" he barked.

Owen froze. It was something he tried not to think about. "There was a—an accident . . . ," he stammered.

"Suicide," Samual said. "Wasn't that it?"

"No . . . ," said Owen.

"Is there a point to all of this?" Contessa asked, her voice cold. She obviously didn't approve of Samual's questioning, but he ignored her.

"Have you ever heard of Gobillard et Fils?" he demanded sharply, his face almost pressed against Owen's now, his eyes eager.

Gobillard et Fils, Owen thought. That's what was written on the trunk in his bedroom! How did this man know about that? He could feel Chancellor and the others watching him intently.

"N-no," he stammered, "no . . . I've never heard that name before. . . ." The lie was out before Owen knew what he was saying. Why had he not admitted that he'd heard the name before? The blood rushed to his face. Would someone notice?

He was saved by the Sub-Commandant. "The boy is not a prisoner to be interrogated, Samual. That is enough."

Samual looked for a moment as if he would defy the Sub-Commandant. Then he thought better of it and turned away.

"You may go, Owen," the Sub-Commandant said gently.

Owen's mouth was dry and his head was spinning, but he knew that there was one question he must ask before he was made to leave the hall. He turned toward the Sub-Commandant and his voice was no more than a whisper.

"Please," he said, "what has happened to all the people?"

There was a long silence, then Contessa spoke.

"You are thinking about your mother, of course. I will explain it as we understand it. In turning back time, the Harsh intend to go back to a time before people. The minute they started the reversal, the people disappeared as if they had never been. So nothing has happened to them, but they have never been. Except for us, stranded on an island in time—as you now are."

"If we stop the Harsh, you'll get your mother back!" It was Cati's voice. She had somehow evaded the watchers on the door. "You'll get her back and it'll all be the same again!"

Contessa gave Cati a stern look, but Owen thought he could see the ghost of a smile hovering around her lips. "That is true. We have stopped them before."

"But this time is different," Chancellor said. "The Harsh are stronger than ever and we are weaker. I cannot see how we can overcome them."

"We are the Resisters," the Sub-Commandant said softly, "and it is our duty to resist, come what may."

Chancellor looked as if he was about to say something more, but in the end he only shook his head and sighed.

"Cati," Contessa said, "you should not be here, but as you are, I would like you to take Owen out of the Convoke. We have many other issues to discuss."

Cati took Owen gently by the arm and the crowd parted again for them as they walked toward the door. Owen wanted to ask more questions. What was the Starry? And what had the Mortmain—whatever it was—to do with him? And why were the Resisters so interested in him, anyway?

Owen glanced toward the armchair beside the fire. To his surprise, the owner of that harsh voice was much younger than she sounded. Pieta was slim with blond hair and a girlish face. She was asleep, snoring gently, and wearing a faded uniform similar to his own, but attached to her belt was an object unlike anything he had ever seen before. It looked like a long, coiled whip, but this whip was made of light—a blue light shot through with pulses of energy, so it seemed a living thing. Beside the woman was an empty bottle and a glass. As Owen stared, she opened one eye and looked directly at him. Her eye was bloodshot and bleary, but Owen felt instantly that she knew everything there was to know about him.

Pieta's lips curved in a brief smile, weary and sarcastic, then her eyes closed again and Owen felt Cati haul him toward the door, which opened for them as they reached it and closed gently but firmly behind them.

Owen felt numb. He had never thought about time before or the fact that it might be possible for it to go backward. "What did Contessa mean by an island in time?"

"That's where the Workhouse is—on an island in time," Cati said. "Time is like a river flowing around us, but the Workhouse never really changes. And we don't change either."

"You mean you don't get older or anything?"

"Course we get older," Cati said with a heavy sigh, as though she was explaining to an idiot. "It's just that we grow old at the same rate as normal people, no matter what time does. You look like you need air."

"I need . . . ," Owen began. But what did he need? A way to understand all of this? Sleep to still his racing mind? A place to hide until it all went away and things returned to as they were before? He was tired, his eyes felt grainy and his limbs fatigued, but an idea was beginning to take shape.

Outside, a mild, damp wind was blowing drizzle in from the direction of the town. He could smell the sea on it.

"Do you want to talk?" Cati sounded anxious.

"No," he said. "No thanks, I'm really tired. I need to sleep, I think."

"You can sleep here. Contessa will find you a bed."

"No!" said Owen, more sharply that he intended. "I want to go back to the Den."

"I understand," she said. "I'll walk there with you."

"I want to be on my own," he said stiffly.

Cati watched as Owen turned abruptly away and walked toward the path to the Den. He felt bad. He didn't want to offend her, but there was something he had to do. As soon as he had rounded the first corner in the path he dived off it into the trees.

Owen climbed steadily for ten minutes. He knew the landscape well, but it was dark and the rain made it murky, and there seemed to be trees where no tree had grown before. By the time he reached the swing tree, his hands were scratched from brambles and there was a welt on his cheek where a branch had whipped across it. He got down on his belly and crawled to the edge of the drop. He looked across the river, but it was shrouded in gloom. Down below he could just make out what seemed to be trenches and defensive positions that had been dug the whole length of the river.

As Owen looked closer he saw that they were hastily dug in parts and in other places there were none. He studied the defensive line and saw that it was at its weakest under the shadow of the trees, in the very place where he had crossed that morning. Silently, Owen slipped over the edge and began to slither down the slope, any noise that he made smothered by the insistent drizzle.

At the bottom of the slope he made his way quietly through the trees. Almost too late Owen saw that there was now a path running along the edge of the river. He shot out of the trees into the middle of the path and as he did so he heard a man clearing his throat. Quickly he dived into the grass at the verge and held his breath. Two men rounded the corner. Both were bearded and carrying the same strange weapon as the Sub-Commandant. They looked alert, nervous even, and their eyes kept straying to the river side of the path—which was just as well, as Owen was barely hidden by the sparse grass at the edge of the trees. They walked past him as he held his breath and pressed his face into the wet foliage. Within seconds, they had rounded the next corner and were gone.

Owen stood up, shaking. He took a deep breath. He had avoided the patrol through luck and knew that it might not be long before another one came along. He darted to the other side of the path and plunged through the undergrowth toward the river.

It was dark on the riverbank; only the sound of the water told him where it was. He felt his way along the bank until he found the old tree trunk that he had climbed across that morning. Suddenly, he felt sick and dizzy at the thought of crossing the black water. He grabbed the tree trunk firmly. If he didn't start across now, his courage would fail him completely.

Breathing hard, Owen swung himself onto the log. It was wet and slick to the touch. Inching forward, he glanced down and saw the water glinting beneath. He shut his eyes and moved again. The sound of the water grew louder and louder. He opened his eyes. With a start, he realized that he was halfway across.

Owen fixed his eyes on the far bank. He had started on his hands and knees, but now he found himself on his belly, slithering along the wet trunk. It was when he was three-quarters of the way across that he felt it—a slight flexing of the tree trunk, barely noticeable, as if there was now some extra weight bowing the wood. He risked a glance back over his shoulder. There was something on the trunk behind him, something small and fast-moving. Panting, Owen tried to move faster, scrambling for grip. He looked behind again. It was halfway across now and gaining fast. He gulped for air and it sounded like a sob. Then he got to his feet and tried to jump the last couple of meters. Just as he jumped, Owen was hit hard and fast from behind. He felt himself gripped and turned in the air, and as he hit the muddy bank with an impact that drove the air from his lungs, a small, powerful hand grabbed him first by the hair, then covered his mouth and his nose so that he couldn't draw the shuddering breath that his aching lungs needed.

"Stupid boy!" Cati hissed furiously. "Where do you think you're going?"

It was several minutes before Owen could get enough air to enable him to talk. Cati crouched beside him, staring intently into the dark.

"We have to get away from here," she whispered urgently.

"I'm not going back," he said. "I'm going home."

"It's not there anymore! You'll be caught or killed looking for something that's gone. Listen to me."

51

"That's the problem," said Owen. "I've been listening to everyone about time turning back and people sleeping for years and great engines and people disappearing. But I have to see. I have to see that my house is gone. I have to see that . . . that . . ." He gulped and turned his head away, hoping that she wouldn't see the tears in his eyes. Stumbling to his feet, he wiped his eyes with the sleeve of his jacket.

"I have to see," he repeated.

Cati gave him a long, level look, then seemed to come to a decision. "All right, but I better come with you."

"You can't," he said. "I'm going on my own."

"Don't be silly. You made enough noise going through the trees to wake the whole Starry, and you left a trail a blind man could see. If I come with you, at least we have a chance of getting back. Not much of a chance, mind you." Cati seemed almost cheerful about the prospect. "Come on then," she said. "Might as well get it over with." And she set off at a crouch, moving fast and silent. Owen had no choice but to follow her along the riverbank.

A few minutes later he thought he had lost her, then almost tripped over her. Cati was squatting on the ground.

"Careful," she hissed. "Get down here." She had a twig in her hand. "Look."

Owen squinted in the darkness. He could just about see the two parallel lines she had drawn in the earth.

"This line is the river," she said, "and this one is the Harsh. We're in between, here. And the place where your house used to be is here, just in front of their lines. We can get to it if we're really quiet and really lucky. But you have to do what I tell you, all right?"

Owen nodded dumbly. He hadn't really thought through what he had set out to do, and now he was feeling foolish and headstrong. Cati had called him a stupid boy and he was starting to feel like one.

"Let's go!" Cati said. He followed her, moving slowly now. They turned left and started to climb the hill toward the Harsh lines. There was more cover than he had expected. Where once there had been open fields there were now deep thickets of spruce and copses of oak and ash trees. Progress was slow. Cati whispered that there might be patrols about, and more than once she glared at him as he stood on a dry twig or tripped over a low branch. He did not recognize anything in the place where he had once known every tree and ditch, although sometimes he stumbled over something that might have been the crumbling foundation of an old field wall.

After what seemed like hours, Cati turned to him and held her finger to her lips. They stepped into a clearing— a patch of low scrub. With a start, Owen looked around him. There was no real way of telling, but his heart said there could be no doubt; he was standing in the place where his house had been.

Was that flat piece of ground with saplings growing in it the place where the road had been? And was that young sycamore the same gnarled tree that had stood outside his bedroom window? Owen moved forward carefully until his foot struck something. Pushing back the vegetation, he found the remains of a wall. He moved along the wall until he reached a corner and then another corner. It was the right size and shape as his own house. In fact, he was standing underneath the window to his own room, if it had been there. The room with the model hanging from the ceiling, and the guitar, and the battered trunk he had stood on to climb out of the window.

"I don't understand," he whispered. "If time is going backward, how come the sycamore tree is getting younger but the house is getting older? Surely the house would turn back into bricks and stuff."

"Living things get younger as time goes backward," Cati said, "but things built by man just decay. It has always been like that."

Owen began to notice that the grass and weeds were crisscrossed with scorch marks and that the leaves of low-hanging trees were blackened and dead. Cati reached up and broke off a leaf, which crumbled in her hand.

"The Harsh have been here," she whispered fearfully. "Searching for something, by the look of it. We have to go."

But Owen wasn't ready. He moved his foot and something clanked against it. He put his hand down into the undergrowth and groped around until his hand closed on an object. He held it up. It was the hand mirror that his mother used when she brushed her hair. The brass back was tarnished and the glass was spotted and milky in places, but it was the same mirror, and as he looked at it, he could picture his mother brushing her hair, her lips pursed, whistling tunelessly to herself. The glass seemed to become yet more faded as his eyes misted over.

Cati said something, but he didn't hear her. And he was only barely aware of the cold that started to steal over him. It wasn't until he heard a faint crackling that Owen glanced up at a small twig that hung in front of him. As he looked, it seemed that hoarfrost crept up the leaf from the tip, then to another leaf and then another, until the stem itself froze and cracked with a gentle snapping sound as the sap expanded.

Owen looked around. The crackling sound was caused by dozens of leaves and twigs snapping in the same way. He turned to Cati, but she was staring off into the trees and her face was a mask of fear. He followed her terrified gaze. Far off, but moving inexorably closer, were two figures, both white, both faceless, and seeming to glide without effort between the trees. Cati's voice, when it came, was no more than a whimper.

"The Harsh," she said. "They're here."

The cold seared Owen's lungs. Somehow he knew that the Harsh were talking to each other in mournful voices full of desolate words that were just out of earshot. The pitch of the voices rose to make a noise like the howling of wolves being carried away on an icy wind and Owen wondered if they had been spotted.

"Come on," he said to Cati in an urgent whisper. "Run!" But it was no good. She seemed to be paralyzed with terror. "Please, Cati," he said. "I think they've seen us."

"No," she moaned, "they don't see well. They can smell us, though. They can smell the warmth."

Owen grabbed Cati by the arm and hauled her to her feet. She stumbled after him. The Harsh were moving sideways, slipping through the trees. They were going to cut Owen and Cati off from the river. Cati wasn't resisting him, but she wasn't helping either. Owen thought he could hear the voices again and he felt a chilly dread steal over him, a sense that things were lost and that there was no point in running. He knew that this must come from the Harsh and was why Cati was paralyzed with terror.

"Come on, Cati," he urged. "You've got to fight it." Owen started to run, dragging her behind him. He could no longer see the two Harsh, but when he stopped for a moment he could hear the gentle crackle of frost attacking twigs and leaves to his right. It was only minutes to the river, but the trees and undergrowth made progress slow. Several times Cati fell and would have lain there if Owen hadn't forced her to her feet again, and all the time he felt the cold dread stealing over him, weighing down his limbs so that it was an effort to lift his feet.

Suddenly, Owen and Cati broke free into a clearing that seemed to lead down to the river. Owen turned. Less than fifty meters away he saw the two Harsh and stopped. The force of their presence dragged at him. Cati sank to her knees as Owen turned toward them. The Harsh made no effort to move nearer. Icy vapor from the frozen ground at their feet curled round them, so they seemed to float in the air. Owen's gaze was drawn to the places where their faces should have been: the blank white spaces. But there seemed to be a mouth to whisper cruel and seductive words, and eyes that bored into him and demanded surrender.

In the distance, Owen heard a shout and knew that the defenders on the other side of the river had seen them. There was a crash and a burst of blue flame close to the river and then another one, but the Harsh did not stir. With one last desperate effort, Owen tore his gaze away. He reached down and caught Cati under the arms. Half dragging and half carrying her, he stumbled down the slope toward the river. Though he dared not look around, he knew that the Harsh had not moved. There was another burst of blue flame and Owen heard men's voices shouting encouragement to them. Even Cati seemed to hear and forced herself to run toward the river. They were just short of the water now and Owen realized they had to cover more ground upstream to reach the log crossing. He risked a glance backward—the Harsh had still not moved. They were almost clear.

Suddenly he felt Cati slow and stop and sink to the ground once again with a moan. Two more Harsh stood less than a hundred meters ahead, blocking off all access to the log and approaching slowly.

Owen looked round wildly. They couldn't go back, they couldn't go forward, and they couldn't stay where they were. There was only one way out. He went toward the low, ruined river wall and peered over it. The water below was black and deep, but at least it would carry them away from the Harsh. He dragged Cati toward the wall.

The Harsh seemed to realize what he was doing and started to move faster. Owen lifted Cati onto the wall and looked down again. He felt sick. He knew that if he dropped Cati into the water, she would not be able to look after herself. She was too lost in fear. He heard a shout from the trees across the way. The bearded man from the Convoke was sitting astride the branch of a tree, shouting, and Owen knew he was telling them to jump into the water. But even summoning up all his strength, even feeling the frost stealing through his jacket and into his flesh, even with his new friend whimpering in his arms, Owen could not do it. And somehow from the knowledge that he could not do it, he drew some strength. He reached to the ground and found a large branch. Turning his back on the river, and pushing Cati behind him, he stood to face the Harsh.

Owen could feel the cold attention of the Harsh on him. And he heard a cold voice inside his head say a single word. Mortmain. Then, as he turned, one of the creatures opened the white maw where its mouth should have been and Owen was hit by a frozen blast of what felt like the coldest sleet he had ever experienced—sleet like frozen knives, cutting through his clothes with a noise like the howling of a terrible wind. Cati cried out. He flung the branch toward the Harsh and saw it turn in the air, freeze, and splinter into a thousand pieces, and then he was driven away from the river.

Somehow Owen managed to turn his back to the blast and wrap his arms around Cati's cold shoulders as the blast grew fiercer. He gasped for air, but it seemed too cold to breathe. He knew then that all was lost. He felt deep calm settle over him. Then the blast stopped.

Owen lay on the ground panting for breath. It was seconds before he could turn his head to see what had happened. The Harsh were still in the same place, but standing in front of them was Pieta. She was about fifteen meters away and she carried the whip of light casually at her side. The Harsh towered over her, so that she looked small and frail, but Owen could see that she was smiling a bleak, dangerous smile. The hand at her side moved quickly. Faster than the eye could follow, the whip of light swung back behind her. Owen gasped as it uncoiled, loop after loop, making a sizzling, whistling noise as it opened out, a living thing of deadly power.

He saw Pieta adjust her stance and with unbelievable power and speed the whip flew forward. She laughed as fifty meters of writhing energy whistled toward the Harsh, hissing as it cleaved the frozen air. The end of the whip stopped just short of the two creatures and, as the whip cracked, Owen had to cover his ears to protect them from the deafening sound, which was followed by a flash of brilliant blue light that illuminated the whole riverbank. There was a smell like iron filings, which stung his tongue and the back of his throat.

When Owen looked again he saw that the Harsh were floating slowly backward, their intense white forms somehow dimmed. He scrambled to his feet. Cati's eyes were closed. She was breathing, but there was a coat of hoarfrost in her hair and round her mouth. The whip cracked again. This time the Harsh dimmed and retreated. Owen saw that the way to the tree trunk across the river was clear. He lifted Cati and half ran, half staggered toward the riverbank. He had to run between Pieta and the Harsh, and for a moment he thought he heard their cold whispering. Then the whip cracked once more, going over his head this time, the force of its uncoiling making him stagger.

He reached the bank. The bearded man was now astride the log and he reached out for Cati. Owen dropped the unconscious girl into the outstretched arms, and with an agility that belied his size the man scrambled back across the tree trunk. Owen looked down at the water, shivering uncontrollably. He knew that he could not balance on the log.

Suddenly he was hit hard in the back. It was Pieta.

"Get across now," she hissed angrily. Looking back, he saw that the two groups of Harsh now stood together. This was too much even for Pieta. Owen felt the cold begin to stream toward them again and he scrambled onto the trunk, Pieta pushing him from behind. Owen threw himself forward and fell. He got up again but this time he slipped. First his foot and then his hand and then his whole body was plunging toward the dark water. He screamed as his foot hit the water, then felt Pieta grab one outflung hand. Effortlessly she swung him back onto the log and pushed him forward. Gasping and half blind from cold and terror, he fell off the end of the tree trunk and landed heavily on the ground.

———

Owen kept his eyes closed, allowing the fear to subside. His heart was beating wildly. When he finally opened his eyes he saw the Sub-Commandant, Chancellor, and Contessa. There were others standing behind, but it was the still form of Cati that brought him to his feet.

"She will recover," Contessa said. "They attempted to freeze her, but they did not succeed."

"No thanks to him!" the long-haired man said angrily, stepping forward. "He took Cati across the river to deliver her into the hands of the Harsh."

"He tried to shield her from them, Samual," Pieta said, her voice ringing across the space between them. "She would now be frozen forever if it was not for him."

"It's a trick," Samual said. "He's trying to fool you!"

"That is enough, Samual," Contessa said, and a dangerous light burned in her eyes. "The young man has just escaped with his life. Now is not the time."

"I saw what happened," Samual said slowly and deliberately. "I saw what happened when his foot touched the water! He couldn't hide the agony on his face."

No one said anything. None of them would look at Owen except the Sub-Commandant, who fixed him with a level, gray-eyed stare that revealed nothing.

Cati stirred. Her eyes seemed dulled and milky, and when she spoke her voice was weak and her breath hung in the air in frozen clouds, the way warm breath does in cold air.

"I . . . I . . . could not move. I was so scared. I followed him . . . I followed him to his mother's house. He carried me. He saved me."

Her head slumped back again. Contessa looked grimly satisfied, as if any question about Owen had been decisively answered. The Sub-Commandant swept Cati up into his arms and walked away swiftly. He did not look back.

"I must make up my mind about this," Chancellor said heavily. "I will sleep on it."

Samual looked as if he would say something more, but instead turned on his heel and stalked off into the darkness.

"Owen needs rest," Contessa said. "This has been the longest day of his young existence, Chancellor. He has been bereft and thrown into another world. His life has hung by a thread this past hour."

"All I did was look for my mother," Owen said, trying to keep his voice steady. "There's nothing wrong with that, is there?"

"No, Owen," Chancellor said, "but do you understand that we are all in great danger? None of us can do what we want, even if your mission is as important as looking for your mother. Do you understand?"

Owen nodded slowly. The cold breath of the Harsh was still fresh in his head. He knew that this wasn't a dream. He shivered. No one had ever wanted to kill him before.

"He will want to go back to his Den," Contessa said,

"but I don't think he should be on his own. He has enemies that he does not yet know about."

"I'll go with him," the bearded man said. "On my way back I can deal with the sentries that allowed the boy and the girl to walk right through the lines." He grasped Owen's hand. "My name is Rutgar. I am the sergeant here, head of the military, such as it is. Come with me."

Owen felt Chancellor's eyes on him as Rutgar steered him toward the path away from the river. The journey back to the Den seemed endless, but each time he stumbled Rutgar caught his elbow. He was too tired to talk, but Rutgar seemed to understand this, although he muttered to himself under his breath as he walked, about the sentries who had allowed Owen and Cati to slip through their lines.

Rutgar knew exactly where the Den was. "There's not one stone of this riverbank I don't know," he said. "Do you think that this is the first time I've had to defend it? Go on and sleep. You'll be looked after tonight."

"I don't want to be watched," Owen said faintly. Rutgar studied him for a minute.

"All right, then," he said. "My men will watch the paths around your Den—and they'd better watch them properly this time, to make sure nothing gets in and you don't get out again." He sounded angry, but as he spoke he clapped Owen on the back. "Go in and get to sleep. You'll need your energy." Owen nodded quickly and ducked into the Den. Rutgar looked after him thoughtfully, then turned away.

In the Den, Owen collapsed on the old sofa. He pulled the sleeping bag over him and kept his clothes on. There was a cold feeling lurking in his bones, but before he could think about the Harsh and their icy terror, tiredness overcame him and he slipped into a deep, dreamless sleep.

Down at the river all was quiet. A sentry called out and another answered in the dark. They did not want to be caught out again. One of the sentries appeared at the end of the fallen log, examined it, and walked on. All was still. Then a shape detached itself from the shadows underneath the trees on the Workhouse side of the river. Keeping low to the ground, the shape moved toward the trunk, looking at first like an animal and then like a human figure hunched under a cloak. It clambered onto the end of the log and then, moving in a fluid and seamless way, crossed the river, slipped off the end of the log, and disappeared into the field beyond. As it did so, a fine lace of ice formed along the edge of the river where the water met the bank. And as the figure disappeared with no more than a rustle into the darkness, there was a whispering noise as the ice melted and dissolved back into the black water.

Owen woke early the next morning and ran straight to the Workhouse without even a drink of water. He ran up the stairs and into the main hallway. Even though people were busy, moving with purpose, he saw more than one curious glance cast in his direction. He found the stairway that led to the kitchen, and he plunged downward. When the stair opened out into the kitchen he found it calmer than the previous day. The great ovens were glowing and many huge pots were simmering on them. He saw Contessa and he half walked, half ran over to her. She turned to him. Her face was grave but she spoke before he did.

"Cati will recover, Owen. I think you saved her. But only just. I had to put her back to sleep in the Starry. She was frozen to the very core of her being. I am surprised that you were not. Perhaps you have a special resistance."

"I was cold," he said. "Freezing."

"The cold they emit is not just physical, Owen. It freezes the very quick of you. Your soul. You're very strong."

"Strong," said a voice. "You'd be good and strong, maybe. But maybe they had fair cause not to freeze you. Them ones could have had cause to spare you."

Owen turned to see a tall, thin youth with a solemn face. His trousers were torn and on top he wore something that might have been a shirt at some time but now was so ripped and dirty that it could have been anything, and was certainly no protection against the cold morning air. When Owen looked down he saw that the boy's feet were bare.

"Wesley," Contessa said sharply, "I won't have malicious gossip repeated in my kitchen."

"It's what people do say," Wesley said, but he grinned in a mischievous way and stuck out his hand. Owen took it and Wesley shook his hand vigorously.

"Wesley," he said. "I do be one of the Raggies. I brung fish for the lady Contessa."

Owen looked down for the first time. There were perhaps twenty boxes of fish on the ground around them, bringing with them a smell of the sea.

"I have an idea," Contessa said. "There are those who wish to ask you about last night, and their thoughts are not kindly for the moment. You would be better out of the way. Would you take him to the Hollow with you, Wesley?"

"I will, lady."

"I want to see Cati," Owen said.

"She is asleep," Contessa said, suddenly seeming taller, her eyes glittering with a dangerous light. "Are you not listening?"

"Come on," Wesley said cheerfully, pulling at Owen's sleeve, "before the lady do devour the two of us." Contessa didn't say anything and her eyes were like stone, but as they walked away with a chirpy "Cheerio, lady!" from Wesley, Owen thought he saw the ghost of a smile tugging at the corner of her mouth.

Wesley walked quickly, even in his bare feet, and Owen had trouble keeping up. They left the Workhouse and Wesley started on a path that followed the river down to the sea, curving toward the town and the harbor. At first Owen fired questions at Wesley, but the boy only turned and grinned at him and pressed on even harder. They came to the place where a new concrete bridge had crossed the road between the town and his house, but there was no bridge and no road. Owen climbed up the riverbank. Despite everything he had been told, he still expected to see the familiar streets of the town.

The town was there, but with a sinking feeling Owen saw that it looked as if it had been abandoned for a hundred years. The houses and shops were roofless and windows gaped blank and sightless. The main street was a strip of matted grass and small trees, and ivy and other creepers wrapped themselves round broken telegraph poles. Where new buildings had once stood there was bare ground or the protruding foundations of older buildings. The rusty skeleton of what had once been a bus sat at right angles in the middle of the street. A gust of wind stirred the heads of the grasses and the trees and blew through the bare roofs of the houses with a melancholy whistling sound.

Owen slipped back down the riverbank. The town was starting to crumble back into time, taking with it the memory of the people who had once walked its streets. He remembered what Cati had said about living things growing young but the things made by man decaying as time reeled backward.

"Never pay no mind," Wesley said gently. "That's just the way it is now. All them things can be put right if we put old Ma Time back the way she should be, running like a big clock going forward. You just stick with us. We'll put all yon people back in their minutes and hours, and Ma Time, she'll put us boys back to sleep again. Come on," he said, lifting Owen to his feet, "let's get on down to the harbor."

This time Wesley walked alongside Owen. The water in the river got deeper as they approached the harbor and Owen found himself veering away from it, which Wesley noticed.

"That's what I heard," he said, with something like satisfaction, "that you can't abide the water."

"Who told you that?" demanded Owen.

"They was all talking about it," Wesley said, "that the new boy, Time's recruit, did fear the water."

"I don't like it too much," Owen said.

Wesley rounded on him sharply, his face close to Owen's, his voice suddenly low and urgent.

"Do not be saying that to anyone. No one. Do you not know? I reckon not. The Harsh cannot cross any water—not fresh nor salt—and the touch of it revolts them unless they can first make ice of it. If any see you afeared of water, they will think you Harsh or a creature of the Harsh."

Owen remembered how the long-haired man, Samual, had reacted when he had seen Owen's foot touch the water. "I think they know already," he said slowly.

"Then it will be hard on you," Wesley said. "it will be fierce hard."

"You don't think I'm one of the Harsh, do you?" Owen said. His voice trembled slightly, but Wesley just threw his head back and laughed.

"Harsh. You? No, I don't think you're Harsh. I think you're like one of us, the Raggies. You been abandoned and the world treats you bad, and even though you ain't as thin as Raggies, I do know a hunger when I see it."

Owen didn't expect the harbor to look the same and he wasn't disappointed. The metal cranes were twisted and rusted. Most of the sheds had gone and the fish-processing factory was a roofless shell. The boats were still tied up, but it was a ghost fleet. The metal-hulled boats lay half sunk in oily water. The wooden boats had fared better and some of them still floated, but the paint had long faded from them, and their metal fittings had all gone.

"It's like they've been abandoned for twenty years," Owen said.

"Longer than that," said Wesley. "Ma Time, she goes back more fast than she goes forward."

Thinking about time made Owen's head hurt. He looked back the way they had come. He could see the slateless roofs of the town, then a white mist where the Harsh camp was, and beyond that, the mountains that hemmed the town into this little corner of land, their tops white with snow. He saw that Wesley was making for the area of run-down warehouses that was always referred to as the Hollow. As they got closer, going out onto what Owen knew as the South Pier but which now seemed to be a causeway over dry land, he saw that the buildings had not changed at all. There were five or six stone-built warehouses with empty windows in the front of them. Owen thought he could see rags or cloths in each window. As he looked, many of the rags started to stir, and then it dawned on him that each one was a child or young person dressed the same way as Wesley. A shout went up from them and Owen thought that there was dismay in the sound. As they closed in rapidly, he saw that they were looking out to sea. Wesley said something under his breath and climbed the parapet of the South Pier. Owen followed.

At the top, Wesley stood staring out to sea, his hand shading his eyes. About half a mile from shore Owen could see a boat, but it was not like any he had ever seen before. It was an elongated shape, copper-colored, but with high sides that curved in at the top, and a single tall mast with what looked like a small crow's nest at the masthead, topped with one of the blank black flags he had seen at the Workhouse. In each side of the boat there were five round holes, and in each hole there was a long, spindly, coppery stick, too long and thin and delicate, it seemed, to be an oar. But as Owen watched, the sticks started to beat violently and the whole craft was suddenly lifted on them and propelled at speed across the top of the water. Owen thought it looked like the insects you saw on ponds, the ones that walked on the surface of the water. The craft splashed back into the water, the sticks beating slowly this time, then it rose and shot forward again.

"Look!" Wesley shouted. Owen followed his out-stretched arm. High in the sky above the strange boat, Owen saw three shapes. At first he thought that they were birds, then he saw they were much bigger. One of them detached itself from the others and dived toward the boat, swooping down in great circles, and Owen saw it was an aircraft of sorts, with two impossibly long and delicate wings that beat slowly. The body of the aircraft was like a very fine cage with a long fin at the back, and at the center sat the figure of a man, crouched over a set of controls and staring down at the boat through huge oval goggles.

As the craft wheeled over the boat, the vast feathery wings glittered with a metallic sheen. Then a blaze of blue light shot from the body of the flying craft and struck the water beside the boat. There was an immense sizzle, and the boat disappeared momentarily in a cloud of steam and spray. When it reappeared Owen saw ragged children clambering frantically over the superstructure of the vessel. Baskets of fish were being passed up at great speed from the depths of the hold and flung over the side. Another of the flying craft swooped on the boat, closer this time. Owen felt sure that the flash of light would hit it, but at the last moment the beating oars raised the hull from the water and flung the boat forward with such violence that it swerved to one side, almost out of control. Once again it emerged from a cloud of steam and spray, but this time there was a long burned streak down its side, and one of the oars hung broken and useless. When it made to move forward again, it began to slew to that side.

"They're dead, dead to the world," Wesley said softly. "They cannot make it ashore." His face was white with fear.

But then a strange thing happened. Owen became aware of a great shrieking. The water around the delicate vessel was covered with the fish that had been thrown overboard and seabirds were converging on the unexpected

meal, thousands of them—herring gulls, black-headed gulls, black cormorants. Within a minute there were so many gulls that Owen could barely see the boat. The spindly aircraft were buffeted in the air by the beating wings of so many birds, and then they too became invisible. More and more gulls blanketed the ocean. Owen could not see the boat, but it appeared that it was still under attack. There were flashes of blue from within the swirling flock and there were dead seabirds among the thousands that squabbled for the floating fish.

Minutes passed and then a great cheer went up from the anxious children onshore. On the very edge of the flock of seabirds, the prow and then the rest of the boat emerged. There were children standing on its deck, some of them sitting along its rail. Many of them were very young, pale and frightened, but the tall, freckled girl at the tiller looked defiant.

The oars beating slowly, the boat swung in against the quay and the girl leapt lightly onto it. Wesley went over to her. Owen followed, hanging back a little. He could see the long scar running down the side of the boat.

"They near got us," the freckled girl said.

"Birds saved your hide," said Wesley.

"That was a good idea, throwing out the fish," Owen said. The girl looked at him curiously.

"That him?" she said to Wesley. Wesley nodded. The girl stuck out a hand. Her eyes were a curious greenish color and she was wearing oily overalls. "Silkie's my name, and I only threw out the fish for to save weight. I never thought about the birds."

"Is she broke?" Wesley said, looking anxiously at the boat.

"She's all right," Silkie said. "She has a bit of a burn on her, but she'll sail again. The little ones is scared, though. Them Planemen was never that brave before; they come pretty close."

"I do think the Harsh is stronger this time and they do push Johnston harder."

"Johnston?" Owen said. "The man who has the scrap-yard? I was playing there once and he chased me with dogs."

"It's a good thing he chased you with nothing worse," Wesley said. "Johnston is a terrible cruel man."

"A man, though," Owen said. "Not one of the . . . the Harsh?"

"No," said Silkie. "You know the way that the Sub-Commandant is the Watcher, staying awake through the years until the Harsh return and it is time to wake the others to fight?"

"I think so," Owen said.

"Well, Johnston is a Watcher too, except that he watches for the Harsh and makes sure that all is ready for their return."

"His own men sleep in their Starry and he wakes them for the Harsh," Wesley said. "The Planemen you seen attacking—they're his men."

"I'm starving," Silkie said.

"You're always starving," said Wesley with a grin, "but you do deserve something to eat for the fright you got from them Planemen. Come on."

Wesley led them into the nearest of the buildings. The ground floor was completely open with a big hearth at one end where a fire of driftwood crackled, a sweet smell of burning wood drifting through the room. A long table with benches on either side stood in the middle. There were children everywhere, all of them dressed poorly. Some of the smaller ones walked straight up to Owen and stared at him with large solemn eyes. The older ones climbed quickly up and down the ladder that led upstairs, or perched in the high windowsills.

Despite all the young people milling about, Owen could see that there was a sense of order. The table was being set with flat wooden plates and food was being carried in. Within minutes all the Raggies had seated themselves round the table and the older ones were serving food. Owen was put at the top of the table, beside Wesley and Silkie. Every plate was full but no one moved to touch them. It wasn't until Wesley pulled his plate toward him that the children grabbed their own and began to eat hungrily. Owen was starving as well. There was fish and fried potatoes. He tried them and thought they tasted like fish and chips. The noise in the room died to a murmur as everyone concentrated on the food in front of them, eating rapidly with both hands.

Within minutes, every plate was empty. While the

younger children carried out the crude wooden plates, Wesley, Silkie, and Owen moved over to sit on the rough stone of the fireplace. As they did so, others sat on the floor in front of them or gathered on the ladders and windowsills. The sun shone through the windows and dust motes floated in the beams. Owen felt warm and full and surprisingly contented. He saw that the children were watching Wesley expectantly.

"We near lost Boat today," said Wesley. "Planemen near got her." No one in the crowd spoke but Owen could feel the wave of dismay and concern that ran through them, almost like a shiver.

"Silkie done well and brung her home," Wesley said. Once again Owen could feel the emotion of the silent children, but this time there was relief and gratitude to Silkie. She smiled and went pink with pride under her freckles. Owen realized that the children could make their feelings be known to each other without saying anything, almost like a crowd at a football match.

"I think we need to arm Boat," Wesley went on, "for if she is sunk, we are all sunk."

This time the feelings of the children were confused. Some seemed angry, others resigned, others seemed to feel a deep, deep sadness. Wesley held up his hand.

"I know that it is against us and the Code of Boat to use weapons, but we done so before and now we need it more than ever. All our crew could've died out there today. This is what I thinks. I thinks we give magno bows to Uel and Mervyn, and them two boys go out every time with Boat. We can trust them, though it is a hard enough task for them two boys."

Children moved away from two tall, solemn boys standing in their midst. Owen felt that the crowd was questioning them with love and concern, asking them if they wanted to do this thing. "Brothers," Silkie whispered in his ear. "There used to be three, but one of them got killed in fighting with Johnston. They don't like fighting. That's why Wesley is asking them. He knows they'll only fire if they have to."

The two brothers looked at each other before nodding slowly. Owen could feel the relief and approval in the room. The children round the two boys touched them on the shoulders and took their hands, and they smiled shyly back. Wesley removed a wooden box from an alcove in the fireplace. He unlocked the ancient lock on it with a key that hung from a chain round his neck. Owen saw that the box was full of small bows, like crossbows. Wesley removed two and carefully locked the box again. He brought it back to the alcove, then returned with a smaller box, which he unlocked with the same key. As he did so, Owen examined the crossbows. They looked very old and deadly, made of age-darkened wood with a brass-colored metal spring, the wood engraved here and there with silver writing too small to read. Wesley had meanwhile removed handfuls of crossbow bolts from the other box. The bolts were brass arrows, about the length of Owen's forearm, and instead of a point, they had a small glass vial filled with a tiny amount of the blue substance that Owen had seen everywhere in the Workhouse. Owen decided that he would ask about it later.

Wesley called Uel and Mervyn forward and gave them each a bow and a handful of bolts. The boys seemed reluctant to touch them, but when Wesley told them to make sure that the crossbows were working properly, they handled them in a way that left no doubt that they knew what they were doing.

The children started to drift away. Wesley said he was going outside to look at the damage to Boat. Silkie asked Owen if he would like to look around. He followed her up one ladder and then another, leading from room to room, most of them taken up with sleeping quarters. There were wooden beds and coverings stitched together from strange, rough materials that Owen did not recognize, with drawings of stars and crescent moons on them. The rooms shared by younger children had bright drawings on the walls and wooden toys that looked as if they had been made by the older ones. There were horses and dollhouses and many different versions of Boat in many sizes. Looking at Boat made Owen think of the question he had.

"You know the blue stuff you see everywhere?" he said. "What is it?"

"Oh, you mean magno," replied Silkie. "I can't tell

you just what it is, for I don't know, but I can show you what it does."

She reached into her pocket and took out a small brass box. Inside was a little piece of the blue material held by two sturdy brass bolts. Silkie pointed it toward a lump of iron in the corner that looked as if it came from a ship and would take four men to lift. She gripped the box tightly. Owen saw the metal begin to rock backward and forward, then start to slide toward them, slowly at first, then faster and faster, and at the same time Silkie was drawn across the floor, her shoes slipping on it, almost out of control until it seemed that she must collide with the heavy metal. Quickly she slipped the lid back on the box and the lump of iron stopped abruptly in the middle of the floor.

"It's a magnet!" Owen said excitedly. "You do everything with magnetism!"

"I don't know," Silkie said, frowning. "All I know is that it is magno. It does lights. It makes Boat work."

At the top of the first building they crossed a makeshift ramp that led to the next building, Owen trying not to look down. Silkie opened a door at the far end and they stepped off the ramp. It was dark and it took Owen's eyes a little time to get used to it. After a while he saw that they were standing in a room that resembled the Starry at the Workhouse, where he had seen all the beds and the people still sleeping. This room was much smaller, but there was the same pale gleam, as if of stars, from the ceiling. The beds were smaller because these were for children and young people, but, as in the Starry, some of them were still occupied, and on each pillow there rested a blue cornflower. Sign of remembering, Cati had said. In the corner two girls were sleeping. They looked like sisters. Silkie stopped by one bed. A small boy slept in it. He had the same sharp, freckled face as Silkie. She brushed his hair back from his face with a sad smile.

"My brother," she said. "He never was good at getting up in the morning." Owen could see that she was trying to make a joke of it, but there were tears in her eyes. "Come on out of here," she said gruffly.

As he hurried toward the door, Owen stumbled slightly and his hand brushed against the forehead of a small girl. He had not expected the skin to feel warm. He looked down at her. The little face looked pinched and careworn. He wondered what she was dreaming about, or if she dreamed about anything.

"Come on," Silkie said shortly, and he hurried after her.

Silkie brought him up to the roof of the building. Far below they could see that Wesley and others were busy repairing the broken oar on Boat, if oar it was, thought Owen, remembering the way the craft had almost flown across the water. The wind was cold, blowing hard from the north, but they sat in the lee of the parapet, where the sun had warmed the stone.

"Where do you come from?" Owen asked.

"Me?"

"No, I mean the Raggies. Where are all the adults?"

"The story we tell is this. That there was a man called Smith who was put in charge of all these children. And each child was given a gold coin for their future. But Smith was a bad man. He wanted the money for himself. He abandoned the children and took their money, leaving us on this shore forever."

She spoke in a singsong voice, so Owen thought that this was the explanation that was given to the younger children by the older ones. He felt sorry for them, losing their parents, being all alone in the world. Then he remembered that he too was alone.

They sat on the roof until it started to rain. The rain was icy, blown in by the north wind. Looking down on the causeway, Owen saw that the waves were now pounding against it. Peering through the spray, he saw a small figure darting across the causeway. It was Cati. They went down and found her in the kitchen, dripping wet.

"You shouldn't be here," said Owen. "You're supposed to be sleeping, Contessa said—"

"Contessa's great," Cati interrupted, "but she's a bit of a mother hen. I was bored to the back teeth."

"She said you were frozen," Owen said slowly.

For the first time the hint of a shadow crossed his friend's face.

"I was . . . I think," she said slowly, then more

83

brightly, "But I'm going to freeze now for definite if you keep me standing here!" Owen jumped out of the way as she darted across the big room and went to the fire. She stood warming her hands, steam beginning to rise from her clothes.

"They're looking everywhere for you, by the way," she said. "Far as I can see, you're in big trouble." She seemed to relish this idea.

"Why?" he said. "It was Contessa who told me to come here."

"That explains it," she said. "Samual's the one who is stirring up all the trouble. Keeps saying you're one of the Harsh. Got some people believing him too."

"Why do people keep saying that?" Owen said. "You don't think I'm one of the Harsh, do you?"

"Me? No. You've got a face, for a start—a fairly ugly one, it has to be said, but a face all the same. I never saw one of the Harsh with a face before."

"That's a relief at least," Owen said sarcastically.

"You see," Cati continued, ignoring him, "Contessa hates Samual, so she's not going to tell him where you are."

"How did you know where I was?"

"I heard Contessa telling my father. They thought I was still asleep. Besides, I more or less knew you'd find a bunch of scruffs like yourself."

"What am I going to do?"

"Not to worry. You've got Contessa on your side, and

84

my father. And Pieta likes you for some strange reason. Pieta doesn't like many people. It doesn't help that there hasn't been any sign of the Harsh all day. They're up to something. We'll have a talk with my father when we get back tonight."

"You'll be going nowhere tonight," Wesley said, coming in. He seemed completely unaware that he was soaked through and that his hands and feet were blue with cold. "Look."

They went to the door. The causeway was now almost completely underwater, wave upon wave crashing in great foaming bursts over the rock.

"High tide and the storm," Wesley said. "You'd best stay here tonight."

"Contessa . . . ," Cati began, alarmed, then stopped and shrugged. "I've only known you for two days," she said to Owen, "and you've already got me into more trouble than in the whole of the rest of my life." She turned to Wesley. "What time's dinner? I'm starving."

Dinner consisted of lobster and the same kind of potatoes Owen had eaten that afternoon. Once again, the children waited for Wesley to begin. After the meal was over, they gathered round the fireplace, the little children playing games, the older ones talking together. It was cozy in the big room with strong wooden shutters closed against the howling wind, the firelight casting flickering shadows on the walls. Wesley started to tell Cati about the attack on Boat. Owen left them and slipped over beside Silkie, who was braiding a piece of rope with strands of what looked like dried seaweed.

"Tell me more about . . . what did you call it? Magno?"

"Why do you ask me?" Silkie said. "There are others who can tell you more."

"Who?"

"Dr. Diamond could tell you."

"Who is he?"

"Dr. Diamond works the Skyward. He knows about things."

"What things?"

"Just things. The proper places for things and what happens to things and where magno comes from and where time goes to." It sounded as if Silkie was reciting something she had been taught.

"So he makes magno?"

"Nobody makes magno," Silkie said slowly and patiently, as if she had taken an idiot in hand out of the kindness of her heart. Owen thought that when he got back to the Workhouse he would keep his eyes peeled for this Dr. Diamond.

After an hour or so, Wesley stood up and clapped his hands. The younger children formed into groups, with an older child at their head.

"He puts everyone to bed," Cati whispered. "We'd better follow."

Wesley said goodnight to each of the Raggies by name, ruffling the hair of the youngest. As they moved off, Owen could hear the low murmur of the oldest child's voice as she began to tell a story.

The whole process took more than an hour, by which time some of the younger children seemed to be asleep on their feet, and Owen was beginning to feel his own eyelids grow heavy. He had started to wonder whether his encounter with the Harsh had drained more energy out of him than he had thought. At last they reached an empty room and Wesley ushered them in.

"Sleep well," he said solemnly. "May old Ma Time bear thee gently till morning."

"Night," Cati said, stifling a yawn.

"Goodnight," Owen said. Wesley grinned at him and patted his arm.

A tiny piece of magno in a glass case on the wall cast a dim light over the room. There were two beds in it. Cati jumped straight into one.

"I can hardly see, I'm so tired," she said, yawning again. Owen climbed into the other bed and slipped his clothes off under the blankets. The mattress was a little hard and the bedding a little scratchy, but he was too tired to care. Besides, the room was warm and the thick walls and shutters closed out the howl of the wind and the noise of the raging sea. He lay still for a moment. Cati's breathing was slow and even.

"Cati?"

"What?" she said sleepily.

"Time is going backward, isn't that right?"

"Yes."

"Well . . . how do we make it go again?"

"The Puissance," she replied.

"The what?"

"The Puissance. The Great Machine in the north makes the Puissance, and the Puissance makes time go back. It has to be stopped."

Owen waited for a moment, listening to the distant howl of the wind.

"How do we do that?" he asked eventually, but Cati's only answer was a gentle snore. Owen put his head down on the rough pillow. Images from his old life came into his head. His school. His old bedroom. The guitar that he had been so fond of. But everything seemed such a long time ago and, strangely, seemed almost dusty in his mind. He remembered the old photograph his mother had carried around. He'd been a member of a family then, a happy, smiling family. If only things could be like that again, just once. But the photograph was lost. Things could never be the same. A wave of tiredness rushed over him and soon he too was asleep.

The wind could not be heard in the Starry far above their heads. The breasts of the children rose and fell imperceptibly, lost in the sleep of centuries. It was warm, for the temperature in the Starry did not change. It was quiet, because the sounds of the outside world did not penetrate the thick stone walls. And still they slept, dreaming who knew what dreams. They slept, except for one child. The little girl whose head had been touched by Owen. Her eyes were open, gleaming gently in the darkness.

Owen was woken by a hand on his shoulder, shaking him insistently. It was Wesley.

"Message from the Sub-Commandant," Wesley said urgently. "Owen's got to go to Dr. Diamond. Samual's asking you be arrested."

"What will Dr. Diamond do?" Owen said, sitting up and trying to put his trousers on under the sheet, aware that Cati was watching him with an amused expression.

"The people trust Dr. Diamond," she said. "If he says you are who you say you are, then Samual won't dare go against him. Hurry up!"

When they got downstairs, Owen noticed a small figure standing stock-still by the fireplace, half obscured by Wesley. He moved to the side to see better.

90

"Is that . . . ?" he said.

"The girl from the Starry," Wesley said. "She must have wakened sometime last night. She was standing there when we came down this morning. Haven't been able to get a word out of her. I'm not sure, but I have a notion that this is the first waking she's had for many a year."

The little girl stood perfectly still. Her feet were bare and the dress she wore was threadbare. Her pinched little features were solemn and unmoving.

"She looks like she needs somebody to pick her up and hug her," Cati whispered. Owen knew what she meant, yet neither of them made a move toward her.

"There is a fierce need there," said Wesley, frowning, "but I cannot work out what it is." He did notice, however, that as they moved about getting ready to leave, the little girl's eyes followed Owen everywhere. And when they crossed the causeway, Owen turned to see her standing at the window, her large eyes, so dark they seemed almost bruised, still following him.

When they got to the Workhouse there was tension in the air, groups of men hurrying toward the river looking grim. Pieta was walking up from the river with the magno whip coiled at her waist. When she saw them she gave Cati a sardonic wink and blew a kiss in Owen's direction. He felt his face turning red and Pieta laughed as she strode past him.

"I don't know why she has to be so unkind," Cati muttered.

"I think she's just sad inside about something," Owen said.

"Since when did you become the big expert on women?" Cati said, a little crossly. "Come on. I have to see Contessa."

Before Owen could answer, she was off racing through the big doors. He ran after her. They crashed through the kitchen door together, then tumbled onto the floor, laughing. When they looked up they saw Contessa standing over them, watching with a calm, measured look that made both feel mildly embarrassed. They picked themselves up from the floor, brushing off their clothes.

"I'm glad to see that you're both alive and obviously none the worse for your experiences the other night." She took Cati's face in her hands and looked long and hard into the girl's eyes. Then she took a small metal rod from her pocket. "Open your mouth."

Contessa slipped the rod under Cati's tongue and waited for a moment before taking it out and looking at it. Owen could see fine markings on it and realized that it was a thermometer. Contessa seemed to look at it for a long time.

"Your temperature is now a little lower than other people's, Cati. It will stay that way for the rest of your life. You can't be assailed by the Harsh like that without consequences."

"Does it matter?" Owen asked, suddenly anxious for his friend.

"Physically, not really. But in the mind . . . the soul, I

suppose, who knows? You can expect dreams of terrible cold, feelings of emptiness . . ." Contessa's voice trailed away. She shook her head and wrapped her arms around her shoulders as if she suddenly felt cold.

"You are to see Dr. Diamond," she said to Owen. "Perhaps you had better go straightaway. Morning is a good time to see him. Sometimes, later on, his head gets . . . congested." Cati giggled.

"Go on," Contessa said kindly. "I don't think you have anything to worry about."

"Where are we going?" Owen asked when they got out of the kitchen.

"To the Nab," Cati said. "Dr. Diamond works in the Skyward. You'll like him. He's very intelligent. Although sometimes things get a bit confused."

"Confused in what way?" asked Owen suspiciously.

"You'll see," Cati said with a grin, skipping ahead of him before he could ask any more questions.

It was a long climb to the Skyward, not helped by the way the Nab groaned and swayed alarmingly every time there was a gust of wind. Once they got halfway up, Owen could see the other side of the river. Or rather he couldn't see it: the whole area was shrouded in a cold, white mist. He could also see how the Workhouse defenses had been strengthened. More trenches had been dug right up to the river, and all approaches from the river to the Workhouse seemed to have been sealed.

They eventually reached the top of the Nab. It couldn't

come soon enough for Owen, who was starting to feel seasick from the swaying of the slender tower. They stepped onto the broad platform on which the Skyward stood. The glass walls gleamed softly. Peering through the glass, Owen could make out instrument cases, strange spindly machines, all shape and manner of objects, and in the middle of the room a long spike pointing down with what appeared to be a clock hanging from it.

"Are we going in?" he said.

"We have to wait until the doors are lined up," said Cati.

Owen suddenly noticed that the contents of the Skyward were in a different position from the last time he had looked. Although the outside glass wall had not moved, the interior was slowly revolving. There was a door in the outer wall and one in the inner wall that was turning, and in a few moments the two doors would be lined up.

"You have to move quickly," Cati said. She grasped the door handle, which was shaped like a long, thin hand with narrow brass fingers. "Ready?" There was a loud click as the two doors lined up. Cati swung the outer door open and hauled Owen through behind her. They fell on their knees inside and the doors clicked shut behind them. Owen picked himself up. He was getting used to being thrown around by Cati.

He looked about him. He could see delicate instruments in cloth-lined cases. Copper piping flowed round the room in complicated and delicate patterns, but much of the machinery seemed to have been scavenged and put to some other purpose. Liquid flowed through a glass pipe into an old vacuum cleaner that turned itself on with a self-important cough every few minutes and spewed warm, green-colored liquid into a glass jar. Tiny plants grew under controlled conditions on an old record turntable that was revolving very slowly. A set of heavy levers coming out of the floor looked as if they belonged in a railway signalman's hut. A chair that looked like an old airplane seat was bolted to the floor in the middle of them. Two chrome hubcaps set on spindles whirled on some unknown business.

As Owen stared, he noticed a man standing in front of what appeared to be an ordinary domestic fridge, except that it was producing extraordinarily cold conditions. The man was of average height with long black hair fastened at the back. He was wearing blue overalls like a garage mechanic. The overalls were tied in the middle with a leather tool belt, except the tools in this one were of all sorts of shapes and sizes and mostly looked as if they had just been invented. The man was wearing huge leather gauntlets and holding a long-stemmed red rose in his right hand. Cautiously he extended the hand into the interior of the fridge, from which cold vapors wreathed to the ceiling. There was a vicious crackling hiss and he jumped backward, slamming the fridge door. He looked down at the flower, which had been turned into an ice rose, cold and glassy. The man smelled it, then yelled "Ouch!" as it touched his nose. He began to rub the place vigorously as if there was a danger of frostbite.

Cati cleared her throat. The man whirled round. He had strange, sloping green eyes, which were watering profusely.

He stared at Cati, then broke into a smile, still rubbing at his nose.

"Hello, Dr. Diamond," she said.

"Again you see to good it's, Cati, hello," Dr. Diamond said.

Owen stared. What had the man just said?

"This is my friend Owen," Cati said.

"You about me telling been they've. You meet to pleased I'm, yes oh."

"What's he saying?" Owen whispered furiously.

"Excuse me, Dr. Diamond," Cati said kindly, "I think you're talking backward again."

"I am? I mean, am I? Yes, of course you're right, Cati. I'm thinking in backtime."

"It's the time going backward," Cati told Owen in a loud whisper. "He thinks that by going backward he's going forward, if you know what I mean. He does it when he gets a bit flustered." Owen didn't have a clue what she meant by this.

"I'd give you the rose," Dr. Diamond said apologetically, "except it's super-frozen now, take a month or two to thaw out, and there's a danger of frostbite in the meantime." He rubbed at his nose again, then turned to Owen.

"Now, young man, Chancellor sent me a note about you. I'm supposed to have a look at you or something. Where is that note? I put it down somewhere five minutes ago. Or am I going to put it down in five minutes' time?"

"He's always trying to work out the way that time works going backward," Cati whispered. "He says the more you think about it, the more complicated it gets."

As Dr. Diamond looked for the note, Owen examined the big clock in the center of the room. At least he thought it was a clock, although it wasn't like any clock he had ever seen. It had five faces all looking different ways, and each face had one hand on it, each hand moving at a different speed. But the hands didn't keep moving at the same speed all the time. Sometimes one of them would speed up and go really fast, then slow down. Sometimes they would all be moving at different speeds. Cati started to say something to him but he hushed her. He didn't think his head would take any more complicated theories about time.

Dr. Diamond found the note from Chancellor. He read it and then stood lost in thought for a moment. Then in two quick strides he was in front of Owen, face to face, staring at the boy with his intense green eyes. Owen felt himself flinch, as if he was staring into the eyes of a fierce hawk. Dr. Diamond's arms were holding Owen's upper arms. Owen remembered that Cati had said the doctor was very intelligent, and he realized that she did not mean intelligent like somebody brainy in school, but something far more—an intelligence that was like a deep, deep well, something dark and mysterious and bottomless.

"Let me see," Dr. Diamond said. "Water, yes. Afraid of it. Harsh try very hard to kill Cati. Understand that. Try very hard not to kill Owen. Mystery there, but perhaps if . . ." He let go of Owen suddenly and whirled round to a desk, seizing a pencil and a piece of paper. He wrote furiously for several minutes. Owen, looking over his shoulder, saw columns of figures and theorems and equations composed of complicated mathematical symbols. Finally Dr. Diamond stopped and examined his calculations.

"I think I comprehend," he said slowly. "Well, at least that which is open to comprehension. I think I know a little more about your friend, Cati."

"He's not Harsh, is he?" Cati said quickly.

"No," Dr. Diamond said slowly, "but not everyone will accept my word for that. And that does not mean that there isn't danger. However, Chancellor's letter simply asked me to work out if you are Harsh and that is what I have done. Now. Your turn, young Owen. Ask me a question for a change."

Owen thought for a minute. He didn't want to hear some complicated theory on time that would make him look stupid when he didn't understand. "What's magno?" he blurted out.

"Ah, magno," Dr. Diamond said, casting a shrewd look at Owen. "Magno is the Force that Binds."

"The Force that Binds," repeated Owen, trying to sound intelligent.

"The Force that Binds, that propels, that powers, that pulls, that pushes, that casts light in the darkness, that defends . . ."

"Is it the same as magnetism?"

"A very astute question," Dr. Diamond said, looking at Owen thoughtfully. Owen returned the look, not feeling very astute at all.

"Yes, Owen, it is very like magnetism. But I can see your head is getting sore with trying to understand things. My advice is to just try to understand one thing a day. It's easier on the brain." Dr. Diamond paused and cocked his head, as if he had heard something.

"What is it, Dr. Diamond?" asked Cati.

"You don't happen to know if Johnston's been over the river to talk about a truce yet, do you?"

"I don't think so," Cati said.

"Well, then, he is on his way. Let us go out and have a look."

They followed Dr. Diamond out onto the balcony. He was right. As they looked across the river, they could see that the white mist had parted slightly, and through the mist the man that Owen had known as the scrapyard owner, Johnston, strode onto the riverbank. He had not changed from the day that he had set his dogs on Owen to chase him from the scrapyard, and the boy shivered at the memory.

Johnston's face was big and fleshy with small eyes,

red-black hair slicked back, and huge sideburns that almost met at his chin. He was tall and as solid as if he had been carved out of a single block of stone. Owen was used to seeing him in blue overalls, but this time the overalls had white epaulettes on the shoulders—obviously part of a uniform. Johnston surveyed the riverbank calmly. He carried no weapon, but Owen was aware that behind him in the mist there were more men, perhaps twenty in all, each dressed like Johnston and with the same massive sideburns. Owen counted as the mist swirled around them.

"Look," Cati said. Rutgar stepped out from the trees on the other side of the river. Although they were too far away to hear what was going on, it seemed that the two men were negotiating. Rutgar turned away suddenly and disappeared into the trees. Johnston waited.

"He is looking for a parley with us," Dr. Diamond said.

"What's a parley?" asked Owen.

"A talk," Cati said, "probably about us surrendering or something."

"I would imagine so," Dr. Diamond said.

"I won't surrender to him," Cati said fiercely, clenching her fists, "not even if he has a thousand Harsh over there."

"I didn't think you would," said Dr. Diamond, patting her shoulder in a kindly manner. "Nevertheless, Chancellor and the others might reckon it their duty to consider whatever offer is made. . . . That didn't take long."

Rutgar had come back. He beckoned to Johnston. The big man sprang onto the fallen tree like a cat and ran lightly across.

"Where is he going?" asked Cati, sounding as if she couldn't believe that Rutgar had let Johnston across.

"He is going to meet our leaders at the Convoke," Dr. Diamond said, "and they'll give him safe passage to do it."

"He'll see our defenses!" said Cati.

"He has seen them anyway," Dr. Diamond said. Then he added in a meaningful way, "I know that if there was some way I could get in to see what was going on at the Convoke, it would be very interesting."

Cati looked at Owen. "Somewhere to watch . . . come on!" she hissed. She turned to Dr. Diamond. "It's been great to see you again, Doctor."

"And you, Cati," he said with grave courtesy, "and to meet your new friend. I would be grateful if you would bring him back to talk about magno and other things."

"Unless . . . unless I've already been here in backtime," Owen said, feeling he was getting a grasp on things.

"Yes," said Dr. Diamond with a twinkle in his eye. "Yes, indeed."

"Come on!" said Cati.

Dr. Diamond suddenly looked thoughtful. He produced a book that looked to be full of important equations from one pocket and a battered notebook from the other. He read rapidly, then started to scribble in the notebook.

"See you soon, Dr. Diamond," Owen said, but the scientist and philosopher seemed to be totally wrapped up in what he was doing, and didn't answer. Cati grabbed Owen's arm and started to haul him toward the ladder. Dr. Diamond did not look up. But as they were on the fourth flight down a head appeared over the rail at the top.

"Don't forget what I said about coming back," he shouted, and Owen waved back.

It took them fifteen minutes to get to the secret hiding place looking down on the Convoke. At one stage Cati saw Samual stalking along the path, and hauled Owen into the bushes to hide. Samual was muttering to himself as he walked along.

"I'm sure he's up to something," Cati said.

They waited until Samual had passed out of sight, then ran to the door of the Starry. As they passed through the sleeping forms, Owen remembered the little girl who had woken the previous day. Had the fact that he'd stumbled and touched her something to do with her waking?

They took the stairs two at a time, Cati leading, until they reached the top and went out onto the little balcony. They looked down to see Johnston standing in the middle of the hall. Chancellor, the Sub-Commandant, Samual, and Contessa stood together facing him. The head of the guard, Rutgar, stood at the door. And Pieta stood behind her chair at the fireplace. Even at this distance Owen could sense the stillness, the dangerous tension in her. If Johnston was aware of it, he showed no sign. He stood with his legs spread wide and his hands on his hips, looking about him with a lazy arrogance.

"You didn't come here to admire the hangings," Chancellor said. "State your business."

"I apologize, Chancellor," Johnston said. "It is such a long time since I have seen the old hall." The words were polite but the tone was not, and Owen knew that the man was mocking Chancellor.

"Get on with it, Johnston," Pieta growled. The man put his fingers to his lips.

"Hush, little one," he said. "Such a long sleep."

Owen didn't know what he was talking about, but he heard Cati's sharp intake of breath, so he knew it was serious. He expected to see the long whip of magno snaking out toward the man. But Pieta bit her lip and turned away, burying her head in her shoulder as if to hide a terrible grief.

"Make your parley, Johnston, and go!" snapped Rutgar.

"Yes," said Johnston, "the parley. That is the reason I'm here. I am ready to offer terms."

"What terms?" asked Chancellor. There was anxiety in his voice.

"These are the terms. You abandon all defense of this place and I will return you to the Sleep, long and dreamless, for eternity."

"And what advantage is there in that?" the Sub-Commandant asked.

"My Watcher friend," Johnston said softly—Owen

103

felt that there was respect mixed with loathing in his tone—"how long have we Watched each other over the centuries, not growing old, but growing weary? You alone of these people know me and know when I am speaking the truth, so listen to me now. The other choice is dying here, for we intend to annihilate you and all of your works. But if you let me put you to sleep, then at least you are alive and have—not hope, for there is no hope, but the illusion of hope that a new day might come and you might wake again."

"It is an offer we must consider," Samual said.

"Consider nothing!"

A voice cut across the debate like a whiplash. It was Contessa's, Owen was surprised to notice. She strode across the room until she was standing eye to eye with Johnston.

"You think he would put us to sleep? Maybe he would. And the next thing would be a blade in the throat, or carried out into the everlasting cold and frozen to death. What he is offering is not a choice."

"I would certainly keep you awake a little longer than the others," Johnston said in a musing tone.

"I agree with Contessa," the Sub-Commandant said.

"I agree," Pieta said quietly.

Samual shook his head and said nothing.

"I agree also," Rutgar boomed.

Chancellor looked at the floor as if he might find wisdom there. After a long time he lifted his head and spoke. "It seems as if I too have to agree."

"You haven't seen the forces I have gathered," Johnston said in a menacing voice. "The largest and strongest I have ever had, and if I am not mistaken, you are weaker than ever. Your little incursion across the river the other night will not have seen any of our strength. If that was the reason for it." He looked at the Sub-Commandant with a raised eyebrow, then gazed about the hall.

Although Owen and Cati knew that he could not see them, they both shrank back into the shadows, and Cati whimpered as if she could feel the cold again. Owen put out his hand to touch hers. Her skin was cold to the touch, very cold, and he remembered what Contessa had said about the effects of the Harsh being permanent.

"It is time for you to leave now," the Sub-Commandant said. His voice was quiet but there was steel in his tone.

"Fair enough," Johnston said, "but we won't be seeing each other again, Sub-Commandant. This is the last time."

There seemed to be sorrow in his voice, but his eyes were glinting under their heavy brows. Johnston turned and strode from the hall, Rutgar keeping pace close behind. Even from a height, Owen could feel the tension drain from the hall. He saw Contessa go over to Pieta and put an arm around her shoulder, whispering to her gently.

"What's wrong with Pieta?" Owen said.

"Her children sleep and do not wake," Cati said. "Every night she sits over them and calls their names and still they do not wake."

Owen said nothing. He thought about Pieta standing

over a child in the Starry, calling and calling, and suddenly the fierce warrior seemed smaller and less fierce. He could see her loneliness and sorrow in the slump of her shoulders until suddenly she shrugged Contessa off, almost in anger. She walked swiftly from the hall. Contessa reached out a hand to touch her as she stalked past.

There was a final flurry of defense building by the river and then everything seemed to slow down. Nothing happened for two weeks, or what felt like two weeks, for Owen was increasingly uncertain about time and the way it worked. He decided to draw a rough calendar on the wall of his Den, where he marked in sunrises and sunsets, for at least that happened in the normal way.

He went up to the Nab to see Dr. Diamond again. The scientist and philosopher showed him the complicated clock with five faces, each one with a single hand, and told him that it was measuring the speed at which time was going backward.

"The five faces measure the five different kinds of

time," Dr. Diamond said. When he saw the look on Owen's face, he went on hastily, "But we only have to concern ourselves with the big face, which is time as we commonly know it."

Owen could see that the single hand of the clock was going backward, opposite to the normal way. It was also moving very slowly.

"That's because time is going backward very slowly at the moment. It doesn't always go at the same speed, you see," Dr. Diamond said. "Sometimes even the Harsh have difficulty in keeping the speed up. And sometimes they manipulate the speed to their own purposes."

"What way does time move at the Workhouse?"

"That's this clock," Dr. Diamond said, tapping the smallest dial. "We're on what you've heard people call an island in time. Not exactly accurate, but near enough. Most other time flows round us. Kind of sloshes backward and forward, in fact. There are plenty of islands in time, but most are tiny, maybe one or two people on them, being born and living and dying, and an hour is an hour and a minute is a minute the same as it always was, even when they step outside the island."

"I think I get it," Owen said slowly, "but what I still don't understand is, where are all the people? I mean, the whole town, for all I know the whole country, even the whole world . . . where did all the other people go?"

"That is complicated," Dr. Diamond said. "The Harsh long for emptiness, for cold nothingness. A time before people. Before history. That is the reason they have turned time backward—to get back to that place. It seems that their Great Machine does away not only with time but also with the idea of human life itself."

"So they've already done away with life?"

"It seems so. Nobody has died; they have just never been."

"So they got rid of life and now they're getting rid of time. Kind of a mopping-up operation."

"I wouldn't have put it like that. But yes, essentially you're correct." Dr. Diamond knelt down in front of Owen, his eyes examining the boy's face. "I know you didn't give the right answer to Samual when he asked you about Gobillard." He put up a hand to stop Owen from speaking. "Your instinct was, I think, correct. There is dangerous knowledge involved, however I—"

The door opened behind them. It was Samual. His face darkened at the sight of Owen.

"Time to go, Owen," Dr. Diamond said swiftly, standing up.

Owen slipped by Samual without meeting his eyes. Whatever Dr. Diamond had to tell him would have to wait.

The Sub-Commandant and the others were busy and preoccupied, so Owen was grateful for the company of Wesley and Cati. Much of the countryside was wooded now and there were mushrooms to be picked in the morning, and wild berries and fruit, and hazelnuts on the banks. The weather felt like autumn, with dew in the morning and cold, crisp days. There seemed to be a mellowness in the air. Sometimes the wind would blow hard, but it never reached the strength of the storm that had trapped Owen in the warehouses. Wesley brought fish and prawns from the harbor. At night they would build a fire in front of the Den and cook fish or rabbit stew, and eat it with potatoes that grew wild in forest clearings.

Owen slept deep, dreamless sleeps, and when he woke in the morning the cold nipped at his hands and face until he had lit a fire. He had a good stock of tea bags, but he knew they might be his last, so he was miserly with them. Wesley and Cati tasted the tea and made faces. They drank only water, or thin wine, or a warm drink that tasted of honey. Owen was surprised at how quickly the Den became a home and how much he liked to lie dozing and listening to the sound of the wind swaying the trees. He missed his home and his room, and he missed his mother, but he did not miss the miserable tension that had seemed to lurk in every corner and crevice of the house.

He realized too that he felt fitter than ever before. One day, as they raced down the forest paths, he was surprised to find himself pulling easily away from Cati. And when he looked in the mirror of the old dressing table he saw a fuller, more cheerful face looking back at him.

At night they sat round the fire after they had eaten,

the flames casting shadows about them. Sometimes they sat in companionable silence and sometimes they talked quietly, Owen telling them about his life and the town, and Cati and Wesley talking about the Resisters. Owen started to understand that the Resisters had emerged many, many times to battle the Harsh, but of those battles he learned little. Cati had only a dim memory, for she had been born on the island in time and was growing up among them as any child would. However, Wesley had stumbled into the Resisters in much the same way as Owen. He had fought on several occasions, but he did not like to talk about it and would fall silent if pressed.

Sometimes Owen saw the Sub-Commandant and Chancellor in the distance. Both men seemed strained. In the evening the Sub-Commandant would stand on the roof of the Workhouse, shading his eyes and staring across to the other side of the river as if to penetrate the white mist, which grew ever more ominous.

Wesley liked to go down and look at the defenses that had been thrown up along the river. " 'Specting the troops," he called it. Owen went with him and was amazed at the small, stone-buttressed forts that stood every hundred meters or so. Rutgar's soldiers had built them. Good with their hands, Wesley said with respect, although it didn't stop him from pointing out imaginary flaws in the stonework within earshot of the bearded men, who grinned and threw friendly insults at the two boys. There were no friendly insults from Samual's soldiers, though. The brightly dressed men and women patrolled in grim silence, passing Rutgar's men without a greeting or even a sideways glance.

From what Owen could see, these troops lived a hard life. When they were not patrolling they were working in the fields they had carved out for themselves on the slope behind the Workhouse. The fields were well kept and crops were already starting to appear, even though they had not been planted for long, and despite the autumnal weather. But every morning the forest had encroached on the fields during the night, and teams of men and women had to be set to slashing and burning round the margins. There didn't seem to be much laughter among them.

In contrast, Rutgar's men had set up a row of small gardens right up against the wall of the Workhouse. They would work in them in the evenings, or sit talking, wrapped in coats against the evening chill.

One morning toward the end of the second week, Owen got up and lit the fire. He boiled water and made some tea. He took a hunk of bread that had been given to him by Contessa and smeared honey on it. He heard a movement on the path, then Cati's head appeared in the opening. Without saying anything she sat down and helped herself to some of the bread and honey. As she started to eat, they heard a noise, a faint droning.

"What's that?" asked Cati through a mouthful of bread. They got to their feet and went out to the path.

Looking up through the canopy of trees they could see, high in the sky, a single Planeman, wheeling in lazy circles above the Workhouse.

"He's out of range," Cati said. "I never saw one fly so high before." They watched the spindly craft in silence, the bread forgotten in their hands.

Later that morning, Owen looked out to see Rutgar walking down the path toward the Den. He held one of the metal tubes with the glass end that the fighters carried. His smile when he saw Owen was friendly enough, but he looked tired, Owen thought.

"I brought you something to defend yourself with," he said. "It looks as if you're going to need it, although if I judge you right, fighting will not be your main part in all of this. Don't misjudge what I'm saying," he added, seeing Owen's expression. "I know you're brave. It's just that fighting alone won't defeat the Harsh."

He thrust the metal tube into Owen's hands. It was lighter than it looked. Owen examined it. There was what appeared to be a pair of sights at one end and some kind of a trigger mechanism, shaped like a crooked finger, at the other.

"Put it to your shoulder," Rutgar said, "and aim at something."

As Owen did so, he could feel the interior of the tube warm up and the weapon began to emit a low humming noise. A dangerous sound, Owen thought, like something woken from sleep that should have been left alone.

He sighted along the tube and almost pulled the trigger in surprise. Instead of the bare metal sights, a square grid with a small dot in the middle had formed itself out of magno.

"Line the mark up with a rock," said Rutgar. Owen moved the weapon until the dot was centered on a rock.

"Now move it away," Rutgar said. Owen moved the weapon, but the dot stayed centered on the rock. "You have to move the whole square off the rock to change your aim."

Owen did so and the dot repositioned itself in the center of the grid. He aimed the gun at a tree. The dot lined itself up again. He moved the barrel, but the dot stayed fixed on the tree. He wondered what would happen if he pulled the trigger. For the first time since he had come here, he felt powerful. He could see the spiteful face of Samual in his mind's eye and for a moment he could hear the cold and grim summons of the Harsh. Rutgar spoke again but Owen did not hear. His finger tightened on the trigger. The metal tube seemed to sear his cheek, so he jerked it away, and a bolt of blue light shot from the glass end of the gun and struck the tree. The tree seemed to vibrate for a moment, then, with an earsplitting crackling and popping sound, it fell in upon itself and collapsed to the ground.

Owen stared at the weapon in his hand. It was almost too hot to touch now. Rutgar leaned over and removed it from his grasp.

"It's not a toy," he said gently, and Owen felt his face flush.

The air smelled of iron filings, and ash drifted slowly away from the felled tree, even though, as far as Owen could see, it had not burned.

Rutgar sat down beside Owen and explained the principles of the weapon, the way to aim it properly, how to make it safe when carrying it. It was powered by the same magno power as everything else. Rutgar's tone was gentle and serious and it made Owen feel even worse. He remembered the two Raggie boys and their reluctance to even touch a weapon, and the sense of duty with which they had done so.

"Used to be you would take a month to learn what I'm telling you, before you were even allowed to touch this," Rutgar said, standing up to leave. "But we don't have a month. We don't even have days, I think."

Owen and Cati watched Rutgar walk away. "What do we do now?" asked Owen.

"Let's go and see Dr. Diamond," Cati suggested.

In the Skyward, Dr. Diamond lay on his bed, perfectly still, his eyes closed. The sky outside seemed to darken and a gust of wind threw a handful of sleet against the windows. Dr. Diamond's eyes opened and he turned his head sharply toward the big clock. The clock's single hand suddenly leapt into motion, flying round the clock before coming to rest. It began to move backward again, but this time its movements were jerky and sharp. Sleet rattled against the window.

"The attack is on us," Dr. Diamond said softly to himself. "Johnston rides on the Workhouse. Can the Harsh be far behind?" He sat up. "The children are coming!" he exclaimed to himself, and raced to the door.

Owen and Cati were halfway up the Nab when the sky darkened. They paused uncertainly. They could see little of the riverbank, but they could hear sudden shouts and muffled explosions and terrible screams.

"The fighting has begun!" Cati shouted. "We need to get down again."

As they started down the circular stairs, there was a terrible whirring sound in the air. Owen looked up, startled. As he did so the long figure of Dr. Diamond cannoned into him. Dr. Diamond pushed Owen to one side as a barbed lance, over a meter long and made entirely of ice, glanced off the handrail beside him. With terrible force it crashed against the brass wall of the Nab, making a deep clanging sound and leaving a large dent in the handrail. The lance had broken in two pieces. Owen bent to lift one but Dr. Diamond stopped him.

"It would freeze your hand," he shouted. "You'd lose your arm or worse. It is not ordinary ice and probably poisoned. Run!"

They ran, Dr. Diamond coming behind them, urging them on, half carrying Cati when she slipped. The noise of battle grew louder as they descended, and smoke started to drift up to them. They were halfway down the Nab when Owen heard an odd humming sound, followed by a warning shout from Dr. Diamond. He turned to see a Planeman astride his flying craft, coming up behind them and gaining rapidly.

Close up, the craft was bigger than Owen had thought, a complicated structure of long spars and struts, with blades that stirred the air and looked too fragile to bear their great length. The craft drew alongside, the blades almost touching the Nab. The Planeman turned his head to look at them. He was crouched behind the controls wearing huge goggles, and Owen felt that they were being looked at by a giant, hungry insect. The Planeman was wearing an oil-stained leather jacket and matted fur leggings, and Owen could see under the goggles the sideburns that all Johnston's men sported.

Abruptly the Planeman wheeled away to the left. "He's coming in to attack!" Dr. Diamond shouted. Sure enough, the craft turned in the air above them and started to descend rapidly.

"Try to keep the tower between us and him," said Dr. Diamond. They descended in a deadly game, trying to anticipate the Planeman's movements. Twice the man fired a long ice harpoon at them, and twice it shattered harmlessly against the side of the Nab. But the ground was getting closer.

They almost made it. Owen thought that they had given the Planeman the slip. He could almost feel the earth under his feet, but the goggled man was an expert and cunning pilot. As they slid onto the last platform the deadly craft rose from beneath it, the ice cannon pointed straight at them. Owen could see the mouth beneath the goggles, the yellow teeth bared in an ugly grin.

"The gun!" Cati cried. Owen had forgotten he was carrying it. "The gun, the gun!" Cati made a grab for it. She missed the barrel; her hand caught the trigger mechanism instead. A bolt of blue light shot from the barrel, cannoned off the brass side of the Nab, and glanced off the edge of one of the plane's wings. The aircraft yawed wildly as the man fought with the controls.

There was a nasty noise coming from the plane now, and as Owen watched, it rose high in the air, higher and higher, the pilot fighting the controls wildly. Its ascent became faster and faster, the plane turning in tight little circles. The two children looked on in fear and pity as it grew smaller and smaller, until in the end it was a tiny speck and then nothing at all.

"The poor man," said Cati.

"He was about to kill us," Owen said.

"I know," she said, but still she watched the empty space where the plane had disappeared.

"Come on," Dr. Diamond said, gently but firmly.

As they ran down the path toward the riverbank, they met wounded men going back to the Workhouse. Most of them were able to walk, although there were broken arms and ugly, blue-lipped wounds from the ice lances. But at one point on the path they had to stand back in silence and watch as a stretcher was carried past bearing a man who did not move or open his eyes. He was one of Samual's men and the red of blood had been added to the color of his gaudy clothes.

"I'm taking you two to the Workhouse," Dr. Diamond said. When they started to protest he turned to them with a grave face. "I want your solemn promise that you will stay in the Workhouse and not go down to the riverbank," he said.

Reluctantly they agreed. In the distance they could hear shouts and explosions and they were simultaneously afraid and drawn to the action.

"If you go upstairs in the Workhouse," Dr. Diamond said, "you'll be able to see everything. And since I have your promise, I will leave you here."

They turned and ran toward the Workhouse. Dr. Diamond watched them for a moment, then turned back toward the Nab. He had learned a few new things that day and he had work to do.

The Workhouse building showed signs of attack when the children reached it. There were scars in its crumbling stone and shards of ice lay on the ground. They ran through the doorway just as there was a loud whistling sound and a huge ice lance struck the wall above their heads. But it would take more than even the coldest ice to penetrate its great walls, and as Owen and Cati ran on, the sounds of attack faded. Passing the door of the Convoke hall, they saw that it had been turned into a temporary infirmary and that there were already more than twenty soldiers on low pallets on the ground.

On and on they ran up one of the Workhouse's endless staircases until it seemed that the fighting must be over by the time they got to the top. They arrived breathlessly at an old room just under the eaves. The room was full of strange and wild stone carvings, weathered until the marks had almost faded back into the stone. Owen could make out the figures of men and women, some peaceful, some looking as if they were engaged in a terrible struggle.

Cati hardly spared them a glance. "They used to be on the roof," she said, "but everyone thought they were so moldy that they would fall off on people's heads. Come on!"

They ran to the window. The fighting had intensified. Owen saw that Samual's troops were holding their trenches by the river as wave upon wave of Johnston's men waded across the river and attacked them. The air was full of jagged bolts of magno, and ice lances fell like rain, some flung by Johnston's men, but other, bigger ones, being flung from the white mist that covered the ground behind them, arching upward as if thrown by machine. Of the Harsh there was no sign. That worried Owen. And above it all the Planemen wheeled and turned and sought targets among the defenders.

"Where's Rutgar?" asked Cati.

"Look!" Owen said, pointing downriver. Hidden from the Planemen by an outcrop of rock with pine trees on it, a band of soldiers led by Rutgar had crossed the river and was making its way silently toward Johnston's lines— hoping, Owen could tell, to mount a surprise, flanking attack. Using the low ground by the river, they crept forward. They were almost there when Owen saw something else. A body of men lay in a shallow depression twenty meters inland from Rutgar. There were more men than Rutgar had, and even at this distance Owen could make out Johnston's unmistakable bulk. He heard a hiss of breath from Cati.

"It's a trap!" she exclaimed. "They'll get Rutgar from behind."

The two children leapt to their feet, waving and shouting, but it was useless against the noise of the battle. They watched, horror-stricken, as Rutgar continued to creep forward, while Johnston staged the surprise attack that would wipe out Rutgar and his men.

Owen grabbed the magno gun, which had lain forgotten against the wall.

"What are you doing?" cried Cati. Owen didn't reply. He got down on his stomach, the little holosights appearing in his vision as soon as he sighted along the barrel. His hands were slippery with sweat and he was finding it hard to focus. Settling himself, he sought the little floating bead and fixed its aim.

There was no more time. He felt the barrel of the weapon become warm in his hands, even before his finger closed on the trigger, as if it knew that he was going to fire. He squeezed tighter and tighter; the barrel suddenly surged with heat and he felt the searing bolt leap from the muzzle.

It missed Rutgar by centimeters. A rock in front of him splintered and he leapt backward. He turned in shock to see who was firing on him from his own lines. Owen jumped up at the window, shouting and gesticulating toward the shallow depression where Johnston and his men lay hidden. Rutgar realized what was happening. With a warning shout he swung around. At the same moment Johnston's men sprang from cover.

With a noise that Owen could hear high above the river, the two bands came together. They were too close to use their guns and ice lances, and they fought instead with the long bayonets from their belts. The fighting was fierce and Rutgar's soldiers were driven backward, but Johnston had lost his element of surprise and he could not break Rutgar's line. For a moment Johnston and Rutgar were facing each other, and the two men struggled toe to toe before a knot of fighting men drove between them.

The two groups fought for close to an hour. Owen could see that Rutgar's men were tiring.

"Johnston's got too many men," Cati said.

"He's getting between Rutgar and the river," said Owen.

It was true. Bit by bit, Rutgar's retreat to the river was being cut off. They could see that many of Rutgar's men were bleeding. Some of Johnston's men went down and did not get up, but Rutgar's men were also falling. They were fighting with desperation now.

"Look!" shouted Cati. One of Johnston's men had one of the Resisters on the ground. He had raised a bayonet to stab when a long arc of light uncurled almost lazily toward him, wrapping itself around the man, then flinging him high into the air.

"Pieta!" Owen exclaimed.

Methodically Pieta worked her way through the attackers, who fell left and right. Owen could see Johnston snarling at her, keeping well out of the range of the powerful whip. Johnston's men fell back; some of them dropped their weapons and ran rather than face Pieta. Just then the fighting seemed to pause. There was a loud, mournful hooting noise, rising and falling, and Owen knew from its cold, empty tones that it was the voice of the Harsh. Cati put her hands over her ears and hung her head.

Down at the riverbank, Johnston's men had started to retreat, step by step, the defenders fighting them all the way across the river. As they did so, the white mist crept forward, enveloping the attackers for a moment only. When it retreated, Johnston's men were gone.

The bottom floor of the Workhouse was crowded when Owen and Cati got down the stairs. Men and women who had been fighting all day were eating and casualties were being attended to. They saw the Sub-Commandant looking anxiously about him, then his relief when his eyes fell on Cati. She waved at him, but then a messenger approached him and he turned away. The children pushed through the crowd of tired fighters, making their way toward the door. As they reached it they heard a shout and turned to see Samual striding angrily toward them.

"Stop that boy!" he shouted. Several of his men at the door turned in surprise, but when he repeated his command, one of them caught Owen by the arm. Samual stopped in front of Owen and Cati.

"Do you think I didn't see what you did?" he demanded. His face was white with anger and his hand was on the hilt of his bayonet.

"He didn't do anything!" exclaimed Cati.

"I was right about you all along," the man snarled, "and I should finish you here and now!"

"What is going on?" a stern voice demanded. It was Chancellor. "What's all this about finishing?"

"I saw this boy in the high window," Samuel said. "He

fired on Rutgar's flanking party. Not only did he almost hit him, but the shot told Johnston where Rutgar was. If not for Pieta, they would all be dead."

"Is this true?" Chancellor said.

"Yes, but—"

"He admits it!" cried Samual.

"He was trying to save Rutgar," Cati said angrily.

"Some of my friends were killed in that sortie," came a voice from the crowd that had gathered. Owen's tongue was stuck to the roof of his mouth. There was an angry murmur from the crowd, and it would have gone badly for Owen if Rutgar had not appeared in the doorway. There was a dirty, blood-soaked rag tied round his head.

"What's all this?" he growled.

"Samual saw Owen shoot at you," Chancellor said.

"Shoot at me?" Rutgar said softly. "Shoot at me?" There was a dangerous gleam in his eye. "If Owen had not fired to warn me, then Johnston would have attacked us from the rear and wiped us out. Owen saved the sortie. Leave the boy alone and consider something else."

"What?" asked Samual suspiciously.

"I would like to know how Johnston found out we were going to try to flank him. Why was he waiting in that exact place? He had to know our plans. It was the same all day—everywhere we went, they were there. Every time we tried an offensive it seemed that they knew in advance. They knew all our plans."

"A spy?" Chancellor said.

"A spy," said Rutgar heavily. He was looking straight at Samual.

The richly dressed man snorted contemptuously. "Your plans are too predictable. A child would know that you would try that flanking movement."

The two men glared at each other. Chancellor made an impatient movement with his hand. "Enough! We haven't seen the Harsh yet; does anybody think there's something strange about that? There's more to come. Something is afoot. I think that was only a softening-up attack. Get something to eat and go back to your posts."

Samual wheeled away. His men released Owen, and Rutgar clapped the boy on the back.

"Never mind that Samual. He was born wicked. I won't forget what you did today. Now let me go and get this head cleaned up."

They watched Rutgar walk away, but Owen could tell that many people weren't satisfied with what he'd said. He was aware of people turning their backs on him as he and Cati walked toward the kitchen.

The kitchen was chaotic. Even Contessa did not look her normal calm self and she hardly spared them a glance as they helped themselves to food. When they left the kitchen, Owen saw Samual glowering at him. "Let's go back to the Den," he said.

"Right," said Cati. "I couldn't eat properly with old sourchops Samual staring at me."

They walked back along the path, meeting only a few weary men who barely glanced at them.

"I'm tired of it," Owen said.

"Tired of what?"

"People being suspicious of me. I haven't done anything to Samual or any of his lot."

"It's not you exactly that they're suspicious of," Cati said slowly.

"What is it, then? My shadow?"

"It's what you are, or what you might be, if you follow me."

"No, I don't follow you," said Owen crossly.

Cati sighed. "Every time I say something you just get crosser and crosser. I think we'll eat this, then go to Dr. Diamond. And then we'd better go and see how Wesley is."

"Were the Raggies in the fighting?" Owen said, worry replacing his anger.

"I heard that the Planemen attacked them again," Cati said.

"Let's hurry, then." Owen broke into a trot. He did not know that much would happen before nightfall, and that they would not be going to see any of their friends.

At the Den, Cati managed to get the fire going from a few embers and Owen put on water for one of his remaining tea bags. He opened out the cloth he had been carrying. There was fresh crusty bread and cheese. Cati had snatched some pickles and preserves, and two slices of rich almond cake. They ate greedily and in silence, and when they had finished they stretched out on the soft moss floor of the Den while the fire warmed them.

Owen was just about to remind Cati that they ought to get going when they heard it—a low sound at first, but building in intensity, a hum that got louder and louder and then turned into a shriek, finally bursting forth with a racket like a hundred fire sirens. The noise drilled into their heads and drove out their thoughts till it seemed that the only thing to do was to lie down with their hands over their ears.

"What is it?" Owen roared at the top of his lungs. Cati shook her head. It was clear that she had never heard the sound before. She ran outside and Owen followed. They scrambled up the bank to the swing tree. For the first time in many days the white mist had drawn back and a great object stood on the far bank. It was like a cathedral of ice and in it, as if imprisoned, he could see the shapes of the Harsh—perhaps ten of them. Above the point of its frozen spire, lightning crackled and small but violent blizzards swept along its gleaming walls.

But even if the Harsh were frozen inside, they were still moving, their arms waving slowly and rhythmically, their mouths open in the terrible howl the children had heard. And this howl, it seemed, had taken shape in a white beam of absolute cold, now pointing straight across the river, freezing and destroying. Every object it struck was frozen, then exploded from within. Trees and boulders detonated as soon as they were touched. The beam gouged great icy trenches in the ground and in the bank where Owen and Cati stood. The air was full of shards of frozen tree and icy slivers of rock. Far below, they could see the shapes of men and women crouched in terror and awe.

They watched for over an hour. It was clear that the beam was concentrated on the river defenses, which were gradually being flattened. Owen saw Samual lead a small sortie. They crouched in the lee of the riverbank, then at a signal they rose and fired the magno guns at the ice cathedral. The bolts of magno glanced off harmlessly and then the beam swung in their direction. Owen did not like Samual, but there was no denying his courage. The red-robed man fired twice more as the beam moved swiftly toward him. Just in time he ducked under the riverbank and, bent double, ran downstream with his soldiers as the beam fell with savage cold on the place where he had stood, leaving a hole in the ground from which icy vapor rose.

Owen heard a noise and turned. Dr. Diamond was coming across the slope toward them. He hunkered down beside them, surveying the scene.

"What is it?" Owen shouted.

"I don't know exactly," the scientist said, "but at a guess I would say that the Harsh are joining their thoughts together. They don't think the way we do. In fact, you could say that their thoughts are frozen drafts blowing about their heads. There's a lot about the Harsh that we don't understand."

"You mean they're thinking about us?" said Cati. Her face was pale and strained.

Dr. Diamond nodded. "Something like that."

"What happens when it hits the Workhouse?" asked Owen.

"The Workhouse is very old and stronger than it looks," Dr. Diamond said, "but if they destroy all the defenses, will the Workhouse stand? I don't know."

Cati stifled a sob. Dr. Diamond looked at her with concern.

"Owen," he said, "your friend is very strong, otherwise she would not be here, but their sound is hurting her. You had better take her to the harbor, where she'll be out of its range."

Owen was going to object, but one look at Cati made him realize that Dr. Diamond was right. With a tenderness that surprised even himself, he put his arm around her and led her gently away.

As they walked toward the harbor the terrible noise faded and Cati brightened. "Sorry about that," she said. "I just get this frozen feeling inside when I hear them."

"They scare me too," Owen said.

"Do you think we can stop them?"

"I'd say Dr. Diamond is cooking up a surprise for them right this moment," Owen said with as much confidence as he could muster.

At that moment the scientist was clambering into the

131

big chair surrounded by levers in the middle of the Skyward. Frowning with concentration, he started to manipulate the levers. The polished exterior of the Skyward
started to move, slowly at first, then faster and faster until
it became a blur, then faster again until it seemed like a
flashing disc of light in the darkening sky.

Inside the Skyward, something had changed. An observer would have noted that only one of the five time
clocks was now moving. A device that looked for all the
world like a submarine telescope came down from the
ceiling. (Indeed, it was a submarine telescope that Dr.
Diamond had adapted from a U-boat.) Dr. Diamond
took the handles and put his face to the eyepiece. For ten
minutes he turned the periscope to and fro. Then he
closed the handles and the periscope rose into the ceiling
again. Dr. Diamond started to manipulate the levers. All
five clocks started again. Outside, the revolving Skyward
started to slow down. Dr. Diamond pushed the last lever
back into place and lay back in the chair. His face was
thoughtful.

The warehouses had been attacked by the Planemen and there were holes in the roof and great gouges in the stonework. But Wesley had led most of the children to the basement, and the shooting skills of Uel and Mervyn had kept the Planemen at a distance. All in all, Owen thought, the Raggies had fared better than the defenders at the Workhouse.

Owen and Cati told Wesley what had happened. Wesley's face was grave. He looked toward the Workhouse. The air overhead seemed to be full of a fine sleet. "I've never heard of this. And you tell me they fired on the Workhouse?"

"They're attacking the defenses," Cati said.

"They do be looking to take the Workhouse whole,"

said Wesley. "Could be they want something . . . the Sleepers in the Starry, I would reckon."

Wesley gave them food but they didn't want to eat. It was getting dark now. The noise made by the Harsh got louder. Cati sat as close to the fire as she could, looking miserable. As darkness fell, an eerie dome of ice hung over the Workhouse.

"They need help," Wesley murmured, "but who will help them?" They stood at the door and stared mutely toward the battle. Then Owen stood up.

"I have an idea," he said. "I have an idea, but I can't do it on my own."

Wesley looked at Cati. She was dozing in the heat of the fire. "Looks like it'll have to be me then," he said eventually.

"Let's go," said Owen.

The two boys ran all the way. They could feel the cold on their faces as they got close to the Workhouse and there were small chunks of ice floating in the river.

"What's your idea?" Wesley gasped. But Owen was too out of breath to tell him. They ran under the town bridge and on, the air full of ice granules. They skidded round the last corner and gazed openmouthed on the battle scene.

Johnston's men had crossed the river and were fighting in front of the Workhouse. The Resister men and women had gathered in a hollow in front of the building where the ice cannon could not get them and were fighting hand to hand in an icy sleet that enveloped the whole area. Owen even saw Dr. Diamond in the middle of it, wearing an ancient karate suit, dealing out spidery kicks and blows.

They saw the beam from the cannon that had already devastated the landscape and now roamed restlessly, searching out targets.

"Perfect," Owen said. Wesley looked at him as if he had lost his mind. "Come on!" Owen urged, and ran off at full tilt without looking to see if Wesley was following.

They charged down the path to the Den, leaping over trees that had been cut in two and pieces of boulders strewn in their way. The Den seemed unharmed. Owen ran over to the old dressing table and gasped, "Grab the other end." Wesley's eyes widened, but he did as he was asked. Together the two boys heaved the dressing table outside.

"Up there," Owen said, pointing toward the swing tree. Together, inch by laborious inch, the two boys pushed and heaved, their task made more difficult by the trenches gouged by the beam. Once the beam swung in their direction, making a terrible tearing, icy noise.

"Down!" Owen hissed. "We don't want them to see us yet!" Wesley ducked, clearly not liking the sound of that "yet." With a cold, malevolent roar, the beam passed them by and they resumed their struggle. Once Wesley lost his footing and the dressing table slipped back down the hill, picking up momentum until Owen threw himself behind it and somehow managed to stop it.

"Get it under the swing tree!" Owen shouted. "Turn it round so that it's facing the river." He adjusted the mirror slightly. "All right," he said calmly. "Ready now." To Wesley's amazement, he started to jump up and down and wave his arms in the air, shouting.

"Over here!" he yelled. "Come on, ice-cube brains!" Wesley stared at him, then an inkling began to form in his mind and he too began to jump up and down.

"Here! Bet you can't hit us with your damn beam," he shouted. "Get away on out of this place. Go on!"

Then the Harsh spotted them. The beam swung toward the boys, greedy for their warmth, and Owen felt a shiver go down his spine. Faster and faster the beam moved, roaring as it tore up the ground, thirty meters away, twenty meters, ten, and then it was on them.

"Now!" Owen shouted. The two boys threw themselves behind the dressing table. But as they tried to turn it toward the beam, Wesley slipped. Owen watched in horror as Wesley sprawled down the slope in front of them. The beam moved forward slowly as though following a trail. Frozen debris peppered Owen's face, drawing blood. Then the beam seemed to sense Wesley and started moving toward him, picking up speed. Wesley lay still on the ground and Owen saw blood on his temple. The beam would be on him in seconds.

Without thinking, Owen threw himself down the slope, trying to draw the beam to him, but it didn't deviate from its path. In desperation, Owen ran right under it, so close that he could feel the material of his clothes

136

turn hard and frozen, so close that he could feel the vibration of the terrible power projecting from it.

And then it became aware of Owen. He could almost feel its attention turn to him. Not only that, but it felt as if it knew who he was. With lightning speed the beam turned on him, and he barely managed to leap out of its way. Again it sought him out, and again, striking like a snake, eager for his warmth. He ran up the slope, slipping, gasping for breath, the air around him full of frozen earth and shattered timber. With his last strength he threw himself at the dressing table. The beam seemed to rear above him, and he could feel its sense of triumph at cornering its prey. With the strength of desperation, Owen pulled the dressing table across his body and felt the terrifying jolt as the beam hit the mirror, just above his heart.

For a moment there was nothing except the sound of the beam, then it doubled on itself, reflected back along its own path, back toward the Harsh and their ice cathedral. It struck like a thunderbolt. The Harsh's voices changed. The structure began to vibrate violently. The Harsh's movements became frenetic and their voices changed to an eerie wail. At the same time the mirror shattered and the cathedral structure exploded with a terrifying boom.

Owen was thrown backward. Shards of ice rained on him. He scrambled to his feet. Down below, the attackers were looking about them uncertainly. The men and women defending the Workhouse seemed to shake themselves as though waking from a nightmare. Standing at the very front of the Resisters was Pieta. Even from a distance Owen could see the light of battle in her eyes. She raised the magno whip above her head and in one easy movement flicked it forward over the heads of the attackers, the lash extending until the tip of it covered the first three ranks. She threw her head back and laughed, and as she did so the attackers' uncertainty turned to fear. The rest of the Resisters, no longer afraid, started to laugh as well and, raising their weapons, started forward in a wave. Johnston's men dropped their weapons, turned, and ran.

Wesley was dazed but unhurt. By the time Owen got him to his feet and back to the Workhouse, the sounds of battle had faded into the distance. Johnston's men had been driven back across the river. The landscape in front of the building was unrecognizable, broken stone and trees scattered all over, the ground churned up into frozen ridges of earth. In the Workhouse they were tending to the wounded. Exhausted men and women sat everywhere. The Sub-Commandant and Dr. Diamond stood in the entrance to the Workhouse.

"I saw what you did," the Sub-Commandant said. "It was brave and it was clever. Thank you. If you are not too tired, perhaps you would find Cati for me and bring her here."

"It wasn't just me," said Owen, "it was Wesley as well." He saw gratitude in Wesley's wary eyes. Wesley had gone along with him without ever questioning what he was doing.

"Cati's at the warehouses," Wesley said. "I'll go." The Sub-Commandant smiled and turned away.

Owen suddenly realized he was starving. But as he turned to Wesley to suggest going to the kitchen first, Dr. Diamond drew him aside. "Good fight," he said enthusiastically. "That was a clever thing you did. Wouldn't have thought of it myself." Owen felt a glow of satisfaction. Perhaps people like Samual might start accepting him now.

"Come with me now, Owen," Dr. Diamond said. "There will be a Convoke in the morning and hostility to you. I want you to be prepared."

Owen groaned inwardly. He thought that his trick with the mirror would have convinced them that he was on their side. Part of him had even secretly hoped that he would be carried shoulder high into the Convoke.

"Never mind," Dr. Diamond said in a kindly voice, as if he had read the boy's thoughts. "You do have friends as well."

Owen followed Dr. Diamond up the Nab until they reached the gleaming Skyward. Once they were inside Dr. Diamond disappeared, reappearing a few minutes later with a large plate of excellent cakes. Neither of them spoke until every crumb was gone. Dr. Diamond brushed the fragments off his karate suit and looked at Owen seriously.

"I have some idea of what will happen in the morning

at the Convoke, and it is time for you to know some of your story. For that you must know something of the Mortmain. And of Gobillard et Fils."

Owen remembered the cold voice of the Harsh in his head from the night he had crossed the river, the way it had spoken the word *Mortmain*.

"I have heard of it," he said, "but I don't know what it is."

"The Mortmain has been many things to different people through the ages. It has taken many shapes as well, but usually it is an object about twice the size of a man's hand, made of brass or bronze. Quite often it is in the shape of a household object or a tool and appears quite battered until you look at it carefully."

"What does it do?"

"For the Resisters it is always the means to turn back the advances of the Harsh. Either it points the way or it fulfills some purpose. In our present case, I suspect that it is the object that can be used to turn off the Great Machine in the north and set time back on its proper course—or courses, since we know of at least five different states of time."

"But Dr. Diamond," said Owen, as much to stop another bewildering lecture on time as anything else, "if we could find it, we could stop the Harsh and I could go home. Where is it?"

"Where is it?" Dr. Diamond's face was grave and he leaned forward and studied Owen, his eyes suddenly dark and gleaming. "Where is it?"

"Is it missing?" Owen said, suddenly feeling unaccountably worried.

"Is it missing?" cried Dr. Diamond, getting to his feet and towering over Owen. "Yes, it is missing and that is the central part of the problem, the nub, the crux, the salient point. It is missing, and the reason it is missing, Owen, is that your father took it!"

There was a long silence. Owen could hear the ticking of the five clocks and the moan of the wind against the brass walls of the Nab. How could his father have taken it? And yet . . . In a part of his memory something stirred.

"When your father was a young man, he used to come fishing in the river. He met the Sub-Commandant as the Harsh were threatening. The Sub-Commandant had just Woken us, for he had detected tremors in the fabric of time. We had to be cautious. Something was interfering with time, but life—your life—was going on as normal."

"What was he like?" Owen could hear the tremor in his voice.

"What was . . . ? Did your mother not . . . ?" Owen shook his head mutely. Dr. Diamond looked surprised.

"They say he . . . they say he killed himself," Owen said miserably.

"Suicide?" Dr. Diamond stroked his chin thoughtfully. "No, I don't think so. Not your father. He was brave, like you, and resourceful as well. He was, well, he was a happier person than you, I suppose, but that can't be helped. He fought side by side with us and we succeeded in repulsing the Harsh one more time. We were puzzled by that attack at the time, but now it seems it was part of a grander scheme, and that its purpose was for the Harsh to get their hands on the Mortmain. At which, of course, they failed."

"Where was I?"

"You were a baby. At home with your mother."

"What happened then?"

"We had a gathering in the Convoke, as we normally do before we go back to Sleep. Usually everybody is a little distracted, thinking about the long Sleep to come. Nobody missed your father. One minute he was there, the next he was gone. And with him the Mortmain."

"Are you sure it was him?"

"What people say is that it must have been, otherwise why did he sneak off?"

"And what do you think?"

If the question discomfited Dr. Diamond, he didn't show it. "If your father did not take the Mortmain, then we have somebody very dangerous in our midst. If he did take it, he must have had a very good reason."

"I don't remember my father," Owen said quietly.

Dr. Diamond put a hand on his shoulder. "Then you aren't in a position to judge him. Let's deal with the present and let the past—or is it the future?—look after itself."

"What about Gobillard?"

"I almost forgot," Dr. Diamond said, frowning, "and time is short. Gobillard was the first Navigator and the Keeper of the Mortmain. Much of the knowledge about him is lost, as is his lore about the Mortmain."

"But the chest in my bedroom!" Owen burst out. Quickly he told Dr. Diamond about the old chest.

"Your father's?" asked Dr. Diamond. "I'm afraid I do not know what it means. And remember, it is gone, lost in time along with many other things. We may never know how the chest might have helped us. But quickly. I brought you here for two things—to give you information about your father and the Mortmain, but also to see what you can discover yourself. I want you to sit in that seat."

When Owen got into the tatty old leather plane seat he thought that the levers were familiar-looking.

"I adapted them from gearsticks belonging to old school buses and lorries," Dr. Diamond said proudly. Owen was starting to get used to the way that Dr. Diamond adapted things.

"What's it for?"

"It's for . . . let me think how to describe it . . . I can't say it's for looking back in time, because once you're out of the present, of course, there is no backward and forward." Dr. Diamond stopped, seeing the blank look on Owen's face.

"I'll try again." He frowned with effort, then brightened. "I know—it's like turning on a television and flicking through the channels with the sound turned down so

144

you have to guess what's going on. Except the television here is time itself."

Owen thought he knew what Dr. Diamond was talking about, and the man was looking at him so eagerly that he nodded.

"You might see something useful and you might not," Dr. Diamond said, "but it's worth a try. Now, concentrate!"

Dr. Diamond began to move the levers and the Skyward started to rotate, slowly at first, then at bewildering speed so that Owen could feel his own head starting to spin.

"Now!" cried Dr. Diamond, hauling back on a lever. The periscope started to descend from the ceiling. As it reached Owen, he grabbed the handles on either side of it and, feeling like a submarine captain from an old film, pressed his face to the eyepiece.

At first he could see nothing. Or rather what he thought was nothing but was in fact nothingness, which was a different thing altogether. It was like he imagined outer space to be, except that was cold and black and this was just . . . well, he thought, no temperature at all, really, and no color.

"Turn the periscope," Dr. Diamond said, his voice seeming to come from a great distance. At first the images were a blur but then Owen realized that he could catch them if he went very slowly. There was a vast herd of some kind of deer silently crossing a frozen tundra. He saw a building with flames coming from its windows

145

and a flag fluttering from its highest point. He saw a boy and a girl holding hands beside a sun-dappled pond.

"You're getting it now," said Dr. Diamond. "Concentrate!" Owen didn't know what he was supposed to concentrate on exactly, but he kept rotating the periscope. He discovered that if he turned the left handle it acted like the focus on a camera. As he turned it, he momentarily glimpsed a house and knew that it was his own home. Then he lost the image and tried to go back to it, but he couldn't find it.

"Keep going," Dr. Diamond said urgently. The next image that came up was of a man's hands, one on the steering wheel of a car, the other shifting gears urgently. After that, the images came faster and faster. Something dull and gold flying through a window and landing with a clank on metal. The swaying sensation of a car being flung round corners. Owen was aware that Dr. Diamond was shouting to him, but he couldn't hear the words. In his nostrils it seemed that he could smell salt water, and then it was as if he was floating through air, and the image was of the world outside the car, spinning upside down.

The final image was the most frightening. The car was filling with dark water. There was sunlight coming through the windscreen, but it took on a greenish tinge and started to fade. The water rose higher and higher, and Owen imagined that it was rising toward his nose and mouth and he shouted out. As he did so, he saw the hands that he had seen on the wheel desperately hammering at the side window until it broke. Then he knew what was happening. That he was the person in the car and that the hands belonged to his father. The hands lifted him and thrust him through the broken window. For a moment all was watery darkness, then sunlight flooded the eyepiece of the periscope. Owen felt Dr. Diamond gently removing his hands from the handles. He lay back in the chair and his chest rose and fell as he drew great shuddering breaths.

11

It was almost half an hour before Owen recovered enough to tell Dr. Diamond what he had seen. Dr. Diamond looked troubled.

"It seems that you were in the car with your father, being pursued. In great danger, if I'm not mistaken."

Owen could almost still feel the hands thrusting him through the broken window of the car. "The hands seemed huge," he said. "Far bigger than normal."

"That is because you were a small child, Owen. A man's hands seem vast to a very small child. Somehow the car crashed into water, and your father saved you by breaking a window and pushing you through it."

"But my father was never found. He just disappeared. Would they not have . . . ?"

"Would they not have known where to look for the car and found his body when they found you? Is that what you are thinking? But perhaps you weren't found at that spot, or some other factor came into play. We don't know what happened."

"But I do know what happened," another voice intervened. Owen looked around, startled. The Sub-Commandant was standing right behind him. Owen had not heard him enter, but Dr. Diamond seemed to know that he was there.

"Then tell us, please, Sub-Commandant."

The little man cleared away a mess of soldering irons and circuit boards and motorcycle workshop manuals and sat down.

"You know, Owen, that I am the Watcher?" Owen nodded. "When the Resisters go to sleep, I fade so that ordinary people going about their business cannot see me. I step back into the shadows of time, if you like. But there is a little time when I am in both worlds. I was down at the harbor that day. The world had woken up around me. There were cars and people everywhere— what you call normal life, Owen."

"Could people see you?" Owen asked.

"Yes, and touch if they wanted. But I tried to stay out of their way. And this is the point, Owen. I could still touch people in your time. And on my journey back I found a baby, soaking wet but fast asleep, at the edge of the harbor. Listening to what you have just said about the car going into the water, I know now that the baby was you."

"What did you do?" Dr. Diamond asked.

"There was little time," the Sub-Commandant said. "I was fading fast. I dried the child as best I could and carried him to the little shop near your house."

"Mary White's!" Owen said.

"Yes. An old woman, but she sees a lot. In fact, I think she saw me leave the child at her back door, but she made no move to talk to me. Perhaps she thought I was a ghost, for I was fading fast into the shadows of time."

"You didn't see what happened?" Dr. Diamond asked anxiously.

"No, but it must have had something to do with the Mortmain," the Sub-Commandant said.

"It must have," agreed Dr. Diamond. The two men fell into an anxious silence.

"Come on," the Sub-Commandant said at last, getting to his feet. "I'll take you home." Owen noticed for the first time that the man was limping and there was a smear of dried blood on his cheek.

Dr. Diamond said goodnight and they climbed down the stairway in silence. And in silence they walked along the path toward the Den. Miraculously, the area around the path seemed to have remained untouched and Owen welcomed the familiar shadow of the trees.

The Sub-Commandant stopped at the entrance to the Den with a further thank-you for his swift thinking in thwarting the Harsh.

"Did it . . . did it kill them?" Owen asked.

"I don't think so. I don't think they can be killed. But

I suspect you sent them fleeing north in disarray—I cannot sense their presence anymore. It is a long time since anyone did even that much. Goodnight, young Owen, and sleep free of fear."

"Wait . . . wait a minute, please," Owen said. "Nobody said what happened to him. My father . . . Did you see?"

"I don't know," the small man said gently, "but it would seem that he did not get out of the car."

"They never found the body."

"I cannot say for certain, but if I answer truthfully, then I believe that he drowned." He watched Owen carefully, but the boy only felt numb. "Do you want me to come in with you?" he asked. Owen shook his head.

He watched the Sub-Commandant walk off deep in thought. He suspected he knew what was on the man's mind. The one thing the two men had not mentioned in his story. The dull glint of metal thrown from the car. The Mortmain, he thought. It had to be.

As he entered the Den a shape moved in the dark. He leapt forward and tussled with it, but a swift kick to his shins sent him hopping about in agony. His lamp came on. It was Cati.

"Sorry about the shin," she said, "but I thought you were going to strangle me."

"Why didn't you put the light on?"

"I didn't want my father to find me. He would have taken me back to the Workhouse for the night and I wanted to know what had happened to you."

151

Tired as he was, Owen took Cati through the events of the day. She gasped at his account of the Harsh and what Owen had done with the mirror. She told him that the Planemen had come back to attack the warehouses. They had been driven off, but many children had been injured. Owen went on to tell her about the Skyward and how he had seen his father.

"Your father's a hero," Cati said indignantly. "He saved your life."

"I suppose so." Owen didn't sound convinced. He yawned. "I have to get some sleep," he said. "You'd better stay here tonight. It's not safe to walk back on your own. There's spare blankets over there."

Owen fell onto the old sofa fully dressed and pulled up his sleeping bag. Cati made a nest out of her blankets and crawled into it. The fire had not been lit and it was cold, but Cati had enough blankets and the little Den was safe and she soon felt sleep stealing over her. For one moment she thought she heard a stifled sob from the old sofa. She listened but did not hear the noise again, and in a few minutes she was fast asleep.

They had just woken the next morning when an unwelcome visitor arrived. Owen had lit the fire and there were oatcakes cooking on an old pan, and water boiling.

"This is all very domestic," an unpleasant, drawling voice said. Owen looked up to see Samual in the doorway. Samual took in the Den, the old sofa, the broken wing mirror on the wall, the old boat propeller, and the empty space where the dressing table had been.

"What do you want?" said Cati.

"Just being neighborly," said Samual. "I wanted to see how our hero was doing this morning." There was a sneer in his voice.

"We're just having breakfast," Owen said, not looking at Samual.

"Ah yes, got to keep our strength up. Particularly for the Convoke this morning." The man stepped further into the Den. Cati glared and Owen stood up. "Do you think that this is the end of the Harsh? Do you not think that Johnston is gathering his men to crush us? And do you realize that we are helpless? That without the Mortmain we cannot defeat them?" He was face to face with Owen now and the boy could see the hatred in Samual's eyes.

"It's not Owen's fault that the Mortmain is missing," snapped Cati.

"No?" the man said silkily, his eyes not leaving Owen's for a moment. "But when the father is treacherous, does not the stench of treachery linger around the son?"

Cati, furious, grabbed a branch from the pile of firewood and drew back as if to hit Samual. But before she could swing at him, Owen grabbed the branch from behind. Samual laughed.

"Get out," Owen said in a low voice. "You aren't welcome here."

"You can say that again," said Cati, struggling to tug the branch out of Owen's grip.

"I have things to do," Samual said, "but just remember: some people may think you are a hero, but there are many who can see beneath the skin." With one final contemptuous look at Cati, he turned and was gone. Owen released the branch.

"Why didn't you let me at him?" Cati demanded.

"I nearly did, but the thing is, he's right, Cati. My father did take the Mortmain. Even Dr. Diamond thinks so. He was trying to say stuff about my father having had good reasons for doing it, but I knew what he meant."

"Your father saved you," said Cati angrily, "and he's not here to speak for himself. He needs you to defend him."

"I wish I could," Owen said quietly.

"I can't believe you're talking like this!" Cati's eyes were fiery and bright spots of red glowed on her cheeks. "When you needed him he was there. And now he needs you and you're coming out with all this 'I don't know if I can trust him' stuff. Well, if you can't trust him, then you can't trust me either and I can't be your friend."

Cati stormed out. Owen sat down on the sofa. He felt tears pricking his eyes. He didn't know what to think. He went back over what he had seen in the Skyward. The hands working frantically at the steering wheel. The dull golden object thrown from the speeding car. It had to be the Mortmain. If only he knew where it had fallen.

Suddenly he knew what had to be done. He stood up

and scattered earth over the remains of the fire. He stuffed the oatcakes into his pocket and set out toward the Workhouse.

Preparations for the Convoke were well under way. He saw Contessa going in, and Chancellor, and Rutgar. To his satisfaction he saw Dr. Diamond coming down from the Nab, taking the steps two at a time. Owen ducked as the man passed him. He seemed to be reciting mathematical formulas to himself. Owen didn't know much about mathematical formulas, but they sounded suspiciously backward. When Dr. Diamond was out of sight, Owen sprang onto the steps and ran up them.

Trying to stay low so that he wouldn't be seen, he ran up and up, onto the roof and then onto the swaying pillar of the Nab itself. He was out of breath and his legs ached, but he forced himself upward until he had reached the walkway surrounding the polished cylinder of the Skyward. He was afraid that Dr. Diamond might have locked it, but he need not have worried. When the two doors had aligned, he dived through them and fell onto the other side.

The place hadn't been left entirely unguarded. As Owen picked himself up, a hatch in the ceiling fell open on what sounded like rusty hinges. An ancient-looking Polaroid camera on a broom handle dropped down, turning this way and that like an owl woken from sleep. The broom handle fell further down until the camera was in his face. The flash went off right in his eyes, blinding him. Owen made a swipe for the camera, but as he did so it shot back up into the ceiling, the hatch door banging shut after it with what sounded like an alarmed squawk.

Dr. Diamond would know that he had been there, Owen thought, but it couldn't be helped. He seated himself in the leather seat and looked at the levers. He had watched carefully as Dr. Diamond had manipulated them, and he thought he could make them work. But there might be things that he had not seen. There might be dangers that he had not heard of. Taking a deep breath, he pushed the first lever forward and then the second.

For a moment nothing happened and then, slowly at first, the Skyward began to rotate. He pushed the levers further forward and the Skyward moved faster and faster. He pushed them to their limit and the outside quickly became a blur. There were five other levers. Three went forward and one back and the last one brought the periscope down. Owen looked at them. What if he couldn't stop the machine? What if he got stranded somewhere in time? But he had to go back to the time he had seen before. He had to find out what had happened to the Mortmain. Quickly, before he had time to change his mind, he manipulated the first four levers, then pressed the last one. The periscope began to descend from the ceiling. When it got to him, he folded out the handles. Gulping a little, he put his face to the eyepiece.

For a moment there was the same nothingness Owen had seen before. Then his mother's face appeared; not the sad, worn face that he had seen so often in the past few years, but a face in which a secret smile still lingered. She was looking at something that he could not see, but he was sure it was his father. Other images floated in as he turned the handles—his school, a toy car lying in the yard. His thoughts were drifting when suddenly an image of a man came into view—a man holding a knife, his face covered in blood and a look of terror on his face as he backed away from an unknown enemy. Quickly Owen spun the handles and the man faded away. Concentrate, he thought. That was what Dr. Diamond had said.

He tried to summon the image of the dull golden object spinning away from the car. He turned the handles slowly and a landscape of scrubby trees came into view. There were old tires and broken windscreens and bits of engine scattered among the trees. He concentrated again, willing the picture to open out. He saw wrecked boats, piles of rusty scrap, and oil cans. There was something familiar about it. . . . Then it came to him. It was Johnston's yard! And just as this realization sprang into his mind a car appeared; a silver Alfa Romeo, his father's car, the passenger door flapping open, speeding toward the yard gate, and behind it Johnston aiming a rifle and squeezing off shots. The car had almost reached the gate; it only had to turn sharply left to avoid an old truck chassis. But as Owen's father turned the wheel the passenger door was thrown violently open and something dull and golden slid off the seat, through the open door, and bounced off into the piles of scrap.

The Mortmain! Owen thought.

The car slowed down. A bullet struck the roof and ricocheted off. His father looked into the back, and Owen saw a small figure in a baby seat and knew that he was seeing himself. His father turned back to the wheel and the car sped out of the yard, leaving the Mortmain behind. A moment later Johnston and several other men sped after him in a truck, passing by the spot where the Mortmain had fallen without slowing.

The Mortmain. Somehow it had been in his father's possession, but he had lost it and now it was somewhere in Johnston's yard. Owen shut his eyes and tried to fix the spot in his mind. There was a pile of broken batteries and the hulk of a steel boat in a trailer to the left of the spot. He opened his eyes and recoiled in fear. It seemed that he was staring right into Johnston's eyes, which burned as they glared at him, the man's face filling the screen.

Terrified, Owen spun the handle until Johnston disappeared. He was about to stop searching, but something made him look at one more image, one that he wished he hadn't seen. Cati was standing on what seemed like an island. The wind tore at her hair. He couldn't see what she was looking at, but tears ran down her cheeks and her face was a mask of grief. Before he could focus in on her, the image started to slip away. Fearing that Johnston's face might come up again, Owen tore his gaze away from the eyepiece and pushed the handles back into place. Working quickly, but trying to remember the right sequence, he pulled the levers back into place. The periscope slid back into the ceiling and gradually the Skyward slowed and came to a halt.

Owen tried to leave things as he had found them. Dr. Diamond would know he had been there, of course, but perhaps not immediately. Moving quickly, he slipped outside and down the steps. He did not want to miss anything of what was happening at the Convoke.

At the bottom of the stairs he ran toward the door of the Starry. He couldn't be seen at the Convoke. He would climb to the little gallery that Cati had shown him, and for that he needed to go through the Starry.

He opened the door and slipped inside. The place was as he remembered it, quiet, as if the quiet had accumulated over centuries, the starlit glow of the ceiling throwing a gentle light on to those who slept on below. Owen had a strange feeling that he was not alone in the place, or at least that he was not the only person awake in the Starry.

He crept quietly forward until he reached the middle of the floor. At the other end he saw a woman bending over one of the beds. Creeping closer, Owen saw that it was Pieta. She was standing over a boy and a girl. The boy was about ten years old and the girl was perhaps fourteen. Pieta was gently brushing the girl's hair. Both children were rosy-cheeked and peaceful but they showed no sign of waking. It was a private moment and Owen tried to slip away, but as he did so, the magno gun hanging forgotten over his shoulder clanked against an empty bed. Pieta's head snapped round.

"Who is it?" she said in a low, dangerous voice. "Who is there?"

"It's me, Owen," he said, feeling unaccountably guilty.

"What are you doing here?"

"I was on my way to . . ." He hesitated, but something told him that it would not be a good idea to lie to Pieta. "I was on my way up to the little balcony so that I could watch the Convoke without being seen."

"Without being seen," she said softly, and he thought he sensed a bleak smile in the darkness. "Come here." Owen walked over until he was standing beside Pieta. "Look at me."

Owen's eyes met hers. They were green and fathomless. She held his gaze for a moment, then her eyes dropped away to the two children. They had the same white skin and fine bone structure as their mother.

"You are going to spy on the Convoke?"

"I'm not a spy!" he said hotly.

"No?" she said. "I suppose you're not. You just don't want them to stare at you, not knowing whether you are bringing good or evil to them." Owen nodded dumbly.

"And sometimes it's hard to know your own heart," she continued, "and whether you are a good person or a bad person." Her voice had dropped and it seemed as if she was talking to herself. For a moment the fierce warrior dropped away and she just seemed like a mother gazing on her sleeping children with love in her eyes.

Without thinking, and not really understanding what he was doing, Owen reached out and placed the palm of each hand on the forehead of each child. Pieta watched him. There was a question in her eyes, but she didn't try to stop him. He took his hands away and stood up. He waited for her to say something, but those strange green eyes merely studied him.

Owen turned away from her. He felt very tired. He started to walk away but stumbled slightly. Pieta's hand caught his elbow. He recovered his balance and continued to walk toward the stairwell leading to the little balcony. He could feel her eyes on his back all the way.

Owen took the stairs two at a time and his legs were aching by the time he ducked through the little door and rolled out onto the balcony. He could tell straightaway that the Convoke was tense. Samual faced the others. Chancellor looked troubled, as did Contessa. The Sub-Commandant's face was harder to read.

"Look what damage they did in one attack," Samual was saying. "They nearly overran us. We can't hold out. Now is the time, when we hold a little of the upper hand, to seek terms."

"So that Johnston can put us back to Sleep, and then kill us where we lie? Is that what you're saying, Samual?" said Contessa softly.

"The offer of Sleep was a negotiating ploy!" Samual said. "We can force Johnston to improve his offer, give guarantees of our safety."

There was a murmur of approval from the crowd. Owen looked at them for the first time. Many of them were injured, some of them still wearing bloodstained clothing. They looked tired and frightened. He could see that the prospect of another attack filled them with dread.

"I'm not letting no Harsh put me to sleep, I do tell you that for nothing!" Wesley had been standing quietly in the crowd but now he strode forward.

"Me neither," Cati said bravely, her cheeks reddening as people turned to stare.

Samual snorted. "This is what I mean. We can't turn back an attack with a half-dressed boy and a skinny girl."

The Sub-Commandant's cool stare fell on him. "No matter how courageous," Samual added.

"I'm with the youngsters." Rutgar was gruff. "My men and women will stand as long as there is breath in them!" The words were brave, Owen thought, but Rutgar's eyes were red-rimmed and there was a bloodstained bandage on his head.

"These are issues that need to be discussed," Chancellor said. "We cannot decide them overnight. Perhaps the Mortmain can be found."

"The Mortmain should never have been lost . . . or stolen," said Samual slyly.

"It was never stolen!" Cati cried. "And the only reason it was lost was because he was trying to save—" She was interrupted by a loud bang followed by an alarming fizzing noise coming from the direction of Dr. Diamond's leather baseball cap. Dr. Diamond took the cap off. Wisps of smoke rose from it.

"Direction finder," he mumbled. "Prototype . . . needs work."

"I think we should end the Convoke," the Sub-Commandant said. "We all need food and rest. It will take Johnston a few days to regroup, at any rate."

Chancellor nodded in agreement. Samual didn't say anything but he tilted his head at Cati and seemed to study her. The malfunctioning baseball cap had stopped Cati saying too much about what Owen had seen . . . if indeed it had been a malfunction. But Samual knew now that she had information about the Mortmain. Owen rolled off the balcony and ran down the stairs. He wanted to be well clear of the Workhouse before the Convoke emerged. He was worried about what he had seen. Samual wanted them to come to terms with Johnston and at least some of the people backed him. The Mortmain had to be found if the Workhouse and its Resisters were not to be surrendered. There was no sign of Pieta in the Starry and he ran lightly through it, not wishing to feel sleepy, particularly now.

Outside it was dark and Owen was surprised that he had spent so much time watching the Convoke. The night air made him shiver. It was much colder suddenly. He made his way back to the Den without meeting anyone. There he packed some food he had set aside, slightly stale bread and a little pie. On the bed lay a coat. Someone had been here. He picked it up. It was made out of leather, lined with some kind of silky fleece. It had a hood like a parka, lined as well. It was heavy and didn't smell as good as it might have done, but he remembered the cold outside

163

and slipped it on. Owen stood in the middle of the Den and looked around. He wondered if he would ever see it again. He put the bag containing the food over his shoulder and lifted the magno gun. He walked through the door and out onto the path, where he turned toward the river. As he did so a single snowflake touched his face. He shivered and pulled the coat closer around him.

There was a different quality to the cold, Owen thought, that told you that it was more than just a dip in temperature, that it was here to stay.

He stayed clear of the log bridge. He knew it would be guarded. But he thought there was another way across the river, a little way downstream toward the harbor. Using the debris of the attack for cover, he skirted the Resister defenses, coming so close he could hear them talking quietly.

After ten minutes' walk, most of it bent double or on his hands and knees so that his back ached, he arrived at the place he had seen from the Nab. A tall pine tree had been struck by the magno cannon at ground level. The tree hadn't fallen, but it leaned over the river at an improbable angle and the very tip of it hung over the opposite bank. He didn't know how he was going to get down from it, but at least he would be on the other side. Pulling the parka tightly around him, he started to climb.

The tree didn't feel at all secure. If he moved too fast, it swayed from side to side and up and down, so he felt seasick. And once, when he got to the middle, he felt the roots shift and the whole tree drop by several meters. Fear welled in his stomach as he saw the black water below. Owen clung to the tree trunk for several minutes before he was able to force himself onward. As the tree narrowed toward the top, it became harder to climb until in the end he reached a point where he could go no farther without his weight snapping the slender trunk. Yet he was still about seven meters in the air, unsure as to whether there was water beneath him or the dry land of the opposite bank.

Owen hung there quietly, trying not to look at the water and scanning the bank for signs of Johnston's men. He could see no one, nor had he seen anything from the Nab. They'd retreated right back as far as the area around the scrapyard. Owen looked down. If he let go, he might just land on the bank. But then again he might land in the water. And if he landed on the bank from the height he was at, he might break a leg or an arm and then he'd be helpless. The tree had been a bad idea all along. There was no way he could get to the opposite bank unseen. With a sigh he started to inch back until, with a terrifying creak, the roots let go.

Owen seemed to be in the air for ages, the ground rushing up toward him. Long enough for him to see that he was going to hit the ground and not the water. Long enough for him to realize, with a blinding flash, that he was scared of the water not because he was Harsh but because he had come close to drowning as a baby. "Idiot," he muttered to himself, just as the the frozen, rock-hard soil of the bank rushed up and met him. And then he was aware of nothing more.

At the moment Owen lost consciousness, something else happened. In the warm dark of the Starry there was a stirring. Slow at first, an eyelid flickering, a change in the slow breathing of one who had Slept for perhaps hundreds of years. And then something more definite. A leg moving, a hand opening—a girl's hand. Then eyes opening—the same strange green eyes as those of Pieta, first one pair and then another. And then the slender girl who had been sleeping under her mother's watchful gaze that morning sat up, stretched, yawned, and turned to smile at her brother as he too stirred and yawned.

Owen opened his eyes. He was lying on his back staring up at the night sky and his first thought was that he had never seen so many stars nor seen them so clearly, each of them sharply defined and seeming to rain light down on him. His head was pounding and his limbs were aching and he felt as if he was lying on a very springy bed. But he knew that he couldn't be because it was freezing cold. He turned over onto his side, moving carefully, and realized that the springy bed was in fact the branches of a pine tree—and then it came back to him, how the tree had fallen and he had fallen with it. The pine branches had cushioned his fall.

Very carefully Owen got to his feet. His head felt like

somebody had hit it with a hammer, his right arm was so bruised he could barely move it, and it took a few minutes to get his legs working properly again, but he was across the river and that was the important thing. He stepped out of the tangle of branches and tried to get his bearings. Most of the fields that had been here had turned to dense forest, but he had a good idea of how to get to Johnston's yard, providing he didn't run into any of Johnston's men on the way. Owen made his way toward the edge of the trees. As he did so, he heard a soft whirring sound in the air high above his head. He threw himself facedown and lay as still as he could until it had faded into the distance. He didn't know if the Planemen could see in the dark, but he didn't want to take any chances. Cautiously, he got to his feet and slipped soundlessly into the forest.

Cati didn't know what to do with herself. She had gone up to the Nab and got under Dr. Diamond's feet. He had sent her to the kitchen to get some flour for him, but she knew that he was really trying to get rid of her. She hung about the kitchen until Contessa told her that the kitchen was a place for working, not mooching, and there were injured fighters who needed to be tended to if she really wanted something to do. Cati was miserable without Owen and she knew that she should go to the Den and make things better. But that would mean saying she was wrong, and Cati did not like saying she was wrong. Particularly when she knew she was right.

She was going out of the front door of the Workhouse when she met the Sub-Commandant.

"Come with me quickly," he said. "There's something I want you to see." He walked on without waiting to see if she was following. Shaking off her mood, Cati hurried after.

The Sub-Commandant threw open the doors of the Convoke and strode in. Pieta was sitting by the fire on her own. There were several bottles on top of the fireplace and her eyes were bleary when she looked up. The Sub-Commandant walked quickly over to her. He went down on one knee and started speaking urgently into her ear. Her head straightened. She looked at him with what seemed to Cati like distrust. Her father spoke again. Taking Pieta by the hand, he made her rise to her feet and led her gently across the hall. She stumbled several times, but the night air outside seemed to revive her.

They went round the side of the Workhouse to the little door of the Starry, where the Sub-Commandant stopped. Almost hesitantly, Pieta went in ahead. Cati stood in the doorway beside her father. Almost against her will she took his hand, something she had not done since she was a small child. As her eyes got used to the gloom of the Starry she saw a boy and a girl holding hands. They were smiling shyly. Pieta knelt in front of them, making small sounds of wonder. The two children dashed toward Pieta and flung their arms round her neck. The Sub-Commandant, smiling, drew Cati backward, closing the door gently behind him.

"That's not for us to watch," he said gently. His hand held Cati's tightly. They walked in silence.

"Are they her children?" Cati asked.

"Yes. They fell asleep many, many years ago and did not wake, and the pain and the bitterness gnawed at Pieta."

"What will happen now?"

"I hope she will be healed. And if she is healed, she may not be the great fighter that she was. But no matter. Without the Mortmain we haven't much of a chance anyway."

"But we do have a chance?" Cati said anxiously.

"There's always a chance," said the Sub-Commandant, seeing her anxiety. "We have fought the Harsh many times and each time we've held the line. Now," he went on, "what about young Owen? How is he getting on?"

"Well . . . ," Cati began. The Sub-Commandant noticed her hesitation.

"What is it?" he said.

"We had a fight," she said, her voice low.

"Tell me about it." He didn't look at her, but Cati could tell that he wasn't pleased. She told him what had happened. How Owen had doubted his own father and how she had stuck up for the man. The Sub-Commandant sighed.

"You have to understand, Cati. So many things have let Owen down, including his sense of reality. Even time has let him down. Then people tell him that his father is a thief. Worse than a thief. A traitor. He's angry and bewildered and he blames his father. He thought that his father had killed himself. Dr. Diamond thinks that he did not and I agree. But either way, Owen feels abandoned."

"I think I understand," said Cati slowly, "and I should have kept my big mouth shut."

"Exactly," the Sub-Commandant said firmly. "Now, what we have to do is to go to the Den and see Owen, and make sure that he doesn't go to sleep miserable. Do you think that's a good idea?" Her father's tone was light, but Cati knew that she wasn't really being asked a question. She nodded without speaking, and they turned away from the Workhouse and onto the path to the Den.

Her father knew straightaway that something was wrong. He paused at the entrance to the Den and Cati saw his eyes narrow. With one hand on the weapon at his waist he crept forward, Cati following. He went through the little entryway and held up his weapon, his finger on the trigger so that it emitted a low, blue light, enough to illuminate the scene of devastation. Owen's sleeping bag and sofa had been torn apart and the contents strewn over the floor, which itself was full of holes as if someone had been digging in search of something. Loose stones had been ripped from the walls, and the car radio and lorry wing mirror had been smashed to pieces.

Cati found candles in the debris and lit them. The Sub-Commandant examined the scene with great care.

"Is there anything missing?" he asked.

"Not that I can think of," Cati replied. "It's hard to tell. Have they taken Owen?"

"I don't think so. There's no sign of a struggle. Just a search."

"What were they looking for?"

"The same thing we are. The Mortmain. Which is good."

"How can this be good?" Cati said, looking at the mess around her.

"It's good because it means that the Mortmain is still lost. If the Harsh got their hands on it then the end would be near."

He took one of the candles and began to examine the walls of the Den.

"Where is it, then?" asked Cati.

"If it fell from the car at Johnston's, then the chances are that it is still there, among the scrap, unless . . ." His voice trailed off.

"Unless what?" said Cati impatiently.

"Unless someone picked it up by mistake," the Sub-Commandant said slowly. "Unless they mistook it for something else." He bent to pick up an object.

Cati could not see what he was looking at. She ducked round the broken sofa until she was standing beside him. The Sub-Commandant was turning the object over and over in his hands, something with a dull gleam.

"That's only an old boat propeller!" Cati exclaimed. "Owen picked it up at Johnston's scrapyard. . . ." Her voice trailed off as she realized what she was saying.

"Is it?" the Sub-Commandant said, almost under his

breath, and his eyes gleamed in the candlelight. "Is it only an old propeller? Look!" He thrust the object under her nose. There were three blades just like a propeller, but the round hole in the middle, where the driveshaft would have gone, did not look like it belonged to an ordinary propeller. It had been etched and grooved in patterns that seemed at once completely random and very precise, and when you moved the object a line would seem to disappear and reappear somewhere else, some of the lines running to the edge of the round hole and seeming to pour out of it like liquid; others were like moving shadowlines that you could only see out of the corner of your eye but which disappeared when you looked straight at them.

"It is, isn't it?" whispered Cati.

"It is the Mortmain," her father said, his eyes bright with amazement. "Owen had it here all along and did not know it."

He turned it over in his hands again and Cati gazed on it, astonished at the way it transformed itself from a piece of tarnished metal into a marvelous object, gleaming with hidden fire and meaning, then mutating back into an old propeller.

"What do we do?"

"It's not for us to decide. There will have to be a Convoke."

"What do you think?"

"I think that in this case the Mortmain is a kind of a

key. I think it is the key to the Great Machine in the north. Someone will have to take it there, is my guess, and use it to stop the Machine."

"Who will take it?"

The Sub-Commandant hesitated. A cold breeze blew through the Den and Cati shivered. "It should have been Owen," he said finally. "It should have been. History dictates it. But something warns me that it will not be. That Owen is already gone."

"Gone where?"

"I saw him earlier, going toward the river. I thought he was going to see Wesley at the harbor. I should have gone after him."

"Gone where?" Cati insisted.

"They say that the sins of a father should not be visited on the son, but I'm afraid sometimes they are. I think Owen has crossed the river to look for the Mortmain."

Owen found it hard going in the trees. It was dense, old-growth forest. The trees were gnarled and mossy, and half-rotten trunks lay across his path, hidden by undergrowth, so that he stumbled often. Ivy and creepers hung down, brushing his face like cold hands, making him jump. And there were noises as well. An owl hooting, a nightjar, and strange rustling noises. Once something large pushed through the undergrowth near him and he stood very still and held his breath until it had gone. He didn't know what it was, but he noted that it wasn't afraid to make noise.

It was about a mile to Johnston's house, and before time went backward it would have taken Owen fifteen minutes walking through open fields. But now he had been in the forest for over an hour. The branches of the trees were bare, but little starlight filtered through them. After three-quarters of an hour he had stumbled out onto a well-used path. He knew that he couldn't take it, that it was probably the route used by Johnston's men to get to the riverbank. It was too risky, so he backed into the woods again and tried to steer a course close to the path, but far enough away so that a passing patrol would not hear him crashing through the undergrowth.

As he pushed on, his face scratched by twigs and his muscles aching from the fall from the pine tree, Owen thought about Cati. He regretted quarreling with her. He had few enough friends in the Workhouse as it was. And if he hadn't quarreled with her, she would be with him now. Then perhaps it was a good thing they had fallen out, he thought grimly. His father had lost the Mortmain and it was up to Owen to get it back, not Cati. Still, he wished he had someone who would make a joke or talk. Anything to help lighten the gloom of the forest.

He pushed on, more and more slowly, bumping into tree trunks, briars wrapping themselves round his legs so he had to stop and unwind them. It was almost as if the forest was alive and full of malice. An image of Dr. Diamond came into Owen's head and he almost laughed out loud. He wondered how Dr. Diamond would react if you asked him for the right time. The answer wouldn't be simple. A cold wind rattled the branches above and Owen wished that he was back in Dr. Diamond's Skyward. Then he thought that Dr. Diamond would be angry with him for breaking into the Skyward and using the machine.

The full loneliness of his position became clear. Rutgar would be mad at him for getting through his defenses and crossing the river. The Sub-Commandant would side with Cati. Samual hated him anyway. Chancellor seemed to think of him as a mere boy and his father's son at that. Contessa, he thought. Perhaps Contessa would speak up for him. And Wesley, even if it was only for the sake of annoying the others. It wouldn't be enough, Owen knew. Even if he had the Mortmain, it wouldn't be enough. And if he returned without it, they would surely brand him a spy. He sighed.

After another half an hour he started to slow. The undergrowth was getting thinner and Owen took that as a sign he was reaching the edge of the forest. He didn't want to stumble into one of Johnston's patrols. After a few minutes he could see lights through the trees and then he was at the edge of the forest. He could see that the trees in front of him had been slashed and burned to create a clearing. Owen crept forward to the very edge of the trees and knew that the light he had seen was Johnston's house, far bigger than he had remembered, although it had been hidden behind trees. But there were no trees this time and the huge manor dominated the ground around it. All the windows blazed with magno light. To the left of the massive front doors were French windows, larger even than the doors. These lay open and music drifted out. The house resembled an ocean liner sailing through the night.

To his right, he could see a large encampment of tents, laid out like a small town with streets between blocks of tents, and open spaces. For cooking, he thought, for large fires blazed here and there. The streets were strewn with rubbish, and Owen wrinkled his nose at the smell drifting toward him. To his left, he could see the place where the scrapyard had been, but little of the scrap remained. All that was left were bits of brass, old fenders, copper water tanks. That was where he had to go.

Before Owen had a chance to move, he heard voices. He ducked back into the trees as two men walked past. They were both tough-looking, with the long sideburns that Johnston's men wore. One of them had a rose behind his ear, although where he had got a rose in winter Owen could not tell. He waited until the two men had gone, then started to edge through the trees toward the scrap. He knew he would have to cross the open ground, but he meant to get as close as possible before he did so. The wind, which he had barely felt in the forest, was stronger now, and the treetops shuddered and shook. He felt small icy particles stinging his face. Owen moved quickly, the noise of the trees masking his passage, and within a minute he was level with the scrap. He could see a copse of small scrubby trees growing in the middle of it. Once he got there, he thought, he could get his bearings and see if he could work out where the Mortmain might have fallen when it was thrown from his father's car.

He crouched at the edge of the trees, looking up and down. He couldn't see anyone coming. The icy wind carried a burst of harsh laughter down from the tent town, and somewhere, faintly, he could still hear the music coming from the open French windows. He tried to gauge the distance, perhaps two hundred meters, exposed to anyone who might come out of the tent village, and overlooked by Johnston's manor. A great gust of wind brought a fine cloud of icy particles and for a moment the house and village were obscured. Owen thought it had to be now. He exploded from the trees, arms and legs pumping.

It was farther than he thought. Much farther. And the icy blast that had helped hide him died down before he was halfway across. He felt terribly exposed and the trees seemed to get no nearer. Owen waited for the shout of a guard, heavy feet running behind him. He felt the blood pounding in his ears and his breath was coming in great shuddering gasps. Stumbling, almost weeping, he fell into the shelter of the trees. He lay still, fighting for breath, his sides aching. He couldn't remember ever having run so fast. His heart thumped madly, but gradually he was able to get his breath and sit up cautiously.

Owen had a mental picture of the way the scrapyard

had looked when the Mortmain had fallen from the car. The driveway from the house still led through the scrap and the sharp corner where the door had swung open was still there, perhaps a hundred meters away. If he went on his hands and knees, he thought, or crawled on his belly, he could reach it. He moved to the edge of the trees. And as he moved he felt as if a great shadow was falling over him, and then a crushing weight, so that he was pinned to the ground. He struggled and then lay still. Rough hands turned him over. He found himself looking into the dark, fathomless eyes of the man he had seen earlier, the rose still behind his ear. Owen could smell an oily perfume, and the man's voice when he spoke was low and strangely accented.

"Now, Pretty," he said, "still yourself. Where is Pretty going? What is Pretty looking for? I think we must talk with Johnston. Johnston will know."

13

The Convoke was crowded, but there was little noise. Shadows from the fire danced round the ancient walls. The Mortmain was on a low table in front of the fire, gleaming softly. The Resister leaders stood round it. All, that is, except Pieta. She sat in her usual chair by the fire. But this time she wasn't slumped with a bottle. This time her back was straight and her eyes were bright and each hand rested on the shoulder of a child, a tall yellow-haired girl and a solemn yellow-haired boy, each with a look in their eyes that said that they had lived in their dreams for many, many years.

"The first thing we must say," Chancellor began, "even before we start our discussion on what must be done, is how glad we are that Pieta's children have awoken from their long sleep."

There was a murmur of agreement from the crowd. Pieta did not smile, but her eyes flashed and the children seemed to stand even more ramrod straight, proud and haughty like their mother.

"I agree," the Sub-Commandant said, "but time is short. We must decide what to do with the Mortmain."

"There is only one decision," Pieta said, "and well you know it, Sub-Commandant. The Mortmain must be taken to the Puissance, the Great Machine in the north, and a way must be found to reverse it so that time flows the way it should."

"I agree," the Sub-Commandant said.

"I agree also," said Contessa. Rutgar nodded sharply, and Dr. Diamond too. Wesley looked amused at the prospect. Even Samual did not disagree.

"Well, then," Chancellor said, "we have agreed that much. The next question is, who will go?"

"Owen must go," Contessa said. "It is his duty and his right." Chancellor looked uncomfortable.

"What is it, Chancellor?" asked the Sub-Commandant.

"I fear I have bad news about Owen."

"He is gone," the Sub-Commandant said. "I knew that."

"That is not all," Chancellor said, his tone grave. "Not only has he left, but he has gone over to Johnston's side."

There was a gasp from the hall. Cati cried out, "No!" Samual looked pleased. The only person who did not react was Wesley. He kept the same sardonic smile on his face.

"How do you know this, Chancellor?" said Contessa.

"I am not at liberty to say who gave me this information," Chancellor said, his voice dense with sorrow, "but Owen was seen on the other side of the river—with Johnston. And Johnston had his arm around his shoulders. Owen was smiling."

"A spy all along," Samual said with satisfaction.

"No!" Cati shouted, jumping to her feet. "Owen was never a spy!" She burst into tears. People stared at her, but no one moved to comfort her. It was Wesley who walked over and put his arm round her, gently putting her back into her seat.

"This is grave news," Contessa said. "I find it hard to believe."

"I had difficulty believing it myself," agreed Chancellor.

"Like father, like son," Samual said. Cati leapt to her feet again, her face red, but Wesley hauled her back down in her seat and put his finger to his lips. She stared furiously at Samual but didn't speak.

Wesley leaned over to her. "Had to of been that Samual that made up thon story about Owen and fed it to Chancellor. He's the only one crosses the river for to spy." Cati intensified her glare at Samual.

Wesley noticed that Dr. Diamond was now sitting beside Pieta, talking urgently into her ear.

"I think we should not judge until we have had a chance to speak to the young man," the Sub-Commandant said firmly. "The point is that Owen should have been the one to take the Mortmain to the Puissance. Now he cannot, so who is to take it?"

There was a long silence. The Sub-Commandant waited patiently. When an answer came, it was from an unexpected source.

"Big snows coming," Wesley said lazily. "Looks like you lot will need Boat. So that'll be me going for a start."

"I'm going too," said Cati defiantly.

"The child can't go," Samual said. "She'll get all of you into trouble if she runs into any of the Harsh."

"I'm not a child!" Cati said.

"Where I go, Cati goes," the Sub-Commandant said.

"I think I'll go along too," said Dr. Diamond. Rutgar started to speak, but Contessa stopped him.

"Someone will need to stay here and defend the Workhouse, Rutgar. I think that is our job." Rutgar nodded heavily.

"I will go also," Chancellor said. "I have a responsibility in this matter."

"You done pretty well making up them minds of yours," said Wesley, getting to his feet. "I'd say we should be fit to go first thing in the morning, if youse lot can get yourselves ready by then."

"He's right," the Sub-Commandant said. "The sooner the better. The weather is closing in."

"I'll get a stock of food together," Contessa said. "You'll need plenty to get you there and back."

"There, anyhow," Wesley muttered. "There mightn't be no back."

"Does anybody know how far it is?" asked Cati quietly.

"No," answered the Sub-Commandant, "nor has anyone here ever seen the Puissance."

"Owen would have been able to find it," Contessa said.

"That is open to question," the Sub-Commandant said. "Nothing has been proved."

"Owen is not here," Chancellor said, his voice harsh, "and I do not wish to hear his name spoken again. He has betrayed us. So our only option is to sail north and hope that luck leads us to it, or we find other Resisters who know where it is."

Wesley jumped to his feet. "Youse lot might have time for chatter, but us lot got Boat to get ready. I'll see youse at dawn at the harbor." He turned and slipped rapidly through the crowd, but not before he gave Cati a warm look.

Cati didn't know why Wesley had stood up for her. Or why he had stopped her speaking. She had the impression there were things going on that she didn't understand. The Convoke was breaking up and Cati allowed herself to be carried along by the crowd as they swept out of the room, talking excitedly about the voyage to come and about how the young man had been a spy all along, falling silent when they realized that Cati could hear. She thought of unleashing a stream of bad language at them, words she had picked up from Rutgar and his soldiers, but her heart wasn't in it. As the crowd passed the doorway that led to the kitchen, she stepped inside.

The kitchen was her favorite place at night, when everyone had finished. Cati liked the dim light, the gleaming pots lined up behind the stoves, the heat still retained in the giant ovens. Sometimes she would take a leftover piece of pie from the cold room and squeeze in behind the biggest of the ovens, where it was warm. When she was small she had called it her house. She was too old for that now, but it was still a safe place to go when she had something on her mind. Also, since her encounter with the Harsh, she seemed to be a little cold all the time, and this was the warmest and coziest place in the entire Workhouse. And she definitely had something on her mind.

Cati squeezed into the tiny space and leaned her cheek against the warm stone. Why had Owen been with Johnston? If he was such great friends with Johnston, then who had ransacked the Den? And if he was not with Johnston, then where was he? Her father had thought that Owen had gone searching for the Mortmain. Was Owen playing some game, pretending to be friendly with Johnston?

The heat of the oven was making Cati drowsy. She felt

her eyes start to close and had to shake herself awake. She didn't want to fall asleep behind the ovens. As she started to wriggle out of the space, she heard footsteps. Contessa, she thought, coming to prepare food for the journey the next day. Then she realized there were two sets of feet. The footsteps stopped close to the oven. The first voice she heard was Contessa's.

"You are sure about this course of action? It will be hard on the children."

"I have explained to them," replied the low, harsh voice of Pieta. "They understand that I have to repay my debt."

"What if Owen has gone over to the other side?"

"Do you think so? He can wake the Sleepers. It points to him being the Navigator. And if he is, he can find the Puissance. That is our only chance."

"Other people have come along who could wake the Sleeping."

"I have to try. He woke my children when no one else could. I have to find him or at least find out what happened. You will be the guardian of the children, if you will do it."

"Of course I will, Pieta," Contessa said.

"Take care of them, Contessa." There was a pleading note in Pieta's voice that Cati did not associate with the stern warrior. "They have slept for so long and are still half in the shadows."

"I will treat them as if they were my own," said Contessa.

The two women moved away, still talking, but Cati could not hear them anymore. She slipped out from behind the oven and went past the sinks so that they wouldn't see her. Supplies for tomorrow, she thought as she ran silently up the steps. She had almost forgotten about the long journey to the north. She shivered, half from excitement, half from fear. And then there was the word that Pieta had used about Owen. She said it over and over in her head. Navigator . . . Navigator . . . What did it mean? And if he was the Navigator, did it mean that he had not crossed over to the enemy? And what was Pieta planning, in order to pay back her debt to Owen?

Several miles away, Owen was shivering too, but not with excitement. The man with the rose behind his ear had grabbed him by the sleeves and started walking toward Johnston's manor. He walked at an unbelievable speed and, Owen found, was incredibly strong, for when Owen tripped and fell, the man kept up the same rapid pace, dragging the boy behind him effortlessly. The man marched Owen straight to the front door of the manor, which opened as he approached it. Owen half staggered, half tumbled up the steps, cracking his shins on the stone.

The door swung open onto a long corridor. There were more of Johnston's men in the corridor, lounging around on battered chairs and looking bored. Weapons were stacked everywhere: magno guns, knives, hatchets, bicycle chains, bottles containing what looked suspiciously like acid. The men watched with interest as Owen was hauled down the corridor at tremendous speed, making comments as he passed.

"Passionara caught himself a rat, so he did."

"Fine big rat."

"What you say, rat?"

"Catch yourself on, Mariacallas. Rat don't talk."

"Rat do big squeak."

"Go on, rat, do squeak." This last was accompanied by a hard kick that made Owen gasp.

"Weren't no squeak, that."

"Sounds like a boy to me."

It would have been a relief when Passionara stopped in front of a large ornate door if Owen hadn't felt twice as scared of what lay behind it. It was something important, he knew, because there was a fat, grizzled man with a white beard sitting at a battered card table. He was wearing a bandanna and a sweat-stained cummerbund. There was a ledger on the table and he opened it as Passionara and Owen came to a halt.

"Name?" he said in a harsh voice.

"You know my name, Whitwashisberd," Passionara said.

"Not your name, you damned wearer of flowers," Whitwashisberd growled. "Name of fancy rat you dangle from your honeyed fist."

"Name of fancy rat is . . . Pretty!" Passionara said. But the corridor had other ideas.

"Rat!" they roared. "Rat! Rat! Rat!"

"Name of boy is . . . Pretty Rat!" Passionara exclaimed,

to a chorus of cheers from the corridor. Whitwashisberd grunted, but bent to the ledger and laboriously wrote "Pretty Rat" in the first free space. Craning his neck, Owen could see that the ledger was crowded with names, most of them, worryingly, crossed out, with a small skull drawn in beside them. Then, with a bored expression, Whitwashisberd waved Owen and Passionara through.

Passionara opened the door, and Owen realized that this was the room that the music had been coming from. A battered old record player was playing opera music, an old scratchy recording of a man singing. The ceiling was covered with ornate plasterwork of angels and cherubs and great plaster bunches of grapes dangling in the corners. A massive cut-glass chandelier lit with magno hung from the center of the ceiling. A log fire blazed in the fireplace. The only furniture in the room was a huge black leather reclining armchair. Johnston was sitting in the armchair, sideways on to the door.

Owen had not noticed quite how big Johnston was before, but now it seemed that he filled the room. Everything about him was big: the head, the sideburns, the boots, the great tufts of hair sprouting from his ears and nostrils. His eyes were closed and one massive hand moved gently as if conducting the movement. Passionara stuck his boot in Owen's backside and propelled him into the middle of the room, where he landed on his hands and knees. Behind him, Owen could hear the door closing gently. Johnston held up a hand. Owen understood. He wasn't to interrupt the music.

Owen stayed on his hands and knees for what seemed like hours, although it could only have been minutes. The music swelled and died away, swelled and died away, then swelled again until it reached a crescendo, then gently and finally died away. There was a long silence broken only by the needle scratching round the old record. Finally Johnston opened his eyes.

"Caruso," he said. Owen looked at him, not knowing what he was talking about. "At La Scala," said Johnston, as if that explained everything. He got up and moved swiftly over to Owen, towering over the boy. He reached down and grasped Owen's chin and raised him to his feet, tilting his head back until he looked directly into his eyes. Johnston's eyes were dark brown with gold flecks and full of life, like the eyes of a hunting animal. Owen felt that he was being probed for weaknesses. The man smelled of garlic and engine oil. Like a French garage mechanic, he thought, and fought the urge to break out in hysterical giggles. But it was Johnston who smiled. He straightened and with a flicking motion sent Owen sprawling across the room.

"The mirror was a good trick," he said, showing great tombstone teeth in a ferocious smile.

"Wh-what?" Owen stammered.

"The mirror. The way you turned the ice light back on the Harsh. Never seen them so put out. Sent them scuttling back north like old maids with their skirts hitched."

"I thought you . . ."

"What? Worked for the Harsh? So I do. But it's contract work, son. You don't have to love them to work for them. Do you know what a Harsh lacks, son? A Harsh lacks a sense of humor. It can get a bit dull around them. They'll win in the end, though, and there won't be much laughing then."

"If they win, that's the end of you too, isn't it?" Owen said.

"Me and the boys is took care of—that's part of the deal. Them Harsh can work time the way a man works a hand of cards. Your Dr. Diamond plays at it, but he's not a patch on the Harsh. Look around you. Time don't change much here, and that's what they done for me. I got myself an island in time."

Owen looked around. It was true. The manor seemed to have experienced no decay. Even Johnston's record player would have ended up as a heap of nuts and bolts if it had been outside.

"Anyway, enough chatting," said Johnston, and suddenly his voice sounded grim. "What are you doing here? And where is the Mortmain?"

"I don't know what you're talking about," Owen said, his voice sounding unconvincing to his own ears. "I came over the river to go to my own house and I got lost."

"Your own house is nothing but a few moldy bricks on top of each other by now, son, and well you know it. No. I know why you're here. You think your father left the

Mortmain here somewhere and you've come to retrieve it. Well, I've a hundred men scouring the ground outside at this very minute. Old Gobillard and his box of tricks couldn't best me, so don't think that a whippersnapper of a boy can."

Owen felt his heart sink. He had crossed the river to retrieve the Mortmain and he had ended up by handing it to Johnston on a plate. And that name again, Gobillard. The box of tricks Johnston referred to—could that be the chest in his room?

Johnston took Owen by the scruff of the neck and propelled him toward the door, which opened. Whitwashisberd looked up at Johnston with a question in his eyes. Owen saw that the pen was poised by his name, just at the place where a skull had been drawn in beside the other names. But Johnston shook his head.

"We're going north tomorrow," he said, "and we're taking this one with us. The Harsh want a cold word or two with him."

For some reason this provoked great mirth among the men in the corridor, and they started to chant. "Pretty Rat! Pretty Rat! Pretty Rat!"

Taking a great key from his belt, Johnston opened an iron-bound door in the opposite wall of the corridor. With a sweep of his hand, he flung Owen through the door and slammed it. Owen tumbled down damp stone stairs and landed with a sickening thud in a pool of water at the bottom. He looked around him. There was only a chink of light from a high barred window, enough to show that he was in an empty stone cellar. A dungeon, he realized, without hope of escape. He had given away the location of the Mortmain and with it the hopes of his friends. And now he was to be handed to the Harsh. Owen buried his head in his hands and felt despair wash over him.

The Sub-Commandant woke Cati gently before dawn. She wrapped up well and grabbed a slice of warm bread and jam from the kitchen, but still she shivered in the cold predawn air. In silence they walked down the river toward the harbor, the Sub-Commandant softly greeting the people coming the other way, Contessa's porters, who had been bringing food for the trip.

The sun was beginning to cast a chilly light by the time they got to the harbor. Boat was tied up by the quayside and the Raggies were loading it, seemingly oblivious to the biting cold. Wesley stood on the bridge with his arms folded. Dr. Diamond was on the quayside with two cases of scientific instruments. He looked excited

and he was trying to get the Raggies to load the instruments.

"I'd better help him," Cati said. Despite everything,
she couldn't help feeling a twinge of excitement at the
voyage ahead.

"Go ahead," said the Sub-Commandant absent-
mindedly, then murmured, "Where is Chancellor?"

After much translation of Dr. Diamond's backward
talk, Cati persuaded the Raggies to load the cases of instruments. Then she went on board herself. She had
never been on Boat before. In fact, she had never been
out on the water before, and it took her a few minutes to
adjust to the slight swaying beneath her feet before she
could take a proper look around.

Boat was about twenty meters long. There was an enclosed wheelhouse, with an outside bridge and another
wheel for fair weather. Beneath the bridge there were
cabins with diamond-pane windows facing out onto the
main deck. There was a forecastle at the front with similar cabins underneath. In the middle of Boat was the
engine. The cover had been taken off and Silkie was
bent over it. She was wearing her ragged and oily overalls and was working with a spanner in the middle of
the huge jumble of coils and belts and flywheels that
transmitted the power of the magno core to the long,
seemingly spindly oars. As she worked, she was cursing
steadily, emitting a stream of bad language that would
have put Rutgar's troopers to shame. But when she

looked up and saw Cati, her oil-covered face broke into a smile.

"Is everything all right, Silkie?" Cati asked.

"Everything's not all right," said Silkie, scowling again. "They sail her too fast and pay never a thought to cam belts. One day a cam belt's going to snap and then where will they be? Down on power like you couldn't believe, that's where. And then they'll be looking for somebody to blame."

"Can you fix it?" Cati asked anxiously.

"Course I can fix it," said Silkie gruffly. "They shouldn't of done it, is all."

Cati realized that something had upset Silkie and she guessed what it was. "They're not going to take you with them?"

"Wesley says somebody has to look after the rest of the children when he's away," Silkie said miserably. There were tears in her eyes. She looked up and saw Wesley looking down at her, and quickly ducked her head back into the engine.

Cati sighed and walked on up the deck. There was a mast in front of the engine with an enclosed crow's nest at the top of it. Cati wondered what it would be like sitting up there, all closed in, with the wind whistling round you. She stepped round the mast and opened a door. The cabin had a low ceiling, with a small bed in the corner and a locker beside it. There was a radiator on one wall, probably using excess heat from the magno. Sunlight fell across the rough bedspread from the diamond-pane window. Cati had her things in a bag over her shoulder and she put it down on the bed, hoping that everyone would take the cabin as being hers.

Back outside, all the supplies were now on board. Uel and Mervyn were sitting at the stern of the boat, looking tense and alert, their magno crossbows in their hands. Dr. Diamond was putting his instrument boxes in his cabin and the Sub-Commandant was pacing the deck. Cati knew that he was worried about Chancellor's lateness. She climbed the little steps up to the bow and from that height she saw Chancellor hurrying down the path. As he did so she felt a snowflake gently touch her cheek, and then another.

"We're in for a big snow, I'm afraid," a voice said. Cati turned to see Dr. Diamond standing beside her. "By my reckoning," he said, "we are now entering the little ice age that occurred circa AD 1130 to circa 1310."

"That's a long time," said Cati.

"Well, it won't last that long because we're going backward so fast, but it will be a few weeks. Are you worried about Owen?" he said, suddenly changing tack.

"Yes . . . yes, of course I'm worried."

"Here," he said, taking a Polaroid photograph from his pocket. It was starting to fade, but you could still make out Owen's face. He was in the Skyward and looking comically surprised as he faced the camera. "He sneaked back to the Skyward to take another look back through

197

time. Whatever he saw there sent him over the river. And I'd say whatever he is after there, it isn't eternal friendship with Johnston."

"Why didn't you show this at the Convoke and tell them that?" Cati asked.

"Remember, there is still a spy in our midst," Dr. Diamond said.

"S-so you don't believe that Owen is a spy?"

Dr. Diamond shook his head and smiled. "No, Cati, I don't think he is a spy. I think he is an important person, with a part to play in all of this before the end. But I don't want you to discuss this with anyone else. There are undercurrents—"

Dr. Diamond was interrupted by Chancellor, who jumped awkwardly from the quay onto the deck.

"My apologies for being late," he said. "I had a lot to do before we left. Is the Mortmain on board?"

The Sub-Commandant tapped the pocket of the long coat he now wore, a military-looking leather coat with a fur-lined collar and faded markings in what appeared to be Russian on the sleeves. The snow was starting to fall heavily now and visibility was dropping.

"We'll have to go," Wesley said, "or we'll never get clear of the sandbar."

"It'll be a problem setting a course, though," the Sub-Commandant said. "A compass will not work with the distortion in the magno caused by the vortex, and if it snows, we will see no stars."

"I believe I have the answer to this slight problem," said

Dr. Diamond airily, as though he had been waiting for this moment. "A small invention of no great consequence— a compass that works according to the timeline when time started going backward. It remembers due north, in other words." He coughed modestly.

"It'll be no use to man or beast, your fancy compass, if we don't cast off in the next five minutes," Wesley shouted. Cati thought that Dr. Diamond would be offended, but he merely grinned and set about unpacking the memory compass from its box.

The snow was falling in great soft flakes. Suddenly, things started to move very fast. Silkie, working frantically, replaced the cover on the magno motor. Seeing her pale, disappointed face, Cati ran and hugged her. Wesley shouted something and the stern rope was detached, and Uel started to haul it on board. Boat was held only by the bow cable now. With a grateful smile, Silkie broke free of Cati's hug. She stood for a moment on the deck looking up into Wesley's eyes and it seemed to Cati that even though nothing was said a universe passed between them. Then Silkie skipped across the gunwale and down the gangway.

The minute she did so, the gangway was withdrawn. Wesley shouted again and the bow cable was thrown into the water. Boat was free. The long oars moved slowly, barely stirring the water. Cati noticed that all the Raggies were gathered on the quayside, their faces indistinct in the driving snow. She saw others there—Contessa, Pieta, Rutgar, all waving, their faces taut with anxiety. She felt a sudden ache in her breast, almost a physical pain, at the thought that she might not see them again. The great danger they were in had never really struck her before. She tried to call out their names, but the snow seemed to muffle her voice. She tried again, desperately this time, but their faces faded as though Boat was sailing against the flow of time and leaving them behind. Once more she called out, and again there was no reply. Feeling a strong hand grip her shoulder, she turned to see her father. Cati leaned her head against his shoulder and watched the last stretch of gray quayside fade into the snow.

And so Boat and its crew slipped away on their voyage, away from danger and into greater danger. On the quayside the Raggies strained to catch a last glimpse of their ship and its captain. Silkie wept openly. The Workhouse people watched in grim silence.

"The best of us are on that vessel," said Pieta quietly.

"No," Contessa said with a smile, "not all of the best of us."

"You had better go, if you're going," said Rutgar gruffly. "I worry about their plans for Owen. I wish you would let me go with you."

"They'd spot a big tramping goon in a minute," Pieta said with a flash of her old sourness, but Rutgar just shrugged.

"You're right," he said mournfully. "They'd smell me before they saw me."

"We'd better get back," Contessa said, but still they stared into the snow with the Raggies, who had not moved, the snow starting to settle on their hunched shoulders, gazing after the vessel that carried the hopes of the world that had been and the hopes of the world to be.

Owen also woke early, if he could have been said to have slept at all. The cellar was half flooded and he had felt around in the dark until he found a low stone shelf above the water. He huddled on it miserably, half dozing, until daybreak, a thin, cold light coming through the high window. He pulled his sodden clothes round him and stood up on the narrow shelf, pacing up and down for warmth, until at last the door at the top of the stairs opened. It was Passionara.

"Get up out of the mire, Pretty Rat," he jeered. "There's rat grub for you."

His limbs barely working from cold, Owen hauled himself up the stairs, shivering uncontrollably. Passionara lost patience with him and grabbed him by the hair, lifting him off his feet and slinging him into the corridor. At the same instant, he slammed the door of the cellar shut. As the door closed, a weak beam of sunshine crept through the high window, shining across the dark cellar to the far corner, where the black water was deepest, glancing off something as white as bone. The sunlight seemed to disturb something in the dark, and after a moment, a large dark rat crossed the deep water, jumping lightly across what appeared to be smooth stepping-stones. But, as the uncertain sunshine strengthened, it became apparent that they were not stepping-stones but skulls, their dead eyes staring unseeing into one more cold dawn.

There were delicious smells in the corridor. Owen was pushed into the kitchen. Mariacallas, the cook, was standing at the stove with a spatula in his hand, watching anxiously as a tray of scrambled eggs with smoked salmon, toast, Earl Grey tea, and grapefruit was hoisted shoulder high and carried toward Johnston's room.

"Spill one drop, I cut your liver out. I fry her for eat," Mariacallas screamed at the man carrying the tray as he left the room.

"You got feeding for Pretty Rat? Johnston says feed the rat," Passionara said.

"No time for feed rat!" Mariacallas screamed furiously.

"Is very pretty rat," Passionara said, "Johnston wants to keep it fresh for Harsh." Mariacallas scowled but opened a cupboard and threw some hard bread and cheese on the table.

"There!" he said. "Food for rat."

Owen was ravenous. Despite the fact that the bread was stale and the cheese was hard, he wolfed it all down, drinking water from someone else's dirty cup that had been sitting on the table. He thought with longing about the tea bags he had left in the Den.

As he ate, Johnston's men came and went, carrying supplies. For the journey north, Owen thought with a shiver. He wondered how they would be traveling and how long it would take. From the quantity of supplies he knew that it was going to take some time.

As the men worked, Mariacallas screamed at them for leaving the door open or muddy footprints on his kitchen floor. One man left a trail of flour from the cooker to the door. When Mariacallas saw it, he whipped a long sharp knife from his belt. Owen did not see his hand move, but the knife whirred through the air. The man, without looking back, ducked and the blade struck the door just above his head and stuck there, quivering.

Passionara seemed to have wandered off. Mariacallas was preoccupied with packing spices and condiments for the journey. Owen eyed the door. He thought about making a bolt for it, but each time he did, his eyes returned to the long knife, which was now back in Mariacallas's belt. It was warm in the kitchen. After the sleepless night in the cellar, Owen could feel his eyes starting to close. The sounds of the kitchen grew distant. He put his head on the table and slept.

Passionara woke him by the simple means of grabbing him by the hair again and pulling him to his feet. Owen had been dreaming about the Workhouse, of sitting in the warm kitchen with Cati, and he looked around him bewildered before he remembered what had happened.

"You ready for big trip north?" Passionara said, grinning. "Holiday!"

"Winter holiday!" Mariacallas exclaimed, and the two men hooted with laughter.

"Hurry," Passionara said, clipping Owen on the back of the head. "Mustn't be late."

"Johnston will leave without you."

"He hopes!" Once again the two men screeched with laughter. Owen didn't think there was anything funny about their jokes at all, but he thought it best to smile politely, in case they took offense. A shove from Passionara took him to the back door, and another shove propelled him through it.

"Watch step," Passionara said. "Johnston never find no Mortmain. Not in good mood."

The world he fell into bore no resemblance to the place he had been the previous night. Snow whirled through the air so that you could barely see twenty meters away. The scrap and the tent village had all been covered, and the manor looked like something from an old painting. There was a sense of anticipation in the air as well, with men hurrying to and fro. Owen thought he could make a bolt for it now, but he wouldn't know which way to go. Besides, as soon as the thought entered his head, Passionara seized him and dragged him off toward the sheds at the back of the Manor, leading him down a bewildering warren of stone-cut buildings, containing forges, armories, workshops of all kinds. Owen had no idea that the Johnston operation was so big. He thought about the sparsely manned defenses of the Workhouse and the casualties they had taken, and wondered how long they could hold out.

At last they turned the corner into a large cobbled space. Passionara halted. "There," he said, "is how travel to north."

It took a moment for Owen to take in what he was looking at. It was the oddest vehicle he had ever seen. It had a wheel at each corner, but they weren't ordinary wheels. They were a bit like bicycle wheels, he thought, thin bicycle wheels with spokes, but the astonishing thing about them was their height. Each wheel had to be twenty meters tall, almost as high as a three-story building. And between them, halfway between the ground and the tops of the wheels, was slung what Owen supposed you would call a pod. It looked like the body of an airplane without the tail or wings, but with the same round windows and windscreen at the front. A long, narrow ladder led from a door in the side to the ground.

"Q-car," Passionara said happily. "Skip up ladder, Pretty Rat." He swung a boot lazily in Owen's direction. Not needing to be told twice, Owen grabbed the bottom rung of the ladder and hauled himself onto it. He felt Passionara get on the ladder after him and he climbed hurriedly upward, knowing that he was liable to get a thump if he didn't move quickly enough. The ladder swayed as Owen climbed, and the snow blew down his collar and into his eyes, rendering him half blind by the time he got to the top of the ladder. He felt for the outlines of the door and pulled himself through, blinking the snow out of his eyes as he did so.

The interior was wider than it appeared from outside. Comfortable leather seats were grouped round tables. The interior walls were also covered in leather. There was one seat where the pilot would have sat on an airplane, and a set of complicated-looking controls that looked more like those of a ship. There was a copper-bound wheel and a series of brass levers and pedals. At the rear of the fuselage was a small galley.

"When are we going?" he asked.

"Shut up, Pretty Rat," Passionara said, and threw himself down in one of the chairs. Owen decided that he wouldn't risk any more questions.

They waited in silence for twenty minutes, Owen feeling more and more tense, until at last he felt the whole body of the Q-car begin to dip and sway, as if somebody extremely heavy was climbing the ladder. Probably

Johnston, Owen thought, almost with relief. At least Johnston would end the terrible silence.

But it wasn't Johnston. After several minutes Whitwashisberd's head appeared in the doorway. He was breathing heavily and he had his ledger under his arm.

"Take book!" he shouted to Passionara, who did not move. "Take book, foul flower wearer!" the man shouted again. But Passionara did not stir. It was Owen who darted forward and took the heavy ledger so that the man could climb through the doorway.

"That'll earn you no favors from the maker of records," Passionara said sourly. "If there's a skull to put beside your name, then a skull it will be."

Whitwashisberd took the ledger back from Owen and went to the back of the craft. He sat down heavily, opened the ledger on the table in front of him, took out a pen, and waited.

He didn't have long to wait. The craft lurched again and Mariacallas climbed on board, closely followed by Johnston.

"Snow gets bad," Mariacallas said.

"We'll follow the Harsh Road," said Johnston. "No need to stray off it, Passionara."

Passionara nodded and moved to sit down at the controls. Owen tried to sidle past Johnston to get a better look at what Passionara was doing, but Johnston caught him round the neck with a huge hand. Owen couldn't breathe. He struggled helplessly.

"Just because the Harsh want me to make a present of you doesn't mean that I have to. You could get killed trying to escape."

"Accidentally on purpose," Mariacallas said, and roared with laughter. Passionara joined in. Even half strangled as he was, Owen was tiring of their terrible sense of humor. Johnston's grip tightened even more. Owen's vision was blurred but he thought he could see Whitwashisberd's hand hovering over the last page of the ledger.

"Where is the Mortmain?" Johnston bellowed into Owen's face.

"In the car," Owen gasped. "When it went into the water. My dad's car . . ."

"Maybe he's right," Johnston said, stroking a long sideburn thoughtfully, seeming to forget that he was strangling Owen with the other hand.

Abruptly Johnston dropped Owen to the floor, where he lay fighting for breath. Johnston went up to Passionara and stood over him while he performed what seemed to be last-minute equipment checks. Owen heard murmurs about "barometric relativity frequencies" and "temporal torque." Still gasping for air, he half walked, half crawled to the back of the cabin. He crept onto a chair that was as close to Whitwashisberd as he dared. There seemed to be no love lost between him and Mariacallas and Passionara, so Owen hoped they would keep away.

From nearby, Owen was able to study the ledger. It

was very old and enormously thick, and its pages were incredibly thin. There must have been thousands of pages in it, perhaps even tens of thousands. He wondered if his father's name was in it. He wondered if there was a skull beside it. Owen decided that, if the chance arose, he would try to get his hands on the book. Meanwhile, he had to think about escape. At that moment he glanced up and saw that Johnston was looking straight at him, a mocking smile on his lips, as though he had read Owen's mind. Fortunately, Johnston was distracted just then. There was a faint humming noise and a crackle, and Johnston whirled around.

"Did anybody stow the ladder?" he yelled. Mariacallas dived toward the open door, avoiding a fist the size of a turnip aimed at his head as he did so. Quickly he pressed a lever. Owen peered through the door and saw the ladder folding itself into sections, then rising until it was out of sight under the belly of the Q-car. Just as the last of the ladder clattered out of sight and Mariacallas slammed the door, the pod seemed to rise and sway between the four giant wheels. Owen saw Passionara ease the lever forward and the Q-car lurched into motion. At the same time loud music began to blare from speakers mounted under the pod.

Johnston was standing with one hand on Passionara's shoulder, and with the other he conducted the music furiously. The big wheels turned slowly, yet still they were covering a lot of ground. Owen moved to one of the round windows. Through the snow he could see Johnston's men, hundreds of them, cheering the great machine as it moved through the camp. Owen looked to his left. Whitwashisberd was painstakingly writing: "Departure 8:34 a.m. Conditions: snow."

The snow eddied and flurried, and momentarily Owen caught a glimpse of the Workhouse towering grim and defiant over the river, the tottering pillar of the Nab clearly visible, the Skyward glittering at the summit. Then the weather closed in again. The wind threw snow against the Q-car with renewed ferocity, obliterating not only the Nab but also the faces of the cheering men below. Owen looked out of the window but could see only whiteness.

On the other side of the river Pieta kissed each of her children gently on the cheek. The older child, the girl, blinked a little, as if emerging from a dream, and threw her arms round her mother's neck, but the boy only smiled a vague, secret smile. Contessa stood with a hand on each child's shoulder as Pieta walked off. As the snow began to obscure her, the girl called out. Pieta turned and spoke the child's name into the wind and snow, then turned again and disappeared into the blizzard.

She reached the river and walked carefully down the bank. The snow did not seem to concern her. She examined the tree bridge, then moved on. After twenty minutes she reached the pine tree where Owen had crossed. She examined the base of the tree in silence for a moment, then climbed onto the trunk and moved across the river slowly, pausing every few meters to examine it. When she got to the other side, she spent ten minutes examining the place where he had fallen. She stood up. For a moment Pieta stared back across the river, pain in her eyes. Then she turned back and plunged into the forest.

The Q-car moved slowly but relentlessly through the driving snow all that day. As far as Owen could see, there were pine trees to either side of the vehicle, but it was moving on a clear space. The ride was incredibly smooth. After a while Johnston had retired to the back of the Q-car with Whitwashisberd. The two men pored over the ledger as if they were looking for something. Maria-callas was asleep in one of the chairs, his legs and arms sprawled out, his head thrown back and his mouth open. Owen moved slowly up to the front of the Q-car, hoping not to attract Johnston's attention.

"Come to see how her work?" asked Passionara. The man was squinting out of the window into the snow, making tiny adjustments to the wheel as he did so. Gauges and dials flickered in front of him and he referred to them constantly.

"Go damn fast, Q-car," Passionara went on. "Got to go slow for now. When we reach proper Harsh Road she go like crazy."

"What happens if you hit a rock or a snowdrift?" Owen asked.

"No problem for big wheel. Ride right over anything you like. Rock, big snow, tree even. Look at wheel." Owen looked out of the window and saw that the wheels were riding up and down, constantly bumping over obstacles, but the cabin stayed steady all the time.

"How come the cabin doesn't go up and down as well?"

"Big spring on wheel," Passionara said with a shrug. "Gyro in cabin."

Owen thought that Passionara looked relaxed driving the Q-car. He seemed happy to tell Owen anything he wanted to know about it and Owen was happy to keep him talking in case he learned something useful. In fact, Owen almost forgot who he was talking to, but there was a sickening reminder to come.

Through an eddy in the snow, Owen saw a deer standing in the middle of the road. Passionara saw it at the same time. With a whoop he pushed one of the brass levers forward and the Q-car leapt toward the deer. The deer froze momentarily, then started to run. Go on, a voice in Owen's head said. Go on! But the deer had no chance against the speed of the Q-car. Passionara swerved violently off the road, ignoring the curses of Johnston from the rear. The deer made one last desperate bound and then the Q-car was on it. With a sickening jolt, first the front wheel and then the back wheel crashed over the animal. Passionara was cheering wildly now as he swerved back toward the road.

His cheering woke Mariacallas, who joined in mindlessly, even though he hadn't seen what had happened. Owen looked out of the side window. He could see the body of the deer lying in the snow. Without looking at Passionara, he turned back toward his seat. But Johnston brushed him aside. Without breaking stride, one giant fist caught Passionara on the side of the head. Passionara toppled from his seat like a felled tree and lay motionless on the floor.

Johnston handed the controls to Mariacallas. "Do a better job than this," he said, indicating the semi-conscious Passionara. Mariacallas watched Johnston walk off, then turned to Passionara and delivered a vicious kick to his ribs. He giggled and did a little dance to himself, then took the controls. The Q-car lumbered off into the snowy dusk.

As the Q-car disappeared from sight a shape detached itself from the forest on the other side of the river. Pieta, running swiftly and tirelessly, seemed to glide lightly across the top of the snow. She reached the place where the Q-car had killed the deer, and bent to examine the body. Then she started to run again and soon she too was lost in the gathering dusk.

The Q-car drove on through the night. Passionara woke up and made his way groggily to the back of the cabin and promptly fell asleep again. Johnston produced his record player from the pile of supplies and started to play classical music very loudly. Owen covered his ears as best he could. Whitwashisberd had fallen asleep and did not seem to be bothered by the music. Owen put up with it for almost two hours and then fell asleep himself. When he woke it was quiet. Quiet, that is, except for the snoring of Whitwashisberd and Johnston and Passionara, which was enough to wake the dead. Outside, the snow was still falling and Mariacallas peered into the night, the road almost invisible despite the help of several huge spotlights that had been turned on.

Owen thought that this was his chance to get a look at the ledger. He crawled under the tables until he was at Whitwashisberd's table. The man had enormous feet and it was with great difficulty that Owen got past without touching them. His snores were deafening from this near, and Owen could feel the table vibrating and rattling. Cautiously he put his hand up over the edge of the table and felt around. He touched something cold and flabby. It was Whitwashisberd's hand. He froze. The man grumbled in his sleep and Owen had to scramble out of the way as the enormous feet swung round under the table. But gradually he settled again and the snoring fell into a steady rhythm. Owen felt about again and this time his hand touched the ledger. Slowly and painstakingly, for it was very heavy, he pulled it toward the edge of the table. Then, using both hands, he eased it down.

The cover of the book was battered and stained. There was writing in a strange language on it, but the gilt of the lettering had long since worn off and it was impossible to decipher. Owen opened the book carefully. It even smelled old. There seemed to be tens of thousands of entries. Hundreds of thousands, perhaps. Owen started to wonder just how old Whitwashisberd actually was. He turned to the last entry. As far as he could see, names were recorded on the left-hand pages and events on the opposite pages. There were skulls in fresh ink drawn beside many of the names on the left-hand pages, and Owen guessed that these were men who had fallen in the battle at the Workhouse. He spotted one entry that read "Frizzell Gruntion, Planeman," and Owen remembered the Planeman who had attacked them at the Nab.

There had to be a system to the book, but Owen couldn't work out what it was. It couldn't be done by date because time was going backward, which made nonsense out of that system. It didn't seem to be done alphabetically. After a while he reckoned that the names must bear some relationship to the events recorded on the right-hand page. Most of the time the events were described by pictures rather than words. For instance, there was a clock that was cracked down the middle, which Owen thought must be the day that time had turned backward. He flicked back through the pages, wondering what event would relate to the time that his father had been with the Resisters. There were so many pages and his eyes began to grow tired, squinting at the small writing in the half-light under the table.

Owen was almost ready to give up when he found it. A small drawing of a car half in, half out of the water. And when you looked closely, you could see the crudely drawn figure of a man in the front seat and the unmistakable round features of a baby's face in the back. Owen felt his blood run cold. With a shaking finger he traced a line across to the left-hand page. He read his father's name. There was a skull beside it. A dull pain seemed to settle across his chest. He felt tears start in his eyes. He closed the book and squeezed his eyes shut in an effort to stop the tears. When he opened them again he saw Passionara's thin features peering at him under the table.

"Now, now," he said softly, "what is Pretty Rat doing under the table?"

Owen flew at him.

Passionara tried to defend himself, but his reflexes seemed to have been slowed by the thump he had received from Johnston. Surprised, he fell backward over one of the chairs and Owen was on top of him.

"Stop calling me Pretty Rat!" he yelled. "Stop it! Stop it!" His arms flailed at the man's face. Some of the blows were landing, but they weren't hard enough to do any damage. He could see that Passionara was grinning now, a thin, evil grin. He opened his lips and his tongue slid out. To his horror, Owen saw a small but deadly-looking razor on the man's tongue. Quick as a snake, Passionara snatched the blade from his tongue with one hand, grabbing Owen by the hair with the other and yanking his head back so that his throat was completely exposed. Owen could see the blade clearly, its rusty edges. He could almost feel it tearing at his throat. Passionara grinned but there was nothing funny about it. The blade arced through the air. Owen could hear his own heart beating, loud as a drum.

"What do you think you're doing, you flouncing popinjay?" Johnston roared, appearing as if from nowhere and snatching Owen up as the blade swooped through the space where he had been. Johnston straightened, Owen swinging from one fist as though the older man was about to use him as a club to beat Passionara.

"Boy attack me!" Passionara wailed, with a sneaky look of dislike at Owen that didn't bode well for the future. He was circling Johnston, trying to cut at Owen with the razor blade. But Johnston kept him dangling just out of reach. At least he called me boy, not Pretty Rat, Owen thought. As Passionara made a lunge, his arm passed too close to Whitwashisberd. With a lazy kick, the white-bearded man knocked the blade out of Passionara's hand and it clattered onto the floor. Johnston swiftly picked it up and put it in his pocket. When he was satisfied that Passionara couldn't hurt Owen, he dropped him heavily on the floor. Dazed, Owen could hear Mariacallas giggling with excitement.

"Quiet yourself!" Johnston said. He turned to Passionara. "You hurt this, even one fingernail, I'll be giving you to the Harsh along with it, you got that?" Passionara nodded sullenly.

"Whitwashisberd," Johnston went on, "tie the creature up, bind him hand and foot, and keep him there beside you." Whitwashisberd nodded grimly.

Within minutes, Owen was trussed up like a turkey, barely able to move a muscle. Whitwashisberd showed a great expertise with knots, wetting each one before he pulled it tight so that it would shrink and become even tighter when it dried. Passionara prowled just out of reach, urging Whitwashisberd to pull the ropes even tighter, and when Whitwashisberd eventually put Owen on the ground, Passionara lay watching him, his eyes alert and full of malice. Owen groaned inwardly. Now there was no chance of escape.

The first few days on board Boat were strange. It took Cati some time to find her sea legs, even though the swell was light. Snow gathered in the rigging and on the decks and had to be swept off, and all sounds were strangely muffled. Cati knew that the great empty sea was all around them, for Wesley had said that he was putting far out to sea. Yet she had no sense of it, just of the small community on board. And that small community consisted of one more than had been intended. They had cleared the bar at the harbor and had been sailing for several hours when Wesley shaded his eyes and frowned and peered forward.

"How did the lassie get on board?" he said. The solemn little girl who had been woken by Owen was standing in the prow of the boat, facing out to sea.

"I don't know," the Sub-Commandant said. "I didn't see her come on board."

"Shall I ask her?" Cati said.

"No," the Sub-Commandant said thoughtfully, "leave her be."

"Nothing we can do about it anyhow," Wesley said. "I'm not putting about now to bring her back."

The little girl stayed in the prow of the boat until nightfall, despite the driving snow. When the Sub-Commandant saw that she was gone, he sent Cati to look for her with some bread and beans and cake. But Cati could not find her.

"There's a hundred places such a small lass could squeeze into and you'd never find her," Wesley said.

"Take the food and wrap it well and leave it in the bow," said the Sub-Commandant. Cati did as she was told.

Wesley and Dr. Diamond had built a small case to enclose the memory compass and were now engaged in a long and serious conversation on the nature of time. The motor beat soundlessly and slowly. "If we're going to run into something in this snow," Wesley said, "best we don't run into her too quick." Chancellor had agreed with him, then retired to his cabin.

At dusk they had dinner in the stateroom under the stern. The stateroom had big windows looking out at the wake of the boat. It was lit by candles. Dr. Diamond cooked and served the meal himself on big white plates, with starched linen napkins.

Cati thought it was romantic, eating under candlelight, with the ship swaying gently, snow gathering on the windowpanes. Dr. Diamond and Wesley resumed their conversation about time. The Sub-Commandant ate quietly by himself and Chancellor stayed in his cabin, saying he had a headache. At the end of the meal Dr. Diamond dramatically produced a replica of Boat made with spun sugar. As they were eating it, Cati felt her eyes beginning to close and she yawned.

" 'Twill be the sea air," Mervyn said. "Does make you tired when you're not used to it." So when she had finished her piece of spun-sugar boat, Cati said goodnight and, yawning, crossed the deck. She checked in the bow and saw that the food was gone before she went down to the little cabin. The blankets were old and much patched, as was the sheet, but it was clean and smelled of fresh air, and she slid under the blankets with a sigh of contentment. Looking out through the little windows, she could see the snow slanting down onto the deck. She thought about Owen, wondering where he was. Cati hoped he wasn't alone in the cold night; she thought about him warm and safe, and held that thought as she drifted off to sleep, in the hope that by wishing it, it would come to pass.

The next morning the snow still fell. Cati slept late and had breakfast on her own in the stateroom. When she went out on deck, Chancellor was pacing up and down. He greeted her cheerfully enough but he looked strained.

"Are you all right?" she asked.

He sighed and ruffled her hair. "Just hoping that our plans come to pass, Cati, and worrying that there is something more that could be done."

"It'll be fine," she said cheerfully. "We won't be beaten by a bunch of snowmen with icicles for brains."

He smiled at her and turned back to the rail, trying to see out through the blinding snow. Cati suddenly thought about the little girl and looked up into the prow. She was standing there, in her thin dress. Cati ran into her cabin. There were much-patched oilskins hanging from a hook on the wall. Cati took her own warm coat and an oilskin coat and hat. She scrambled up the ladder that led to the top of the forecastle. When she got there the little girl still had not moved, but she turned and looked at Cati as she put the coat over her shoulders, and allowed her to button the oilskins round her and put the hat on.

The girl's expression didn't change. At first Cati thought it was a blank look, but then she started to see a level of trust there, a sea of trust, which frightened her. She wanted to tell the child that you couldn't trust the world that much. It wasn't right. There was too much out there to hurt you.

But instead of speaking, Cati slid down the ladder again. She ran into the kitchen and made up a bacon sandwich and brought it out to the girl. The child was looking out to sea again, but she took the sandwich and bit into it. Her eyes moved ceaselessly, although there was nothing to see except snow.

"What are you looking for?" Cati asked. The little girl did not reply and did not stop staring into the dead whiteness ahead of them.

Cati slipped away. As she walked across the deck, a large snowball exploded on the top of her head. She looked around startled, but couldn't see anyone. Then she heard a voice from high above her. Wesley in the crow's nest.

"Come on up!" he yelled. Cati didn't hesitate. She had never been afraid of heights. At top speed she flew up the ladder that was bolted to the side of the mast. Within three minutes she emerged into the crow's nest. It was surprisingly roomy, with a low roof and a glass screen that you could slide across to cut out the wind.

"For spotting fish," Wesley said, "a few of us do stay here. You do look for gannets diving and the like."

"I wish Owen was here," Cati began wistfully.

"He'd be stuck, like as not, same as the rest of us, sailing north, blind as bats," Wesley said.

"Not if he's the Navigator," said Cati defiantly. Wesley looked at her, his eyes narrowing.

"What is it you do know about the Navigator?" he demanded.

"N-not much," she stammered. "I heard Contessa and Pieta talking one night. . . . What is the Navigator anyway?"

"Don't rightly know. People do whisper. Old tales that was once told say Navigator can save us."

"Could Owen be the Navigator?"

"Might be, might not. Anyhow, Chancellor, he lets on it's all a bit of a cod, that there's no such thing as Navigators anymore. Fair and sharp he was about it too."

"Then I suppose we're on our own. Looks like somebody's going to be spending a lot of time up here looking for the Puissance, whatever that looks like."

The next morning Cati woke early and realized that something had changed. The motion of the craft seemed different, and the light that flooded through the little windows was different too. Quickly, she slipped into her clothes and ran outside. The snow had stopped. All around them the sea stretched out, vast and silver-gray, flecked with white. A sharp wind whipped foam off the top of the waves and she could taste salt in her mouth. The sky was filled with leaden cloud, heavy and menacing, and a flurry of snow whipped across the deck as if to remind them that this was only a respite. To either side of Boat the oars were working faster now, and the bow rose and fell, crashing into the waves and sending spray high into the air.

"It's a bit clearer now!" Wesley shouted to her from the bridge.

"It's amazing," Cati called. "It's . . . it's so big!"

Wesley slid down the stairs to where she was standing.

"Right enough, you never seen the sea like this before, out of sight of land."

"No. This is great!"

"Maybe it is," Wesley said, "and maybe it isn't. Take a look."

Cati followed his gaze and realized that Uel was lying on top of the bridge with his eye to the sight of his magno crossbow. He was facing astern and the bow was pointing toward the sky. When she looked to where the gun was pointing, her blood ran cold. Far off in the cold, gray sky, small but unmistakable, were the menacing shapes of four Planemen.

"That's right," Wesley said grimly. "Somebody told on us. They knew where to find us."

Cati followed Wesley back up to the bridge. The Sub-Commandant was standing with Dr. Diamond.

"How long have they been there?" Cati asked Wesley.

"I'd near say they were there all the time, we just couldn't see them."

"Will they come any closer—I mean, attack?"

"I think we're safe enough," the Sub-Commandant answered, "for the time being, at any rate. The wind is blowing in their faces and they're having trouble making headway against it."

Dr. Diamond produced a pair of binoculars that had a suspiciously homemade look about them. "I think you're right," he said.

"Can I look?" Dr. Diamond handed over the binoculars.

Cati scanned the sky until she could see the Planemen and took an involuntary step backward, so close did they seem. They had been in the air a long time, she could see. Their clothes and beards were matted with ice, their lips chapped and cracked. Behind the rimed glass of their goggles she could see their bloodshot eyes. The machines bucked and twisted as they fought the wind for control, but there was a grim determination about the way the Planemen hunched over the controls that told her they would never give up.

"We're all right as long as the wind holds," Dr. Diamond said cheerfully, taking the binoculars back.

"As long as it holds," said Wesley, "but the minute it drops . . ." He drew his finger across his throat in a cutting gesture.

"Don't listen to him," said Dr. Diamond. "Even if the wind does drop, they'll not come near us as long as Uel and Mervyn are here."

"But a watch will need to be kept," the Sub-Commandant said.

"I can do that," said Cati. "In the crow's nest."

"Good. You can cover the rest of the day. Tomorrow we can do it in watches."

Cati nodded, feeling glad to have something to do, although wishing that it could be something less threatening.

"Where's Chancellor?" Wesley asked.

"In his cabin," replied Dr. Diamond. "He started to feel seasick when we picked up speed."

"We'll have to manage without him, then," the Sub-Commandant said. "We'll have to take Uel and Mervyn off normal duties. We need one of them ready to shoot and one of them resting at all times."

All that day the Planemen hung in the sky, not gaining any ground but not losing any either. Chancellor remained in his cabin. Dr. Diamond stayed in his. The Sub-Commandant sent Cati to bring food to him. When she went in he was almost invisible behind a large, ancient-looking book and he barely glanced up when she put the plate down beside him.

Outside, an occasional flurry of snow hid the planes, but they were always there when the snow died away again. Because she was watching, Cati had to eat a quick meal standing up. The sea had got rougher, and apart from the Raggie boys, who were busy, no one else was comfortable with the idea of the crow's nest as it swayed sickeningly from side to side. Bringing her food out onto the deck, Cati could see the sun setting in the west, a great glowing orb, tinting the dark clouds round it a foreboding orange. Looking up, she saw that Wesley was strangely agitated. He walked to the rail on both sides and looked at the oars, then returned to the helm, still obviously unhappy. As she watched him, Cati felt a tug on her sleeve. She looked down to see the little girl standing there. The girl tugged again, then turned and walked away. Cati followed her.

The girl went through the open door in the rear bulkhead. Just beyond the door, steps led down to the hold. It was dark and Cati had to hold on as she went, although the girl seemed able to keep her balance easily. They got to the bottom and walked along a short companionway. The girl stopped. She pointed at the floor. At first Cati didn't know what she was doing; then she saw there was a brass ring set into the floor. Cati grasped the ring and a hatch swung open. As it did so there was a loud gurgling noise. Peering into the dark, Cati could see a stopcock set into the hull, a kind of tap going through to the outside. That was the source of the gurgling, Cati realized. Someone had opened the tap and water was flowing in from outside! Looking into the darkness beyond, she could see that bilges were already full of dirty, oily water.

Cati desperately tried to close the tap, but she wasn't strong enough. She turned and ran up the gangway calling for Wesley. Seeing the look on her face as she burst onto the deck, Wesley vaulted over the bridge rail and landed lightly on the deck. He ran down the companionway, followed by Cati. When she reached him he was already on his knees, wrestling with the brass valve of the stopcock. The flow of water diminished to a trickle and then stopped. But the damage was done.

"Will it sink?" Cati asked anxiously.

"Sinking's not the problem," said Wesley, his voice tight and angry. "She'll float with the hold full of water.

It slows us down, though, slows us down something desperate till we get the water out. I knew I could feel something on the wheel."

Cati heard footsteps behind her and turned to see her father. The small man looked into the bilge without expression.

"This was done deliberate," Wesley said, and his eyes flashed with fury. "This isn't no accident. Thon stopcock never opened itself."

"We need to form a human chain," said the Sub-Commandant, "to get rid of the water as fast as we can."

Wesley stirred himself. He ran back up on deck and called to Uel and Mervyn. Then he ran up to the bridge. Dr. Diamond came out of his cabin. Even Chancellor came out, looking pale and ill. Emerging into the daylight, Cati could feel that the vessel had slowed and was wallowing slightly, taking longer to recover from the waves.

"Come up here, Cati!" Wesley called out. When she got to the bridge, he told her to take the wheel.

"I've never—" she started.

"You have to," he interrupted. "You're the lightest of all of us, so you'll be the least use slinging buckets."

Cati felt her face grow red and she clenched her fists, but she held her tongue. She knew that he was right. She put her hands on the wheel, which twitched and turned so much that it felt like a live thing. A live thing carrying a great burden, for she could feel the dead weight that had pulled Boat lower down in the sea. Instinctively, she turned to look behind. She could make out the Planemen in greater detail now. They were definitely closer.

The other six crewmen formed a chain as best they could, Wesley scooping out the water from the bilge with a bucket, then passing it up the line to the next man. Cati could see that there weren't enough of them and that Chancellor was weak and slow. It was going to take a long time. She turned to look at the Planemen again. Although they were hard to see in the fast-closing dusk, they were closer still. The wind in her face freshened and she could see Dr. Diamond looking up hopefully.

"What are you looking for?" asked Cati.

"Smith had a daughter," the doctor murmured, almost to himself.

Smith? The man who had abandoned the Raggies? Cati was familiar with the story, but she didn't see what it had to do with what was happening now.

Darkness fell. Cati peered out into the night. Below her the men worked tirelessly. Looking toward the bow, she could see the little girl standing there. After an hour she saw Chancellor sway and almost fall. Dr. Diamond sent him to his cabin and the others redoubled their efforts. Cati had an itchy feeling at the back of her neck and every five minutes she turned to stare, but the night was starless and she could see nothing. It seemed to her that the wind stayed fresh and she hoped against hope that it was enough to stop the Planemen.

As the night went on the temperature dipped. Cati couldn't feel her nose or her hands anymore. Then she realized that she could go into the wheelhouse and take the wheel in there. She strapped up the outside wheel and stepped inside. The wheelhouse was warm compared to outside, and she felt guilty looking down at the others working in the cold and dark. As the night stretched on, the wheel became lighter in her hands as the water level in the bilge fell. The buckets went up and down from the hold in a slow, weary rhythm. Her eyes felt grainy and sore.

Close to dawn, Cati could sense a definite change in the way the craft handled. It was dancing over the waves instead of plowing through them. At the top of a wave she could see a cold glimmer of light in the east. Down below, the rest of the crew worked on, gray and exhausted. Cati looked over her shoulder. It was still too dark to see the Planemen, but she was sure now that they were traveling at their old speed. She heard Wesley call out that they could stop bailing. None too soon, Cati thought as a fresh flurry of snow, blowing horizontally in the stiff breeze, blocked her view of the deck. The last thing she saw was Dr. Diamond slumping onto the deck, Uel and Mervyn leaning wearily against the mast.

That was when they came, the Planemen, screaming in under cover of the snow. Blue flame blazed across the deck. Cati was dimly aware of Mervyn and Uel scrambling over the bridge, weariness forgotten. The Planemen wheeled about the masthead like spindly, evil birds and then dived to attack again. The water alongside the craft boiled, and she felt a hard jolt through the wheel. Desperately Cati spun the wheel away from them. She felt strong hands grab the wheel away from her and was aware of Wesley, white-faced, alongside her. In his hands Boat came about, faster and more agile than she would have believed possible, but still the Planemen came.

Another flash seared the deck and through the snow she saw Dr. Diamond thrown heavily against the base of the mast. She turned to the left. The snow cleared momentarily and she saw one of the Planemen skimming the wavetops, heading directly for the wheelhouse. Closer and closer he came so that she could see the gaunt features, the rime-crusted beard, the cracked and frozen leather jerkin, the grim, staring, red eyes, and the great hands grasping the controls and moving, she knew, to trigger the terrible power of the magno cannon.

Cati stood fixed to the spot and she knew that she could no more have moved than she could have snatched the Planeman from the sky. Suddenly, a burst of blue flame shot from the roof of the wheelhouse above her. The Planeman veered wildly to the side to avoid it, but the bolt of magno seared the side of the plane and struck his shoulder a glancing blow. As he dipped dangerously close to the waves, Cati could see a jagged rip in the shoulder of his leather jacket and smoke rising from it.

Grimacing with pain, he eased the craft into the air, turned, and flew away from Boat.

Another Planeman came skimming across the waves astern of the boat, firing as he came. Cati saw flame streaking toward the windows of the dining cabin and heard a great crash of crockery falling to the deck, but both Mervyn and Uel were firing now and the Planemen were having to use all of their skills to avoid their fire. One of the Planemen raised his hand in a signal and they all wheeled about and flew swiftly away. The snow began to ease. Boat rose on a wave and Cati heard another crash as more crockery came down.

Dr. Diamond! she thought. She had seen him hit! Shaking herself out of her stupor, Cati ran out of the wheelhouse and down onto the deck. Dr. Diamond raised himself gingerly onto one elbow. There was a deep gash on his temple, and he was deathly pale.

"Are you all right?" she asked anxiously.

"Am I think I," the scientist said, looking groggy. He swayed and Cati reached out to support him. "Hap . . . What happened?" he asked, making an effort to correct his speech.

"The Planemen attacked. They must have got ahead of us during the night."

"Now I remember," he said. As Boat crested a wave, Dr. Diamond swayed again and Cati had to grab the mast to stop them both falling over.

"I think I'd better lie down," said Dr. Diamond. Cati

helped him across the deck to his cabin, trying to avoid the great scorched furrows left in the deck by the Planemen's guns. He lay down on the bed and Cati wet a cloth and bathed the gash on his head until she was sure that it was clean.

"Thank you, Cati," he said softly. "I think I'll stay here for a while." Turning at the door, she saw that the man was almost asleep already.

She went back to the wheelhouse. Wesley was still at the wheel. He was talking in low tones to the Sub-Commandant. Both of them looked gray with exhaustion.

"They must have known we were leaving," he was saying, his voice angry. "They couldn't have guessed it."

"Possibly," the Sub-Commandant said, "but perhaps they picked up our trail by accident."

"What about the stopcock?" Wesley demanded angrily. "How did it get open?"

"I admit that it is strange," the small man said.

"It's a whole lot more than strange," said Wesley. "There's someone aboard this here—"

"Cati," the Sub-Commandant interrupted. "How is Dr. Diamond?"

"I think he's all right. He's doing a bit of backward talking, but I think that's just the bang on the head. He's lying down."

"That's one good thing," Wesley said. "We're going to need all the help we can get, not that it'll make any difference anyhow."

"Why's that?" asked Cati. "They didn't put a hole in us, did they?"

"Might as well've," Wesley said. "Take a look at thon." He pointed toward the oars on the left-hand side. A deep scorch mark ran across the top of them and two of them were splintered, not yet broken, but bending out of shape each time they touched the water and threatening to snap. Cati remembered the hard tug on the steering she had felt when the Planeman attacked down that side and she realized that was what she had felt.

"If that goes," Wesley said, "it's the end of us."

Boat limped on through the day. The Sub-Commandant insisted that they keep up the same pace.

"Fair dos," Wesley said, "but if the weather gets up a bit, she'll snap."

"Does that mean we have to stop?" asked Cati. The Sub-Commandant explained that they could still keep going, but they would have to disengage the two damaged oars and two oars on the other side, opposite the damaged ones, otherwise they'd end up going round in circles.

"Them Planemen would catch us in a second," Wesley said. Behind them, a line of Planemen hung in the frozen sky, a kind of terrible patience to the way they were flying now. Cati noticed that one of them was flying slightly lower than the others and seemed to have difficulty keeping his place in the line.

Dinner that night was subdued. The sleepless night had taken its toll. Dr. Diamond had stayed in bed for most of the day and was now managing, with difficulty, to get his sentences the right way round. Uel and Mervyn looked tense and tired. Chancellor could barely lift his head to eat. Only Wesley and Cati's father seemed alert: the Sub-Commandant calm, eating methodically, Wesley's eyes darting suspiciously round the table, scrutinizing each face in turn.

"Stop that," Cati whispered to him.

"What?"

"Looking at me like that. I didn't open your precious stopcock."

"Somebody did."

"Well, it wasn't me. You probably left it open yourself."

"Whatever the two of you are squabbling about, please don't," the Sub-Commandant interrupted. "We're all tired. We'll take four-hour watches tonight, in twos. Wesley, you can take the first one with me."

Wesley looked at him with approval. If two people were working together, then there was no chance of anyone interfering with stopcocks or anything else without being seen.

The night passed without incident. The Sub-Commandant took his watch, with Wesley. Uel and Mervyn took the four hours in the middle of the night. Cati took the dawn watch with Dr. Diamond. She shivered when she walked out onto the deck, not with cold, although there was a deathly chill in the air, but with awe. The night sky had cleared and every star shone as brightly as they must have done at the beginning of the world, the great constellations stretching off into infinity. Slowly she clambered up to the wheelhouse, reluctant to step into the shelter, for the movement of the boat made the stars seem to spin and wheel in the dark sky.

"Fascinating," Dr. Diamond said when she entered the wheelhouse. "Do you see anything different, Cati?"

"Just that the stars are so bright."

"Yes, they are bright, but they are also different. The constellations are not where you would expect. The Milky Way should be over there. The Plow should not be visible in that quarter."

"Why's that?" Cati asked.

"Well, if you interfere with time, then you also interfere with space. Things are dragged out of place in unexpected ways."

The night passed without incident. Cati found herself holding the wheel, almost dozing, while Dr. Diamond made measurements from the stars with a series of sextants and protractors and other oddly shaped instruments he had brought from his cabin.

When the dawn came, the air itself seemed to glint and sparkle with cold. The sky was cloudless and the sea was a deep, cold green flecked with white. When Cati went out onto the bridge ice particles stung her face.

"The wind carries the foam off the top of the waves," Dr. Diamond said, "and it freezes in the air."

They looked back along the wake of Boat. The Plane-men hung in the air at the same distance as before. Except that this time there were only three of them.

There is one good thing about being under Whitwashisberd's table, Owen thought, and one bad thing. The good thing was that he had been thrown almost on top of a small inspection window, so he could see out. The bad thing was the proximity to Whitwashisberd's feet, from which emanated an almost indescribable stink.

Despite the tightness of his bonds, Owen managed to get his face up against the window. The snow had stopped. He could see pine trees stretching out silently to either side of the Q-car. The huge wheels enabled the craft to move through the trees, but it swayed and bumped as it went. Earlier, he had heard Johnston tell Whitwashisberd that they would be reaching the true Harsh Road soon and that they would pick up speed then. Owen wasn't sure if he liked the idea of that. He was tired and he pressed his face against the cold glass to wake himself up. As he did so, he thought he saw a black shape moving through the trees behind the Q-car. He looked again. There was definitely something there, running lightly and tirelessly in the snowy spaces between the pines. Someone, he thought, who is following the car.

Owen felt his heart leap. The figure was carrying something in a coil at its waist. A long whip. It was Pieta! She was keeping pace effortlessly, but what would happen when they reached the Harsh Road?

There was a sudden stir in the cabin. "Harsh Road coming up!" Passionara sang out. "Get us some speed. Get the boy quick to freezebones Harsh." This provoked gales of mirth from Mariacallas. Owen thought that he would like to strangle both of them.

The ground was more open now. The trees had given way to scrub and then to clear, featureless snow. As it did so, the Q-car started to pick up speed. He saw Pieta clear the edge of the trees and accelerate as she realized what was happening.

Then Owen saw something odd. The edge of what seemed to be some kind of crash barrier protruding from the snow. He saw what was unmistakably a motorway sign, bent and aged, but still recognizable. Ahead, a long, snow-covered space led off into the distance. It is a motorway, he thought. The Harsh had taken a motorway and turned the whole thing into an island in time.

Things started to happen quickly then. The Q-car

leapt forward as it hit the road. Owen could see that Pieta was running at full tilt now, but it wasn't fast enough. Just as she started to fall back into the darkness, he saw her reach to her belt. The Q-car bounced onto the motorway, the jolt of it throwing him backward. By the time he had got back into position at the window, Pieta was gone. No one could help him now. He was being delivered to the Harsh, who could turn time backward and make an entire motorway an island in time. Owen closed his eyes and let despair wash over him.

On and on through the night the Q-car sped, moving so fast that the landscape through which they passed was reduced to a blur. Owen was exhausted but he couldn't sleep. His legs were tight with cramp and his arms were bound so tightly he could no longer feel them. Passionara was driving. Johnston and Mariacallas sat at the rear of the cabin, drinking gin and playing whist. Whitwashisberd drank gin as well, then fell asleep. The floor on which Owen lay vibrated with his snores, adding to Owen's misery. With the first glimmer of dawn he fell into a disturbed sleep, punctuated by the drunken yells of Johnston and Mariacallas.

Owen's fitful sleep was finally broken by loud shouting. It was Passionara.

"Hey, wakey wakey, gents! You want me drive all night to hell?"

There was no answer from the others. They were all drunk and snoring. Passionara let the Q-car coast to a halt. He got out of his seat and walked back down the cabin. Owen quickly shut his eyes and pretended to be asleep. After a moment he could sense the man leaning over him, feel his breath.

Owen remembered the look of hatred on Passionara's face after Whitwashisberd had kicked the razor blade out of his hand. He had never felt more helpless in his life. The man stayed there for a minute and Owen squeezed his eyes shut even tighter as if he could block him out. In the end Passionara merely muttered something under his breath and Owen sensed him move away. Cautiously Owen opened one eye. Passionara was examining the sleeping men. He bent over Johnston and fiddled at his neck. Johnston grunted, but did not wake. Passionara straightened, holding a key on a chain, and did a silent jig to himself. He went to a small cupboard under the rear bulkhead and opened it. It was the gin store. Passionara picked out a bottle and put it in his pocket. Then, moving cautiously, he replaced the key round Johnston's neck and started back up the cabin. Owen squeezed his eyes shut once more.

Owen did not open his eyes again until the Q-car lurched into life. Passionara was at the controls, but this time he was swigging from a bottle of gin as he drove. Owen stared out of the window. The sun shone brightly and the whiteness of the snow outside was almost unbearable. The wind blew fine powdery snow against hidden objects, creating strange shapes and making the world outside look like no country he had ever seen. As the morning wore on, Passionara started to sing. He shouted back to Owen.

"Hey, Pretty Rat, you like songs from time of shows? You like that damn fine Vera Lynn? Tell me. I sing for you. I cut throat after."

In fact, Passionara had a good voice and his singing took Owen's mind off the danger he was in. Passionara introduced songs from Sandy Shaw and the Sandpipers, and lots of other people Owen had never heard of, but then things started to go wrong. Passionara started to repeat verses. Then he began to forget the words. Finally, he went completely out of tune and was reduced to humming loudly off-key. The gin bottle rolled past Owen's nose. It was completely empty.

In the end there was no more singing. Gradually, Owen realized that another snore had been added to the chorus in the cabin. Craning his neck around as far as it would go, he saw that Passionara was fast asleep, slumped over the controls. They were careering down the Harsh Road at terrifying speed with no one in control.

The end wasn't long in coming. The Q-car started to veer away from the center. For several minutes it traveled down the snow-covered motorway on what would have been the hard shoulder. Then it struck a road sign buried under the snow. With a ringing sound the sign snapped and flew high into the air. The Q-car turned sharply sideways and ran at high speed right off the road and into the countryside, snapping trees like twigs, crashing over hidden obstacles. Johnston stirred in his sleep, but it was too late. Owen saw a huge wall rearing up in front of them. Before he had time to brace himself, the Q-car struck with a massive crash. The force of the collision propelled Owen the length of the floor. With a sickening impact he hit the bulkhead beside the sleeping Passionara. Mariacallas hurtled down the floor after him and struck Owen with an impact that drove the breath from his body.

For several moments there was chaos. Swearing and sweating, Johnston plucked the drunk Passionara out of the driver's seat and simply flung him the length of the cabin. Mariacallas seemed a bit dazed and was dancing around the cabin with a long thin knife in his hand looking for imaginary foes. Whitwashisberd was awake with his book open in front of him, and by the way he was looking at the still-sleeping Passionara, it was open at the page featuring the drunk man's name, Owen thought.

It turned out that the wall they had struck was made of soft snow piled up by the wind, and there was little actual damage done, although the Q-car was almost buried in it. Johnston took the controls and drove the Q-car forward and back until he had got it clear. He lay back in his seat looking terrible. His great sideburns were matted, and his eyes were red and veined.

All at once he sat up and looked through the side window of the cabin, then leapt to his feet. He suddenly seemed to become aware of Owen and with half a kick and half a push he propelled the boy back down the cabin until he fetched up under Whitwashisberd's table again. Then he threw open the hatch and unfolded the long, spindly ladder. Johnston clambered down followed by Mariacallas, and Owen could not see them for a few moments. When they reappeared in his window, they were trudging across the snow toward a large flat area. Reaching it, Johnston took something out of his pocket and threw it. There was a blinding blue flash and a large noise. When the fine haze of ice that hung in the air after the explosion had cleared, Owen saw that there was a small lake underneath the ice, the water black and cold against the snow. Johnston and Mariacallas threw off their clothes and, with whoops and wild curses, plunged into the freezing water.

Whitwashisberd saw what they were doing. With what sounded like a grunt of enthusiasm he clambered to his feet and lumbered toward the hatch. Owen could feel the whole Q-car shaking as he went down the ladder. Then the man reappeared in the window, almost running across the snow, shedding his clothes as he went. Owen looked away. He felt bad enough without being put through the ordeal of seeing a naked Whitwashisberd.

On the outside of the cabin, a piece of ice stirred—a piece of ice that seemed to have eyes that glittered with determination every bit as cold and adamant as the frozen earth over which the Q-car had traveled. When Pieta had seen the Q-car reach the edge of the Harsh Road she realized that she would not be able to keep up. With one swift movement she had reached for the magno whip at her waist. She lashed it backward and forward over her head until she had woven a rope of burning blue flame. Then one immensely powerful flick had sent it speeding toward the back of the Q-car. With a hiss, the end of the knotted cord of light wrapped itself around the jutting tailpiece of the Q-car. Still running at full tilt, Pieta had flicked the whip again. A great shiver had run along its length and she was lifted off her feet as the light cord contracted at great speed, hurling her through the air as if she was flying until she landed, feetfirst, on the rear of the speeding vehicle.

There she stayed through the night, using her belt to bind her to the riveted bulkhead of the Q-car so that she would not be thrown off. So frozen were her clothes that you would have thought she was a statue were it not for those green eyes, stern and unblinking even in the icy gale that buffeted her.

Owen heard a noise at the hatch. He turned to see a head coming through, but a head unlike any he had ever seen. It seemed sculpted from snow, with long, stiff hair of ice. The ice person moved quickly into the cabin and Owen shrank back as it approached. Then he saw the eyes. The same eyes he had seen, bold and fierce, in the battle with Johnston's men; the same eyes he had seen narrow with sarcastic humor at the Convoke; the same eyes he had seen soften with love at the sight of her children. Pieta.

She unwrapped the cloth round her face.

"Pieta, I—" he started to say.

"Can you walk?" she interrupted him brusquely.

"I don't know. I can't really feel my legs."

Pieta took out a small knife and began to cut through the ropes. At first Owen couldn't feel anything, but moments later the blood began to flow back and he had to bite his lip to stop from gasping out at the pain. With a quick glance at the unconscious Passionara, she hauled Owen to his feet and slashed the cords on his arms. Her clothes crackled with frost as she bundled him quickly toward the hatch. His legs were numb and weak and she had to support him. Pieta looked quickly through the hatch. The three men were still in the water.

"I can't climb," Owen said.

"You won't have to," said Pieta, giving him a shove between the shoulder blades. Unbalanced, and with his arms too weak and numb to catch the sides of the hatch, Owen tumbled through. Looking up as he fell, he saw Pieta jumping after him. He landed in a deep snowdrift. Pieta landed beside him. She urged him to his feet. He got up, his still-numb legs almost useless in the deep snow. Pieta put her arm round his shoulders and half dragged, half carried him away from the Q-car.

Owen felt terribly exposed as they moved slowly across the snow. Pieta was making for a low ridge several hundred meters away. He glanced over his shoulder. The three men were still in the water. He could hear Mariacallas's high-pitched laughter. At least he wouldn't have to put up with that terrible sense of humor again, he thought.

As they approached the ridge, feeling gradually returned painfully to Owen's legs and he was able to carry more of his own weight up the slope.

"Keep low," Pieta said as they reached the top of the ridge, but no matter how low they kept they were silhouetted against the skyline. Owen waited for an angry shout but none came. Almost on their hands and knees, they crossed the ridge and fell onto the other side.

"Rest for a moment," said Pieta, "but then we have to move."

"They'll see our tracks," Owen suddenly said. "They'll find us straightaway!"

"I'm not so sure," Pieta said quietly. "Look." She pointed north. Owen could see great yellow snow clouds massed on the horizon.

In the Q-car Passionara woke up. He shook his head and spat out a tooth with an expression of disgust. He looked around. He was on his own. He went to the window. In one direction he could see footprints leading away across the snow. He went to the other window. He saw Johnston, Mariacallas, and Whitwashisberd still in the black water. He looked under the seats in the car. He went back to the window and counted the figures in the water. He went to the other window and looked thoughtfully at the footprints. He went to the driver's seat and started the engine. The car trundled across the snow toward the lake. Johnston looked up in surprise.

Owen found the going easier after his brief rest and Pieta only had to stretch out an arm now and then when he stumbled. It helped that they were on the windward side of the ridge so that the snow was not as deep. Ahead of them they could see the dark mass of the tree line.

"If we can get under the trees, we'll be able to hide," Pieta said.

"Is everybody all right?" asked Owen. "Cati and the rest?"

"They have gone north," Pieta said. "They have the Mortmain with them. They are looking for the Puissance."

"But that's no good. Even if they reach it, they won't be able to find the right place; they won't know what to do." Pieta looked at him strangely. Owen felt his face burning. Why had he said that? What did he know about the Puissance and how to make time go back the right way?

Two things happened then that stopped Pieta questioning him further. A fat snowflake drifted down and landed on Owen's cheek. And behind them, the Q-car crested the ridge. Johnston had opened a hatch at the top and was scanning the ground in front of him with one hand shielding his eyes. He pointed and they heard a distant shout.

"Run!" Pieta said. "Run like you've never run before!" Owen ran, stumbling and falling and picking himself up again, a great lung-bursting, nightmarish run where, it seemed, the trees did not get any nearer and the

252

Q-car gained on them every second. The snow will save us, he thought desperately. The snow will hide us. And yet the snow drifted down in large downy flakes, not thick enough to conceal them or their tracks.

And then they were nearly at the tree line, but the Q-car was almost on them. Pieta turned and lashed the magno whip across the surface of the snow. A huge curtain of white rose from the ground, a spiraling blizzard, and the Q-car disappeared behind it. Owen could hear Johnston's bellow of rage and then they were in among the trees.

Safe! thought Owen. Safe, that is, until he realized that they had not reached the forest as they had thought. The place they had reached was not that of the deep forest, but a line of trees only five or six deep. Owen stopped and teetered and would have fallen if Pieta had not caught him by the arm.

They stood on the brink of a sheer gorge and, far below, at the bottom of a cliff, was the green-blue water of a fast-rushing river. They were trapped. Following Pieta, Owen started to run along the top of the gorge, keeping in the shadow of the trees. Behind them he could hear the Q-car crashing through the trees like some large and angry beast. They reached a stand of tall Scotch pines. Pieta uncoiled the whip. The blue flame lashed out with the speed of a snake striking. There was a crack and a sizzling sound and then, with a mighty crash, the tallest of the trees fell right across the gorge, forming a long, smooth bridge.

"We have to cross at a run," Pieta said. The Q-car was very close now. Owen looked down at the coil of green water below them and felt the familiar sick fear rise in his throat.

"I can't," he said. "I can't."

Pieta didn't hesitate. With a flick of her wrist she drew the whip across the back of Owen's legs. He yelped at the searing pain and she flicked her wrist again. The pain and shock were indescribable. Owen saw her flex her wrist again and he recoiled onto the fallen tree. She swung at him again. And so he crossed the bridge at a run, driven like a beast, tears of pain and humiliation in his eyes.

Halfway across, he heard a roar of triumph. He could not help stopping and turning to see, half expecting the lash again. But Pieta had done what she had set out to do. The Q-car emerged from the trees; Johnston, face and sideburns coated with snow, yelled again. Passionara was driving. He turned the vehicle to cut them off, setting a diagonal course. Too late he saw the gorge, and they heard Johnston's enraged cry. The Q-car stopped on the very edge of the gorge, teetered and righted itself, teetered once more, and once more righted itself. Owen could see Whitwashisberd sitting in his usual place. The ledger was open in front of him.

The Q-car teetered again, but through the windscreen Owen saw that Mariacallas had come to the front of the vehicle. In vain, Passionara tried to push him back. The extra weight was enough to turn the teeter into a slide, and the slide into an uncontrollable descent. Owen stopped his ears against Johnston's roar of terrible anger. But as the Q-car slid past them Owen could see Whitwashisberd writing something in the book with an air of calm satisfaction, and Owen knew he was drawing a tiny skull next to his own name. There was a bang and the rumble of rocks falling into the gorge. And then the Q-car was gone.

On and on Boat sailed and still the damaged oars held. Wesley kept looking back at the three Planemen following them. If they stopped for two hours, he could have put a splint on the oars, he said, but everyone knew that they couldn't halt and risk another attack from the Planes. Cati spent most of her time in the crow's nest. When she was on deck, she kept looking into people's faces and wondering which one of them had opened the stopcock. She even wondered about Dr. Diamond, then felt ashamed for doing so.

Besides, she liked being in the crow's nest. She brought up some blankets to keep her warm and sat all day huddled in them, watching for danger and for the Great Machine in the north, although she had no idea what it might look like. And then there were the strange things she saw. A great iceberg, dirty white on top and a deep sea-green where it met the water, which sailed past them like a stately palace of ice. There were plenty of ice floes as well—growlers, Wesley called them—and once she saw one float past with a great white bear standing on it, looking as through it was the most normal thing in the world to be floating on a big piece of ice in the freezing, inhospitable ocean. Then there were the whales: small ones that swam alongside Boat, and the huge ones she saw in the distance, their backs looking like blue-black mountains as they surfaced.

On the fourth day since the attack Cati climbed the mast as usual. She could see Wesley at the wheel and the little girl standing in place at the bow. Far below her, tendrils of smoke curled out from under Dr. Diamond's door and were snatched away by the icy wind. Mervyn was crouched behind the wheelhouse, watching the Planemen. Cati couldn't see Chancellor or her father. She hauled herself into the crow's nest, the skin of her face stinging from the ice particles carried by the wind, particles that had scoured every exposed surface on Boat until they shone as if they had been polished daily.

Cati scanned the sea around the ship but it was empty. Then she looked toward the horizon. For a moment she thought she saw something—a tiny black tendril right on the limit of her vision that seemed to curl upward. She rubbed her eyes but it had disappeared. She was about to call down to Wesley when she realized why she couldn't see the horizon anymore. It was obscured by a black cloud, which, even as she watched, grew larger, seeming to race toward them. As it did so, the register of the wind seemed to alter, going from a steady roar to a vicious whistling sound. By the troubled look on Wesley's face, Cati knew that he had already seen the cloud.

All afternoon the black cloud built on the horizon and Wesley stayed in the wheelhouse in worried debate with the others. When Cati came down to eat, she asked Dr. Diamond if anything had been decided.

"There are a few choices, none of them good," he said, scanning the horizon. He looked peculiar, as he was wearing a pair of heated ice goggles of his own invention. "We can keep going as we are and hope that the storm blows the Planemen off course. Or we can turn back and ride in front of the storm, and with luck keep the oars intact. The problem with that is that we have to go under the Planemen."

The seas continued to build. The bow of Boat rose and plunged, sending sheets of icy spray high into the air. Wesley slowed the craft a little, and bit by bit, the Planemen got closer, although you could see that they were having difficulty controlling the planes in the high wind. Mervyn and Uel were both crouched in the sheltered spot behind the wheelhouse now, the magno crossbows following every movement of the planes.

"They can't hold them off forever," Chancellor said.

"True enough," replied Wesley.

Night fell. But it wasn't night the way Cati knew it. As they went farther north, it seemed that the sun didn't set properly, so it was never completely dark. Dr. Diamond said it was always like that in the far north, but Cati preferred it when night was dark and day was light. When the storm finally struck, no one could see anything anyway. One minute they were cresting the waves, the next the sky seemed to be blotted out and Cati had to close her ears against the terrifying shriek of the wind as the sea seemed to rise around them, mountainous and boiling.

Cati ran to the wheelhouse. Uel and Mervyn ran in behind her, for to stay on the deck was to be swept overboard.

"Where's the little girl?" Cati asked, having to shout to make herself heard above the noise of the storm.

"It's all right," Uel shouted back. "I saw her go below."

Cati had to hold on to the door frame to stop herself being thrown to the floor. Down below she couldn't see the deck for boiling, seething water. Wesley's face was taut with concentration as he fought to control the wheel. Through the window Cati could see rank upon rank of vast, white-crested waves advancing on them. Boat took an age to climb each one before plunging down the other side with dizzying speed. Dr. Diamond stayed on the left-hand side of the wheelhouse where the damaged oars were, peering anxiously though the spray and angry foam in an attempt to see how the oars were faring.

"Don't fret, Doctor," Wesley said with a tight grin. "I'll know about it if them oars snap."

On through the dark, tempestuous night Boat sailed, and still the oars held. And each time they thought that the storm could get no worse, the wind blew stronger, the waves grew bigger, and the wind shrieked still louder.

The Sub-Commandant took Dr. Diamond aside. "The oars can't possibly hold," Cati heard him say.

"If they go, then there will be three oars working on one side and five on the other," Dr. Diamond said. "Wesley won't be able to steer straight."

"We have to take the oars off the other side so that there are three on each—" the Sub-Commandant said, but before they could act, they were interrupted by a gasp from Cati and a curse from Wesley. In the distance, and bearing down on them with the speed of an express train, was the biggest wave any of them had ever seen. Cati thought it was like a mountain of water, vast and threatening with icy spume like lightning flying in great sheets from its leading edge. In a moment it was on them and the oars beat frantically as Boat began to climb what seemed to be a sheer cliff of water. Up and up they went, Boat tipping further and further backward until it seemed to Cati that they would tumble down and be lost in the boiling water. And still they climbed. Then, they were at the very top, teetering on the crest of the wave for what seemed like eternity.

They almost made it, but just at the very moment that

Boat tilted forward for the race down the other side of the wave, there was a loud crack, followed closely by another. The damaged oars had snapped. Boat's bow dropped and it slewed around so that it was racing in a diagonal line across the back of the wave. The side with the broken oars rose higher and higher into the air as the craft tilted onto its side. Cati was thrown against the wheelhouse door. A locker full of maps and charts fell open and the contents rolled about the floor. As the tilt got worse, the chart table snapped its moorings and followed the charts, striking Cati a heavy blow on the leg. Just when it seemed that Boat could not tip over any further without capsizing, Wesley gained control again and Boat straightened—just in time to face the next wave.

"I can't hold it like this for long," he gasped. The wheel shuddered with every stroke of the oars and his shoulders were knotted with effort.

"Someone will have to disconnect the other oars," the Sub-Commandant said.

"It would be suicide to go out on deck," said Chancellor. "You'd never reach the engine hatch."

"True enough," Wesley said.

"What about under the deck?" asked Dr. Diamond.

"No good. You wouldn't fit in the space." Another wave hit the bow of Boat and Wesley wrestled with the wheel, beads of sweat breaking out on his forehead. He managed to correct Boat's course and turned back to the others.

"You wouldn't fit," he added, "but she would." He inclined his head toward Cati. "It's fair and tight, but she'd get in there all right."

"I don't like it," the Sub-Commandant said. "The linkages are powerful. If Cati gets caught in one . . ."

"We've no choice," said Dr. Diamond gently.

"The girl wouldn't be strong enough," Chancellor said.

"She'll have to be," said Wesley. "I can't hold Boat much longer."

"The magno motor is powerful, but perhaps we can cut it for a moment or two from the wheelhouse," suggested Dr. Diamond.

"Dangerous—" the Sub-Commandant began.

"Stop it!" snapped Cati. "Stop talking as if I'm not here. If the job has to be done and I'm the only one who will fit, then tell me what to do and I'll do it."

Dr. Diamond gave her a long, considering look. The Sub-Commandant shook his head but said nothing.

"Right," said Cati, "how do I get to the motor?"

Wesley tapped the floor behind him with his foot. "Uel and Mervyn," he said, "lift them boards." The two boys sprang forward and started to pull up the floorboards.

"I have a plan," Dr. Diamond said. "It will take you about five minutes to get to the motor. The two forward blades are attached by a hook. We'll turn the engine off for exactly two minutes so that you can unhook them."

"How will I know the time?" Cati asked. Dr. Diamond produced two identical hourglasses from his pocket.

"The Harsh haven't been able to make sand run backward yet," he said. "When the motor stops, turn this on its end."

"You damn well better hurry," Wesley said, and she could hear the strain in his voice. "Crawl straight and crawl quick."

The Sub-Commandant helped Cati down into the dank hole revealed by the lifted planks. When the time came to release her hands, he did not let go and she had to gently break his grip. With a quick smile she ducked into the dark space.

There was only just enough room. The underside of the deck grazed her head and she couldn't straighten up enough to crawl so she had to wriggle. Filthy, cold bilge water swirled around and within a minute her clothes were soaked. As Cati began to crawl under the exposed deck, she could feel the wood above her head thrumming with the power of the storm. And each time a wave struck she was thrown sideways against the unforgiving beams that supported the deck. The only thing that made it bearable was the faint glow of magno from the engine compartment ahead.

Dr. Diamond had said five minutes, but it felt like half a lifetime before she reached the motor and was able to stand up. Cati could see the magno core of the motor, contained in a kind of brass case, open on top. To each side there were five levers. On the left side the levers were attached to five oars, and they moved smoothly, like a rower's arms and elbows, but to the other side only three of the oars worked properly. The other two had splintered stubs of oar attached to them. Just as Cati registered this, the engine stopped. She froze. They should have given her more time. Wesley must not be able to hold it anymore. The motion of Boat changed immediately, the rising and falling movement being replaced by wild corkscrewing.

Cati knew she was wasting time. She took the hourglass from her pocket and placed it upside down beside the motor. She saw straightaway that the link between the oar and the lever was a giant hook and eye arrangement. She grasped the hook on the front left oar and heaved on it. It didn't budge. She tried again. The sand is running through the glass far too quickly! she thought. She also realized that if the motor started with her arm in it, the arm would be crushed. Desperately Cati pulled at the hook. The sand was half gone and she hadn't even got one oar off. She shifted her grip to the lever and pulled. Still nothing. She moved the lever around a bit and then realized that if she pushed it down, it seemed to go without resistance. She pushed down and down, and then there was a creak of protest and the oar came loose.

There was still time for the other one. Cati grasped the lever with confidence this time, but it wouldn't move. Scrambling to her feet, she looked down at it. The metal below the lever seemed to have corroded and jammed it. Frantically she looked around. There was a monkey wrench hanging from a peg above the motor. She grabbed it and hammered with all her might at the lever. It shifted, but the sand was almost gone, the last few grains trickling into the bottom of the hourglass. She grabbed the lever and it moved downward, not smoothly, but moving. It was almost free, but as it moved the last centimeter, the motor started again. Instinctively, Cati thrust the wrench into the motor. The lever, which was descending like an axe, stopped. She pushed and it came free. She snatched her hand back, and just as she did so, the strong brass wrench snapped like a twig and the lever plunged through the space where her hand had been seconds earlier.

Cati lay back against the ribs of the little vessel. She could feel it start to rise and fall again. Her heart was pounding. Owen would be impressed with her, she thought, then felt the return of a dull ache. Owen would never know.

The journey back to the wheelhouse seemed longer. When she reached the other end, filthy and exhausted, the Sub-Commandant lifted her out of the hole and held her for a moment.

Dr. Diamond beamed. "You did very well."

"Sorry about that," Wesley said. "I couldn't hold her anymore. We had to start the motor again."

"That's all right," Cati said with a weak grin, remembering the sound that the wrench had made when it snapped.

The Sub-Commandant said nothing but rested his hand on her shoulder.

It still took all of Wesley's skill to keep Boat on course since it was now short four of its ten oars, but at least, he said, he didn't have to fight Boat as well as the sea. However, his face was pinched with fatigue by the time dawn came. If it could be called a dawn. For despite the fact that the sun didn't really set this far north, the sky was completely hidden by heavy black clouds, and the waves were so high that even if there had been a horizon, you wouldn't have been able to see it. In the end, the Sub-Commandant persuaded Wesley to step down and let Mervyn take the wheel. The Sub-Commandant had insisted that they all stay in the wheelhouse, so Wesley lay down on the floor and wrapped himself in a blanket. Cati was able to do no more than doze on the hard floor.

"At least there's no sign of the planes," said Dr. Diamond.

"The wind will have blown them miles away," the Sub-Commandant said. Suddenly, there was a shout from the corner. The Sub-Commandant whirled round. Chancellor, who had been sleeping, was sitting bolt upright, his eyes staring.

"The Mortmain!" he shouted. "Where is the Mortmain?" The Sub-Commandant was beside him in an instant, placing a gentle arm on his shoulder.

"It's all right," he said. "It's all right. The Mortmain is safe."

"The Planemen will have it!" Chancellor shouted. "The Planemen must have it or send it to the bottom of the sea!"

"The Planemen are gone," the Sub-Commandant said gently but insistently.

Chancellor blinked, then slumped back against the wall. "I was dreaming," he said weakly. "I thought the Planemen had taken the Mortmain."

"The Mortmain is safe and the Planemen are gone. The wind took them in the night."

"Maybe not," Dr. Diamond said quietly. They followed his pointing finger. Just a few hundred meters off the bow, the three Planemen rose into the air from behind a wave. Their leather jerkins were so coated in ice that it seemed as if they were wearing frozen armor. There were signs of damage to the planes—a bent vane, a ragged tailpiece, and long icicles hanging from their undercarriage—but they were intact. And Dr. Diamond could see that they were hunting now.

Pieta urged Owen across the tree bridge, but her urging was gentle this time. He was numb and exhausted, and the back of his legs felt on fire. She made him sit on a large rock, giving him some flat cakes that she took from a small bag slung over her shoulder. He realized that he couldn't remember the last time he had eaten. As he ate, she knelt beside him and rubbed snow into the burning welts on the back of his legs.

"There was no time," she said, looking up into Owen's face. He knew she was right. While he was hesitating, paralyzed by his fear of falling in the water, the Q-car would have been on them. Pieta finished tending to his legs. Her touch was gentle. She took a cloth from her bag, tore it into strips, and wrapped it round his legs.

The snow was still falling sparsely, but Pieta looked around her, as if smelling the air. She seemed worried.

"There is a lot more snow coming," she said. "We should move, try to find trees we can shelter under. We can't use the Harsh Road. They will wonder what happened to Johnston. Maybe they will come looking for him."

They set off, Pieta leading the way, Owen walking as best he could in her footsteps. They walked all morning and into the afternoon, but there was no sign of trees. Pieta stole worried looks at Owen. The boy had taken far too much physical and mental punishment, and now he stumbled along as though in a dream. As she began to recognize the sort of place they were in, her worry grew. There were icy pools everywhere, small clumps of scrubby birch and elder. The ground beneath their feet was frozen and Pieta believed they had found themselves in the middle of a bogland—a great icy fen where there would be little proper shelter.

As the afternoon wore on, the snowflakes became smaller, turning hard and sleety so that they stung Owen's face. At the same time, the wind from the north became stronger, stirring up the surface of the snow and flinging it in their faces. They pressed on, not because they had any aim or destination but simply because Pieta knew that if Owen stopped and lay down, he might never find the will to get up again.

They had been walking on smooth ground for some time—smooth ground without shelter, it was true, but at least it was easier to walk on. Then, as it began to get dark, Pieta suddenly realized why the ground was so smooth and shelterless. Kneeling quickly and scooping away the snow, she revealed hard, black ice. They were walking on the surface of a lake, frozen and bleak. Behind her Owen swayed and almost fell. She put her arm round him. He mumbled something and leaned against her shoulder. Night was coming and the temperature was plummeting. There was one last desperate hope. Something Pieta had once learned about another level of Resisters. Something proud and bitter and dark of thought. And these marshes and fens and boggy lakes were the stronghold of this resistance.

Stumbling now with tiredness, for she had run day and night after the Q-Car, Pieta pushed Owen forward into the storm and the growing night. On and on they went, beyond any limit she had ever known, and when Owen fell, she picked him up and put him over her shoulders and carried him. Until at last a small mound of earth reared in front of them, ringed in ancient whitethorn bushes. Pieta pushed through them, the sharp thorns tearing at her clothes and skin, and fell exhausted. With one last effort, she took the whip from her pocket and sent a searing flame up the trunk of one of the trees.

She waited, but nothing happened. She noticed that the falling snow had covered Owen and brushed it away from his face. "The debt of my children is repaid now," she said. "There is nothing else I can do."

The boy's eyes were closed and he did not answer.

Pieta staggered to her feet. Her hands and legs were frozen and useless. She made to move forward, but her legs gave way and she fell onto her knees. As she did so something hard and merciless wrapped itself round her neck, choking off her breath. Frantically, she tried to twist and throw off her attacker, but it was no use. As she struggled, she was aware of a ghostly shape, bent over her.

Suddenly the pressure eased slightly. Then Pieta heard a female voice, harsh and gravelly and full of dark authority.

"You said to the boy the debt of your children you have repaid. You burned my tree. Now you have to start paying him for your own life, for you would surely be dead now if he was not here."

The pressure round Picta's neck grew again and she felt her sight grow dim, her limbs grow weak, and she pitched forward into the snow and knew no more.

21

All day they tried to hold off the planes, but without the extra speed it was useless. The Planemen had realized that they could hold their craft steady for long enough to fire on Boat, whereas Uel and Mervyn had only the wildly pitching deck from which to fire. The planes swooped and dipped around the boat, firing carefully and steadily. They were too far away for any one shot to do massive damage, but at the same time, each shot did a little harm. Bits of the railing were carried away. The deck was scorched and cracked in places. The hull had been hit several times. In the midafternoon, one of the bolts of magno plunged through the wheelhouse glass, exploding shards around the crew and burning a half-meter hole in the back wall. Wesley risked an expedition across the deck and down into the bilge. He reported that they must have sprung a plank, for there was water in the hold.

Uel and Mervyn did their best, but too often their shots arced wildly off into the dark sky. Then another shot from the Planemen hit the deck beside Uel. He rolled onto his side, white-faced, with a jagged wound in his right hand. Cati bandaged it as best she could, but he couldn't operate the crossbow anymore. The Planemen grew in confidence, sweeping in at wave height and firing across the deck, and this time their fire was doing real damage. On one sweep the forecastle was set alight, and Dr. Diamond and the Sub-Commandant had to brave the open deck again and again with buckets before they had it under control.

The water was still pouring into the bilges, and Cati could feel that the weight of it was slowing Boat again, and still they were tossed around by the huge waves. Cati marveled at the ability of the little craft to take so much punishment, but she knew that it could not go on. She remembered what Chancellor had said about the Mortmain being sent to the bottom of the sea. Why had he said that? The scene in the wheelhouse was chaotic now. Dr. Diamond and the Sub-Commandant ran from place to place putting out fires, but still the woodsmoke stung her eyes. Sleety spray came through the broken window every time they crested a wave. The injured Uel crouched miserably in a corner, clutching his hand. The Planemen were like angry birds as they swooped over Boat.

"We'll try to make it to nighttime," Wesley said through gritted teeth. "They might let up then."

But what will happen after that? Cati thought. They'll simply come back at dawn. Just then, she looked to her left and saw that the little girl was standing there, staring out across the waves, seeming completely unperturbed by what was going on around her.

Cati followed her gaze. She thought she could see something, a shape perhaps, something that seemed to blend with the gray and stormy sea. Probably something belonging to the Harsh coming to finish us off, she thought miserably. Maybe it was the little girl who had undone the stopcock. Cati looked at her again, but she kept her calm gaze fixed on the sea.

The Planemen withdrew and took up position behind Boat. They seemed to be talking among themselves, taking a rest before a final attack, Cati thought. Wesley's attention was taken up with Boat now, but suddenly he straightened and peered out into the storm.

"What is it?" the Sub-Commandant asked.

"Damned if I know," said Wesley, "but I'd say it's with them lot of Planemen behind us."

As it got closer, they saw that it was a ship of some kind. Cati could see that the Planemen were aware of it too. After a while one of them rose in the air and flew off toward it.

The ship was much closer now, moving at tremendous speed. It was big, so big that it barely rose and fell on the waves, and even when it was still a mile away, the great prow reared above them.

"A freighter of some kind," Dr. Diamond said. But as it neared, they could see that there was something strange about it. For a start, it was red with rust and hadn't seen paint for many years. Whole sections of its huge metal plates were missing. The giant mast lay broken across the deck. There seemed to be tangles of broken equipment and overturned oil drums lying everywhere. So much of the huge ship's superstructure was missing that you could see right through it in places. Great gouts of oily black smoke billowed from its funnel as it bore down upon them at speed.

"What is it?" asked Cati.

"I think I know," Wesley said, and there was a strange expression on his face. "I think I know."

"It is the Grim Captain," the Sub-Commandant said quietly.

"The Grim Captain is just a story," said Chancellor shortly, but Cati thought that if there was such a thing as a Grim Captain, then this was the grim kind of ship he would command.

The Planeman who had gone to investigate rejoined the others. He spoke to them quickly and then without warning they swooped on Boat, this time in a furious attack, no longer caring for their own safety. Mervyn landed hits on them, and one of the planes trailed fire, but their own bolts of magno were landing everywhere on Boat. They felt the deck vibrate beneath their feet.

"We can't stay afloat much longer!" Wesley shouted.

A great wave crashed over the deck and extinguished the flames that licked at it, but as it did so half a dozen other fires sprang up. Mervyn fired desperately and the damaged plane was hit again. It shot across the bow of Boat and landed in the sea with a great hiss. One of the remaining planes slewed in the air to avoid the stricken plane and struck the mast with a clang. It hung there, tangled with the mast, its pilot struggling to free himself. The remaining plane swooped in and the trapped Planeman grabbed its undercarriage. As he was hoisted aloft, Mervyn's last shots seared the air around them. But it was too late. The overloaded plane climbed high into the air, hovered for a moment, and then turned slowly back the way it had come.

Their work was done. The deck was full of holes and flames were starting to lick up through them. Boat was listing badly to one side and barely moving. And the ship was almost on them. The massive bow bore down on their frail craft. Cati was sure that it must plow over them until, with its engines shrieking in protest, water boiling at its stern, the ship shuddered to a halt alongside.

In the lee of the ship the storm seemed almost to have disappeared. A wall of rusty and scarred steel reared up above them, and Boat banged gently against its side. As Cati stared, a rope ladder suddenly tumbled down from the freighter. The ladder had been mended and knotted all over; some of the rungs seemed rotted and others had snapped.

"It could be a trap," cautioned Chancellor.

"I'm not climbing that," Cati said.

"You don't have a choice," said Wesley, and his voice was serious. They looked down. Water was oozing through the deck at their feet and the motor had stopped completely. But still they looked doubtfully at the rotted hulk beside them and the dangerous-looking rope ladder dangling beside the bridge. Until, without a word, the little girl walked to the end of the rope ladder, grasped it, and started to climb confidently.

"That's it, then," the Sub-Commandant said. "You next, Cati."

One by one they took hold of the ladder and climbed. Wesley paused before he climbed, taking a long look around the ruined Boat that had sailed proudly out of the harbor. Rubbing the handrail and muttering something under his breath, he began to climb without looking back. Not even when the Sub-Commandant, supporting the injured Uel, got onto the ladder and the burning Boat turned on her side, then slipped beneath the waves with a gentle hiss.

It was a long climb up the side of the ship. The rope ladder swayed against the rusty and jagged metal plates, scraping Cati's knees and elbows. Every so often a plate would be missing and she would find herself staring into the dark void that was the booming, cavernous interior of the ship. She didn't know what was down there, but she found herself scampering up the ladder away from it.

When finally she fell over the rail onto the deck, Cati

lay there for a moment, exhausted, then lifted her head cautiously to reveal a scene of terrible squalor. Empty barrels and paint tins littered the deck, which was splintered and broken in places. There were deep rents and missing hatch covers. There were tangles of rusting cable and broken winches. Broken chains dangled from splintered masts. Cati turned toward the bridge. It was, if anything, in worse shape than the rest of the ship. It was a towering structure, as high as a ten-story building, with many windows, all of which were broken. There were large holes everywhere, and part of the roof seemed to be missing. But the worst thing was that the entire structure was bent to one side, leaning out over the water as if it had been nudged by a giant elbow. The wheelhouse itself seemed to have suffered the worst devastation. All its windows and their frames were gone and the interior was full of tangled metal, and every piece of buckled metal bore the scars of a thousand storms.

And then in the middle of it Cati saw him—the Grim Captain—the wheel of the ship gripped in his icy hands, as it had been gripped for countless years and countless icy seas. The man was tall and heavyset and motionless, as though carved from a block of stone. His face was hidden by a massive white beard streaked with brown and black. And above the beard his eyes burned with a fierce light. Cati felt her knees go weak and felt her heart hammering in her breast, with fear, yes, but also with a terrible pity, as if all the loneliness in the world had been given to one man and he had carried it as a burden for time out of mind.

She sensed Wesley standing beside her and knew that he felt the whole thing.

"The Grim Captain," he breathed, seemingly unaware that he had spoken. Just then the Sub-Commandant and Uel tumbled over the rail. The Grim Captain raised one hand and grasped a lanyard above his head and pulled it. The ship's siren rang out and Cati had to cover her ears. He rang it again and again, three times in all they heard the note of the ghostly horn, long and sad. Then, accompanied by loud moans and clangs deep in the bowels of the ship, they started to move again, slowly at first, then picking up speed, the whole ship shuddering and creaking as it crashed through the waves.

"There's somebody knows where they're going," Wesley said. They followed his gaze. The little girl was once more standing in the bow, looking out across the storm-tossed ocean. Chancellor leaned wearily on the rail, until Mervyn pointed out that the stanchion holding it was almost completely rotted through. The injured Uel was shivering uncontrollably.

"He needs to be out of the wind," Dr. Diamond said. There was a doorway in the front of the wheelhouse, its metal door sagging on the one hinge that was left, but none of them felt any eagerness to enter the dank space beyond.

"I must ask the Captain if we may take shelter," the

Sub-Commandant said. Wesley looked at him as if he was mad.

"Are you sure?" Dr. Diamond said.

"I have to speak to him," the Sub-Commandant said. "We have work to do and I need to know if he will help us."

"He'll freeze your blood," said Chancellor.

"I don't know," Cati said slowly. "I don't think so." Unless, she thought, terrible sorrow can freeze your blood.

They watched as the Sub-Commandant stepped through the doorway and into the darkness beyond.

Several minutes later they saw the Grim Captain turn from his station at the wheel, but Cati could not see the Captain's face. It seemed that they talked for a long time. Cati was getting worried about Uel, who was sitting on the deck, pale-faced. With five minutes' swift work Dr. Diamond had converted his ice goggles into a makeshift heater, which he put under Uel's jacket, but it didn't seem to help.

At last the Sub-Commandant came back. He seemed stooped with fatigue, and his expression was that of someone who had been given terrible tidings.

"He will give us passage," the Sub-Commandant said wearily. "He will take us to the Great Machine in the north."

"Did he ask a price?" Chancellor demanded. "Is there a tariff?" The Sub-Commandant shook his head wearily.

"There is something he wants," he said, "but he won't

say what it is. It is something that must be given freely, without being asked for." Dr. Diamond said nothing, but he shook his head as if the Sub-Commandant's words had confirmed something he already suspected.

The Sub-Commandant turned and beckoned to them to follow him through the door. Cati shivered as she stepped through. But it wasn't as bad as she expected, if you didn't count the water slopping about, the discarded tools and junk that littered the corridor from one end to the other, and the groans and bangs and coughing sounds echoing up and down.

After a minute the Sub-Commandant led them down a twisted metal staircase. Then a most peculiar thing happened. Cati was at the bottom of the staircase one minute, and then there was a kind of a flicker and she was back at the top again. She looked round alarmed.

"Don't worry, Cati," Dr. Diamond said, "it's nothing to do with the ship. It's a sign that we're getting close to the Great Machine in the north. When you interfere with the fabric of time, you get distortions—little slippages like the one you just noticed. It will happen more and more as we get nearer."

They stopped in front of a set of doors that once had been carved and varnished but now were dilapidated. The Sub-Commandant pushed them open. Inside were the remains of what had once been a beautiful stateroom. The walls had once been paneled with leather, although only strips of it remained now. A chandelier sagged drunkenly from the ceiling, many of its glass pendants either shattered or missing. Expensive furniture in various states of disrepair lay on the floor. To Cati's surprise, she saw a stained marble fireplace on one wall. Dr. Diamond walked through the room, examining the furniture and various broken objects, muttering things like, "Louis Quatorze, very fine," and "Early art deco . . . impressive . . ."

Wesley, meanwhile, started to pile broken pieces of furniture into the fireplace to make a fire. Dr. Diamond looked as if he was going to object.

"It's all broken anyway," Cati whispered to him, and he nodded and smiled a little wistfully. Soon Wesley had a blazing fire going and Uel seemed to revive a little.

"Who is he?" she whispered to Dr. Diamond. "I mean the Grim Captain."

"We all thought that he was a legend. But that's the problem with being adrift in time. Legends have a habit of turning up. The story is that he did a great wrong, but in the process threw away the one thing he valued above all else. And now he cannot rest."

"Like the Flying Dutchman?"

"Just like the Flying Dutchman, except in the Grim Captain's case it is his own mind that drives him; the memory of what he did will not let him rest."

"Can he not do something to make up for it?"

"I don't know. There are some crimes for which there are no amends. Perhaps his is one of them."

They made themselves as comfortable as they could in

the ruined stateroom. They were exhausted, since they had not really slept the previous night. One by one they all slipped off to sleep—except for Chancellor, who sat by the fire and stared into it. And the Sub-Commandant, who watched him from the shadows, his eyes stern and unblinking.

Owen woke up in what seemed like a smothering dark. He sat bolt upright and realized that he was in a bed with dark drapes pulled round it. Vaguely, he could see the flicker of a fire. Something told him that he was underground. There was a certain smell, but he couldn't put his finger on it—earth and roots and buried things perhaps.

Cautiously he moved one of the drapes aside. He could see a fire flickering in a large stone fireplace. Pieta was curled up beside it on the floor, sleeping like a cat. He stuck his head out cautiously. He was in what seemed to be a very large room, its ceiling lost in the shadows. At first he thought that the room was covered in vast drapes sweeping down gracefully from a height, but then he realized that they were not in fact drapes, but cobwebs, accumulated over hundreds of years. But Owen also knew that the shapes could not be natural, that some hand had created them, woven them even. The light was eerie too. There was no magno here. The walls seemed to emanate light, a greenish phosphorescence. He moved to get a better view and suddenly his arm was seized in a clawlike grip and with ferocious speed he was plucked from the bed.

Owen found himself standing in front of the tallest woman he had ever seen. She was wearing what appeared to be a ball gown. When she moved, gorgeous flower patterns showed, but it was so faded with age that the designs seemed to come and go. Her face was long and haughty and brown as oak, and her eyes were a golden color. Like an eagle's, Owen thought. Her feet were bare and her black hair was piled on top of her head. When she turned her head slowly, he gasped. One side of her face was riven with a scar that ran like a fissure from the temple to the edge of her jaw, a scar that reminded him of the old tree on the riverbank that had been struck by lightning.

"I am Long Woman," she said, her speech rapid and accented, her voice harsh. "You are Navigator."

"M-my name is Owen," he stammered.

"You are Navigator," she repeated in a tone that told him not to contradict her again.

"Where am . . . Where are we?"

"You in my place. I find when they bury me in bog."

"Bury you? Are you . . . I mean, alive, or . . ."

"Alive? They bury me, no?" She tossed her hair back and laughed, a harsh sound like a rook cawing. "Now come eat," she said. "You not have much time."

"What about Pieta, my friend?"

"She sleep, not wake; she lead you freeze in storm." The Long Woman made a gesture of contempt.

"It wasn't like that. She rescued me from Johnston. It wasn't her fault."

"Right, right, you say. Maybe I wake her later." The Long Woman didn't sound all that interested one way or another. She led Owen through a doorway into another room.

If the first room with its cobweb drapes had been strange, then this one was more eerie still. The walls were moist and boggy, with mosses and lichens growing on them. In the middle of the room was a table set with the strangest feast that Owen had ever seen. Each place setting had a plate, a knife, and an oddly shaped fork with two prongs. The centerpiece of the table was a large bowl filled with eels. As Owen watched, one of them lifted its head and then slithered over the others so that they all writhed.

There were bowls piled high with mistletoe berries. Inside a tall glass bowl, snails moved slowly over the glass, leaving a trail of slime behind them. Other plates had mounds of evil-colored fungus, carefully sliced. There were sickly puffballs and plates of jellylike aspic that quivered as though there was something living inside. There were pale and lacy toadstools that seemed to be pickled in bluish liquor. Each place had a large silver drinking vessel, and as Owen looked, something seemed to dive from the rim of the nearest one, landing in whatever liquid filled them with a distinct plop.

"I not make you eat," the Long Woman said with her harsh laugh. "This food for other guests, come later."

All Owen could think was, whoever they were, he didn't want to meet them. The Long Woman led him through the room into a pantry. This time, he saw with relief, there was nothing that crawled or oozed on offer. Instead, there were boxes of wrinkle-skinned sweet apples, hazelnuts, hard-skinned cheese. He ate hungrily and, at the Long Woman's order, filled his pockets.

"Can I ask you something?" he said.

"Ask question," said the Long Woman.

"Why did you call me Navigator?"

"Because you are Navigator. Only one to bring all back to right time, unless Harsh kill you stone dead."

Owen shivered at the thought of the Harsh. He couldn't believe that he had almost forgotten about them. "How do I do it?" he asked. "How do I bring everyone back to the right time?"

"Use Mortmain. You have it?"

"No. I went to look for it, but I couldn't find it."

"What hell," she said with an elaborate shrug. "Maybe it find you."

"They were taking me to the Harsh, to the Great Machine in the north. Johnston was going to give me to the Harsh," Owen said.

"They take you to Puissance; that where you must go. Only place to use Mortmain."

"I don't understand. What do I do? Where is the, the . . . Puissance?"

"You not know?" she said disbelievingly. "You not know!" And her mocking laughter filled the whole room.

"How should I know?" he said angrily.

"Do not be cross with me, my dear friend," the Long Woman said, suddenly stooping to him and taking his face between her thin, strong fingers, her face hovering over his so that she looked like a snake ready to strike. "Do not shout at me or I snap your neck like small twig. You pay attention?"

"Yes, yes . . . I'm sorry." Owen did not doubt for one moment that she meant what she said. She scrutinized his face, as if to make sure that he really was sorry.

"Better," she said. "Your father not tell you where Puissance was?"

"My father is dead."

"I see now. Father should tell son these things. I tell you. You are on frozen lake now. River not freeze, go too fast. Lake freeze. Frozen lake goes all the way to coast. There is Puissance. Many mile."

"How are we going to get there?" Owen said, his heart sinking.

"I look after how. You know what to do, you get

there?" He shook his head. "Who help you? Your friend, she good for fight, not for think."

"Can you help me?"

"Not like that. I cannot leave lake. Is forbid. But I can show you a little." She knelt on the floor and took a long pin from her hair. Using the tip of it, she traced out a map. First of all a jagged coastline, then an inlet, which showed a lake narrowing to a thin neck, then open sea. Opposite the mouth of the inlet she drew an island.

"Island is like mountain outside, like castle inside. Stone underneath, very deep. Great Machine is down in rock, very deep." She drew another wide line in the sand going from the coast to the ice island. "Is ice bridge for Harsh to get to island. They no like water. Like ice."

Maybe I could cross the ice bridge as well, Owen thought, shivering at the idea of the sea.

"Come with me," the Long Woman said, standing up swiftly. "We have to get you quick to coast." They walked up a long passageway and she opened the door at the top. They stepped out into a blizzard, snow driving at them horizontally across the lake.

We'll never get to the coast, Owen thought as he tried to shield his face against the icy blast. But the Long Woman led him on until they reached an enclosure of living willow.

She opened a gate and motioned Owen inside. He stepped in and she closed the gate carefully behind him.

It was calmer in the enclosure. The willows broke the force of the wind, although their straight trunks looked suspiciously like bars. The Long Woman looked upward and whistled softly. Owen was surprised to see several dogs sprawling across the branches of a large tree growing in the middle of the enclosure. The dogs were like massive greyhounds with long hair and handsome, aristocratic faces. They were different colors, but one was coal-black, and this was the one that the Long Woman summoned.

"Arcana," she called softly. The black dog stood up, stretched in an almost catlike way, and turned his head toward them. Owen took an involuntary step backward. The dog's eyes burned red like hot coals. "Arcana, there are guests for journey."

Arcana stretched again and gave a single sharp bark. Suddenly the snow that lay deep on the floor of the enclosure started to stir. Other dogs were sleeping under it, and one by one they stood up and shook off the snow. Owen realized that the Long Woman had kept one hand on the bar of the gate. The dogs were all facing toward them, and from one of them came a low growl.

"Not to be trusted," the Long Woman said softly. "No, not to be trusted. Arcana!"

The black dog uncoiled and slid to the ground in one easy movement. It stood with its back to Owen and the Long Woman. One by one the other dogs backed away and sat down, except for one brindled dog who stared past Arcana at Owen, her eyes burning. Arcana took several paces forward. Without warning the brindled dog lunged at the black dog. But her teeth clicked shut on air, and suddenly Arcana was on her back, his teeth buried in her neck, driving her down until her growls turned to whimpers and a trickle of blood ran from the spot where Arcana's teeth were fixed. When he was satisfied that she was subdued, Arcana released her. With her tail between her legs, the brindle dog slunk off to join the others, although not without a sullen and dangerous look over her shoulder at Owen.

The Long Woman then opened the gate and led them all out into the snow. Suddenly Owen understood what she was doing. Standing in the lee of the enclosure was a sleigh, incredibly long and thin, consisting of a carriage mounted on two long, narrow blades that curved up at each end.

"Is ice runner," the Long Woman said. She took down a long harness that was hanging from the willows and started to put it on the dogs, each of which stood patiently in its place. Arcana took up position at the front. "Dogs will run all day all night. You start now. Get to Great Machine Puissance in time."

"What about my friend?"

"You want take her? Maybe she no go. Maybe she stay for dinner." The Long Woman smiled, showing sharp little teeth, and Owen shuddered as he remembered the strange feast he had seen laid out.

"No, no . . . I'll take her with me . . . if that's all right."

When they got back to where Pieta lay sleeping in front of the fire, the Long Woman leaned over and whispered something in her ear. There was a pause, then Pieta leapt to her feet, looking around her mistrustfully.

"It's all right, Pieta. This is the Long Woman. She is helping us."

"I know who the Long Woman is," Pieta said. "I called her to help us."

"Good thing I hear," said the Long Woman, "else Navigator die in snow, all lost forever."

Owen saw the startled look in Pieta's eyes, although she tried to hide it. The Long Woman saw it too. "You not know boy Navigator?"

"Some of us thought he might—"

"Who else could boy be?"

"Some . . . some people didn't want to believe it," Pieta said.

"They said my father stole the Mortmain." Owen felt anger wash over him.

"Navigator cannot steal Mortmain. Navigator is Keeper of Mortmain. Cannot steal what you own."

Owen was more confused than ever, but Pieta was nodding thoughtfully.

"Is time to go," the Long Woman declared. "Dogs get tired waiting; they eat each other for entertain."

"I'm not going anywhere until you tell me what the Navigator is," Owen said.

"Not time," the Long Woman said in a cool, dangerous voice, but Pieta held up her hand. "Quick then, quick, quick."

"The Navigator is the person who forms a link between the temporal world—your world, Owen— and the islands in time. The Navigator has the power of waking the Resisters from Sleep."

"The Navigator is Keeper of Mortmain," the Long Woman said. "The Navigator is forever bound to the Resistance. The Navigator is the faithful. The Navigator is the betrayer."

"Betrayer?" Owen said, bewildered. "I've never betrayed anybody."

"The Navigator has betrayed the Resisters in the past," Pieta said gently. "That's why Samual was so hostile when he suspected that you were the Navigator."

"And my father? They thought he betrayed them as well."

"Yes, but I did not believe it then and I do not believe it now."

Pieta and Owen followed the Long Woman out into the snow. The dogs were whining and snarling, eager to be off. Pieta looked at them suspiciously.

"Get in," the Long Woman said. For a moment Owen thought that Pieta was going to refuse. Quickly he got in, hoping she would follow him. It was surprisingly warm in the sled. A hooped leather cover kept the snow off, and underneath the cover were warm, soft skins he could pull up to his throat.

"Come on," Owen urged. Reluctantly Pieta clambered in. The Long Woman handed a set of reins to Owen.

"You will not need them," she said. "Arcana knows what he has to do. Take this." She handed Owen a crude iron knife. "Cold iron. Harsh don't like it. Stick it in door, they can't open it." Owen put the knife inside his coat.

"Also this." The Long Woman took a pin from her hair, a small one this time. She bent to the ground and dug in the snow with her long hand. Owen looked down. She had uncovered a tiny white flower. She plucked it and pinned it to his coat.

"What is it?" he asked.

"Fleur-de-lis," she told him.

The dogs were getting anxious now. One of them started to howl and suddenly they all lifted their heads and howled, the hair on their backbones standing on end. Owen thought he could see the static crackling in their coats. The Long Woman suddenly seemed even taller. Her long shadow fell over them, so black and hard that Owen could almost feel it. Over the howling of the dogs she spoke out in a terrible and ancient language. The dogs howled even louder and pulled at their traces until she raised her hand and brought it down in a slicing motion. First Arcana and then the rest of the dogs leapt forward.

The Long Woman leaned over Owen as the sledge shot past her and it seemed that he could smell her perfume, heavy and cloying, with something of the earth about it, something of the grave. A look of terrible regret was on her face, a look of anguish endured over years. Owen drew back from her, and even Pieta drew her breath in sharply, and then they were gone. The snow around them flew up into the air and there was a sound like a great sigh. For a moment they were blinded and when the snow fell to the ground again and Owen looked back, he could see nothing but a little wooded island breaking the vast flatness of the lake. The island dwindled even as he looked, the only sound the runners of the sleigh as they hissed across the ice.

Three miles south, a river ran parallel to the lake, going toward the sea. It was a fast river, tumbling through gorges, and its speed and savagery meant that it would not freeze. A careful watcher might make out a dark shape being carried downstream by the furious current. It was a raft. At the front of the raft sat Johnston. Mariacallas was steering the boat with a crude oar. Passionara sat in the middle of the boat, maintaining a stream of venomous cursing. Johnston was grim-faced and there was a bandage about his head. He carried Whitwashisberd's ledger under his arm.

23

Try as she might, Cati could not get used to the little fluctuations in the flow of time, which increased as they went north. One minute she would have just got into the bed she had made for herself, ready to go to sleep, and the next she would be back standing on the freezing floor. Or time would flicker the other way, forward, when she was about to take a bite out of an apple, and then she would find herself standing there with an apple core in her hand. It got so that she couldn't remember what she had done and when she had done it, even if she had done it at all. Wesley looked bewildered every time it happened to him.

Only Dr. Diamond didn't seem to mind. He spent all

his time at the rail with his binoculars, studying the twisting shape on the horizon.

"What is it?" Cati asked him.

"I think it is what we are looking for," he said quietly, "although I still don't know what we're going to do when we get there." He weighed the Mortmain thoughtfully in his hand.

"And the Harsh will be waiting for us," the Sub-Commandant reminded them.

On and on they sped. The Grim Captain never seemed to leave the wheel. His eyes were fixed on the horizon. Cati saw the three Raggie boys gather often just beneath the bridge, talking intensely among themselves. She asked Dr. Diamond what they were talking about, but he just smiled—sadly, she thought—and said that if the Raggies wanted to tell her, then that was their business.

The weather had settled into bitter cold, with little wind, and at night the stars shone brilliantly, although Cati noticed that sometimes they seemed a bit elongated, stretched out of shape as though they were painted on some flexible material and somebody had pulled it. And still the shape on the horizon grew, so that it was now a funnel, narrow at the bottom and wide at the top. Except that this funnel twisted and writhed and seemed to go on without end into the sky.

After two days on the ship, Cati overheard Dr. Diamond and the Sub-Commandant talking together anxiously.

"I haven't seen him since last night," Dr. Diamond said.

"He hasn't been himself lately," said the Sub-Commandant.

"Have you searched?"

"Yes, but it's a big ship. If you don't want to be found, you could hide for days. But he is somewhere on board. I can feel it."

Cati knew that they must be talking about Chancellor and she realized that she hadn't seen him since the first night they came on board.

"It's very worrying," Dr. Diamond said gloomily.

"I know where to find him," said a voice beside Cati, making her jump. It was Wesley. "I know where he is, and I reckon it was him tried to sink my Boat. Come on!"

"Shouldn't we tell the others?"

"I want to have a word with him about Boat first. Are you coming or not?"

Cati turned and followed Wesley. He led her through the door in the bridge and past the stateroom. They went down one stairwell after another, each one colder and gloomier than the last.

"Where are we going?"

"Engine room," said Wesley grimly, "and be careful."

The condition of the ship down here was even worse. There were great jagged holes in the gangways, and broken metal stairways spiraled off into nothingness. And all the time Cati could feel the booming and clanging of the engine getting nearer and nearer. Finally, they reached a massive steel door. Wesley threw his weight against it, and with a rusty protest it swung open. They stepped out onto a gangway above the engines. The engine room was a vast cavern of dangling cables and open sumps and broken dials. Pipes leaked great gouts of steam or oozed oil. Massive piston rods rose and fell, making the ground shake. Tappets clattered. In the middle of the engine room, two great boilers roared and hissed and flared.

"Come on!" Wesley shouted. Cati followed him. They went down a metal stairway until they reached the floor of the engine room. The heat was intense. Wesley walked purposefully toward the giant boilers. Huge fires blazed at the foot of the boilers. Even at this distance Cati could feel a sheen of sweat on her face, but Wesley kept going forward and she followed.

As they clambered onto the final catwalk, Cati could see the boilers glowing a dull orange, burning who knew what kind of fuel.

"Look," Wesley said. At the foot of the biggest boiler and dwarfed by its bulk, a figure crouched. Chancellor. He did not see them as they approached. They were three meters away from him and the heat was like a wall. They stopped. Even above the noise of the engine room they could hear his voice, thin and piercing.

"Cold," he moaned, "so cold, so cold."

"Chancellor!" Wesley called out.

The man spun around and as he did so he put his hand on the railing beside him. Cati was also holding the rail, but she snatched her hand away as sudden cold seared it. She looked down. Despite the heat, the rail was covered with frost. She looked up. Chancellor's face was whiter than anything she had ever seen.

"What do you want, Raggie?" Chancellor demanded. "Can a man not get a little heat in a cold world?"

"It was you tried to sink Boat, weren't it?" Wesley said. Chancellor did not reply. "And no one ever seen Owen with Johnston," Wesley went on evenly.

"We thought it was Samual!" exclaimed Cati.

"All damn lies," Wesley said, his fists bunched now.

"There was a spy all along," Cati said. "It was you!"

"Johnston got told every move the Resisters did make," Wesley said.

"I don't understand," Cati said. "Why are you working with the Harsh? After everything . . . all they want to do is freeze us forever!"

"No," Chancellor said, "they aren't like that. You don't understand. They wanted to make an island in time for us. I went to see them, to save us."

"They wouldn't save us," Wesley said. "And even if they did, what about everybody else?"

"All the people who lived all through time," Cati said, horrified. "What about them?"

"That is true," Chancellor said, and this time his voice was full of sorrow. "All those people." Great tears welled in his eyes, which froze as he bowed his head. Wesley and Cati watched as the tears formed into long icicles.

"We would have taken care of the future," Chancellor said. "There would have been someone left alive. There would have been hope. A small hope, but still a hope."

Cati thought of the loneliness of the man as he tried to make terrible decisions for the good of everyone. Chancellor raised a hand to his face as though to wipe away the long icicles that had formed on his eyes. Then, in one sudden movement, he snapped off an icicle and with a vicious flick of his wrist, his eyes filled with hatred, he sent the icicle speeding through the air, a stiletto of ice, with its long blade aimed precisely at Cati's heart. There was nothing she could do. It seemed she could hear the whistle of the ice blade as it cleaved the air, and she closed her eyes and waited for it to strike her.

Time flickered.

Cati opened her eyes. Once again she saw Chancellor reach up as if to wipe the ice tears away, but this time she knew what was going to happen. And so did Wesley.

"No!" he shouted, and lunged toward Chancellor just as the man started to flick the tear toward Cati. Wesley's shoulder hit Chancellor on the hip, throwing him off balance, and the deadly tear, instead of hitting Cati, struck the pipe at her shoulder with an icy clang.

Chancellor stumbled, his arms flailing as he sought to regain his balance. He reached out for a pipe to stop himself, but the ice that formed on the pipe the second he touched it formed a glaze so that his fingers slipped off. Cati and Wesley could only watch in horror as he staggered backward toward the fiery mouth of the ship's furnace.

"No! No!" he cried out. Cati hid her eyes, wishing that time would flicker again and bring them back to before all of this happened. There was a roar, a huge hissing sound, and the heat of the furnace dimmed. Cati opened her eyes. The furnace was almost black now, and it seemed as if the cold in Chancellor's bones had almost extinguished it. Then suddenly the flames leapt up again and a huge cloud of boiling steam billowed out at them.

"Come on!" Wesley yelled. "Let's get out of here." He pushed Cati in front of him as they dashed toward the exit, just ahead of the scalding steam. They stumbled through the door and Wesley threw his shoulder against it. With a protesting creak, it swung shut. Wesley slumped to the floor.

"Is he . . . is he gone?" Cati asked. Wesley nodded.

"Like ice thrown on a fire. Good thing the way time flickered when he threw the tear at you. Or else . . ."

"He must have been working for the Harsh all along," she said.

"Aye. Remember the fight by the river? The way they always knew what we were going to do next?"

"He always took the other side against Owen too, acting like he was just being reasonable."

"He done the stopcock as well. They turned him good. You got to watch them Harsh. There's more to them than ice. . . . What's that?"

The ship was slowing, the great engines juddering to a halt, the hull creaking and groaning with a sound of rivets popping. They ran quickly up the gangways, trying not to slip on the oily deck or fall into one of the gaping holes. Eventually they burst into the open air. Cati gasped in astonishment. Even Wesley swore quietly to himself and took a step backward. Somehow they had reached the Great Machine in the north, and the object they had seen on the horizon towered above them, bigger than anything Cati had ever seen, a great whirling, twisting mass that grew bigger as it went up and up, rising from a point on an island. As it disappeared into the sky, massive storms raged, sheets of lightning crackling about it. And as it spiraled upward, a roaring filled the air. On and on it went, its vastness humbling and terrifying. If it had been night, Cati thought, then even the very stars would be sucked into it.

"Goes on for ever," Wesley breathed.

"Yes, it does," the Sub-Commandant said. "It goes on to eternity. In a way, it is eternity."

"It's like a giant waterspout or something," Cati said.

"That's a good comparison," Dr. Diamond replied, "except it's not made of water, it's made of time." The scientist's face was pale with excitement. "Look closely."

Cati stared at it as it writhed over them. It seemed that she could see vast oceans appearing and fading, stars being born, planets dying. There were continents covered in trees that seemed to wither in an instant. A great city went from shining citadel to ruins in the blink of an eye.

Dr. Diamond's notebook was in his hand and he was scribbling furiously. Cati saw that her father was looking at her.

"What is it, Cati?" he said quietly. "What's wrong?"

"It's Chancellor," Wesley said. Quickly he told the Sub-Commandant and Dr. Diamond what had happened. The Sub-Commandant turned away and bowed his head. Dr. Diamond opened his mouth to say something, then he too turned away. They stood in silence for several minutes. The ship drifted on the cold, black ocean and chunks of ice struck its hull with low thuds.

"He betrayed us all," the Sub-Commandant said bitterly.

"He went to the Harsh to parley and was corrupted," Dr. Diamond said. "Don't be too hard on him."

"I should have seen it." The Sub-Commandant's fists were clenched. "I should have read it in his eyes. It was there, you know. His treachery was there to be seen for those who looked."

"He was a proud and subtle man," Dr. Diamond said. "He knew how to hide his duplicity from us."

They might have stood there forever had the sound of the great spout of time not changed, adding an ominous and ever-increasing shriek to its tumultuous roaring.

"We have to hurry!" Dr. Diamond exclaimed. "Or the Puissance will reach a pitch that we can't stop."

"We have to get to the Machine itself," the Sub-Commandant said.

"Where's that?" asked Wesley.

"The part at the bottom is the Great Machine," Dr. Diamond said. "It generates the Puissance, which is the vortex—what Cati called the waterspout." He hesitated. "Chancellor was a traitor in the end, but I think the Harsh exploited his desire to do good, to save something from the ruins."

Dr. Diamond took out a small pocketbook. Between the pages was a pressed and faded cornflower. "You were a friend and comrade once," he said. "This is how we remember you."

He cast the cornflower into the sea. For a moment it floated on the frozen ocean, a symbol of spring and hope, and then it disappeared beneath the black water.

Owen had lost all sense of time passing as the sleigh sped silently across the ice. The cover was stiff with ice, but it was pleasantly warm beneath the skins and he dozed on and off, waking once in the night and looking up to see a clear sky and thousands of stars. The dogs ran tirelessly, their breath streaming out behind them like pennants in the cold air. The next time he woke it could not have been more different. It was gray dawn and it was snowing hard. Pieta had pulled down the cover behind them so that it acted as a roof, leaving a thin slit through which they could see. They shared the food that the Long Woman had given him. It was warm in the sleigh and Owen started to wish that the ride would last forever.

Pieta had thawed a lot from the ferocious warrior he had first met, and he felt brave enough to question her about the Long Woman. She told him that there were many islands in time, some small, some large. Some were dedicated to resisting the Harsh and their allies, and some were devoted to other, unknown purposes, like that of the Long Woman. "But if the Workhouse ever falls," she said, "all of them will fall."

After a while Owen slept again. His body had taken a lot of punishment and he hadn't slept much since he had been captured by Johnston. But when he woke it was night again and he was confused.

"I didn't sleep all day, did I?" he asked.

"No," Pieta said with a frown. "Time is changing fast and both day and night are short now. I hope we aren't too late."

That dawn the snow cleared and they could see a great writhing column on the horizon. Arcana slowed the dogs to a halt. He sniffed the air cautiously, then lifted his muzzle and howled long and loud. The other dogs joined him and their cries split the air. Then the ice runner leapt forward again, twice as fast. A spray of ice crystals from the runners hung in the air long after they had passed.

The ship moved slowly forward as Dr. Diamond studied the Puissance with his telescope. He had spotted the ice bridge that led from the mainland to the island.

"They'll be guarding that," the Sub-Commandant muttered. "We'll have to land on the island somehow." He seemed preoccupied and sad since the death of Chancellor.

Overhearing this, Wesley went hunting for a boat to take them ashore. The ship had once had lifeboats but now the shattered remnants hung from davits fused with rust. On the foredeck, though, Wesley found a small boat that had probably been used for painting the hull, for it seemed that gallons of multicolored paint had been spilled on it. Fortunately, the spilled paint had preserved the woodwork, so Uel and Mervyn started to repair a few sprung planks and fashion oars from old bits of timber they found around the place. The little girl stood in the bow and did not turn around. The Grim Captain stood similarly unmoved at the wheel.

Slowly they inched nearer to the island. Cati could see the mainland clearly. It was bleak and treeless. There seemed to be an opening into an estuary or a lake, and a fast-flowing river emptied into the sea not far from it. As she watched, an object emerged from the mouth of the river. There were people sitting on it.

"Look!" she said to Dr. Diamond, but he was engaged in a complicated calculation and did not turn around. "Wesley!" she called. Wesley came over and followed Cati's pointing finger. He looked, then deftly plucked the doctor's binoculars from his coat pocket.

" 'Scuse me, doc," he said, although Dr. Diamond didn't hear. Wesley looked through the binoculars, then whistled softly.

"Here," he said to Cati, "take a look for yourself."

She put the binoculars to her eye.

"That's Johnston, isn't it?"

"And two of his men. Looks like trouble for somebody."

Cati swung the binoculars around. At the mouth of the lake inlet she saw more movement. Then suddenly a sleigh came into view, a sleigh traveling at breakneck speed and pulled by a team of the biggest dogs she had ever seen. Cati focused on the back of the sleigh. There were two people in it. Suddenly she felt her heart jump. She could barely speak.

"Wesley . . . W-Wesley . . . ," she stammered, "it's Owen and Pieta!" Wesley grabbed the binoculars.

"You're right, girl," he said, "and they're headed straight toward Johnston."

It was true. Even without the binoculars Cati could see that Johnston's raft had beached itself on the icy margin where the lake met the sea and that the sleigh was heading straight toward it.

"Owen!" she shouted. "Owen, look out!" Wesley joined her in jumping and waving, then Dr. Diamond and the Sub-Commandant, but it was to no avail. Their voices were shrill and tiny against the monumental howl of the Puissance.

"Quick, boys," Wesley said. "Let's get that boat into the water." He ran over to Uel and Mervyn, who were struggling with a rusted davit as they tried to lower the little boat.

"They're nearly past. They'll escape!" Cati shouted. She could tell that Johnston hadn't seen the sleigh yet.

Then time flickered again, and on this occasion it was not helpful. Johnston turned in time to see the sleigh, and it was obvious that Pieta and Owen had not seen him yet. Johnston grabbed a magno gun from the raft and leveled it at the sleigh, ready to blast its occupants as it swept past. Cati watched, not able to tear her eyes away.

Then suddenly three long, loud siren blasts split the skies. Cati looked up. The Grim Captain had sounded his siren in warning. Pieta and Owen heard it, or at least the dogs did, for the sleigh skidded to one side and came to a halt, just out of range of the deadly gun.

Behind, Cati heard the light splash of the boat slipping into the water.

All that day Owen and Pieta had seen the whirling column of the Puissance get larger and larger, until now it seemed to fill the sky. Owen could not take his eyes off it, could not look anywhere else, the howling mass of it riven with bolts of lightning. And, like Cati, he caught sight of moments in time, half-glimpsed images of shining seas that emptied and turned into desert in an instant, planets flaring up and shrinking to dull, cold ashes. Pieta spoke to him several times, but he ignored her, mesmerized by the sight of time being undone.

And so they came to the edge of land, the dogs wild-eyed with exertion but still leaping onward, driven on by the great red-eyed Arcana. The sleigh reached the sea and turned smoothly without dropping speed to follow the line of the shore. Breakers crashed on the shingle beach and huge chunks of ice crashed and growled. Owen could see to his right the ice bridge that the Long Woman had talked about, a sinister-looking structure, although elegant, one single curve of ice, solid to the sea floor, for otherwise the Harsh could not cross the open water. It was his only way in as well, for he knew that he could not force himself to cross the angry sea. Yet the Harsh guarded the bridge. And even if he crossed, he did not have the Mortmain. And even if he did have it, he didn't know what to do with it.

They swept around the shore. Ahead of them Owen could see the mouth of a fast-flowing river rounding a point, a natural harbor formed in its crook. Owen found that he had picked up the reins, which had lain unused for the entire journey, so sure was Arcana of his leadership. But now the black dog seemed to hesitate and check his stride.

"Something's wrong," said Owen. As he spoke, he heard three siren blasts, long and loud and sorrowful. Arcana came to an abrupt halt and stood staring ahead, lips curled back. Owen followed the dog's eyes and saw Johnston.

If they had gone another thirty meters, they would have been sitting targets, Owen realized. Then Pieta was out of the sleigh, her magno whip in her hand. There was a flicker and to his astonishment Pieta was back in the sleigh, climbing out again. He heard Johnston laugh a heavy, sneering laugh.

"You see what the Harsh have done to time, lad?" Johnston said. "Another while and it'll all be sucked in."

"Pretty Rat come to put time right," said Passionara, and Mariacallas cackled with laughter. Arcana growled and took a step forward. The two men jumped back, almost tripping over each other in their haste.

"Good doggy, good doggy," Mariacallas said nervously.

Arcana's red eyes bored into him. But Johnston did not seem concerned by the dogs. He kept his eyes on the whip in Pieta's hand.

"Let us past!" Pieta said. Owen looked over Johnston's shoulder and saw the source of the siren blasts.

A massive ship stood off the coast. A ship with holes in it and a bridge that tilted to one side. A ship that he would have thought derelict except for several small figures on her deck. And then, rising and falling on the waves, Owen saw a small boat coming toward them.

Just then, one of the people it carried stood up and waved. Cati? he thought. It couldn't be Cati—she was many miles away. But something in his heart told Owen that it was Cati. He could see that the boat was headed for the pier, and knew that was where they needed to be.

He looked up again. Johnston had taken another step forward. Both weapons were still at the limit of their range, but Johnston was edging forward, and Owen knew that the magno gun would come into range before the whip. Johnston knew it too. He moved forward in a stalking motion, keeping low to the ground. Passionara and Mariacallas followed. Pieta tightened her grip on the whip. Owen felt a cold, clear anger flood over him. All he wanted to do, he thought, was see a friendly face again. He was fed up with being thrown around the place and tied up by Johnston. Even Pieta's grim companionship was too much sometimes. He stood up in the sleigh and brought the reins down hard on the dog's backs.

"Arcana, go!" he shouted. The dogs exploded forward. Owen was thrown backward and landed on his back. Pieta, caught by surprise, just about managed to grab on to the sleigh and was dragged behind it as it flew straight toward Johnston. There was nothing the man could do except dive out of the way. Arcana, in passing, made a lunge for Mariacallas. With a frightened yelp the man leapt headfirst into a snowdrift. And as Pieta was dragged behind the sleigh she managed to free one hand and catch Passionara around the legs with the whip. Passionara tumbled head over heels high into the sky, until he too landed in the snowdrift, right beside Mariacallas.

Owen could see that the boat had docked. Wesley and Mervyn stood on the dock, beckoning to him, and as he watched, Cati joined them. He could see the Sub-Commandant holding the boat against the quay. For a moment he thought that the dog team was going to charge straight over the edge of the quay, but at the last moment they swerved sideways and came to a dead halt. Owen jumped out and ran over to Cati and Wesley.

"I can't believe it, I—"

"No time for sentimental stuff," said Wesley gruffly. "Get your backside into that boat or Johnston will have us." The big man had recovered and was charging in their direction.

"I can't," Owen said, "I can't." His mouth felt dry. His stomach lurched as he stared at the seething water below him.

"Come on!" Wesley shouted, but Owen could not move. All seemed lost until the little girl, who had been sitting unobserved in the bow of the boat, stepped ashore. She took Owen by the hand and led him to the edge of the dock and together they stepped into the boat. The Sub-Commandant and Dr. Diamond exchanged a glance.

As they rowed back to the ship, Owen quickly tried to tell them what had happened—Johnston's yard, the Q-car, Pieta, the Long Woman. There was too much. And then Wesley shoved an oar in Owen's hand and told him to stop gabbing and start fending off the ice growlers that were starting to threaten the little boat.

As they approached the ship Cati whispered to Owen, "Are you still mad at me?"

He shook his head. "No. You still mad at me?"

She looked at him for a moment. "Don't know," she said. "I'll have to think about it." She turned away, but not before Owen saw the smile on her face.

Owen stood up and looked back at the land. He could see the ice runner speeding up the hill behind the pier. When it reached the top it stopped and he heard a distant howling. He raised an arm in salute. The howling intensified briefly, then the dogs leapt forward and the sleigh disappeared over the crest of the hill.

Then they were up beside the ship and all hands were needed. The Grim Captain had turned his ship to give them shelter, but the ice clanged against the hull and threatened the boat again and again. It took a long time to get everyone on board and hoist the boat. But as soon as they did, the ship started to move, painfully at first, then building up speed. Owen looked down at the water as though seeing it for the first time.

"How did I do that?"

"You had some help," Cati said.

"That little girl . . . ?" They looked around but could not see her.

Time was flickering more and more now. Added to that, day and night were passing with bewildering speed. Owen felt he was in an old black and white film that flickered and jumped as he watched it. The ship went faster and faster, crashing through the waves, heading straight for the island. There was so much juddering and banging that Cati was sure that bits of the ship would fall off. And then she realized that they *were* falling off. First a bit of plate, then a piece of handrail, then one whole chunk of the leaning bridge fell into the water. But still they sped.

"Listen to me," Dr. Diamond said urgently. "I calculate from the angles of diminution and the various defined, though highly mobile, interstices of the Puissance vortex that the source of it is approximately 293.44 meters below sea level."

"What's he saying?" Wesley asked impatiently.

"It means that we have to get down to the source of the vortex, right down in the middle of the island," said Cati.

"Not we," Owen said, surprising even himself, "me. I

am the one who has to reach the source. I am the Navigator."

They all turned to look at him. Nobody said anything for a moment. Then the Sub-Commandant took the Mortmain carefully from his coat and handed it to Owen.

"This is yours, then, and your father's before you," he said, meeting Owen's eye for a moment before stepping back.

"Land ahoy!" shouted Mervyn. They were in the lee of the island. The ship slowed and all eyes were drawn upward to the towering Puissance, the vortex spinning with almost diabolic speed now. The Sub-Commandant was the first to tear his eyes away. He saw that the island was a crag growing out of the ocean, the top of an underground mountain perhaps with a crater at the summit, like a volcano. It was into this crater that the Puissance disappeared. At the foot of the island was a little stone jetty, and stone steps led upward.

"That's where we need to be," the Sub-Commandant said.

"Let's get the leaky tub into the water, then!" shouted Wesley over the roar of the Puissance.

As they struggled with the rusted davits again, no one noticed Johnston's raft halfway between the island and the shore, Passionara and Mariacallas rowing furiously. By the time they were in their own boat and rowing for shore, Johnston had almost reached the island.

The water was still choppy and the currents were

strong, and they had battled for several minutes in silence before Cati looked around worriedly.

"Where's the little girl?" she said. "We've left her behind."

"I think she'll be all right," Dr. Diamond said. "Look!"

They turned and saw her. She was standing on the bridge beside the Grim Captain and his hand rested on her shoulder.

"That was the thing that he wanted," the Sub-Commandant said, "the thing he wouldn't ask for."

"A bit of company," Wesley said, and sniffed.

"Or forgiveness," Dr. Diamond said quietly. "Do you not see it, Wesley? He was not always known as the Grim Captain. In the mists of time his name was Smith."

"What?" Wesley gasped. "The man who did abandon the Raggies? And me on his boat. I should've—"

"Perhaps, Wesley," Dr. Diamond said gently, "but when he put the children into an open boat and abandoned them all those years ago, he lost the only thing he truly loved."

"His daughter," the Sub-Commandant said. "For she sneaked onto the boat when he wasn't looking and was lost along with all the other children. For centuries he has wandered the seas seeking her, and now she is found."

As they watched, the Grim Captain caught the little girl under the arms and lifted her. She reached up for the siren and pulled it three times. The Grim Captain set her down. He looked down on the little boat, raised one hand, and touched the peak of his cap. Then the ship turned and started to steam away, picking up speed as it went. By the time they had reached the pier and scrambled onto dry land it was almost lost in the night.

25

"If I'm not mistaken," Dr. Diamond said, "then the objects that resemble stone beehives at the top of the steps are in fact entrances."

"Entrances to what?" growled Wesley.

"To the home of the Harsh. But also to the source of the Puissance."

"I'm damn well worried about something," Wesley said. "We haven't seen any of them Harsh yet."

"They'll be waiting," the Sub-Commandant said grimly. Pieta loosened the magno whip at her belt.

"Best get going, then," Wesley said. Owen checked that he still had the Mortmain in his pocket. Wesley told Uel and Mervyn to stay with the boat, for what he described as the unlikely event of them returning.

"One thing to remember," Dr. Diamond said. "On no account must you touch the vortex. Remember that."

Owen turned to Cati. She was shivering.

"Are you all right?" he asked.

"The Harsh," she said. "I can feel them. Nearby." Owen touched her forehead. It was icy cold.

They set out on the long climb to the top. The path was old and crumbling, and howling winds generated by the Puissance threatened to sweep them off it. But that was not the worst part. The time flickers increased to such a rate that Owen barely knew where he was or whether he was about to say something or had just said it. Everything was confused, nightmarish, and the sound of the vortex above them became more and more threatening. At one point he slipped and fell. He got up and slipped and fell again, then once more, the flickering of time making him repeat the motion painfully. At the last, he thought he wouldn't get up. He would just lie there. Then he felt his arm being squeezed and looked up and saw Cati smiling a small brave smile at him, and he felt ashamed. He climbed to his feet and went on.

After what might or might not have been a very long time—there was no way of telling anymore—they reached the top and found themselves right beside the Puissance itself, majestic and terrifying beyond all knowing. Owen felt his mouth go dry and his knees go weak. Dr. Diamond took out a notebook but did not write. All of them stared at the black, writhing surface through which they could see, like a film moving at incredible speed—flashes of history, yes, but more and more darkness punctuated by the light of a few stars, as though all of the world's history had already been sucked into the hole, and now they were seeing what had gone before, the events that were close to the void.

"Time much . . . we haven't much time!" Dr. Diamond shouted.

"Get to one of the entrances!" the Sub-Commandant commanded. Then, without warning, they were under attack. Passionara leapt onto the Sub-Commandant's back and Owen whirled to find himself face to face with Mariacallas.

"Hello, Pretty Rat," he hissed, and Owen suddenly became aware that he was being pickpocketed, the man's hands searching his clothes at incredible speed.

"Is this what you're looking for?" Owen heard Dr. Diamond say. The scientist was holding up his heated ice goggles. Of course, Owen realized, they were looking for the Mortmain but didn't know what it looked like. Greedily, Mariacallas swung round toward Dr. Diamond. To his right, Owen could see the Sub-Commandant struggling with Passionara, who had steely fingers round his throat. Pieta had her whip in her hand but could not get a clear shot.

Mariacallas darted toward Dr. Diamond, but Dr. Diamond backed away again, to the very edge, holding the goggles as high as he could. Mariacallas made one last lunge. Swift as lightning, Dr. Diamond threw the goggles off the edge. Mariacallas threw himself after them and disappeared with a despairing cry.

The Sub-Commandant struggled desperately with Passionara. He was too small to shake off the steely-fingered man, but suddenly another small figure flew toward them—and Cati landed on Passionara's back.

"Leave him alone! Leave him alone!" she screamed, pulling at his fingers and, when that did not work, sinking her teeth into his wrist. Passionara cried out and his grip loosened. With one final desperate effort the Sub-Commandant wrenched free. Passionara stumbled backward, still with Cati wrapped around his neck. Dr. Diamond shouted a warning and Owen saw what was happening. Passionara was overbalanced and falling toward the vortex. The Sub-Commandant reacted fastest. With lightning speed he reached for Cati and tore her from Passionara's back. With a wail, Passionara toppled into the vortex and was snatched away. But as he did so, his hand reached from the vortex and grabbed the Sub-Commandant's sleeve. With horror Owen watched as the man's hand was drawn toward the whirling mass, his fingertips just touching it before he pulled away.

There seemed to be silence then, although the flickering and howling did not stop. Cati looked at her father in disbelief. Owen thought that there was something transparent about him.

"What . . . what will . . . ," she began, her voice trembling.

"Be still, my child," the Sub-Commandant said in a gentle, sad voice. "It is time for me to go now."

"Go where? Not . . ."

"No, not death as such, but I have been touched by the Puissance, and I belong to time now. I have to go, otherwise I will die here, in the next few minutes."

"You can't go!"

"You must let him go, Cati," said Dr. Diamond.

The Sub-Commandant put his arms around his daughter and held her. "You will be the Watcher now. Watch well!" he said.

Owen now understood why Cati was treated as special by the others—she was a Watcher too.

"Owen," the small man said urgently, "I have to tell you something. It was me who gave your father the Mortmain. He didn't steal it. I suspected he was a Navigator, so it was his to guard. I also thought we had a traitor and I wanted to protect it. I never thought it could be Chancellor."

Owen said nothing. Cati started to weep. The Sub-Commandant touched her face. "Just as you will watch the world from the shadows of time and look out for danger, I will be watching you too, from the deepest shadows of all, the shadows at the beginning of all things."

The Sub-Commandant turned, and with one last warm smile to Cati, a smile from which it seemed all the care had gone, he stepped into the vortex and was gone.

They stood there for a long time, or what seemed like a long time. Dr. Diamond held Cati tight. Owen felt numb. He had not realized how close he had become to the small, serious man. "Somebody a body could respect, somebody a body could respect," Wesley was muttering over and over again, and Owen knew how he felt. Pieta made a choking noise and turned away. Then there was an ominous crackling sound and Owen looked at the Puissance. It was now running all black.

"Better hurry," said Wesley, "or there'll be nothing for Cati to watch over."

"Quickly!" Dr. Diamond exclaimed, leading them to one of the beehive huts. "Just step inside."

Owen watched as Dr. Diamond, Pieta, and Cati ducked through the little door, Cati turning a tearstained face to him as she did so.

"Notice something?" Wesley said as he ducked inside. "I seen the monkeys, but I never seen the organ-grinder."

It was true, Owen realized. They had not seen Johnston. Then he stepped inside and found himself falling through blackness.

They were in a kind of chute, Owen thought, a steep chute, black at first but turning lighter as they fell, lighter and colder. Finally he recognized it as ice. He was aware of the others in the chute with him at first, but just as the chute started to level, he came to a fork. As he slid toward the right-hand fork, he caught a glimpse of Cati's foot in the other fork. Desperately he made a grab for the rim of the chute, but it was too late. His fingers clasped the smooth ice momentarily, then lost their grip, and his momentum carried him on. He was on his own. The descent went on for another minute or so. With relief Owen noted that time had stopped flickering. And then, with a heavy thud, he was out of the chute.

He leapt to his feet, fists clenched. But there was no one to be seen. He was in a room filled with extraordinary-looking objects. There were delicate mechanisms shaped like hourglasses, tiny trembling gauges capable of measuring the finest variation, a long metronome consisting of metal so fine it seemed like filigree. The walls were covered with brittle cog mechanisms, all moving. On a fine glass screen, numbers appeared and disappeared as if someone had breathed them onto the glass on a cold day.

Owen stepped forward. The room looked out on something, protected by a glass screen. He crossed the room to the screen and peered through. It was the Puissance, spiraling down through a tunnel, black as jet now. And around it a staircase led down and down. I have to reach that, he thought.

There was a plain wooden door in the wall. Owen opened it and stepped out into a corridor. But this was not like any corridor he had ever seen. It was all white. Like ice, he thought, but not ice. Beautiful objects were set into alcoves along the walls: a delicate ice flower, a milky-colored vase with intricate and ancient carvings, rare and beautiful lamps, exquisite porcelains. Like a castle inside, the Long Woman had said.

Owen walked carefully along the corridor. He had never been anywhere so still. Frozen, he thought, although not frozen in the cold sense. Still he walked on and still there was no turning, and then at the end of the corridor he reached a doorway. He put his hand on the doorknob, a wooden doorknob, cool but not cold to the touch. He hesitated, but time was running out. He had no choice. He turned the knob and opened the door, and knew immediately that this was where the Harsh waited for him.

Cati heard Owen call out and realized that he had gone the other way. She was numb with grief and almost paralyzed by the nearness of the Harsh, and she opened her mouth to tell the others, but no sound came. At that moment she was as near to despair as she had ever come. Then she saw in her mind's eye the smile that her father had given her when he stepped into the vortex, a smile no longer weary but full of youth. It seemed to flood her bones with vigor, and she knew that this was his last gift to her. I won't give up, she told herself. They won't freeze me. And then she landed with a bump on something soft.

"Get off me bloody legs," said Wesley. The four of them were standing in a room of ice. There was a slamming sound from over their heads. Cati looked up to see that a lid had closed above them.

"Owen went the other way," she said.

"I know," Dr. Diamond replied. "It was a trap."

He walked over to the walls and started to examine them closely. Pieta took one look at the ice and lifted her whip. She lashed it against the wall. The ice melted a little, then froze again. She lashed again and again, but each time the ice refroze.

"It's not ordinary ice, is it?" Cati asked.

"No, it's not," Dr. Diamond said, "and as a trap, it's pretty ingenious. Look." They looked and saw a film forming over the surface of the ice and disappearing. It happened again.

"What is it?" asked Cati.

"It's our breath," Dr. Diamond said. "Each time we breathe out, the moisture from our breath freezes on the ice. Each layer of ice that is added, our cell gets a little smaller. Until eventually, as long as we have breath . . ."

"It'll squeeze the rullocks out of us," Wesley said.

"If it is a trap, then they have Owen," Pieta said. "We have to find him."

"Any ideas, doc?" asked Wesley.

Dr. Diamond was fishing around in his pockets. He pulled out what looked like a small gyroscope. "I call this an infinite sonometer," he said proudly.

"Does it work?"

"I don't know. In fact, I've never tried it."

Wesley sighed heavily and theatrically. Dr. Diamond placed the device on the floor and started it spinning. It gave off a low hum at first. The sound built and built, until first Cati and then the others had to cover their ears. Then the sound stopped.

"Ultrasonic now, you see," Dr. Diamond explained.

"Better work pretty quick, doc," Wesley said. "We're breathing out a fair bit of moisture by the look of them walls."

Owen thought about turning and running, but his legs wouldn't carry him. He was trapped. The Harsh had waited for him, confident that he would come to them. There were eight of them, white shapes sitting in a semicircle. Then he looked again and stifled a gasp of shock. The white shape was merely a kind of white dust—ice, perhaps—that floated in the air around them. The Harsh were people, he realized, and not only that, they were young people, or seemed to be anyway. A little bit older than him, sixteen or seventeen, perhaps. They had brown eyes and high cheekbones and blond hair. And very, very white skin. They looked . . . *bored* was the word that sprang to mind. One of the girls, curled up on a chair, yawned and examined her fingernails. Each one of them was beautifully dressed, in pale, cold colors. Then they started to speak.

"That's him. That's the boy who broke our beam." It

was a boy's voice, low and modulated. It might have been pleasant if it hadn't been for the sneer in it.

"It was a very nice beam," a spoiled, petulant-sounding girl's voice said.

"It was a nice beam," the boy agreed, "but he broke it with his mirror." Owen realized they were talking about the ice beam he had bounced back at them at the Workhouse.

"You were trying to kill us!" Owen said, and immediately regretted it. The Harsh might look like spoiled rich children, but they had great power.

"He singed my hair and my shoes were absolutely ruined!" the smallest girl said. She gave Owen a peevish look and some of the white dust around her billowed toward him. He felt a terrible pain in his chest, as though an icy hand had grasped his heart, and he fell to his knees. The girl tossed her head and returned to examining the ends of her hair. Owen felt the grip relax.

"Now he's going to try to break our Puissance machine," the oldest of the boys said.

"And we worked so hard."

"Soooo hard."

"Well, not all that hard, actually," the little girl said, and they all started to giggle, and for all that they had pleasant voices, there was something grating about the sound.

As they giggled, Owen started to think. They were obviously incredibly powerful and clever. But they were so . . . *immature.* Then he heard a voice that was deep and hard and anything but immature.

"So the little Navigator navigated his way here after all."

It was Johnston. The man had entered the room behind Owen and stood there now, regarding him with cold amusement.

"You shouldn't have let him come in here, Johnston," one of the girls said.

"No," agreed another. "You shouldn't have. What do we do now?"

"Freeze him, I suppose," Johnston said. His voice was casual, but Owen sensed a tension in it. "Freeze him, and then I'll take him away and interrogate him, make him tell me where the Mortmain is."

This time Owen could hear the anxiety in Johnston's voice, and all at once it was clear to him. Johnston wanted Owen alive because he wanted the Mortmain for himself! Johnston gave the appearance of working for the Harsh, but really he was trying to double-cross them.

"Yes, I suppose we should do that," one of the drawling voices said.

Suddenly Owen didn't care anymore. He was sick of the Harsh, their cold childish voices, and their toying with time and people's lives as if they were playing a cruel game.

"You can freeze me if you like," Owen said furiously, "but that still makes you just nasty little children."

"I'd be careful what you say to them," Johnston said in a warning voice.

"I don't care! They can turn time back if they like, but they'll still be just as empty. It doesn't make any difference to them what kind of world they live in, whether they live in our world or in their own empty one. They'll still be cold and miserable."

Owen saw that the vapor surrounding the Harsh had started to change, swirling as if they were agitated. Their cold, pinched faces seemed twisted as though with pain.

"They're jealous of us, they're jealous of the heat and the warmth and the light!" Owen yelled. The Harsh seemed to be writhing inside their vapor clouds now, the vapor becoming denser and harder to see through. But as Owen looked, they seemed to age, the childish faces becoming old and sagging, and the room filled with a cold whispering of loss and despair and emptiness. And anger, Owen realized—an anger that was directed at him.

The icy vapor around the Harsh cleared and he could see their real selves clearly now. They were haggard and ancient, with long, wrinkled faces and sparse hair and empty, corrupt eyes. They were time lords, Owen realized, old beyond all imagining, subtle and corrupt. They waved their long, bony fingers as though to ward off his words, and the sound of their voices was a long, evil complaint.

One of the women turned toward Owen and he could feel her gaze like a cold weight on him. She pursed her

331

thin, proud lips, sucked in her breath, and blew. A great freezing maw of icy air blew toward him. Desperately he flung himself to the ground and felt the blast of foul, chilled air pass over his head. Owen's eye was drawn to the open door behind Johnston. He thought he could see part of the shaft containing the Puissance through the door. If only he could get through it.

The knife! he thought. The Long Woman's knife! If he could just get to the door . . .

Suddenly, there was a loud crackling and an enormous crash. Johnston and the Harsh were momentarily distracted. Owen seized his opportunity and ducked under Johnston's arm. He reached the door. He slammed it shut, grabbed the knife from his jacket, and jammed it into the wooden door surround. The Long Woman had said it would hold, that they would not be able to open it. It held. Just. He could feel the strain in the wood, ice creeping across it, as the Harsh bent their will to it. The door remained closed, but for how long? Owen turned and raced down the corridor. The shaft was right in front of him, as was the staircase, and as he looked, Dr. Diamond, Cati, Pieta, and Wesley came racing out of a side corridor.

"The bang," Owen gasped.

"That was us," Cati said. The little gyroscope had worked. It had spun and spun, emitting higher and higher sound waves, until it reached a frequency that even the hard ice could not bear. With a great rending crack, the ice walls had flown apart. They had not known where to go then, but Cati had felt the Harsh nearby and had led them, her face a mask of cold pain.

"Look!" Pieta exclaimed. The door with the iron knife in it trembled. Great bulbs of ice had formed in the apertures and in the lock.

"It can't hold forever," Wesley said.

"Quick, run!" Dr. Diamond spoke urgently. "We'll hold them for as long as we can."

"I can't leave you; they'll kill you," said Owen.

"You have to go, Owen." Cati spoke quietly, and there was a new authority in her voice. He turned to her, surprised. She seemed to have matured in the past hour.

"Would you go on," Wesley said, "till I get a good go at these Harsh." He spat on his hands and rubbed them together.

Dr. Diamond took up a karate stance. Pieta cracked the magno whip by her side.

"Go," Cati whispered. "You are the Navigator. Everything depends on you, don't you see?" Then she gave him a quick peck on the cheek and turned to face the door.

"Run, Owen!" Dr. Diamond said. "Run!"

Owen turned away from his friends and ran to the stairway. He put his foot on the first step and looked at them one last time. If he failed, he would never see them again. And if he succeeded, he realized, he would not see them again.

But I will succeed, thought Owen grimly. I will succeed.

Down he fled, down the staircase that spiraled around the Puissance, all its power concentrated in a writhing coil now, a coil of deep, black nothingness. Down he fled, his heart racing, his legs buckling with fatigue. And from above him came the sounds of battle. He slowed as if something was dragging at him. He knew that his duty was to stop the Puissance, but he had left his friends in mortal danger.

A long, cold, triumphant howl echoed in the stairwell and the sounds of battle stopped. Half running, half falling, Owen cleared the final steps. In front of him was a doorway that seemed somehow familiar. He threw himself through it and slammed it, turning the key in the lock, and let his head rest against the shut door, sobbing for breath. Then he straightened and turned around.

Owen rubbed his eyes. He did not believe what he was seeing. It was all as it had been, but it should not have been here, not at the bottom of a long shaft in an island in a frozen sea. But it was here. In every detail. It was his own bedroom. It seemed as if he could see everything more clearly than he had ever seen anything before. Every faded flower on his bedspread. Every dust mote. The old chest. The guitar. The dartboard. The replica fighter hanging on fishing line from the ceiling.

Owen moved forward in wonderment, letting his fingers trail over the familiar surfaces. He put his hand into his jacket and took out the Mortmain. But what was he supposed to do with it? He looked around but could see nothing new. Desperately he paced the room. A clue, he thought, a clue. Then something came back to him. What was it the Long Woman had said? Look for the fleur-de-lis. The fleur-de-lis was a flower with three leaves, he remembered, and he had seen one before in this room. He went quickly over to the chest and looked at the lettering—J M Gobillard et Fils. What had Johnston said—Gobillard's box of tricks? This had to be it. It had been there all the time. His father had entrusted it to him. He stared at it. Just above the broken lock Owen saw it.

A fleur-de-lis.

He knelt down and looked at it. He saw that there was a tiny opening in the center of the fleur-de-lis, and above it some kind of disturbance in the air. The air was moving round and round, and as he followed it from its tiny beginning to a small hole in the ceiling that he had never noticed before, it got a little bigger, a miniature vortex, and he knew that if he followed it up and up, it would eventually become the raging Puissance that towered over the island. All of time was being sucked into the tiny aperture in the fleur-de-lis. Gobillard had somehow managed to contain in this chest whatever enormous power was needed to turn time backward. But what now? He looked at the Mortmain, and it dawned on him. It wasn't in the shape of a propeller. It was in the shape of a fleur-de-lis. And the hole where the lock had been torn out was in the same shape!

Quickly, he placed the Mortmain in the hole where the lock had been. It fitted! It fitted, and as he watched, it began to turn slowly, then more quickly, then faster than the eye could follow, a blur of terrible speed. Above his head the roof seemed to dissolve until he was looking right up through the center of the vortex, black lightning crackling from one side of it to the other. Owen put his hand on the chest to steady himself. Suddenly he could see scenes of his own past appearing and disappearing in the walls of the Puissance, the Sub-Commandant disappearing into the Puissance, the Long Woman, Johnston, the battle for the Workhouse.

He looked further up, realizing that he could see back in time. The scenes were indistinct, becoming more so, but he could make out his father's car as it veered into the harbor—and was that a figure swimming away? It was too hard to tell. Then it seemed that he heard his voice called. Right beside him in the vortex Owen could see what had happened several minutes ago. And he did not like what he saw, for it was the pitiful remnants of his friends who had fought so that he could get to the chest with the Mortmain. Wesley and Pieta limped in front, leaving a trail of blood on the ground. But behind them came a grim-faced Dr. Diamond, carrying what appeared to be a lifeless Cati.

"Cati!" Owen called out, reaching out to his friend, but as he did so the image faded, the Mortmain tightened inexorably around the vortex, and it became fainter and fainter until in the end he could not see it all.

It was gone. It was over. The Great Machine in the north had been stopped.

The bedroom door flew off its hinges and crashed against the wall. There was a howl of outrage, a freezing blast. But Owen rested his head against the old chest and heard, and felt, no more.

26

It was the sunlight that woke him, streaming in through the high window. He was lying on his bed, fully dressed. He sat up and shook his head. The Harsh, the Mortmain. And then he remembered Cati being carried by Dr. Diamond. If he had dreamed all of it, then why did sadness sweep over him the way it did? He looked around. The room looked as it always had. He jumped to his feet and ran to the door and snatched it open, and saw the corridor, as it had always been, a little dusty, in need of a fresh coat of paint.

Owen jumped up onto the chest and looked out of the window. He could see the rooftops of the town, and beyond it the harbor and the masts of the fishing boats. The empty windows of the Workhouse loomed over the river. And Johnston's scrapyard, half hidden by trees, did not look any bigger. He jumped down. Of course, he thought, the chest! Owen hunkered down and examined the lock. There it was. A lock in the shape of a fleur-de-lis. And yet it looked as if it had always been there, battered and scratched like the rest of the chest. Perhaps it had always been there.

Owen felt as if his head was going to burst. Quickly he grabbed some clothes from the pile of dirty washing on the floor. That hasn't changed, he thought. He couldn't find his trainers, so he pulled on an old pair of boots and ran downstairs.

As he reached the bottom of the stairs Owen glanced into the living room. His mother was kneeling on the floor, looking at something. She turned toward him. "Come here," she said in a calm, worn voice he had not heard for a long time. "Look!" She was holding a photograph of Owen as a baby with his parents. The lost photograph.

The photo had faded, but all three were still smiling, and his mother was smiling now too. She took Owen's hand, squeezed it, and looked into his eyes, and as she did so a weight lifted from him. The mother he had known was back. Things were going to be different now. Then she straightened up and looked around as though seeing the house for the first time.

"Look at the state of this place," she said. "Go on. Get out from under my feet until I get this place into shape." He squeezed past her and slipped out of the front door.

Everything was as it had been: the neat housing estates in the distance, the three fields leading to the river. As fast as he could, he ran across the fields to the water. He straddled the tree that lay across the river and waited for the familiar tug of fear of the dark water below. But it did not come. Had he dreamed that as well? Owen crossed the river and ran to the Workhouse. Its damp stone walls were the same as ever. He went inside, but there was nothing but fallen timbers and grass and young trees growing through the ruins. He went round to the side of the Workhouse, pushing through undergrowth, looking for the door to the Starry, but he could not find it. Neither was there any sign of the fortifications along the river.

Owen searched all morning and then he followed the river down to the harbor, walking under the town bridge and listening to the sounds of the traffic overhead. He went down toward the warehouses, but somebody had put chain-link fencing across the entrance and he could not go any further.

He put his face against the fence and remembered Boat and the Planemen attacking it as the Raggies fished. Or did he remember it?

Owen sat on the harbor wall all afternoon, trying to work out what had happened, if he had dreamed everything. He couldn't have, he decided. There was too much, too much detail. And yet . . .

340

He walked home through the town. As he turned toward the river he saw a scrap lorry laboring up the hill in a cloud of black smoke. From behind he could see an elbow leaning on the driver's door. Owen was sure it was Johnston. But then it wasn't unusual to see Johnston driving a load of scrap through the town.

He went up to the swing tree and looked out over the river, half thinking he might see the Sub-Commandant crouched below him. But there was nothing except the river and the mountains in the distance. He sighed. Disheartened, he walked down the hill toward the Den. It was getting dark. Owen lifted aside the bushes that hid the entrance and went in.

It was a moment before his eyes adjusted to the dark. The propeller, he thought, the Mortmain. He went to the wall. There was a lighter space on the wall where it had hung. He turned then to look at the table and his heart leapt. There, in the middle of the table, was a faded blue cornflower—the cornflower that the Resisters used as a sign of remembering. And beside it a tiny glowing piece of magno! And there was more. As he bent to the table he saw something written in the dust. It read:

Do not forget. From the shadows, Navigator.

And underneath it in the dust, her name:

Cati.

She had survived. Carefully Owen wrapped the magno in a piece of paper and put it in his pocket. The cornflower he pinned on the wall. They were all Sleeping in the Starry now, until they were called again, he thought.

341

Except for Cati. She was the Watcher. What was it her father had said? Stepping back into the shadows of time. She could see Owen, perhaps, but he could not see her. He went outside. It was almost dark.

"See you again, Watcher!" he shouted. But there was no answer from the darkened river valley.

"See you again soon, Cati," Owen said again, almost to himself this time. The wind sighed across the valley and the grasses rustled, and the trees whispered as though in reply.

END OF BOOK ONE

ABOUT THE AUTHOR

EOIN MCNAMEE was born in County Down, Northern Ireland. He is critically acclaimed as an adult novelist, his best-known title being *Resurrection Man* ("one of the most outstanding pieces of Irish fiction to come along in years," according to the *Irish Times*), which was made into a film. He was awarded the Macaulay Fellowship for Irish literature in 1990.

Besides his literary novels, Eoin McNamee has written two thrillers under the pseudonym John Creed. *The Navigator* is his first novel for children.

On the next page, read an excerpt from
City of Time, Book II of the Navigator Trilogy.

Owen walked down the riverbank, straddled the log that acted as a bridge over the water, and shinned quickly across. It was a fine sunny day with a brisk cold wind blowing up from the sea. It stirred the branches of the trees over his head, where the first colors of autumn were just creeping onto the edges of the leaves.

He stopped at the end of the log as he always did and looked up at the dark bulk of the ruined Workhouse towering above him. It was hard to believe that it was only a year since he had stumbled across a secret organization called the Resisters who were hidden inside, asleep until the world needed them.

He shivered at the memory of the deadly Harsh, the

enemies of mankind and of life itself, who had sought to turn back time, spreading cold and darkness throughout the whole world. They had constructed a device called the Puissance, which was like a huge whirlwind, sucking in time. But the Resisters had emerged and Owen had joined with them to defeat the Harsh, imprisoning the Puissance in the mysterious old chest in his bedroom.

When the battle was over, the Resisters went back to sleep in the chamber known as the Starry, hidden under the Workhouse. It was where they waited until they were called again. It was his friend Cati's job to watch for danger and to wake them when it came. She was invisible to the ordinary eye, hidden, as she said, in the shadows of time.

"Hello, Watcher," Owen shouted as he always did, knowing she could see him even though he couldn't see her. He paused and scanned the shadows under the trees, wondering if she was safe and if he would ever see her again. Time, he had learned, was a dangerous place.

He strode briskly along the path toward his Den. Owen had made the Den in a hollow formed by ancient walls and roofed it over with a sheet of perspex he had found. The entrance was cleverly disguised with branches, so it was almost impossible to find unless you knew where it was. He moved quickly. He was late for school, but he had an errand.

He uncovered the entrance and ducked into the Den. Everything was as it had been the evening before. The old sofa, the pile of comics, the battered old kettle and gas stove, the truck mirror on the wall. The only thing that had changed in a year was the empty space on the wall where the Mortmain had hung, the object that he had thought was an old boat propeller, the object that turned out to be the key to defeating the Harsh. It was a magical object, whose properties he didn't really understand. It resembled a battered piece of brass a little larger than a man's hand, with three leaves coming out from the center. When activated, it transformed into an object of wonderful intricacy and power. The Mortmain was now in his bedroom as well, acting as a lock to keep the Puissance in the chest.

Owen looked at himself in the mirror. His face had filled out and the thin, worried boy of last year had gone. His brown eyes were still wary, but that wasn't surprising, given the danger he'd gone through.

Quickly he opened the small box he had left on the old wooden table. He reached into his pocket and took out what looked like a small jagged stone, one that glowed bright blue. It was the piece of magno that Cati had left as a keepsake, the stone filled with a power that the Resisters harnessed like electricity. He had taken it home with him the evening before, but he wasn't comfortable leaving it in his bedroom. It belonged in the Den, close to the Workhouse. He shut the magno in the box, took a last glance around, then left.

Once outside, he climbed up the side of the bridge

onto the road. His mother had forgotten to give him lunch again, so he ran toward Mary White's shop. He had to stoop down to get into the tiny dark shop with the whitewashed front. As always, Mary was standing in the gloom behind the counter wearing an apron and pinafore, her hair in a bun.

"Have you been down at the Workhouse recently?" Mary asked. Owen remembered that the Resisters had spoken of her and seemed to have a great deal of respect for her. How much did she know about them and their battles with the Harsh?

"Be careful down there," she said. "Be very careful." For a moment the shop seemed to grow even darker and Mary's face looked stern and ancient. Then she smiled and things went back to normal.

Owen bought a roll and some ham. He put the money on the counter and Mary looked at his hands, which were unusually long and slender for a boy. *Just like his father's,* Mary thought. *Hands that were made for something special.*

Things had been easier at school since Owen had fought alongside the Resisters. No one knew about his adventures with the Resisters, or that if they hadn't defeated the Harsh, everyone would have vanished from the face of the earth, but he had grown up a lot during that time and his classmates sensed it. He was still a loner, but he was respected. It also had something to do with the fact that his mother was not as depressed and forgetful as she had been, so no longer sent him out in clothes he had outgrown or cut his hair with the kitchen scissors. Now he had the quiet air of a boy who could solve problems, and the younger children in particular often came to him for help.

At lunch he sat in the shelter outside. He had forgotten to buy a drink, so when Freya Revell sat down beside him and offered him a sip of her smoothie, he gratefully accepted.

"Look at the moon," she said. "It's so clear today."

"So it is," Owen said.

"You can see the man in the moon," she said.

Owen looked up and saw she was right. Then he turned back to Freya and felt his blood run cold. Instead of Freya's pleasant features, he saw the face of an old woman, more than old, ancient beyond counting. He felt himself recoil.

"What is it?" she said. "Is there something wrong?"

Owen rubbed his eyes. When he opened them again, Freya's face was back to normal. "I just . . . I just felt a bit dizzy," he said, knowing that didn't sound very convincing. "I have to go now."

He backed away, feeling Freya's eyes following him, her expression puzzled and a little hurt. He looked up again and for a moment the man in the moon did not seem like the kindly face from the nursery rhyme, but instead looked hard and cold.

After school, Owen walked slowly home, trying to rid himself of the image of Freya's face, how it had changed. Was there something wrong with him, or had it been a kind of waking dream?

No. It had happened, and there was no one he could tell.

If only Cati were here.

When he got back home, his mother was in the kitchen. She looked careworn, but she smiled to herself from time to time as though she remembered something funny. It was an improvement on the way she had been, he thought. She had put out tea for him. Well, he thought, she had tried. There was a rubbery fried egg, which looked as if his fork would bounce off it, a bowl of porridge that had set like cement, and tea that came out as hot water because she had forgotten the tea bag.

Owen didn't mind, though. After his father was lost when his car crashed into the sea, his mother had sunk into a terrible depression, barely recognizing even Owen. But when he had broken the hold that the Harsh had on time, his mother had recovered a little, although Owen didn't understand how. She was vague and sometimes hardly seemed to be there, but she was happier.

He put the egg between two slices of toast and gulped it down, then grabbed his schoolbag from the corner, kissed his mother gently on the cheek, and went upstairs.

Owen spread his homework out on the bed, but he

couldn't concentrate. When it got dark he climbed up onto the chest underneath his window and stared out at black trees whipped by the wind. Then he got down and examined the chest, as he did almost every night. It was a plain black chest with brass corners and what looked like an ordinary brass lock and yet he dared not open it. The terrifying whirlwind that had turned time backward and threatened to destroy the world was trapped in it. The tarnished brass lock, the Mortmain, could look dull and uninteresting, as it did now, but Owen knew it was ornate and complicated. *Not made just to be a lock on a chest*, he thought. *No matter how important the chest is.*

He pulled off his trainers and lay on the bed. He shut his eyes, but Freya's old-woman face was the first image that came into his head. Then he saw the moon, with Freya's wizened face on it. He drifted into a troubled sleep in which images of the chest and the Mortmain drifted and merged into each other.

Owen wasn't the only one thinking about the chest. At the far side of the garden there was an ash tree, and in its branches a heavy figure was perched holding a brass telescope in one hand. The man had a broad red face, large sideburns, and a sly look. His name was Johnston and he was a sworn enemy of the Resisters. He was a scrap dealer, but the previous year he had stood shoulder to shoulder with the Harsh, the cold enemy who had tried to crush Owen and his friends.

He peered through the telescope into Owen's room. Reflected in the dressing-table mirror he could see the chest and the dull gleam of the Mortmain. It had taken Johnston all year to work out that the chest contained the Puissance. The Harsh were eager to get it back. He lowered the telescope. This time Owen would not stand in his way.

Cati also lay awake. For a long year she had been the Watcher. There was always a Watcher—one member of the Resisters who stayed awake while the others slept.

She lived in the Workhouse on the river below Owen's house, taking food from the cavernous storerooms and cooking it in the vast empty kitchens. Every day she walked the crumbling battlements of the Workhouse, the Resister headquarters, which just looked like an old ruin to human eyes. She could see traffic moving up and down the road, but the drivers could not see her. She wondered what they would think if they knew that there was an army sleeping in the old building.

Watching other people going up and down the road

was lonely enough, but worst of all was seeing Owen going to and from school or walking to his Den, his brown hair blowing in the wind from the harbor. She loved it when he waved and said hello even though he couldn't see her. She longed to call to him and walk along the river, to laugh and talk the way they had before.

Cati sighed. Her father had been the Watcher before her, but he hadn't said much about what it was like to be awake when everyone else slept. He had never mentioned the loneliness. He'd merely told her that it was a bit like being a night watchman. She sat up in bed. She knew that she'd never sleep that night, so, pulling on her clothes and boots, she made her way toward the stone staircase that led to the top of the Workhouse. *If I'm the Watcher,* she thought, *then I might as well go and watch.*

It was a crisp clear night, with a full moon that seemed to fill the sky over the harbor. Cati shivered and pulled her collar tight around her neck. She listened to the gentle murmur of the river far below. Then she heard the sound of wings. A vast skein of wild geese were flying low and hard toward the harbor. They were flying in a V formation from north to south and Cati could hear them honking. She watched them cross the face of the moon until they were framed in its circle. *They are free and I am not,* she thought sadly.

Then she froze to the spot. A second before, there had been birds on the wing. Now they turned to skeletons, the flesh and feathers gone! For a moment they hung in the sky, a great silent flock of the dead, their bone wings fixed in flight, their beaks agape but noiseless. Then they turned to dust, which fell earthward in a great plume until it was swallowed by the darkness below.

Cati wondered if her heart had stopped. For a long moment she stood staring at the moon, wondering if she had hallucinated the whole thing. But the geese had been real; nothing could have been more real than their wild honking high in the sky. She forced herself to think. No weapon could have reduced the geese to dust. No storm or wind or lightning strike. Only one thing could have happened. Somehow, time had changed them and they had aged many years in a single second.

Her job was to watch for a threat to the fabric of time and to wake the other Resisters if they were needed to defend. Was this one of those times? Her heart told her that it was. She turned and plunged down the stairs.

In two minutes she stood at the doors that led to the Starry, the great chamber where the Resisters slept. As she fumbled at the lock, doubt began to creep into her mind. What if she was wrong? She thought about Samual, one of the Resister leaders. The warrior was a brave fighter, but his tongue was acid and he had not approved of Cati's friendship with Owen. She could almost hear his sarcastic words. *Geese turning to dust? You woke us because you had a silly dream?*

But it wasn't a dream, she said to herself. *It wasn't.*

Cati turned the slender key in the lock and the stone doors opened.

Before her in semidarkness were hundreds of wooden beds, and in each bed lay a Resister. What light there was came from the ceiling, which was domed and covered with tiny lights like a night sky. The air was warm and still and she could hear gentle breathing sweep the room like a great sigh. She looked at the sleeping faces, recognizing every one—young and old, friend and opponent.

She checked on the Starry once every three or four days. It was part of her job, although no one had ever told her so. Her visits were brief: a glance to make sure all was well and no more. To see so many familiar faces only made her loneliness worse.

She had seen her father wake the Sleepers before. He had simply touched each person's forehead and after a moment the Resister would wake, looking around, a little bewildered until they realized where they were. Whom would she wake first to tell about the geese? *Contessa,* she thought. Contessa, who ran the great kitchens in the Workhouse, who was gentle and wise, a mother to them all. She would know what to do.

Cati walked between the rows until she found her. Contessa was tall, elegantly dressed in a wool gown. Her hands were folded on her breast and even in sleep there was a calm authority to her face. Hesitantly, Cati reached out and touched her forehead. She stood for a moment, feeling the warm skin, waiting for her eyes to open.

Without warning, Contessa started to writhe, her back arching, pain written on her gentle face. "No," she moaned, "stop . . ."

Cati jerked her hand back. Contessa's body fell back to the bed and she was asleep again, breathing heavily, beads of perspiration on her forehead.

Something was wrong. Cati placed her hand on another Resister's head, a dark-haired young man. He twisted and moaned as if her touch burned him. She snatched her hand away. What was wrong? She should be able to wake them.

Even as she stood there, bewildered and alarmed, Cati could feel sleep start to steal over her, as it did if you remained too long in the Starry. But this sleep felt different. It seemed . . . *stale*.

She turned swiftly and walked toward the door. As Watcher, she knew it was not the time to fall asleep. She closed the door behind her and locked it, then ran outside, welcoming the cool night air on her face. Outside it seemed as bright as day. The moon over the Workhouse roof shone with a light that was almost dazzling.

Cati sat down on a rock. Something was terribly wrong. There was only one option. She knew that her father had sometimes called upon special people in the ordinary world. She thought that the shopkeeper, Mary White, was one of them.

Owen was another. His father had known the Resisters and Owen had joined them to defeat the Harsh. Owen was called the Navigator, for reasons she didn't quite understand, and it was a title that the other Resisters seemed to respect; even, in some cases, to fear.

She would never try to contact him under normal circumstances. But these were not normal circumstances. She jumped up and began to run.